HAUNTING melody

Chloe Spencer

Tiny Ghost Press

*actual size

*To every girl who ever felt like she was a weed: you are a rose. May
you find the people who will water you and help you grow.*

Content Warning

The protagonist of this book struggles with internalized fatphobia and post-traumatic stress disorder, the latter of which she is receiving treatment for. Although the protagonist does not have a formal eating disorder diagnosis, mentions of disordered eating habits and other fatphobic comments are within this story. Also included: gore (including partial dismemberment, dead bodies, blood, and facial disfigurement), death (including teen death), graphic violence, kidnapping, mentions of drugging someone's drink, mentions of torture, brief discussions of butchphobia, brief depiction of parental abuse, and description/discussion of an emotionally abusive relationship between the protagonist and her ex.

And so Iliony plunged into the abyss marked by Death, her hands outstretched, until she could pluck the blue souls of her Ancestors from it. Once that was done, she cast them into the Beyond, where they were saved, and would watch over her forever.

—"Verse 3: The Ballad of Iliony," *Thistlefeayr Tomes*

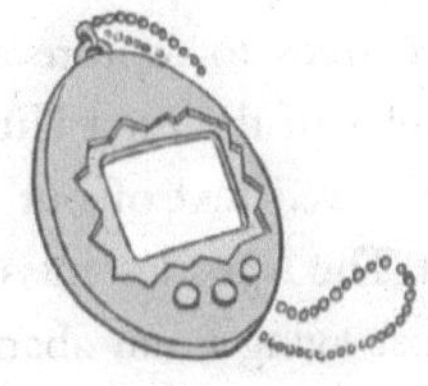

Prologue

Three kisses for good luck. Forehead, nose, and lips. It's a ritual I've shared with Brynne since our sixth coffee shop date two years ago, and I'm all the more grateful for it because tonight is my First Sacred Hunt, so I need all the luck I can get. She holds me ever so briefly before stepping back and letting me put on my gear. Dad upgraded my cap-can before tonight, and the silver hose attachment has been polished to the point of perfection, my reflection visible on its surface. The pockets of my cargo pants are stuffed with bags of freshly blessed salt. All my years of training alongside my parents have led up to this.

I am ready. More than ready. *Born* ready.

So why do I feel so nervous?

Brynne frowns, her lower lip protruding in a childlike puppy pout. She rubs my shoulder affectionately, but there's a stiffness to her touch. "What's wrong?"

"I—I don't know."

Her brow furrows. "Don't psych yourself out, Melody. You've got this. It's one little ghost. You've bagged them on your own before."

Yeah, but that was different. When I was accompanying my parents on a mission, they were there to help if anything went awry. They were always one floor above me, or one hallway over. Tonight, I'm entering this giant Victorian mansion surrounded by foreboding, jagged trees to capture a ghost entirely on my own—such are the rules of the First Hunt as it's written in the *Thistlefeayr Tomes*, the sacred text of our people. Brynne lucked out on her First Hunt. The Apostles' mission for her was to track down a little girl ghost living in an abandoned carnival on the other side of Harbor's Edge, a city about a half hour away from Mountain Ridge. She even figured out how to turn on the carousel and go for a ride while waiting for the will-o'-wisp to appear.

With how wretched this place looks, I'll be lucky if I don't fall through the floor. The foundation is so lopsided, the house seems to quake in the August breeze. Many of the roof tiles are missing, and in their place are clumps of visible spores—an unfortunate side effect of too much ectoplasm in a poorly insulated environment. The fuzzy white masses pulsate with a sickeningly slow rhythm, like the lungs of a chain-smoking cancer patient. Instinctively I pull my mask over my nose and mouth. I'm pretty sure I won't inhale spores from standing here, but the last time I had ectochitis, I was laid up for three weeks, hacking blue phlegm into the trash can beside my bed.

"Melody." Brynne nudges my shoulder a little too aggressively.

She nods in the direction of my parents and our family's Apostle, Simon Wallace, who have gathered at the base of the rickety porch steps. I glance overhead at the crescent moon hanging high in the sky, glowing a radiant amber even through the cover of clouds obscuring it.

It is time.

We walk over to the others and Mom squeezes me a little too hard, forcing all the air from my lungs. Dad smiles at me and tousles my russet-brown hair before giving me a kiss on the head. They're all joyful, except for Simon. For as long as I've known this man—which has basically been since birth—he hasn't liked to smile. Dark expression, dark hair, dark energy. He clears his throat, as if such a display of affection is offensive to him. With watchful blue eyes, he pinches his fingers together, touches them to his tongue (gross), and uses them to flip to the proper page in the *Tomes*. As Simon begins to recite the incantation, my mother rubs my cheeks and forehead with sea salt salve for good luck. The gristly goop seeps into my pores, and I can already feel tomorrow's breakout erupting underneath the surface of my skin. Again—if it'll help me out, I'll take it.

"Spirits in Sanctity, Spirits of the Beyond, and Spirits Ancestral, heed our prayer. Melody Myere, Whisperer in Kind, shall begin her First Sacred Hunt, and on this most precious night, we ask that the Three Bodies watch over her…"

In the light of the moon, listening to the low rumble of Simon's voice as he recites his prayer from the scripture, my heartbeat quickens. Not even the smiling faces of my girlfriend or my parents can comfort me. *What is wrong with me?* I've done this before. I bagged my first ghost when I was ten years old. It's burned into the surface of my memory like a Polaroid. Little boy in a yellow rain jacket, in the heart of the Canopy Woods in the Western Wildlands, his gray paper-thin skin melting into the open receptacle of the roaring hose—

"Melody."

I jerk my head up, my gaze fixing on Simon's unfriendly face. The tome is closed, folded tightly across his chest in the same way a young girl would protect her diary from prying eyes. It would be comical if this wasn't supposed to be so serious. I try to nod my head slowly, like I've been listening this whole time and appreciating the recitation, but Mom knows better. She touches my sticky forehead.

"What's wrong? Are you feverish?" She turns to Dad, the pace of her voice quickening as her anxiety climbs. "Honey, she's hot. I don't think she feels well."

I brush Mom's hand from my forehead. I wish that Brynne would say something, but she regards me with this bizarrely icy look, her pupils mere pinpricks, her jaw clenched like she's chewing a tough stick of jerky. What, is she disappointed with me? Why? I haven't failed yet. No, I *won't* fail.

"I'm fine, Mom." A lie. "Just…can't believe it's really happening." Well, that's true.

I felt like my First Sacred Hunt was never going to happen. When you've known about it from the age of five, but can't do it until your sixteenth birthday, I mean, the anticipation builds and builds and builds—no wonder I feel fit to burst. I'm fine. I double-check the placement of my mask on my face, flick my cap-can on and off to test the battery, and drum my fingers against my chest to quiet my pounding heart. Underneath my button-up shirt, my tactical chain mail vest, crafted from the finest of blessed silver, bears no gaps, tears, or imperfections. And why would it? It's brand new. Bought special for me. Special for today.

"Honey?" Dad asks, his smile kind but his voice stiff.

He's getting freaked out the longer I stand here. So am I. He nods in the direction of the house, encouraging me to go inside and start the ritual.

I hope my eyes are smiling. "I'm all set."

I walk up the steps of the ramshackle house, each one creaking underneath my weight as I go. Once on the porch landing, I take a deep breath, then wrench open the door. It creaks loudly, the hinges threatening to snap off the rotten wood frame, but miraculously stays intact as I maneuver inside. I squeeze my eyes shut as the door closes behind me, and when I open them, I'm greeted by tarnished floorboards, weathered wallpaper roses, and a crystal chandelier with a missing light bulb. Although extravagant, the light fixture is grimy and sad, like an engagement ring that fell down a drainpipe.

Most of the furniture was ransacked over the years, judging from the scuff marks and less dusty spaces outlining where things used to be. Some stuff remains: Sun-faded family portraits hang from the walls, the bleached eyes of their subjects ever watchful, even underneath years' worth of dust. A stained red Persian rug runs down the length of the hallway. Decades ago, I'm sure it was beautiful. It doesn't deserve to rot in a place like this—and rotting it is. The stench of ectoplasm, sticky-sweet but noxious, clings to the walls. I tentatively place a gloved hand against the peeling wallpaper, and a mucus-thin layer of blue goo sticks to it in weblike strings. The resident of this house staked their claim a long time ago, and they probably won't be too happy to see me.

I flatten my back against the wall as I walk by the staircase. This is an easy place for a ghost to jump you from above. *You're always vulnerable going up or down,* Dad told me. *You never want to leave your back exposed for too long.* As I make my way through the foyer, I pull out one of my little bags of salt and sprinkle a trail behind me. Should I need to retreat or retrace my steps, this will keep me protected. Most ghosts don't like salt. For whatever reason, if they touch it, it burns little holes through their forms. Maybe they don't feel pain, but they sure don't like watching themselves disappear.

A ceramic clatter echoes from the kitchen, and I stick my cap-can's hose around the corner of the doorway before looking inside. It's empty, aside from the lone plastic mixing bowl rattling in circles on the counter. Nothing in it. There's a giant gap between the scratched-up marble countertops where a stove used to be, rust and rot staining the wall a putrid shade of brown. No reason to be in this kitchen, but if the ghost is making noise, he's letting me know he sees me.

The end of this mission might come sooner than I think.

I sprinkle a little more salt behind me and walk through the kitchen into the dining room. Scattered newspapers and crumpled-up coupons carpet the floor, signs that someone has been here recently. A pathway guides me into the center of the room, the other side of which is walled off by an overturned dining table, cardboard boxes, and piles of trash. Something is etched on the underside of the table.

SUZIE WUZ HERE
AUGUST '00

I can't help but crack a smile. In creepy, ghost-inhabited spaces, it's always nice to find signs of people who once lived here, no matter how many years ago it was. For some reason, it helps me feel a little less alone. I run my hands over the table, pulling away tiny droplets of ectoplasm. Suddenly, a chill courses through me, and in the pocket of my cargo pants, my EMF reader whistle-whirs anxiously, its pitch undulating.

Someone is in here.

Panic flutters in my chest. I pull back the trigger on my hose, and the cap-can rumbles in warning. No point in staying quiet anymore. This is the part of the hunt where the ghost will try to assert dominance over the intruder—where they'll try to scare me into fleeing the scene. Although there's a dead end in front of me, the wall of boxes looks smaller and easier to push through a few feet down from where I'm standing. I walk over and unceremoniously kick over the boxes, then trudge through. But as my foot hits the ground, something slick grips onto it. *Ew.* More ectoplasm, gobs of it, smeared on the floor. I turn my back to the wall and grit my teeth, trying to free my boot from its clutches, but the sound of something else fills the air. More whirring from my EMF reader? No. Not the same. Then I realize it's not a whirring but a buzzing: a flurry of buzzing from desperate, hungry flies. Swirling through the air ahead of me, a cluster of them is swarming something—no, someone.

Someone is sitting on the ground.

The EMF reader whirs, its shrill screams piercing and painful like a tornado siren. Even the flies are fearful; they disperse immediately, darting toward the wilting rafters overhead. Their absence exposes the face of their last meal: an old man whose bloated blue tongue hangs limply from between his lips. A soft, rose-colored foam nestles at the corners of his eyes and nose. A gaping hole in his chest, its fleshy edges shriveled from dehydration and putrefied blood, serves as a window into his broken rib cage. The splinters of crisscrossed bone inside resemble a bird's nest. Solidified gore, dried after the Spirits know how many days, surrounds the hole, staining the ends of his plaid shirt and denim pants.

I resist the urge to shit myself and instead grab the radio from the holster around my waist. My trembling fingers fumble to press the Talk button, and my heart quakes within my chest when I hear the chattery static.

"Mom, Dad, wrai—"

Before the words can escape my mouth, a hideous screech shreds the air, rattling the walls. My breath comes out in icy puffs as the air rapidly cools. I already know where the wraith is, but I can't help my morbid curiosity.

I tilt my head back and look at the ceiling.

The wraith floats above me, its black cloak billowing around its formless figure like a cloud of smoke. Its face resembles a mummified human, the skin so thin and tattered it's almost skeletal. Eyeless, its sense of smell and hearing are keen—it's the strongest of all the ghost types. Its mouth is full of sharp, crocodile-like teeth: prehistoric and gnarled, but tough, stained red with blood.

Wraiths are born when a living being dies in an extremely traumatic way. It's as though the trauma destroys their minds, leaving their souls lost and left to wander for decades, usually centuries. They're one of the worst ghosts you can encounter, as they are the only type that feels inclined to *eat* humans, despite that they don't need to eat to survive. Another fun fact about wraiths? They can't be sucked up into cap-cans easily. Unlike other ghosts, whose clothes stick to them stiffly underneath the layer of ectoplasm, the cloaks of wraiths are large and tangled— and can easily clog the hose attachment. Now, as for how to capture wraiths? I have no damn clue.

A drop of blood from the creature's mouth smudges my cheek, right above my mask. I grimace but remain still. The blind husk hovers menacingly over me, its spindly hands stretching toward me. I tuck and roll out of the way, which frustrates the creature enough to make it shriek. Spirits, that *shriek*.

Eager for a taste, the wraith claws at my back with sharp, bony fingers, but it hisses in pain and recoils as it grazes the blessed silver. Outside, the panicked commotion of the others grows louder as they realize what's in here with me. My radio crackles and snarls, Mom's cries desperately trying to break through, but the wraith's presence is overpowering it. I take a deep breath, spring to my feet, and sprint back into the kitchen. The bowl on the counter violently rattles and whips in my direction with intimidating force. Somehow I duck just before it hits the wall with a resounding slam, leaving a crater riddled with spiderweb cracks. My lungs feel empty and my eyes are blurry from tears, but I have no choice but to keep running.

Exiting the kitchen, I scramble through the foyer and make a beeline for the door. The salt trail I left behind earlier does not ward off the wraiths; they're tougher than that. The wraith springs after me, its claws digging into the moldy runner that lines the front hall, tearing it seam by seam from the floor, tripping me with a tumultuous wave. I crash headfirst into the railing of the stairs. The trigger for the hose jams and the cap-can switches on.

Head throbbing, I roll onto my back before the wraith pounces on me. It screeches like a pterodactyl, gnashing its teeth, and I scream, gripping its jaws and prying them open.

This is not how I want to die.

As it claws away my mask, the stench of ectoplasm fills my nostrils, and fingernails strip the flesh from my cheeks. The heat gushes from my face and the cold air stings the fresh wounds. For a brief moment the wraith recoils at the sting of the salt salve, then it goes back in for the kill. The tattered ends of its cloak wrap around the lower half of my body like a python—paper thin but constrictive, nonetheless. Over its screams, the cap-can sucks away, high-pitched and shrill. This thing won't hold it, but it's the only shot I've got.

I keep one hand fixed on its bottom jaw and use all the muscles in my arm to keep it at bay. With the other hand, I reach for the hose and jam it into the wraith's head. It screeches, twisting away from me, its sharp claws trying to tear into the hose, but unable to shred the reinforced carbon fibers. Breathless, I stagger to my feet, but I'm woozy, and my vision is whirling before I can make it three steps closer to the door.

Thankfully, someone kicks it open, and everyone who's been waiting outside scrambles in. My mother blows her whistle, which emits sounds at a frequency only specific types of ghosts can hear. The wraith stops screaming but keeps snapping as Dad raises the Phantom Prod high above its head. He brings it down on the creature's skull, and as the weapon cracks against it, purple sparks fly. The creature collapses to the ground in a heap and deflates, the spirit leaving its shell for good. Mom takes her own vac hose and gobbles up the cursed little soul, a blue orb wriggling desperately in midair. It swirls and bounces through the silver-lined tunnel with a loud, wet *SCHOOP*, then finally enters the canister.

Mom switches off the cap-can before enveloping me in her arms, and soon after, Dad embraces both of us. They murmur apologies to me, their voices trembling—terrified yet relieved that I'm somehow still alive. Dad removes a cloth from his pants pocket and ties it around the lower half of my face, but I can feel myself bleeding through it mere moments after it's secured. Dad squishes his hands against my cheeks to try to stop the bleeding and tells Mom to call for an ambulance.

In the corner by the entrance, two people watch us, aghast.

The first—Simon—doesn't surprise me: his standard expression is one of displeasure; his nose is always pinched up about one thing or another.

But the second—Brynne—cuts me just as deeply as the wraith's claws.

Honor can only be earned through valor; such is the way of the spirit whisperer. To outsiders, one would view their society as unempathetic but ambitious. To the spirit whisperers, this is all they know.

—Peggy Harthorne, *My Year of Ghosts: An Anthropological Account of Life with the Spirit Whisperers in the West Province* (1978)

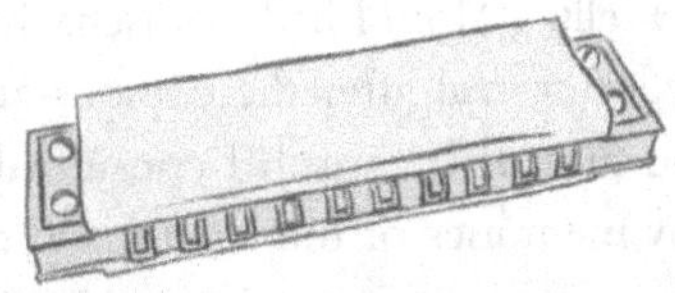

Chapter One

It's rare that someone fails their First Sacred Hunt, and even more unexpected that I, the daughter of two talented ghost hunters, would fail so miserably. Your First Sacred Hunt is supposed to be a rite of passage—a way to demonstrate to the other hunters that you've come of age. It doesn't matter that I faced off against a wraith, which not even an expert ghost hunter would've handled well. That little factoid didn't spread around as much as the reality that I failed. In our small, insulated community, the only thing that counts is appearances: who's a winner, and who's a loser. In their eyes, I'm a loser.

Especially to Brynne, who dumped me shortly after. Not that I blame her—not only did I fail horrendously, but the gnarly scars from where the wraith tore me up have flushed my attractiveness score straight down the toilet. We went to Pyke's Overlook, where we'd had our first kiss. She stared off into the distance as she monotonically told me her feelings had changed, that she wanted to commit her time to other activities, and that I was "honestly too much to deal with right now." I cried into the strawberry cheesecake ice cream she'd bought for me and asked her if we could still be friends. She assured me that we would be, but after that, it was like *I* was a ghost. When I showed up to school the following Monday, she didn't bother to say hi. She stared straight past me and kept on walking. Icy, like the wraith that scarred my face. And our mutual friends followed suit.

So began my stint of wearing stained sweatpants and getting out of school by telling Mom I had stomachaches, which were at first fake but became real after the copious amount of cheese puffs and gallon tubs of ice cream I consumed. My nightmares were plagued by memories of the wraith, and during the day, it felt like anything—a smell, a sound, an object—could send me right back to that house. My parents scrambled to set me up with a therapist so I could regain *some* cognitive function, but in some ways, it was too late. Sure, I learned healthy coping mechanisms, but by the time my junior year ended, my grades and social standing had plummeted—while my weight was at its all-time highest.

In short, I've hit rock bottom.

Tonight I enter the kitchen to see my parents sitting at the table with a take-out bag from my favorite Indian place. After inhaling the mouthwatering savory smells, I cast them a suspicious look.

"It's not my birthday, and I know we're not celebrating my success or anything." I plop down beside them and eagerly open the bag, but don't eat.

Mom and Dad exchange a look of concern. Dad passes me a plate and gingerly spoons chicken dum biryani onto it. The multicolored rice shimmers in the auburn light of our kitchen, but I resist the urge to dive into it.

"You're right," Dad says. "We're not celebrating anything, but we do want to have a serious discussion."

"About…? The suspense is really killing me here."

"Well, the Council contacted us, and they said there's a town in need of our help." Mom launches into her explanation: Murkmore, an isolated island town, is suffering from what they believe to be a ghost problem. Five young men, ranging from their teens to late twenties, have turned up as mutilated, ectoplasm-covered corpses. No one in town can figure out where the ghosts are coming from, but even if they could, there's no community of ghost hunters to take care of the problem.

Being so small and isolated, Murkmore is quite unattractive to our people, as it's harder for us to find business. Islands only have so many ghosts, and while you could probably find business on the mainland, that means hopping on ferries to do anything. Whole lot of hassle when you consider how much equipment ghost hunters need.

But it's not just bad because of the economic reasons, the environment is also kinda-sorta-terrible. Murkmore isn't some tropical paradise. I met a girl from there in school once, and she gave a whole PowerPoint presentation on the place, complete with visual aids. It's woodsy and bug-ridden and iced over in the winters. The kind of island where there's no point to it being an island, since the waters are often too cold to swim in even during the summer. A real shithole that keeps trying to reinvent itself as a tourist trap to the unfortunate and deceived.

If that doesn't convince you it's bad, consider this: up until about a year ago, the place was considered a Fantastical-free zone. That means no one of Fantastical descent—witches, vampires, and yes, also ghost hunters—could live there. Even dismantling its bigoted and dusty old laws couldn't convince folks to move there and revitalize the place. I've wanted to be the first in a lot of things—first to get to class, first place in a competition, first to capture a ghost—but being the first Fantastical teen on an island is not something worth bragging about.

"We know these past few months have been rough for you, and it's been rough for us too. That's the thing about hunters: They're a catty bunch of people. They're unfair and prideful." Mom bites her lip, ashamed to admit this. She looks to my father, and he rubs her hand in support. "So…perhaps it would be good for us to move to a town where we would be the only hunters."

"But we know that that's asking a lot from you," Dad chimes in. "I mean…we're possibly dealing with wraiths there or something worse."

When Dad says the word *wraith*, an involuntary shudder escapes my chest. The face of that soulless monster resurfaces in my mind like a wolf returning to its hunting ground. But I swallow down my fear with the first spoonful of biryani and nod slowly—after all, I've spent enough time in therapy now to at least somewhat control my trauma responses. Besides, I know that my failed hunt reflected poorly on my parents as well. They used to get hundreds of jobs per year and were contracted by a few rural municipalities to be their on-call ghost hunters. But in the last six months those contracts dried up, the phone stopped ringing, and a suspicious number of bills have piled up on the kitchen counter. Hunters make a living based off their reputation with the nonhunters and their governments; they hire us for ectoplasm cleaning and ghost extractions based on word of mouth. If Mom had to go to the Council to get work, shit is really, *really* bad.

"You've also grown up here," Mom murmurs, her eyes sad. "And with you only being a couple years off from going to college, well, we don't want to upend your whole life."

Dad pipes up again. "But we also think this could be a great opportunity for us all to have a fresh start."

He says this so calmly and kindly, yet the undertone cuts through: *Your failure has ruined our lives, and now we're being exiled. There is only one choice; it's time to redeem ourselves.*

What better way to do it than by facing my greatest fear again?

So, that was that. There was no send-off party, no tearful goodbyes. By mid-August, we had sold the house I took my first steps in, boxed up our things, and traveled cross-country to Murkmore.

Four days in a sweltering car and a nauseating forty-five-minute ferry ride later, we've arrived.

Mom and I walk off the ferry while Dad inches the SUV down the ramp, us waving and guiding him along. The boxes and equipment precariously strapped to the top of our car wobble violently as the car crunches onto the hole-speckled pavement. Mom cheers, raising her arms over her head. Dad rolls down the window and gives us both a smug smile.

"Like a pro," he says.

"Like a dork," I reply.

"You want to be grounded on your first day in a new town?" Mom asks.

The first thing that hits me is a foul odor: a deadly combination of rotten fish, salt from the sea, and sulfur, like rotten eggs. The ferry unloads at Murkmore Visitor's Center, which consists of a square white brick building and an asphalt courtyard filled with patches of scraggly trees and flowers quarantined behind ankle-height rusty iron fences. One of the benches has a hole smack-dab in the center of its seat, like some monster took a bite out of it. Discarded bits of bottles and trampled trash form a disgusting caulk for the sidewalk's many crevices. But nothing is quite as impressive as the seagull poop that litters the tops of the suspiciously full trash cans.

What a dump.

We get back in the car, and I can barely buckle my seat belt since stuff has shifted. Dad drives agonizingly slow through the streets, which are empty save for a few kids biking around in their still-wet swimsuits—today is fairly humid, so I guess it's the one time they can take advantage of the "good" weather. One kid, no older than six or seven, sticks his tongue out at me.

Nice.

Eventually, we pull into the crumbling asphalt driveway of our new home, a single-story ranch-style house sitting atop a plot of scraggly grass. We pile out of the car, eager to stretch our legs. Dad jingles the keys as we approach the front door. A withered ivy trellis clings to the wall beside the door. From the stoop, the imperfections in the house are more apparent: Paint chips off the white window frames, and the sconces all have cracks in them. Empty flower beds form graveyards for—ew, what are those? *Dead bugs?* I glance over my shoulder at Mom, whose brown eyes are wide and simmering with excitement at the possibility of finally implementing all those fixer-upper techniques she learned from HGTV. *There go my weekends.*

"It's cute!" she chirps, placing a hand against the trellis. The wood cracks at her ginger touch, and she recoils. "Okay. That might have to go."

I point to the distressed windows. "*All* of it has to go."

Dad rolls his eyes as he puts the key in the lock. "Nothing a fresh coat of paint can't fix."

"You guys got the place inspected for termites, right?"

Dad remains suspiciously silent as he jimmies the key in the lock.

"Cool, cool, cool."

He twists the doorknob, and the door creaks open. The kitchen and the living room are in the same area, separated by a half wall. Piled up in front of the fireplace are most of our boxes and furniture—the realtor agreed to show up a few days before our arrival to help the movers bring everything in.

Mom scrunches up her nose as she approaches the pile of boxes. "I would've thought that they'd…put boxes where they need to go." She picks up one labeled *GARAGE* and points to another labeled *BATHROOM.* I can't help but laugh, and she laughs too.

Dad is way too literal to find it funny. "No. A mover only brings the stuff in; they don't care about putting things where they need to go."

Mom stares. "I know, hon."

"Oh." Dad blinks and looks at me with a grin. "You want to go check out your room?"

"Which one is it?"

"Down the hallway, to the left. There might be a surprise in there for you."

"What is it? A feather duster?"

"Very funny. Humor me and take a peek."

I shrug my shoulders and head in that direction. The hallway is quite narrow, the edges of the cream carpet yellowed and fraying against the walls. I can't tell if that's cat piss or water damage, but judging from the smell of this place, it's both. Behind me the windows shriek and rattle as Mom throws them open; the noise is so bad, it's like they were rusted in place. This house is so damn old I'm surprised it's not haunted. Imagine having to haul boxes around all day long and then having to suck up a soul into your cap-can. I'd lose it.

I walk to the end of the hallway and open the door. The room inside is smaller than my old room for sure, but it should have enough space for all my stuff. I gasp when I see what Dad was grinning about: built into the wall beside the closet is this small enclave, and within it stands a glorious vintage vanity. The white paint is peeling in places and the mirror has streaks, but it's beyond cute. Plenty of drawers for all my things—and wall outlets. It's also got the classic little bulbous lights I love so much. A perfect place to do makeup, unlike the bathroom I used to have at our old house, which had little to no counter space.

Okay. So maybe this house will grow on me.

My bed frame and mattress are already in the room collecting dust, but none of my other furniture is in here yet. After I've helped Mom and Dad unpack the kitchen and bathroom things, they help me move in my furniture, and then leave me to my own devices. I wonder where they're planning on setting up the workshop. At home—well, our last home—they had a dedicated room above the garage. But the garage here isn't meant for two cars, and there's no way Mom would allow Dad to park the SUV in the driveway.

Mom answers my question when she sticks her head in the door. "Can you come help me in the basement?"

"Basement?" I shudder.

I know that place has got to be filthy, given the state of this house. Mom and I tiptoe down the wobbly wooden stairs into the inky-black abyss. It's ten degrees colder down here than it is upstairs.

"Melody, the light."

I fumble in the darkness for anything: a light switch, a control panel, a button. All I feel is grime and layers of dust. My fingers meet wooden grooves—I guess there's paneling on the walls?—and I shudder at the thought of getting a splinter. Mom giggles behind me and suddenly the world erupts in light. I spin around to face her and she points to a string hanging above her head.

"Old school," she says. "But we'll get it fixed up soon enough."

Doubt it. Electrical work probably costs thousands of dollars we don't have. But I know better than to be a smart-ass right now. The movers somehow managed to bring the EctoChamber down here—a spherical object that resembles an oversized light bulb. It's meant to serve as a holding cell of sorts for captured souls, until they can be funneled through the Ingress. Speaking of the Ingress, I have no idea where ours is. Must still be packed up in a box. I'm not digging the musty smell down here, but it beats the uninsulated garage attic we had before.

Mom passes me a broom and tasks me with sweeping up all the dead bugs and dust bunnies while she and Dad haul down box after box. Soon, the space is cluttered yet clean, and Mom and Dad begin setting up their workshop. Dad beams, his smile full of hope.

Hope, which I took away from them by being a total fucking loser.

"Sweetie," Mom says, "do you want to maybe take a break and go into town? It's almost dinnertime."

I nod. "You think this place has an Indian restaurant?"

Mom laughs.

While there are unfortunately no Indian restaurants in Murkmore—a fact that almost brings me to tears—there is a sushi restaurant. This *almost* makes up for the devastating realization that I may not be eating biryani or palak paneer for the next few years (unless I'm willing to suffer through a ferry ride to the mainland, and my gurgling stomach says that I will *not* be prepared for that anytime soon). Since we're right on the water, the sushi's cheap and high quality. Quiet, too. When we walk in there are only a few people eating. Mom points in the direction of a couple of teens clearly on a date, their fingers laced through each other's.

"Look!" she whispers, with the awe of someone witnessing a man walk on water. "Other people your age!"

My cheeks burn. "Mom, don't point."

I would honestly rather spontaneously combust than have anyone my age glance in my direction. I'm still dressed in the sloppy sweats I was wearing earlier, and plus, I didn't put on any makeup today. Maybe I should have made the effort, because the hostess flinches when she notices the scars on my face. 'Least she doesn't stare.

We're escorted to our table, and before long a waitress arrives to grab our drink order. My parents enthusiastically ask for sake while I sip on my water.

"Move-in day—done! Mission accomplished!" Dad cheers, clinking his cup against Mom's and mine.

"We still have plenty to do. So much cleaning." Mom groans and rolls her eyes. "Had I known the place was gonna be this dirty, I would've maybe sprung for a professional to come in and clean."

"No use doing that. The carpets need to be torn out altogether. Vinyl wood floors, baby." Dad takes another sip and smacks his lips in satisfaction. He looks at me with a twinkle in his eye. "You excited to start school soon?"

"Well, it beats spending an entire summer packing boxes."

There's nothing worse than an uneventful summer. Things have been so bad, we didn't even take a vacation this year. The last time we didn't take a trip I was thirteen, and that was because Mom was still recovering from her open-heart surgery. But this is going to be a fresh start. No one here knows about my failures, and because there are no other hunters here, they're not likely to care about them anyways. I'm going to slap on a flawless makeup look, a fave outfit, and walk through those school doors tomorrow a changed woman.

At least, that's my plan.

Once a vibrant fishing community, Murkmore experienced a sharp drop in employment after the 2007 oil spill. The town is now completely dependent on its meager tourism industry, but the current infrastructure cannot support it. And, because of the rising poverty levels, no one can afford to leave their home. Despite their struggles, the residents truly emblematize their simplistic island motto: "To persevere."

—*Nightly News Broadcast*, hosted by Nenario Mthens, East Province News Network (20 Feb. 2007)

Chapter Two

Murkmore High, with its three stories and old-school Grecian columns, casts a shadow down the entire street. Seriously, it's like a solar eclipse over here, and the overcast weather isn't helping. The exterior walls near the school's doors have pep rally posters plastered all over them, and throngs of students have gathered outside. The giant stone sign embedded in the yard bears the town motto: "To persevere." Adjacent to this building is the elementary school, another brick-and-mortar block that would resemble a prison if not for the colorfully rusted playground out front—well, that and the throngs of screaming children. How does this tiny island town need these big-ass buildings? Maybe they're remains from the island's glory days as a fishing industry giant.

I shuffle in place, feeling self-conscious, but stop myself. *No, Melody. Fresh start. Just like you wanted. Own it.* I stand up a little straighter, tilt my chin up higher. Deep breaths. Must've been standing in the way for too long, because a middle-aged lady in a turtleneck wrinkles her nose at me disdainfully.

"Hey! You!" Her blue eyes nearly bulge out of her skull. "Are you waiting for something?"

"Me? Uh…" I don't know what to say. Is it a crime to stand somewhere?

"Do you have your student ID?"

"My—no?"

She rolls her eyes and makes a big sweeping motion with her arms toward a line of kids waiting to get into the building. "If you need your student ID picture taken, you need to get in line. Don't block the flow of traffic."

It's not like kids are completely unable to walk around me, but whatever. Guess she wanted to have a little back-to-school power trip this morning. With a huff, I shuffle over to the line, but after seeing how long it is, I think I'll pass. There's gotta be makeups for this sort of thing, right? Instead, I make my way over to a series of tables arranged on the front lawn. Various tablecloths are adorned in block lettering spelling out the names of clubs: cheer squad, art club—wow, even an honor society. Okay. Maybe I won't wallow in depression for an entire year until I graduate. Maybe once the chaos of this hunt is over, there'll be other things I can do to make the time go by.

"Hey there!"

A stocky teen with a sienna skin tone sits behind a table, completely alone, their hands neatly folded on its surface, showing off an array of rubber bracelets. They've got buzzed pink hair, horn-rimmed glasses, and are wearing a bright-teal—

"It's a tunic," they say, stretching out the fabric to illustrate its shape and style.

"Uh…cool," I say, unsure of how to respond.

"I like your—I like your sweater-vest," they say.

It's a pink-and-white Argyle sweater-vest that I got secondhand from Delaney's thrift store back in Mountain Ridge. I've paired it with a button-up white lantern-sleeve blouse and a black skirt that Mom swears is too short, but it passes the fingertip rule, so I'm going with it.

"I'm surprised you didn't get dress-coded, but I guess Ms. Ruder over there is too frazzled."

"Wait—Ruder? Her name is actually Ruder?"

They smile. "Yep. Really fits the bill, don't you think?" They extend their hand. "I'm Tomai. They/them."

"Melody. She/her." I say this calmly, but inside I'm screaming. Spirits Beyond, I'm making friends already! *Queer* friends! I'm not going to be the only one here! Who knew that having a positive mindset would actually work?

Tomai offers me a red flyer from their stack, and their fingertips feel sticky against mine. "Anyways, welcome to town, new girl. If you think this place is a dumpster fire, consider joining me to clean it up. Apologies for the flyer; I spilled my frappé earlier."

Spunky letters across the top read *MURKMORE HIGH BEAUTIFICATION COMMITTEE*. Clip art of flowers and cutesy birds decorate the margins of the page, surrounding information about the club's meeting room. Clearly graphic design isn't their passion. There's a lot going on here, but not enough to distract me from what they said.

"You know I'm new here? Is it that obvious?"

Tomai gives me a weird look. "I mean, yeah. I've known everyone here since pre-K."

"Oh. Right."

"And I guess that means you're the ghost hunter, right?"

I hear hushed whispers behind them: "Ghost hunter? Oh my God. No, they're talking to the ghost hunter."

Within seconds the others descend on us, eyes wide, jaws slack, ogling me in a way that's both uncomfortable and highly flattering. I mean, I guess after a year of being ignored I can't say the attention is unwelcome. Tomai seems uncomfortable though. Students push and shove until they're in front of the table, blocking my view of Tomai..And then from the sea of faces emerges one, sharp, angular, with cat eyes so fine they could stab a man clean through the chest. She wears box braids that frame her heart-shaped face, showing off her modelesque features even more. Her amber skin has not a single blemish, and her pores are invisible to the naked eye.

Stunning would be a modest word to describe her.

"So you're the ghost hunter girl? That's what you're called, right?" she says, and from the inflection in her voice, I can tell.

She's the queen bee. You know the voice. Perky yet restrained. Brynne hung around these types of girls all the time. Going to a party back then felt like sitting in an iron cage with sharks swimming around you.

"Hi. I'm Melody," I say with a smile. "And yes, that would be me."

She smiles back. Full of teeth, sharp and white. Despite how gorgeous she is, the shark resemblance is uncanny. "Very cool. I didn't know that hunters would, like, go to school."

I don't know why I wouldn't, but I'm not about to ask. While ghost hunters aren't nearly as common as witches or vampires as far as Fantasticals go, we're not unheard of. According to the last Interprovincial Census, we account for like, 2 percent of the population, so we're about as common as redheads. We also live the way most humans do, only our lives revolve around the scientific study, management, and capturing of ghosts.

There are a few key things that separate ghost hunters from humans though: For one, we have a gene that allows us to see ghosts, which are only visible on a certain light spectrum. Ghosts are invisible to everyone else unless they choose to reveal themselves—with us hunters, nothing can hide from us. Secondly, like the ghosts we hunt, we can manipulate certain electromagnetic fields and devices—this is what allows us to power and operate our cap-cans, and to cancel out the powers of ghosts. Third, using our powers, we have the ability to open up the pathway to the Beyond, although I'll be honest, devices like the Ingress and the EctoChamber have largely replaced the grueling, time-consuming rituals we previously used. Knowing the history of this island, I'm not totally surprised these kids are ignorant about our culture…but most people know at least a *little*, even if it's just the basics. It throws me off.

"Anyways, I'm Jackie, your student body president. Pronouns are she/her. Welcome to our sorry excuse for an island." She arches a brow. "I mean it *is*, isn't it?"

"Uh…"

"I bet you've been in places way more interesting. The paper said the hunters would be coming from Mountain Ridge."

My family's move was reported in the paper? There's a paper here? A *physical* paper? What, is the internet connection here ass? Devastating. How am I supposed to read fan fiction?

"Ahh…yeah. Mountain Ridge. Yep."

"Wait," a brunette chimes in, her brown eyes wide and nervous. "Are you going to be helping your family take down the ghost?"

A chorus of voices chimes in from the crowd.

"Yeah, are you gonna be hunting them too?"

"How much do you know about the deaths?"

"Oh shit, guys. What if she's here because the ghost is *in* the school?"

"Shut the hell up, Tyler!"

Okay, maybe all this attention *isn't* what it's cracked up to be. My palms are clamming up and my neck feels damp. That could be my social anxiety, or it could be from the heat of all these surrounding bodies. I search for Tomai's face in the crowd, but I can't identify them in this dense ocean of people.

"I haven't heard anything about the ghosts inhabiting the school," I mumble in response.

Someone's jaw drops. "*Ghosts?* Ghosts, plural?"

"She hasn't heard *if* they live here, but you don't know for sure?"

"We're boned."

The sound of a whistle, shrill like a girl's scream, cuts through the air. Rattled, the crowd turns in the direction of the noise. Stomach churning, I lock eyes with Ms. Ruder once more, her pupils ablaze. Her ruddy complexion grows blotchier and redder as she tries to regain control of the kids.

"Keep it moving, people!" she growls, gesturing in the direction of the other frazzled teachers and parent volunteers.

Mumbling their discontent, the students shuffle toward the school, but Ruder scowls at me like a venomous snake. She wags her finger at me in a come-hither motion. Obediently—and regretfully—I shuffle over.

"Yeah?"

Her brow arches at my one-word answer. "Yeah, what?"

"Uh…"

With a snort, she tosses her head. "Why are you freaking out all the other kids like that? Your family's business is none of their business."

"Well…" I mumble, trailing off. "They asked."

"Yeah? Well, it's clear you don't know anything about it, so I'd keep your lips zipped. Also…" She fumbles in her flamingo-colored fanny pack and withdraws a tape measure. With an expert flick of her wrist, she drops it alongside my hips and shakes her head. *Spirits, what?* She's clearly practiced this! "Your skirt's too short. It needs to be below the knee. We don't follow the fingertip rule here."

"I didn't know that," I whine in response.

"You would have if you came to orientation—or read the student handbook. There was an email."

"M-Ms. Ruder," I laugh breathlessly. "I literally moved here three days ago. I've been helping my family unpack; I haven't had the time to check my email."

That's a lie. I check my email religiously, but I never got a damn email from this school, unless it ended up in my spam folder.

Ms. Ruder remains unfazed. "Not my problem. You need to call your parents and ask for a change of bottoms."

Mom and Dad are supposed to be meeting with the mayor and the force today to discuss the investigation. If they have to stop what they're doing to bring me a change of clothes, they'll flip. In my head, Mom's voice chides me. *You need to* think *before you act, Melody.*

Something heavy presses down on my shoulder, and I glance down to see a perfectly manicured hand resting there. Behind me, a woman dressed in a pressed pink pantsuit stands, blond hair slicked back in a twisted bun. Her skin is white, with a rosy undertone. She smiles kindly, but her eyes seem stiff, like she's had too many Botox sessions or something—at least, that would explain her flawless, shimmering skin. How much highlighter has this lady caked on her face? And where did she get it from because it's *amazing?* When I glance back at Ms. Ruder, all the fire and brimstone is gone, leaving her face flushed.

"You must be Melody Myere," the pink lady says with a smile full of pearly whites. "I'm Principal Redd. I trust Ms. Ruder was welcoming you to our school?"

"Actually, I was being dress-coded. Skirt's too short."

Ruder nods. "She needs to bring a change of clothes."

"On the first day?" The woman crows, pressing a hand against her chest in deep offense. "Oh, no. I think we can let this slide, don't you? That's no way to welcome a student."

Damn. Ruder getting roasted. Her cheeks grow pinker and pinker by the second. Can't say I'm not enjoying it. I bite down on the inside of my cheek, hoping to stop my smug little smirk from spreading across my face.

"Wow, thank you for your *generosity*, Principal Redd," I reply emphatically, glancing over at Ms. Ruder.

Her head shrinks down into the collar of her shirt like a frightened turtle. That's right. *Cower. Cower in fear.*

Principal Redd's smile thins in a way that indicates she knows I'm being a shit, but she's restraining herself from lecturing me. Ruder huffs in response and shuffles away like a dog with its tail tucked between its legs.

"I saw you met my daughter, Jackie."

She gestures to the girl with the sharp smile, now hovering in the background with the rest of her friends, gossiping. I wouldn't have thought they were related, but I can see the resemblance in their facial features—in particular, their blue eyes. *Ahh.* It all fits together, doesn't it? The high school queen bee has power because of her principal mother.

"You'll have to forgive the excitement of the other students. It's not often we get newcomers on the island. Certainly not ghost hunters."

I nod, unsure of what to say. Principal Redd points somewhere inside the school as if gesturing for me to follow her. I stand there a bit confused until she waves her hand in a beckoning motion.

"Shouldn't I get my ID first?"

She smiles. "You can get that later. We have some things we should discuss."

The history of the West Province, although not without its moments of bloodshed, is more peaceful than the other provinces. The exploration of uncharted territory enabled the idea of the "mixed salad" to take root, rather than a melting pot. Individual cultures were celebrated and welcomed.

—Jacob L. Potterwirks, *A Condensed History of the Northern Americas' Nation-State*, 5th ed. (2000)

Chapter Three

Principal Redd's office appears suspiciously nice for something that's financed by the tax dollars of Murkmore's citizens. Warm-coral paint plasters the walls, sans the one that's just exposed brick, like some industrial-chic apartment in a city skyrise. Family portraits and vacation snapshots encased in glittering gold frames hang from their hooks, or are otherwise artfully placed on her bookshelf, which is packed with history and environmental-science books. It looks like she's also got a book on the history of Murkmore, which seems dorky to me, considering she's likely lived here her whole life.

"Would you care for anything? Hot chocolate? Tea?"

Confused, I settle into the velvety armchair across from her desk. She migrates over to a minifridge in the corner—one with a wood-textured wallpaper plastered over it, so it resembles a fancy cabinet—and gestures to the Keurig sitting on top. Pods and tea packets are neatly organized in a three-tiered wire basket embossed with gold. Damn, okay. Don't mind if I do.

She pops a hot chocolate pod into the machine at my request and places a dainty rose-colored teacup underneath the spout. The wet gurgling of the machine is drowned out by the sound of the air conditioner overhead, which vibrates so intensely I fear an air duct is going to fall from the ceiling. It's right over my head, too. Can't help but lean a little bit to the left, (hopefully) out of its way.

Redd winces and takes a seat at her desk. "Ahh, yes…it's quite an old building."

"At least you guys have air-conditioning. At my old school, it went down in April, and by June, it was so humid, we were all sticking to our chairs."

She laughs, and her voice almost sounds musical. I think I really like this lady. She seems like the type of person that's kinda uptight in public, but pretty chill otherwise. She leans back in her chair, her perfect posture slumping a tad.

"So, I don't want to make you feel like you're in trouble or anything. But I overheard what Ms. Ruder said to you, and despite her tactless way of phrasing things, she's right," Principal Redd says. "We'd prefer to not talk about the deaths at the school. The boys who died, well, they were former students here. Marcus Crowley…Wendell Phillips…Tyreese Buchanan. May they rest in peace. They had such bright futures ahead of them."

Damn, *three* people from this school have died? I knew the victims ranged from teenagers to young adults, with the oldest victim I think being twenty-nine, but that number still surprises me.

"We ended up closing the school early and moving to online learning for the remainder of the year. Island-wide curfew. It was hard. Hard on all of us. And I don't want the focus of everyone's year to once again be their deaths." She nods. "That's why the city hired your family, after all. To prevent more deaths from happening."

"I... I didn't mean any disrespect," I say. "I was a little overwhelmed with all the questions. And I get why people would be curious. I mean, they knew them."

"Oh, certainly. But we want to prevent any discussion whatsoever, to the best of our ability."

Steam wafts up from the Keurig, and it finishes dispensing the hot chocolate with a watery hiss. Principal Redd rolls over to the machine, grabs the teacup, and glances back at me.

"Oh, I'm sorry. You don't want any cream or anything in this, right? No? Okay." She hands it to me. "I'm not sure how involved you're going to be in your parents' practice. Do spirit whisperers often let their children participate in hunts?"

"Spirit whisperer..."

"Oh, I'm sorry. Is that not appropriate?"

I shake my head. "It's not necessarily derogatory. It's a little— it's a religious phrase. I haven't heard anyone other than pious people use it."

Honestly, if someone calls me a spirit whisperer, I think they're trying way too hard. It's a term our ancestors used before things like electricity, or paper that wasn't made from animal skin. It's not wrong, it's just really outdated. At my old school there was only one girl who called herself a spirit whisperer, and she was always mumbling verses from the *Tomes* under her breath in between classes or before meals. Probably someone who'd be voted in the yearbook as Most Likely to Become an Apostle.

"Ahh, my apologies, then." She taps her fingers against the desk, and for the first time since I've met her, she looks a little nervous. "We're making efforts to be more inclusive at the school."

I'm surprised Redd knows this much about ghost hunters, when everyone else seems totally ignorant. This is such a weird departure from life in Mountain Ridge. Back there, if you weren't a hunter, you were likely a witch, a vampire, or a terra-elf. The province was a stronghold for Fantasticals for centuries, so aside from a few spats, and of course the Great Chimera War of 1879, everyone learned how to get along pretty quick. My parents warned me about this kind of thing before we moved here: *Mountain Ridge isn't like other places.* Until I left my hometown, I had no understanding of what that meant.

"We—the school administration and myself—would truly appreciate your cooperation in regards to this."

"I totally understand, Principal Redd."

Gotta keep the peace and all of that. But as to her earlier question about how much I'm going to be involved, my parents have yet to explain what kind of role they have in mind for me. They've been pretty tight-lipped about the whole ordeal, and if I ever bring it up, they suddenly act like they're walking on eggshells. Hushed voices, wide eyes. Their bodies tell me what they won't say outright, which is that they think I can't handle it.

But I only agreed to move here so that I can prove them wrong. And I'm hoping they're not going to stand in the way of what I want.

Principal Redd smiles at me fondly, as if she believes my innocence. "I'm glad we understand each other. You should get your student ID after you finish your hot chocolate. No drinks other than water are allowed in our classrooms."

Historically, the island has not welcomed Fantasticals due to its zoning regulations, but these were lifted in order to let the ghost hunters move here. When asked about the change, local resident Stella Brown says it's about time. "Change is a good thing," she says. But does the rest of the island agree, and will the more conservative residents come around? Time will tell.

—Howard Bonevue, "Ghost Hunters Moving In Late Fall; Will Address Island's Ghost Problem," *The Sunshine Standard* (10 Aug. 2024)

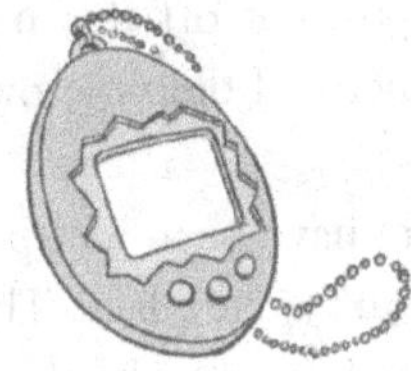

Chapter Four

School is…well, it's school. It feels normal. For the most part my teachers seem nice, and while the students gawked at me at first, no one has asked me any weird questions or been outright anti-Fantastical so far. In fact, no one's talked to me at all. Judging from some of the watchful eyes of the teachers, I can tell they've all gotten the memo from Principal Redd to not ask me any questions about the hunt. Lips zipped shut. Makes me almost miss the overwhelming attention I got this morning.

When I go to lunch, I find Tomai sitting alone at a cafeteria table. They're munching on a sandwich and doodling in their agenda. Embarrassment resurfaces in my body when I remember how they were buried by the crowd this morning. They were so nice to me, and yet, I got separated from them in the chaos. I want to make friends. I want to make friends with people who will bother to be nice to me like Tomai did. I want to build bridges and not burn them like I've been doing for the past six months.

I hope I don't come across as too eager, though. The last thing I need is for more people to think I'm a socially inept dork.

"Tomai!" I call out to them, waving.

They look up, blinking. A reserved smile widens across their face, and for a moment, my heart hammers within my chest. Not a good sign. But then they motion for me to come and sit by them, and I breathe a sigh of relief as I scurry over.

"Hey. Sorry we got cut off this morning." I plop my tray down across from them. "I didn't know people would spot me, like, immediately."

"Yeah…they sure have been whispering about you," Tomai says with a tone I can't quite place. They won't meet my gaze. Are they mad at me? It seems like they're mad at me. Maybe I shouldn't be sitting here. But if they were mad, they wouldn't have invited me to sit, right? "Especially Jackie and her little cohort."

"Jackie…?"

"You met her this morning. Principal Redd's daughter."

"Oh." I frown and tear open my carton of skim milk. It tastes like water, but I'm trying to eliminate as many unnecessary fats from my diet as possible. "Is…that a bad thing? I mean, she seems—"

"She's your run-of-the-mill high school It girl—well, second to Brinkley Davis."

"Haven't met Brinkley yet."

"You will. Eventually. And unfortunately. Especially if you're in the theater crowd."

"What was that?"

Tomai's shoulders tense and eyes widen. A girl is walking down the aisle toward us. Her brown hair is styled in a shaggy wolf cut that grazes the tops of her shoulders, but her outfit contrasts with this grunge aesthetic: wide-legged pink pants paired with a tastefully cropped striped sweater. *Huh.* Wonder if she got dress-coded today. The girl pays no attention to me, hazel eyes engulfed in flames as she stares at Tomai.

She crouches down beside them even as they avert their eyes. This time, her voice leaves her lips in a hiss. "Hmm, I could've sworn you were saying how *unfortunate* it'd be to meet me."

Oh, she is absolutely terrifying.

Tomai's face flushes and they manage to stammer, "Uh-uh, no, Brinkley."

"I thought so." She looks at me like I'm gum stuck to the bottom of her shoe, then leaves, the heels of her boots clicking against the concrete as she saunters to a nearby table. Tomai and I hold our collective breath until she makes her way to a table and sits.

Tomai gives a little flourish of their hand. "Brinkley."

"Figured." I take another sip of milk. "So you're a performer?"

"Nah. Stage crew, baby! I make the magic happen. And when I'm not doing that, I'm focused on saving the planet."

I guess that explains why Tomai is so muscular—long hours lifting heavy set pieces and crawling around in fly towers will do that for you. In my first couple years of high school, I was involved in theater. No big roles or anything, but I enjoyed being in the chorus and playing bit parts whenever I could. Then I started dating Brynne toward the end of my sophomore year and I gave it up so I could spend more time with her. I'd consider doing it again if I didn't need to focus on finding the ghost—or ghosts—responsible for these damn deaths.

"We're always looking for more people to crew, if you're interested."

"I would be, but…" I bite my lip nervously.

Tomai's eyes widen. "*Ohh*. You mean you *are* helping out your family?"

"I mean, I would like to. It's complicated." Personally, I'm hoping if I'm able to get a little head start on the case, it'll smooth things over. "My parents went to meet with the mayor today to discuss the situation. I don't know much about what's going on, except that three students from here are—"

A sad expression crosses Tomai's face. "Yeah. It's been…a rough couple of years."

"Did you know any of the boys that died?"

"I mean, we know everybody here. But friends with them? Nah. Still sad though." Tomai stares solemnly at their lukewarm cafeteria lasagna for a few moments. "Tyreese was always a nice dude. He was the former class president."

"I'm sorry to hear that."

I take a bite of my apple and chew slowly, although it tastes a little old, like sinking my teeth in quicksand: sloppy, heavy, wet-cementy. The flesh is already oxidizing, brown staining the soft yellow insides. Yikes. It's on the verge of going rotten. I drop it on my tray with a grimace.

Tomai notices. "Oh yeah. I should mention—don't get the 'fresh' fruit here. They flash freeze it when they ship it over and then it's defrosted. You're better off getting the little fruit cups instead."

I'd get the fruit cups, but I know those are filled with a ton of sugar and corn syrup. And judging from the number I'm looking at when I step on the scale in the mornings, I want to avoid eating things with unnecessary additives. If I'm going to get back into ghost hunting, I need to get back into shape. I take a bite of my lasagna instead, which is equally unimpressive, but at least the sauce has meat in it, so I'm hoping I'll get a little more protein. I'm not looking forward to the wilted side salad on my plate either; it's full of iceberg lettuce, which tastes like water and has the nutritional content to match. Ugh. Am I going to need to start packing my own lunches? Like I need another thing on my to-do list.

"So…kinda weird no one has reported any paranormal activity. No possession of objects, no electricity on the fritz, no mysterious chills…" I say in between bites of food. "Normally when things like this happen, it's easy to narrow down where a ghost should be, even if y'all can't see them like I can."

"I think it's harder to find a ghost in what's essentially a ghost town," Tomai replies with a wry smirk. "I don't know anything about ghosts, but I imagine there are tons of places for them to be hiding in plain sight, you know?"

Oh. Duh. So much for being a great detective. "Yeah…true. But it's weird to think that there're no connections between their deaths."

Tomai's eyes widen as if in protest to what I've said, and I struggle to contain my excitement, maintaining my poker face as best I can. *Got 'em.* They drum their fingertips on the table anxiously, and their head swivels from side to side, glancing over their shoulder. Ms. Ruder lurks at the back of the cafeteria like a leopard pacing back and forth in an iron cage.

"Sorry," Tomai mutters to me, turning back around. "Ruder is on the prowl."

"What does she do here? Aside from enforce sexist, outdated dress code standards."

"AP Lit and Comp."

My heart drops to my stomach. "Aw, shit. I think I have her."

"Same. We unfortunately cannot escape her fiery wrath." A mischievous twinkle appears in Tomai's eyes, and they lean in closer to me. "So…you're clearly fishing for information."

Heat swells in my cheeks. I know I have to be beet red right now.

Tomai chuckles. "Yeah, sorry, but you're not slick. You've got the subtlety of a six-year-old."

"Damn," I whisper, touching an offended hand to my chest.

"You're trying to help your family out; I get it. But uh…I can tell you my theories, after school. If that's cool with you."

I nod a little too eagerly. Tomai laughs, and although they're poking fun at me, my heart feels warm. It's nice to finally have a friend again. I just hope I don't blow it.

Virginia Green takes a shaky breath. "It was my family's life's work. And although the Lennox Theater has brought a lot of joy to our community, that doesn't mean it's special enough to withstand all the bad luck our businesses have been hit with." She wipes a tear, wringing the handkerchief in her hands. "We do our best to help each other, but it's not enough."

—Howard Bonevue, "Lennox Theater Closes Down: Looking Back with the Founder's Great-Great Granddaughter, Virginia Green," *The Sunshine Standard* (15 Oct. 2012)

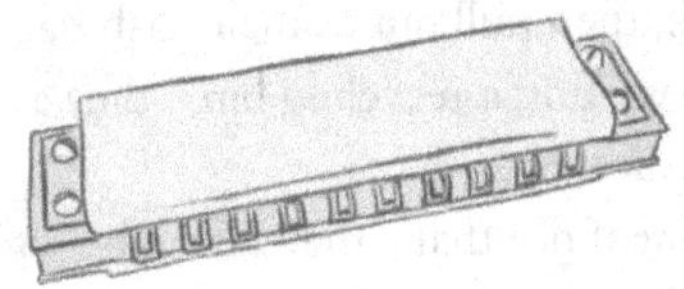

Chapter Five

Miraculously, Ms. Ruder is not a total raging asshole when she figures out I'm a part of her class. We do introductions, go over the syllabus for the trimester, and then we're out for the day. Murkmore is so small there's not even a bus system here, so the streets are a chaotic mess of slowly moving cars and excited children sprinting down the crumbling, trash-laden sidewalks. A couple of kids kick a can back and forth as they continue toward their destination. Kids on bikes dart between the cars with a frightening disregard for their personal safety. I follow Tomai out the school doors and down the street, although I'm not sure where we're going. I text Mom to let her know I'm going to hang out with a friend for a while.

MOM: 🖤🖤🖤 Yay!!! B home by 5:30 for dinner tho!

It's kind of embarrassing Mom is as excited about this as I am, but it's nice she's showing her support. It wasn't too long ago—before my Hunt—she was complaining I was spending too much time out of the house. Brynne had a lot of friends, and most of the time we were either out with them at a party or at Dickey's Diner down the road from our school. Six months into my relationship with her, almost every weekend, I was over at Brynne's.

Tomai grunts underneath their breath as they squat down to pick up a discarded soda can. They grimace as they reach into their backpack, then pull out a small trash bag.

"Just until we find a recycling bin," they assure me.

"Wow. Dedicated."

"I'm nothing if not that," they say with a sigh, then ask, "How do you like it here? On a scale of 'It's really shitty' to 'I'd rather be dead'?"

I laugh. "It's really shitty. But kinda cute, in a way."

"I'm glad you *think* that, but I'd like for it to actually be cute. That's the focus of the Beautification Committee. We—and by we, I mean me—pick up trash, clean roadways, and last year, we *finally* convinced the city council to place recycling bins around town. Can you believe it? Murkmore has been around for a hundred and fifty years and we *just* started recycling."

"That's cool, but I thought that was an environmental club kinda thing? I would've thought *beautification* meant like, painting murals or planting flowers."

They scrunch up their face. "Yeah, except if I called it that, admin would've fought me. Some of those people don't believe in climate change."

"Seriously?"

"I wish I was joking. When I started the club in freshman year, they made me pick that name."

"And no one else wants to join the club…?" I ask, carefully. "You're the only member, right? At least, I didn't see anyone else at the table this morning."

Tomai's expression darkens, and for a moment I think I've struck a nerve, but then they turn their gaze away from me. "We did have other members at one point, but, yeah. I'm the only one left. I think most people are determined to get out of here after school, so they see no point in making it better. They don't *want* Murkmore to have a future; they want it gone." They shrug. "But, like…we're still here. People will continue to be here. I think there's some value in making Murkmore a better place, even if I don't intend to live here all my life. Doing a few little things day by day can make a difference, so why not do it?"

"That's… That's kinda brave."

"Brave? Pfft. You live here long enough, you'll get sick of seeing the trash and dead fish along the shoreline, too. But thank you." They grin. "Anyways, you're from Mountain Ridge, right? Over in the West Province?"

"Yeah." I kick at a chunk of crumbling asphalt in my path. Spirits, the potholes around here are enormous. I bet when it rains you could go swimming in these. Passing cars maneuver around them in drastic spins and turns, like dancers in a chaotic ballet. "Lot different from here. But I'll be honest: I kinda don't miss it."

"No?"

I shake my head and laugh nervously. Is it too early to reveal I'm a total freaking loser? Tomai looks at me expectantly, but I decide to keep it vague, rather than trauma-dump.

"Uh, I mean, it was time for a change of pace. So when my parents said they wanted to move here, I was kinda like, sure, I mean, why not?"

"I can think of plenty of reasons." Tomai laughs and fumbles with the straps on their backpack, which jingles under the weight of all the key chains and pushpin buttons attached to it. It looks like more of an art project than a functional bag, but it's still pretty cool. "I can't wait to get out of here. Hoping to go to Empire City for college, if I can get lucky and get a good scholarship. Otherwise, I'm going to head over to the mainland and do community college for a couple of years until I can transfer—well, I say a couple, but with all the AP I'm doing, I'm hoping it's only going to be like, a year."

I've given no thought to my future this past year. I've been too depressed. Most ghost hunters end up going to an academy where they can practice their craft and eventually get their license. There's an academy in almost every province, most of which aren't too competitive to get into, but the best schools are Thistlefeayr Americas, Empire City East, and Rose Red Row— my parents' alma mater, which they wanted me to attend. But I don't know what my future entails. I know—or at least I *think* I know—I want to be a hunter and carry on my family's legacy, but school seems…complicated. When you pass your First Hunt, you're usually granted a passing certificate, and without it, getting into an academy will be a lot more difficult. It will likely require additional tests, trials, and readings, none of which I've done. My focus these past six months was on getting better and not having a complete and total meltdown every time I was reminded of my trauma. Now that I'm in a better spot, I can focus on helping my parents with this hunt and proving how much stronger I am.

Tomai waves a hand in front of my face. "Melody? Hello?"

"Sorry," I murmur, embarrassed. "I don't know where I'd want to go. Haven't given it much thought."

"Oh. That's totally normal," Tomai responds, shrugging their shoulders. "Don't feel bad about that. I know a lot of other people here are feeling the same. They're thinking about doing gap years."

Honestly, I think my parents would have a total meltdown if I told them I was considering that possibility, although at this point, I probably need it. Or, I need to do something extraordinary—so brazenly extraordinary that the Council, or the Head Apostle herself, would have no choice but to automatically grant me a passing certificate. By helping my parents on this investigation, not only would I be proving myself in their eyes, but in everyone's. Losing to a wraith only to come back and defeat a swarm of them? Oh yeah, they'd have no choice but to let me into my school of choice, whatever that is.

Tomai interprets my silence as nervousness and tries to reassure me. "If you don't know what you want to do now, and it's your senior year, maybe consider the gap year. It's not the end of the world. Plus, since you're doing AP classes, if you *do* decide on where you want to go, you'll have a lot of your schooling done already. Whichever you decide, you'll be in good shape. Or get your gen-eds done. Not nearly as intense or expensive."

Tomai speaks so authoritatively, with such confidence, I'm both impressed and jealous of them. But then I remember why we're here, walking down this path together.

"Not to change the subject, but—"

"You're going to change the subject?"

I giggle. "Yeah."

Tomai glances around once more, then takes my arm as we scurry across the street. We arrive at a small park in the center of town. A cobblestone pathway guides us into the heart of the sparsely green area. The trees wither beneath the weight of their rainbow of autumn leaves. We sit on a bench a safe distance from where a group of children chase each other and crawl through holes in an absurd metallic jungle gym that looks more like a car wreck than a children's play palace.

Tomai digs around in their backpack and withdraws two bags of chips, one of which they offer to me, but I decline. Tomai shrugs and after a few determined tugs, manages to crack it open.

Even though I can smell the salty potato goodness in the air, I resist the urge to ask for the other bag and quell my craving. My stomach grumbles, and I gently place a hand against it to quiet its murmurings. Food, or redeeming my reputation in the eyes of my parents and my people? No thanks. I need to keep my priorities straight.

"So," Tomai says, crunching down on a chip. "The boys. Let me tell you—I have no solid proof, so I never reported it to the cops. Not like they would've done anything with the information anyways. If you ever meet Sheriff Rodgers, I mean, my God, you're *really* gonna understand the meaning of 'The lights are on but no one's home.' He sucks big-time. Always misgenders me."

"Ew."

"Yeah. Ew. Anyways," they say, wiping their greasy fingers on their jeans, "the night Wendell was killed I was walking home alone. It was tech week, so I left school kinda late. Streetlights already on. Neither Dad nor Gran could pick me up, but I was like, whatever, y'know? Plus Yang's, the Chinese place over on eighth, is on the way to my place, and I figured I could stop by and grab a bite. They've got this frickin' *amazing* sesame chicken, dude. You've got to try it sometime."

"I *love* sesame chicken." My stomach gurgles in agreement.

"*Right?* Okay, well, as I was walking—again, no one around, it's the middle of dinnertime, so spooky as shit—I swear to God, I could hear this faint music, like singing. At first I thought it sounded like some New Age gospel music, but then I realized there weren't any words. Just elongated vowel sounds. *Aah-aah-ah, ohh-ohh-oh.* When I tell you I had goosebumps, girl, I mean my hair was standing on end. And I'm looking every which way, trying to figure out where the hell the noise is coming from. I keep walking to Yang's, but as I'm passing by the old Lennox Theater, I realize the sounds are at their *loudest.* That theater has been closed since I was in elementary school, and there was a *light on.*"

"A light? Like—like bluish like a spirit, or…"

Their shoulders slump forward in disappointment. "No. Like, a regular office light. Yellow. But I swear to you, no one's been in there for years. I don't think the bank has the key anymore, because duh, who would buy that place? Burning sacks of money is a better investment."

"What did you do after you saw the light?"

"I booked it." They pump their arms ferociously to demonstrate, and we both laugh. Tomai wipes away a tear, clutching a hand to their chest. "I thought I was a goner for sure. Like, shit, maybe this ghost doesn't discriminate and decided it'll eat a nonbinary person too!"

"Eat?"

"Oh." A more serious expression crosses their face. They lower their voice so the nearby children don't hear. "Yeah. Um. Eat. Every single guy had huge chunks gnawed out of his body. Gnarly shit. No one could have an open-casket funeral." They run their hands through their hair. "And Wendell… Wendell was found a couple of intersections away from the theater the next day."

Fuck. That means they were *for sure* attacked by a wraith. The singing though…that's a little odd. In the ghost taxonomy, there are four main types of ghosts: wraiths, of course, then will-o'-wisps, which are weaker spirits that have trouble maintaining their form and are more of a nuisance than anything else, shades, which have the powers of psychological manipulation, and then there are phantoms, which are the most humanlike. There're all different kinds of subcategories too, but those are the big four. Phantoms are capable of mimicking behaviors they had in their past life—singing, dancing, doing chores. Dad and I once came across one in a restaurant that was a former chef, cooking an entire three-course meal. But a wraith, *singing*? I've never heard of them being able to do that. If a wraith had that ability, that would suggest a kind of intelligence and power far greater than anything I've ever come across. I know one person who I could ask about it—Simon, our family's Apostle. But he's not exactly approachable, and besides, since we moved, I don't think he's our Apostle anymore.

"Did you tell the police any of this?"

"I did, but they told me that ghosts couldn't turn on lights."

I stare at them. "What? Why did they think that? They absolutely can."

"They can?" Tomai's brow furrows.

That's bizarre. Either that's blatant incompetence, or—no, I can't get ahead of myself right now. "Hmm… So the theater. Are you sure the sound was coming from inside the building?"

"Either in there, or around it. I could take you there if you want."

I smile. "I'm sorry, but…that might be too dangerous for someone who isn't a ghost hunter. The type of ghost you're describing is—"

"Really, really bad?"

I nod, biting my lip. "I mean…if it's eating people, it's a wraith, and they're super dangerous."

"Oh. Is that how you…" Tomai lifts a finger to point at my face.

My stomach lurches violently at the not-finished question, and although I'm starving, I'm grateful I didn't eat those chips, because I'd probably throw up right here on the sidewalk. Regret surfaces in Tomai's brown eyes.

"I'm sorry. My bad." Tomai wrings their hands. "Sometimes my mouth gets ahead of my brain and asks things it shouldn't."

"It's…okay. And uh, no. These are birthmarks."

It's an obvious lie, but somehow, even though Tomai isn't someone who would understand the weight of my failure, I can't tell them what happened. If I did, I'd probably start crying, and again—new year, new me, new start. I have to play this cool. I have to be confident, even when I know I'm not. My stomach gurgles angrily as my cheeks burn in shame.

I check the time on my phone, and even though it's nowhere near time for me to leave, I stand up. "Oh, uh, I gotta go. Thanks for the info."

Tomai stands as well. "Melody, I'm sorry."

"No, you're fine. I—I need to get home. We're still unpacking, and Dad might need my help with dinner. I'll see you in class tomorrow, okay?"

Tomai opens their mouth as if to apologize again, but then slowly clamps it shut. They look down at their shoes. "Okay. I'll see you tomorrow."

"Y-yeah. See you tomorrow." I turn on my heel and walk out of the park, no longer plagued by nausea, but a deep sense of shame.

Much like Catholic priests, Apostles aren't allowed to marry, and must take a vow of celibacy as they work to serve their families. Unlike the Catholic Church, however, the Council of the ghost hunters recognized the potential for bad actors and familial abuse when the standard was created. Most Apostles have been women, and in olden times, men who wished to be Apostles were eunuchized. Those rules were uplifted in the early 1970s, which led to an increase of men entering the profession.

—Peggy Harthorne, *My Year of Ghosts: An Anthropological Account of Life with the Spirit Whisperers in the West Province* (1978)

Chapter Six

When I arrive home, my parents' car isn't there, but someone else's is. A tan sedan, its trunk popped open, sits in the driveway. Confused, I stare into the back of it. Boxes of books, and fresh bedding, wrapped up in a plastic bag. I look in the direction of our front door as someone exits, and my eyes widen.

Simon.

It's been months since I've seen him. But here he stands on the front stoop, his black hair somewhat disheveled and slick with sweat, his eyes wide with surprise. He's dressed in the frumpiest clothes he's ever worn: a tattered pair of shorts emblazoned with the Rose Red Row logo and a gray sweatshirt with fraying hems. He places his hands on his hips, as if trying to appear confident, but his lanky form crumples beneath the weight of my heated gaze.

"Melody," he says, and there's an odd pitch to his voice—a real *Oh shit* tone. "Your parents said you wouldn't be back until around 5:30."

"What're you doing here?" I ask.

"Same thing that you're doing here. I'm moving in." He crosses his arms and leans against the front door, his nose tilted upward in an air of defiance. "Your mom and dad didn't tell you?"

"Uh, no. Where are you sleeping?"

"In the room adjacent to your parents'."

Adjacent? Who uses that word in casual conversation? Spirits, he's *so* weird. I inch a little closer to him, still wary. "I thought we would be assigned another Apostle."

"Well, no one wants to move here, so…" Simon shrugs his shoulders.

"And you do?"

"I didn't, uh, have a choice. I thought your parents would have told you, I'm sorry." He ruffles his hair. "It's good to see you. It's been awhile."

I haven't seen Simon since Dad's birthday a few months back. Since I failed my Hunt, my parents have been limiting our contact with him as much as we can without pissing off the Council. Apostles are religious leaders who are also supposed to be like members of the family. They lead ghost hunters in spiritual rituals like the Hunt, but also during other holidays. While Apostles are usually praised for their jovial and nurturing nature, Simon is anything but. Every family photo he's in, he looks miserable. And since he was the one to pick out my Hunt, I've been deeply suspicious of his commitment to our family. Apostles are given the opportunity to choose where they're assigned, so if he ended up here, it's because he *wanted* to be here, no matter how much he tells me no one else wanted the position.

"How was school?" Simon holds open the door stiffly, and it takes me a minute to register that he's trying to invite me inside *my house*. The actual audacity. "You hungry? Want something to eat?"

I open my mouth to protest, but my stomach betrays me, grumbling low and loud like the engine of a Mach 1. A blush rises to my cheeks and Simon grins. He points to the remaining items in his trunk.

"Can you bring those in for me?"

With a huff, I reach into the trunk and head into the house. Simon migrates into the kitchen, and I set his things in his bedroom, which is already organized and full of furniture I haven't seen before. A crammed bookshelf houses various religious texts, and his desk is littered with papers. Framed pictures of our family are scattered across his unmade bed. Spirits, *what?* Some of these are copies from Mom's photo albums. Did she give these to him? How long has he had these? Like I said, whenever we're together, he gives the impression he would rather be anywhere else than with the family. But the fact he has these photos tells a different story. He also has a photograph of himself holding me as a baby, my face red, my little fists clenched, but again, he wears the same stoic expression, even as he gazes down at my face. This is too weird for me. I set down the box of books and dart from the room like my feet are on fire.

"When did this all show up?"

"This morning. When you were in school," he responds. "Come in here. Tell me what you want to eat."

I stomp into the kitchen and stare at Simon through the pass-through window. His sleeves are rolled up to his elbows, and he holds up a bag of crackers and a brick of cheese. Cheese and crackers? Is he kidding? What am I, eight years old?

"I need real food."

"This *is* real food—you know what, I'll make you something," he says with a huff, turning his back to me. "I take it school didn't go too well today, since you've got an attitude."

"No, Simon, it didn't go well because you randomly showed up at our house. And now we're living with you?"

What the hell, Mom and Dad? Why wouldn't you have said anything? I thought it was weird they got a house with three bedrooms, but I chose not to question it. I figured it was the least run-down house we could buy. I didn't realize we'd be living with the dude who sabotaged my First Hunt!

"Again—" he waves a hand in a half circle, a passive-aggressive gesture begging me to shut up—"I didn't know your parents didn't tell you. And I had no idea you would be this upset. I'll talk with them when they get home tonight."

"Are they still with the mayor?"

"I think they hopped the ferry back to the mainland to get some more groceries." Simon shudders. "That damn thing made me nauseous. I have no sea legs."

"Guess you're going to have to get used to it," I remark, taking a seat on the stool.

He digs desperately through the cabinets. All he's able to come up with is a sack of potatoes, which I don't remember bringing inside the house. "Steak fries?"

I sigh. "Sure."

"You mean, 'Yes, please, Simon. Thank you for offering to cook for me, Simon. I'm going to tone it down now, Simon.'" He snorts and begins to wash about five of the potatoes in the sink. He scrubs them so vigorously I worry he's gonna scratch the skin clean off them. "How was your first day?"

"It was fine."

"Yeah? Your mom says you made a friend."

Mom has been *texting* with him? "Yeah, I did."

"Well…your parents might be busy this week, but I'll be around. Please invite your friend over to the house if you wish. I promise not to go all-Apostley on them."

"Maybe." I dig into my backpack and withdraw my homework for the evening. It's light, thank the Spirits, so I'll have plenty of time to plan my strategy for canvassing the Lennox Theater. "They might want to show me around too."

"I saw the boardwalk. It looks lovely. Despite the trash, that is." He places the potatoes on a cutting board and begins to chop them into thick strips. "Reminds me of the time we went to Oceanview."

"I never went to Oceanview."

Simon stops chopping and frowns. "Oh. Oh that's right. That was your dad and I."

I roll my eyes. He's so weird. He stumbles through every conversation he's in, and you can never tell if he's trying to get a rise out of you or what. But he *is* preparing food for us, so I throw him a bone.

"You and Dad? When?"

"Long time ago. I think that was before he met your mother."

Wait, what? Dad knew Simon before he became our family's Apostle? I thought Apostles were assigned to families after people got married, but their relationship *predates* my parents' marriage? Why didn't I know about this? I open my mouth to question this, but as soon as I do, my parents come barreling through the doorway with their arms full of overpacked Kostko boxes. I rush over to help them, but not without serving them a fresh glare.

Mom winces and smiles a little too widely. "Simon! How did your move-in day go?"

"Hello, Rachel." He sets the knife down on the cutting board. "It went well, except Melody here was more than a little surprised to see me."

Mom winces again. Dad stares at the floor, like he's completely mortified. Spirits, they're all so weird around each other. Wish I could escape to my room and flee this awkward situation, but Mom would kill me if I didn't help with putting the groceries away.

"Sorry," Mom murmurs. "I didn't get the chance to tell her, since it was such a last-minute decision."

Simon's expression softens. "Oh." He tosses the uncooked fries into a bowl and drizzles olive oil over them, then begins to fumble through the cabinets for seasonings. "I'm making steak fries. They were going to be for Melody and I, but I can make some for you too, if you want."

"Oh man, I haven't had those in a *long* time," Dad says with a smile. "That sounds good."

"I've got a box full of burgers we can fry up as well," Mom adds, equally cheery.

The evening that follows is quite possibly one of the weirdest I've ever experienced in my life. Mom cooks with Simon, something I haven't seen in two years, since the Blue Moon Reclamation. They chat with one another breezily. Dad breaks down the now-empty cardboard boxes for recycling. Everyone ignores my anger, even as we sit down at the dinner table. Simon recites a short blessing, and we begin to eat. Damn this man. He may be annoying, but he does make good food. Perfect medium-rare burgers, seasoned, and he also prepared a little spicy aioli for the buns.

"So, how'd it go with the mayor today?" I ask.

Mom and Dad exchange a look. They shrug their shoulders. Mom pushes around some of the mixed-berry salad on her plate. Since her heart disease diagnosis, she's largely stopped eating red meat. I feel a pang of guilt when I see it. Maybe that's what I should be eating, instead of this stupidly good burger.

"It's…tough," Mom says. "Normally when we hunt, we have an idea of where to start. But we're going to have to go through every abandoned building on the island."

"Possibly go through the sewer system," Dad adds with a shudder. "One of the victims was fished out of a clogged storm drain."

"We're hoping it's not an infestation, but that's what it's looking like. I mean, wraiths don't usually leave their haunting ground to go out and hunt. Even if they do, they don't go very far. The fact that some of the attacks happened on opposite sides of the island, well…that points to the existence of multiple ghosts."

Dad shakes his head, a sad expression clouding his eyes. I wonder what he's seen. Sometimes my parents are given access to crime scene photos so they can have a better understanding of what they're dealing with. Those are always the hardest days. He crunches down on a fry and takes a sip of his beer.

"At least we'll be busy for a while," he comments sadly.

I squirt a little more ketchup onto my plate. "Well…maybe not too long. I may have a lead."

For a moment, my parents' expressions are blank. Mom takes a sip of her water and arches her brow.

"A lead?" she repeats slowly. "What do you mean?"

"You're not talking to kids at school about this, are you?" Dad asks.

I hold up my hands. "Someone said the night one of the boys died, they heard music."

My parents stare at me quizzically. A small vein pulses on my father's forehead and he takes another sip of his beer. Mom sighs and rubs her temples, an indication that what I've said is going to give her a massive migraine.

"Mel, sweetheart, we think it's best for you to not be involved in this," she says. "This is a big, big case. More dangerous than others we've taken on in the past. And besides, you know if it's a wraith, they can't sing."

Simon pipes up. "Well, actually, wraiths *can* do that, it's just very rare—and usually seen in younger wraiths. The younger a wraith is, the more like their original human self they are. Ghost memories and their understanding of humanity deteriorate as they age."

"When," Dad asks, with heat in his voice, "have we ever come across a young wraith?"

Simon shrugs, surprisingly indifferent to Dad's hostility. Guess he's used to it. "I don't know, I don't hunt ghosts. I only know the *Tomes* and the work of other scholars."

"I think—" I try to speak again, but Dad cuts me off with a furious shake of his head.

"You aren't ready yet."

A cold silence falls over the dinner table, one that stabs my heart with icy pain. He didn't say that, did he? Mom and Simon have shocked expressions on their faces. He did say that.

And he's not sorry about it.

"I don't want you involved in this hunt," Dad continues. "And I don't want you talking to your friends about it. Spirits above, Melody, people are dead. Kids your age are dead. You understand that, right? You don't need to be gossiping with them about it."

"I wasn't gossiping," I retort. "I was trying to get information."

"I don't *want* you doing that," Dad says, his voice climbing in volume.

The anger clouding his eyes disgusts me. Why is he treating me like this? I would've thought that after all the months of lying around the house like a slug they would at least be somewhat open to me helping again—practicing ghost hunting again.

"Dean…" Simon murmurs. He's looking right at me and I hate it; I hate that he's pitying me.

"No," Dad protests. "Melody, didn't we already tell you to stay out of it?"

I stare back at him. "No, you didn't."

"Actually, we didn't," Mom mutters into his ear.

I gape, aghast. "Mom, don't tell me you're taking his side."

"I agree with your dad. You have more important things to worry about than working on this case—your future, for one. If you're going to apply for an academy, you need to work on your application. It's going to be hard enough as it is, given what happened last year."

"You mean when I failed my Hunt?"

Mom winces. "What else would I be referring to?"

"If you're so concerned about my application chances, why not let me help you? This would improve my chances tenfold, especially if it *is* a lot of wraiths!"

"Because," Dad snaps, "it's too dangerous! Look at what happened to you! Do you want to risk something worse?"

Dad's nostrils flare and his face scrunches up like he smells something foul. Tears spring to my eyes. *Look at what happened to you.* Look, as if I don't see it in the mirror every morning when I wake up. As if I don't notice my reflection when I pass by windows. As if I don't *feel* the change in textures on my face when I put on lotion, or makeup, or just to pick an eyelash off my cheek. I already think I look disgusting, but I didn't realize my own father feels that way too. I push back from the table, unable to choke down the sobs escaping from the back of my throat. I rush into my room and slam the door shut. Mom calls out after me, and I can hear Simon hissing, lecturing my father on his wrongdoings.

Mom jimmies the door handle. "Melody, open up. Let's talk about this."

"No," I shout back. "You've made yourselves perfectly clear. You think I'm a disgusting screwup."

"No one said that!"

"No, but it's what you were *thinking!*"

The rage, the anger, the hurt, it bubbles up within my body like an unstable potion in a witch's cauldron, rancid and wretched and all-consuming. It's scrawled across my ugly face. My mind goes blank as I reach for my hairbrush and throw it at my mirror, which splinters into hundreds of pieces. As the shards of glittering glass crumble onto the surface of my vanity, I collapse onto my bed and ignore my mother's pleas for me to open the door.

My parents don't want my help. They don't believe in me. Fine. That's fine. I don't need them. I've got my lead.

I can take on this wraith all by myself.

An Apostle's job is to guide the family in their spiritual journey and help them maintain a connection to their ancestors. Training for Apostles is rigorous and difficult.... While Apostles are still highly regarded within the culture, in recent years, the outdated and isolating nature of their lifestyle has been criticized. This has led to an adjustment in some practices, and even calls for change, but that movement is only growing slowly.

—Peggy Harthorne, *My Year of Ghosts: An Anthropological Account of Life with the Spirit Whisperers in the West Province* (1978)

Chapter Seven

The next morning, Simon knocks on my door. It's 6 a.m., about fifteen minutes before my alarm is supposed to go off.

"Coffee's ready," he tells me. "Come on."

Groggily, I shuffle out of bed, ignoring the messy remains of the mirror that I didn't bother to clean up. Simon's in the kitchen, cooking eggs alongside turkey sausages in a cast-iron skillet. Delightful savory smells waft from the pan. As weird as Simon can be, I think I can get used to living with him if he keeps cooking good food like this. I only hope that he's not using too much butter or salt. The last thing I need is to bloat up bigger than I am right now.

I pour myself a tall mug of coffee and douse it with milk, hoping to eliminate as much bitterness as I can.

"Sleep well?" he asks.

"Meh."

"Me too." He lowers the heat on the stove.

"Where are Mom and Dad?"

"Gone. They left earlier this morning. They wanted to talk to the head of the waste management system about getting into those sewers."

I sigh and take a seat on one of the stools. Simon plates some breakfast for me and passes it over. His eyes lock dead onto mine, and I try to avert my gaze.

"Your father loves you," he says gently. "He doesn't think you're hideous. What happened scares him."

"He didn't have to bring up my face. I already feel horrible about it. I wake up every day and have to look in the mirror."

"Well, at least you have one less mirror to look at."

"Seriously?"

He holds up his hands. "Hey, I broke worse back in my day." He smiles as he takes a sip of coffee. "In high school I smashed out the taillights of a boy who cheated on me."

"A boy…?"

"Oh. Yes. A boy. Why?"

"It's… I thought Apostles weren't allowed to date anybody."

Simon smirks. "Not every teenage boy knows he wants to be an Apostle. Besides, I find the Vow of Solace a bit incongruous with what the *Tomes* say."

"How rebellious."

"Well, times are a'-changing. Even for people like us, stuck in our ways." Simon takes a bite of eggs and wrinkles his nose. "These need more salt. Do you want more salt?"

I shake my head no.

"See, living together won't be that bad. I can tell you all kinds of stories."

"Cable TV can also tell me stories."

"Damn, you are a mean one," he laughs.

It's funny, the last time I heard him laugh was during the Blood Moon Solstice, when he drank a little too much of Mom's homemade elderberry wine. It's an unusual, jarring sound, but not unwelcome.

"Anyway, we can replace that mirror easily. Don't sweat it too much."

"Don't worry about replacing it. A mirror can't fix what's broken."

"Hey"—Simon sets down his mug of coffee, and the ceramic clicks against the granite countertop, as if he's on the verge of breaking it—"you are *not* broken, Melody."

"You don't have a face that resembles a smashed pumpkin, so I would stop with the lecture," I sneer. "I especially don't need it from the person who's partly responsible for it. You were in charge of canvassing for that Hunt."

Simon's face turns a ghostly shade of white. For a moment he stands there, mouth open like a fish on a hook, before it sets in a firm, hard line. He averts his eyes. "Eat your breakfast," he grumbles. "Also, your mom told me to tell you that you're grounded, and you're to come straight home after school."

"What? Why?" I cry out, dropping my fork against my plate.

Simon winces at the clatter of metal against ceramic. "Because you broke your mirror? What, you thought you could do that without consequences?"

Well, no. Okay, kinda. Mom sorta let me cry myself to sleep last night, and since Dad insulted my appearance, I kinda figured I'd be granted a pass. Guess not. But if I have to come home straight after school, that means I have to ixnay the investigation at the Lennox Theater. Unless…

I ditch.

The theater program at Murkmore High may be small, but it is mighty. The sets for this fall's production of Antigone *exemplify this.*

—Sylvia Lonneka, "Murkmore High's Production of Antigone*: A Charming Performance with an Endearing Cast," The Sunshine Standard (15 Nov. 2014)*

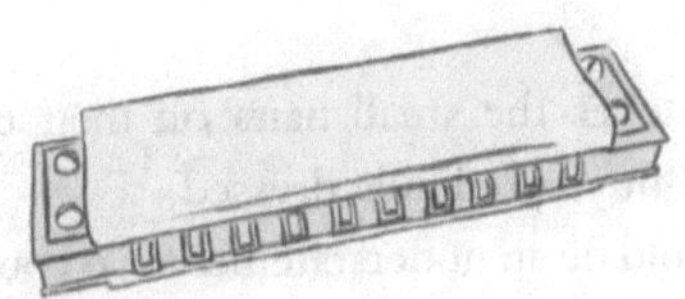

Chapter Eight

"Oh yeah," Tomai says after I tell them my plan. "You should be able to walk right on out."

I smack my freshly glossed lips together, staring at Tomai in my reflection. They're leaning up against a stall in the girls' restroom, arms folded across their chest. Technically, they're not supposed to be in here—they're supposed to use a gender-neutral bathroom—but it's still half an hour till the homeroom bell rings, and not many people are around, so even if someone walks in, I don't think they're going to get weirdly invasive about where Tomai goes to pee.

Only losers do that.

"Really?"

"No." Tomai sighs, disappointed by my naivety.

I don't know how to tell them that if we're gonna be friends they should probably get used to it.

"You'd have to leave out one of the side entrances in between classes. Then you'd have to be careful the school resource officer doesn't catch you. And, on top of that, I mean, you live in a town where everyone knows everyone. Kid is seen walking down the road in the middle of the day, they're gonna know who you are."

"Which means...I need a disguise."

"A"—Tomai blinks, their long eyelashes batting their cheeks—"what?"

"A disguise. What if I looked like a teacher? Couldn't I walk on out of here?"

Tomai scratches the small hairs on their chin, considering this. "I guess. But you're kinda dressed..."

Vibrant would be an understatement. To counteract my shitty mood, I decided to dress overly bright today. Holographic button-up, acid-washed denim jeans with polka dots, white sneakers. I will never regret my bizarre fashion choices, but I do regret wearing this today.

"Would... Would the drama department have clothes that I could wear?"

Tomai's eyes widen, and they snap their fingers enthusiastically. "Yeah, wait a minute. We could find you something in storage. Might smell a little funky, but—"

"But it's better than nothing." I squeal joyfully, laughing as I throw my arms around them. "Tomai, you're coming in clutch!"

They push their glasses up their nose and smile sheepishly. "Least I can do, given what I said yesterday."

My smile evaporates. Oh, shit. I forgot that happened. No wonder they seemed a little weird when I started chatting it up with them this morning.

I squeeze their hands. "Hey. People have said a *lot* worse to me. Don't worry about it."

"You sure?" They wince. "Sometimes I just—I say shit. Like word-vomit. I mean, I *am* curious, but like—damn it, I'm word-vomiting again."

I shake my head. "You're good. It's—it's not wrong to be curious. Not when it's this obvious."

They grin softly. "Maybe you can tell me about it someday. But right now, we gotta get you a change of clothes before homeroom starts."

Eighteen boxes later, I still haven't found a single outfit that is (1) practical and (2) makes me look more mature. The drama department owns *way* too many togas—Tomai says they're from the dozens of Grecian play productions over the years. Some boxes are full of questionably racist Egyptianesque clothing, leftovers from a *Jackalope and the Amazing Technicolor Dreamcoat* production—linens in Egyptian flag colors (*what?*) and gold lamé (*yikes*). And there are also a few too many capes and cowls, likely from a lackluster *Phantom of the Opera* performance. We're fifteen minutes out from homeroom starting, the floor is completely covered in a kaleidoscope of musty clothes, and we're still nowhere closer to finding a halfway decent disguise.

With a frustrated groan, Tomai tears open another box behind me. There's the sound of tape shredding (*shudder*), followed by the shuffling of different fabrics within the box, and then, an odd silence. When I turn to face them, my jaw drops.

"A *leather* tube top and hot pants?!" I cry out. "I thought we were trying to draw *less* attention to me! What show is this from?"

Tomai taps the top of the box. *SPENT – '11. KIKI CLOTHES.* "You don't have to wear the hot pants."

"I cannot wear hot pants. The leather tube top is also a stretch."

"Can you walk in heels?"

"Yes? Why?"

"Are you a size 10 in shoes?" Tomai pulls out a pair of strappy black heels from the box. "Look. You tease your hair, you apply heavier makeup, you wear this getup—we could make you look like a MILF. We can MILF you up."

"MILF? MILF me?"

Tomai nods. They point to the wall clock, ominously ticking closer and closer to the bell. "It's better than nothing, Melody."

I sigh. Unfortunately, they're right.

At the latest town hall, citizens vocalized their concerns over the various abandoned buildings throughout the town, such as the Lennox Theater and the Fables and Sons Department Store. Individuals have proposed transforming one of the buildings into a community center or possibly giving small business owners grants to set up shop in the old spaces. In turn, council members voiced their concern over the cost of these projects.

—Howard Bonevue, "Murkmore's Abandoned Buildings Prove Troublesome for Community Members," *The Sunshine Standard* (10 Jan. 2021)

Chapter Nine

We came up with the rest of our plan at lunch. I'll leave before AP Lit and Comp at the end of the day. Tomai will tell Ruder I went home sick. When the bell rings for fifth period, I scurry off to the bathroom, dig through my backpack, and put on my costume. The heels Tomai gave me have little buckle straps on the sides, and with my clumsy fingers, I struggle to strap them on. Once that's done, I thank the Spirits I remembered to bring my makeup bag today and start caking it on. I fill in my eyebrows with a pencil, apply blush to the apples of my cheeks (older women tend to do this instead of adding it along the upper part of the cheekbones), and smear on dark-purple eye shadow. Then, to finish off the look, a ruby-red lipstick. It is the most atrocious thing I have ever done to myself, but thankfully, I look older—like midthirties chain-smoker older.

Then I realize another problem.

What woman who looks like this wanders around with a backpack instead of a purse?

Aww, shit.

I book it out of the bathroom and make a beeline for the exit closest to me. Some kids look in my direction and I can hear them giggling at me, but thankfully most are trying to scramble into their classrooms before the bell rings again. The straps of these heels are carving little blisters into my ankles, but I grit my teeth and push through the throngs of slow-moving students. My heart skips a beat when I spot the exit door.

"Miss?"

Jaw agape, I turn in the direction of the voice: a teacher—bald, bearded, and wearing a stained shirt. Dark circles ring the undersides of his eyes. The school badge hanging around his neck tells me his name is Mr. Ernest. He looks me up and down with bugged-out eyes, and I can tell he's having difficulty placing whether I'm a student or an adult. I take a deep breath, channel my innermost Oscar-winning persona, and speak.

"I think you mean *ma'am*. Little too old to be a miss."

The noise that comes out of my throat is guttural and raw. Inwardly I scream. *Too old. Too old.* But to my surprise, his eyebrows raise.

"Oh, you're a parent," he mutters, embarrassed.

"Yeah." I hold up the backpack. "My daughter said some kid spilled coffee in this, so I gotta take it home and clean it."

It is the worst lie I've ever told—the backpack isn't even damp—but he's buying it, word for word. Or maybe I look scary enough that he doesn't want to deal with me. Slowly, he nods in understanding, although there's still some confusion floating in his eyes. He offers a smile and doesn't say anything else, so I head for the exit. I burst through the doors, scurry down the steps, and for the briefest of moments, bask in the warm autumn sun.

Then the bell rings and I make a break for it.

My eyes scan the lawn for signs of any school officers, but I don't see anyone. I creep closer to the edge of the courtyard, and when my foot lands on the sidewalk, I sprint. My heart hammers in my chest and some sort of lump crawls up the back of my throat. I have *never* skipped school before, and prior to moving here, I would've never considered it. But this is too important to be concerned about keeping a perfect attendance record. Not only is my life on the line, but the lives of others are too.

The streets are virtually dead, which makes sense since it's the middle of the day and everyone's probably at work. In fact, the only thing that occupies the roadways as I make my way to the Lennox Theater is the grotesque amount of trash. Plastic bags drift through the wind like lost balloons, and unmentionably filthy clumps of wrappers, broken glass, and discarded cigarette butts clog the curbs. Yeesh. No wonder Tomai started the Beautification Committee; this is horrendous.

The building itself is petite yet impressive, the architecture reminiscent of a 1930s movie palace. The exterior is painted gold and teal, still saturated and bright despite years' worth of obvious neglect. Like the high school, there are Grecian columns framing each corner of the building. The lobby windows are boarded up, and an iron chain loops through the handles of the front doors, knotted together with a clunky, rusted lock.

I circle around the theater and discover the side door is chained shut as well. But when I look up? There's a ladder creeping toward a rickety fire escape. It's risky for sure, but it's worth a try—maybe there's an entrance on the roof. The ladder is barely within reach, so to be safe, I might want to find something that'll give me a boost. Looking around some more, I find an aluminum trash can—one that's probably home to several rats, but it's my best shot. I grab onto one of the grimy handles and push it under the ladder. I attempt to climb on top, but with my heels, it's too hard. Grimacing, I put my backpack down on the ground and try to find my other shoes. *My shoes.* Spirits above, where are my *real* shoes? They must be on the floor of the bathroom I changed in!

I shoot a quick text to Tomai.

ME: RED ALERT!!! 📸 I left my shoes on the floor of the bathroom!!!

To my surprise, they message back.

TOMAI: Oh shit. K I'll try to look for them. First floor close to the cafeteria right?
ME: Yess 😭
TOMAI: I got you. Did you get there?
ME: Yessss but Im gonna have to go in barefoot 😭😭😭
TOMAI: No 😖 don't do that
ME: Alas. I have no choice.
TOMAI: good luck 🙏

Spirits above, I hope Tomai can find my shoes. Those were my *favorite* white sneakers. I'd be lucky if someone didn't find them and take them for themselves. I scowl in frustration, examining the sparse grass and mostly dirty ground. This is going to be so damn gross.

I crouch down to remove my shoes. When the straps peel off the back of my heels, the blistered skin stings. Spirits above, I'm *so* going to get an infection. As my raw, sore feet touch the bare ground, I shudder in disgust. I'll have to take a hot shower tonight and scrape myself raw with a pumice stone.

I glance back toward the street to make sure no one's looking, and my heart drops to my stomach. There's a cop car approaching. It doesn't look like it's spotted me or anything, but if it gets any closer, I'll be right in the driver's line of sight. I'm not about to get arrested for breaking and entering in this unstylish getup.

I turn back to the ladder, lift up my leg, and climb on top of the trash can, which rattles under my weight. I have the worst balance, so of course, it begins wobbling violently. I grip the edges of the ladder, which creaks in distress, and wince as my fingers close around the chipping flakes of rust that threaten to prick my skin. I gingerly lift one foot up onto the closest rung, and although it creaks, it seems to hold me okay.

Shit, the car is *so* close. Squeezing my eyes shut, I place my other foot onto another rung, and beneath me, the trash can collapses to the side, its contents spilling on the ground. The ladder groans loudly, and I *swear*, it's swaying in the breeze. The hinges at the top are probably loose, which means that I'm risking it breaking off and falling to the ground—and me along with it.

But my other choice is, y'know, getting arrested for trespassing.

I hug my body to the ladder and take another step up. This time it shrieks in protest, but I grit my teeth and keep going. I wish I didn't have my backpack with me—the added weight is surely making this all worse—but there's no way I'm leaving it for the cops to find. My heart is pounding so hard it's going to bruise my rib cage. Maybe that explains why I can't breathe. As I inch closer and closer to the top, fear floods my body, rushing to my brain, making me woozy. My eyelids flutter and my mouth tastes dry. But finally, I reach the top. I scramble for the brick edge of the building, and push myself up as best I can, but for some reason—

I slip.

A near soundless scream escapes my lungs—the kind of noise you make when the wind is knocked out of you. I dig my nails into the gristly grooves of the building and they scratch against cement, slipping in staccato succession. For a moment, I'm suspended between the top of the roof and the last rung of the ladder. There *should* be another one, but it's rusted away, leaving nothing but two craggy holes in its place. I frantically scramble to find my footing, and when I touch the last rung, I take another deep breath and push. My leg swings over the side of the roof and, gasping, I pull myself up then unceremoniously throw myself to the ground.

I fall hard against the pebbles on the rooftop, panting. My eyes water with relieved tears, and I almost want to kiss the ground. Sweet, sweet land. The ladder is somehow still attached to the side of the building. Come hell or high water, I'm going to find another way out of here, even if it means I have to break the iron chains on all the doors. As to how I'm going to do that, I'll figure that out later.

I remain on the ground for a few more minutes before sitting up and surveying my surroundings. Thankfully, there *is* a door on the rooftop, and it's not padlocked. I guess when they closed the place up, they didn't think anyone would be dumb enough to try that ladder. (Sorry to disappoint, City of Murkmore.) I brush off the bottoms of my feet, and with a heavy sigh, reach back into my backpack for those dreaded heels. I hate them, but there's no way I'm going in there barefoot. Climbing up the ladder was bad enough, but if I step on a nail in this decrepit place, I will have a mental breakdown, and I don't have time for another one of those. After putting them back on, I grab my EMF reader— which hopefully Mom and Dad won't notice is missing from their lab—and enter the building.

Shit it's dark. Duh. I fumble in my pocket for my phone and turn on the flashlight. Red and black graffiti lines crisscross over each other, forming an intricate web that follows me as I descend the creaky steps. My EMF reader chirps when I reach the fifth step, and I turn down the volume. The little bars on the scanner are low and green, but are bumping slightly into the yellow area. Tomai was right. There's something in here.

The staircase from the roof is long and winding, and by the time I reach the nearest floor, my feet are throbbing again. I duck underneath the doorframe and enter a hallway littered with scraps of moldy paper and glittering glass. The carpet beneath my feet is oddly damp and smells of fresh lichen, like the kind I'd find on the trees in Mountain Ridge. I crouch down and brush my fingers against its surface, and a few droplets of blue goo appear. *Yep.* There's a ghost in this building.

I don't have a cap-can with me, but if I can figure out what kind of ghost this is—if it's really a wraith—then I can use that information and come back this weekend to snatch it up and take all the glory. I can't go back the way I came, because I don't want to risk going down that ladder, leaving me with no choice but to go deeper into the haunted theater.

The hallway is long, and narrow, and full of doors. This must be a bunch of projector rooms? I'm not eager to step into a room right now. Ghosts can, and will, close doors behind you so you can't get them open. They love that shit.

I walk forward through an archway that leads to a balcony. There's an overturned desk and some random folding chairs in the area, along with file cabinets, their drawers open and empty. This must have been their makeshift office area. I approach the desk, which is close to the railing, and scan the papers on top of it: discarded pay stubs dating back to 2012, damp playbills from community theater productions covered in grease stains, and crinkled paper tickets.

I pick one up and examine it closely. *Troll Bridge Massacre?* Woof. That brings back memories. This was the first movie I ever watched alone with Brynne, about the second or third time I'd gone over to her house. We snuggled together in her basement; it was so cold we had to huddle together underneath a blanket for warmth.

It was the first time she held my hand.

Suddenly, a loud crash echoes out, shattering the silence, and my heart hitches in my chest. I check my EMF reader, which is now solidly yellow on the scanner. The sound came from downstairs. I fumble in the pocket of my pants for my bag of blessed salt, and make sure it's open so I can dip my fingers in and throw it if needed. In my backpack, I also have a Phantom Prod Lite, which is sort of a cross between pepper spray and a regular Phantom Prod. When you press the button, it emits electromagnetic sparks. It'll help to ward off wraiths, but the kickback from it can be powerful, and I want to avoid accidentally electrocuting myself.

I sprinkle some salt in front of the archway, then make my way down. The Lennox Theater appears so small on the outside, but descending the steps by the front entrance, it expands into something more cavernous. A chandelier lovingly enveloped in dusty cobwebs is suspended above the lobby. Small crystals shaped like teardrops cast ripples of light onto the walls and ceiling.

My heel smashes through the rotten wood of a step, and I gasp, trying to pull out my foot. *Shit, shit, shit.* I grab onto the railing and yank it out of the crevice. Small splinters jam into my ankle, and little pinpricks of blood drip down.

"No, no, no." I flatten my back against the wall and slink down.

Pinching my fingers together, I slowly pull out the tiny splinters. Another clatter rings out, but when I look up, nothing is there, and the EMF reader isn't getting any higher. The ghost is on this level. I try to think of where that side door was in relation to my current location. Probably on the west side of the building. I carefully tread down the remaining stairs, wincing every time I move. Regret pools in the pit of my stomach. *Why did I decide to do this? Why did I think I could do this alone?* If there *is* a wraith in here, I hope it kills me swiftly. At least then I'd die with some dignity.

Now on the ground floor, I examine the front doors. Not chained shut on this side, so hopefully that's the case with the side door too. I spin around to examine the ticket booths and concession stand, somehow all frozen in time. The candy display still has KytCats for some reason. Containers of popcorn kernels rest on the shelves alongside empty paper buckets. My gurgling stomach gets the better of me and I snatch one of the candy bars from the shelves as I sneak past, then peel back the wrapper. It feels…weirdly mushy? The surface of the chocolate is scratchy and white, like it was trampled in dirt. Oh, yuck. I didn't know candy could do that.

More clattering and commotion draws my attention back to the hallway. I dump the candy and approach the first set of doors, then press my ear against it. A frightened shudder escapes my chest when I hear it.

Strings.

Music.

But, after listening for a moment, I can't hear any vocals. None of what Tomai described.

I reach for the door handle and pull it open slowly, each molasses-slow movement of my arm building tension within my body. I peek in, and it's almost pitch black. The music has stopped. I slip inside, careful not to let the door slam shut behind me. I sprinkle salt onto the ground as I walk along the back of the theater, my eyes scanning the darkness and shadows to make sure a ghost isn't lying in wait. Then I see it, underneath the screen: a small office lamp, sitting in the center of the stage, with sheets of paper spread out in a half circle surrounding it. I creep closer, until the lines and markings become visible—sheet music. Notes scrawled in pencil line the margins of the pages.

"Mierda—where is that stupid music stand—oh, *there!*"

The shrill sound of metal and possibly cardboard boxes or some sort of Styrofoam echoes through the air. Someone is moving something. The sound seems like it's coming from offstage, which is hidden by a floor-to-ceiling curtain. It rustles as if it's being moved by a breeze. My heart hits my stomach as I watch a blue hand draw it back, revealing the ghost on the other side. In their other free hand, they hold a rusty music stand, stained orange with age. They're a larger person, with broad, muscular-seeming shoulders, and aren't very tall; they maybe have an inch or two on me. Clenched between their teeth are more music pages. They fumble with the curtain and try to push it out of their way to avoid tripping on it, but it keeps getting stuck on the music stand. In their frustrated dance, they eventually look up. Shock fills their eyes, and their jaw drops along with it, scattering the pages everywhere on the floor.

Before I can get a word out, they scream.

Do I think that ghosts are the same as human beings? No, of course not. That's why they're called ghosts.

—Nataya Brown, Head Apostle, 1972 interview in *Radical Spirits: Ghost Hunter Politics in the 1960s and '70s*, dir. Genevieve Plottergirth (2005)

Chapter Ten

We remain bewitched, rooted to our respective spots: them on the stage, and me in the aisles.

"Who the—who the hell are you?!" they screech, spinning the stand in front of them to wield it like a battle-ax. "How did you get in here?!"

So weird. Their form is corporeal. Most ghosts have little wispy strands of ectoplasmic vapor that trail out from their bodies, but this ghost's outline is rigid and stable. I've never seen that before. I inch a little closer to them, keeping one hand on the bag of salt still tucked away in my pocket.

"Hello!" they snap, shaking the stand as they take another tentative step forward. "Are you going to answer me? It's impolite to keep a gal waiting, y'know!" Oh, this ghost is a girl. She takes another step forward, closer to the light. She squints in confusion. "Why are you—why are you dressed like that? Is that purple eye shadow? You know that's bad luck, right?"

I flinch. "I—"

"Look, I'm not sure what anime convention you dressed up for, but there's no cosplay contest here—"

"Cosplay—what? I'm not cosplaying as anything!" I cry out, the heat rushing to my cheeks.

She blinks. "Leather top, high heels, heavy makeup…"

"Who would wear something *this* tacky intentionally?—"

"You, apparently—"

I stumble backward on a crack in the floor. "Ugh! No! This was a disguise!"

The ghost scrunches up her nose and places her hands on her hips.

"Oookay," she says. "You want to tell me what you're doing here, totally-not-a-cosplayer-girl?"

"Looking for you!"

Her head tilts to the side. "Me? I don't think we know each other."

She lowers the music stand but comes a little too close to the edge of the stage. In an instant I whip a handful of salt in her direction. The pellets smack into her, and little clouds of ectoplasmic smoke float up from where they hit. She hisses and recoils, but to my surprise, doesn't flee, and the salt doesn't pepper little holes into her body. Normally, blessed salt threatens the integrity of a ghost's form. Interesting.

"What the fuck?"

"Blessed salt. Stay back," I snap, holding up another fistful.

I climb up onto the stage. Now we're only a few feet away from each other. She scowls in displeasure.

"Ooh. A white girl with the most basic seasoning known to man. I'm so scared," the ghost sneers, but she moves backward, out of grabbing range. "You seem pretty afraid for someone who said she came here to find me."

"I was trying to see if the rumors were true. If the ghost was here."

"Pause." She holds up a hand, her brow furrowing. "What do you mean by *ghost*?"

A strangled yelp of surprise escapes my throat. She doesn't know? A dark expression crosses her face, and her eyes drift to the floor. It's like she's performing a series of calculations within her mind, and her chest deflates with a heavy sigh.

"You know what? That makes a lot of sense, now that I think about it."

"How could you not know?" I shake my head at her, confused. "You're glowing and blue. It's fairly obvious. Not to mention all the ectoplasm you've painted all over the walls."

She glances down at her body, then shrugs her shoulders, indifferent. "Don't know."

"I'm sorry, but that doesn't make any sense."

She picks up the sheet music pages off the floor. Wait. Picking things up? With her bare hands? Ghosts don't do that. They use their electromagnetic abilities to reverberate the molecules and particles in the air fast enough to move an object. In other words, they pick things up with their minds and not their bodies. Not to mention, she's walking—feet on ground walking, not floating or hovering or drifting above it. And she didn't phase through the curtain either, she pulled it back with her hands. She's acting as if she's still a human being, like a phantom would. But phantoms can't have complicated conversations like this. You challenge them too much, and they get upset, and start throwing things.

What's going on here?

"You didn't notice you weren't breathing, eating, sleeping, any of that?"

She pauses to consider this. "I took a nap once. And I haven't been hungry."

"You haven't been…" I shake my head. "How long have you been in here?"

"Uh…like a few hours? Maybe like, a day, tops?"

Oh *noooooo*. "Um, what year do you think it is?"

"2023."

"That was a year ago."

"What?" Her eyes bug out and her jaw hangs open. "A—a *year* ago?"

"Yeah."

"You're shitting me."

"I shit you not." I place my hands on my hips, watching as she continues to pick up the pages, this time at a flustered, faster pace. Uh-oh. She might be spiraling a little, here. "So, you didn't notice time passing at all?"

She laughs nervously. "No? I mean, I remember coming in here with my violin, and I wanted to play a little bit. Realized the doors to the theater were locked and I couldn't get out, so I was…kinda waiting for someone to find me."

"Waiting for someone to find you? Why would you need to do that? You can phase through walls."

She stares at me blankly. "How?"

"I don't know. But you're a ghost, so in theory, you *should* be able to."

"Meaning I could've walked out of here this whole time?"

I nod.

"My mom's going to kill me," she whispers.

I refrain from reminding her she's already dead, instead focusing on that valuable little detail she shared. She remembers she had a mother. "So you've been here this whole time, and never once tried to leave."

"Yes," she says, a little more annoyed.

"Okay." I drag a hand over my face, aware I'm smudging my terrible makeup. Good for me, honestly. "What month did you think it was?"

"Um…" She squeezes her eyes shut. "October. It was October."

This is…strange. This girl died last year, before the other victims were found. So, who is she? Why hasn't anyone talked about her? Was she a victim of the wraith attacks, or did something else happen? And did she die in here? From what Tomai told me, this theater has been boarded up for years.

The ghost girl calmly stacks the papers, her eyes looking anywhere but my face, pupils wide and wild as she struggles to comprehend everything she's learned. One hand nervously reaches up and unbuttons the collar of her shirt, exposing a necklace with a budded cross. She rubs it with one hand, unsure of what to do.

"Aren't you the least bit concerned I found you?"

"Should I be? The most dangerous thing you have is salt. Not high on my list of things to fear." She shrugs and walks offstage again, disappearing behind a curtain.

I am flabbergasted, stammering nonsensical strings of words in a desperate attempt to form a basic sentence. Most ghosts fear human presence, or are at least annoyed by it—yes, even wraiths. But it's like she has… Oh wait, right. She doesn't know.

"I'm going to give you a few tips. One: you should *absolutely* be afraid of the salt I threw at you, because in case you didn't notice, parts of your body started fizzing."

"Fizzing?"

"Smoking. Whatever you want to call it. You should be *very* afraid of me right now. I'm a ghost hunter."

She pops out once again, this time holding a violin. "A what?"

"Ghost hunter. Spirit whisperer."

She makes an *I don't believe you* face. Eyes scrunched up, tight lips turned upward in a fake-polite smile. "No, you're not."

"Yeah," I say. "I am."

"No, you're not," she insists. "There are no ghost hunters here. Never have been."

"Now there are," I tell her.

"Hmm. Now you mention it, you do look new." She holds the violin in one hand and organizes the music sheets with the other. "Welcome to the shithole, I guess."

"Thanks. It's been real great so far."

"Okay," she says, her tone still far too nonchalant. "So, you're a ghost hunter. What does that mean for me, and why are you here, in this putrid outfit?"

"Have you—have you not heard about what's been going on in town?"

"No. Like we've already established, I haven't left this place since I got here—which apparently was a year ago."

"So you know nothing about all the people that died?"

She flinches, her eyes wide. "Dead? *Multiple* people?"

"Yeah. A bunch of boys were found dead. Eaten. Traces of ectoplasm on their bodies. Looks like a wraith—a type of ghost—did it."

"Boys?"

"Grown men too. But three kids from the high school."

If her face could be any color other than blue, I'm sure it would look pale. That's how shocked her expression is.

"No," she whispers. "Wh-who?"

"Uh…" I squeeze my eyes shut, trying to recall the names of the students. "Marcus, Wendell, Tyreese, and—"

"Tyreese?!" she cries out, horrified. "No! No way!"

"You knew him?"

"Fuck. I did," she says, and her voice breaks. She pinches the bridge of her nose. "Not Ty."

"I'm sorry for your loss."

"I didn't know him too well. We weren't in the same friend group or anything, but he was… He was always so nice…"

She blinks repeatedly and wipes at her eyes, which confuses me profoundly. Ghosts can…cry? Or is this how her spirit remembers sadness? I shuffle uncomfortably in place, unsure of what to say. For as much as I work with ghosts, death is out of my realm of expertise. I don't know how to apologize to someone when they've lost someone they've known their entire life—and afterlife. It's one of those situations where I feel like I'd either not say enough or say the wrong thing, so I don't say anything at all.

When she gathers her composure, she looks at me. "So you… You think I did it."

"Well, I don't *now*," I reply, trying not to sound disappointed.

If she's not the wraith, then the wraith is somewhere else, and that means I'm back to the drawing board.

Unless…

"You wouldn't happen to know of any ghosts other than yourself?"

She blinks. "No. I think I would've remembered seeing someone else in here."

That brings up a good point. What else does she remember?

"What happened *before* you got in here? How did you get your violin? And if you didn't realize you could phase through walls, *how* did you get inside this building when the doors are padlocked shut?"

She considers these questions for a few moments, staring hard at the floor. Then she shrugs her shoulders. "Wish I knew."

"Do you remember—do you remember *how* you died? I mean, you clearly didn't die here, because the doors are shut, and the only way in is the roof."

I would've come across her body by now if she had. And I mean, if her own decaying corpse was in this place, maybe she would've realized she was a ghost. She died somewhere else and came here somehow. Maybe in the trauma of her death, she phased through the walls and forgot she had the power to escape.

She shakes her head in response to my question. She places her chin atop her violin and squeezes her eyes shut, a pained expression surfacing on her face once more. She lifts the bow and presses it against the strings, sliding it back and forth a few times experimentally, as if checking to make sure it's in tune. Then, with a steadier hand, presses down on the strings again, and plays her first chord. It is sweet yet delicate, like a child weeping. She plays another, glances at the sheet music, and then proceeds to lose herself completely—eyes closed, fully immersed. Her fingers move with expertise along the strings, triggering the right notes to follow. Suddenly this decaying theater, rotting from the inside out, feels a little less hollow.

When she finishes her song, her whole body deflates, as if exhaling a massive breath. She lowers her instrument and bow. Her eyes quiver with some sort of emotion. Is it sorrow, pain, or fear? I can't tell.

"I-I don't remember any of that. And I don't have anything to do with their deaths."

"There are people saying they've been hearing mysterious music on the nights of these murders."

"Like I said, it's not me."

This doesn't make any sense. I found a ghost that plays music, but allegedly, she's not the ghost I'm looking for? Then again, if she was, why am I not frightened of her? I remember how violently I trembled in the wraith's presence, both from fear and from the cold air emanating from its body. I may be a little chilly here in this space with her, but not enough for it to be a problem.

"If you're a ghost," I tell her, "you should be able to phase through walls. You're telling me you can't do that?"

"No. Again, this is the first time I'm learning I'm a ghost."

"Can you fly?"

"That would be sick. But no."

"Sonic screams? Electromagnetic manipulation?"

"Also sounds sick, still no." She smiles politely. "Not the ghost you're looking for. Sorry to disappoint."

"You should be more concerned," I say and flinch.

She arches a brow, suspicious.

"Like I said, my family and I are ghost hunters. I found you today, but if my parents find you, you'll be captured and sent to the Beyond."

She scoffs. "Why? I'm not doing anything. I'm not bothering anyone."

"Because we're ghost hunters. That's what we do."

"Wait, so even if someone isn't being a nuisance, you still kidnap them?"

"Kidnapping isn't the word I would use. I mean, you're not a human anymore."

"*Woooooow.*" She draws out the word to emphasize her surprise and disgust. "That's fucked up."

I shrug. "It's nothing personal. Most people see ghosts as the equivalent of rodents or termites, right? If they infest an area, they could make things dangerous or pesty."

"As you can see, I am neither rodent nor termite, you sack of shit," she snaps, her brow narrowing. "Who the hell do you think you are?"

"I'm Melody."

"Well, *Melody.* My name is Cyrus Paredes-Pantazis, and I am as much a human as I am a ghost, so kiss my ass."

"Kiss your—"

"Kiss. My. Ass," she hisses, absolutely seething.

And yet still—no tremors in the building. No telepathically throwing objects in my direction. No odd, inhuman deepening of her voice or discernible increase in volume. She's right. She doesn't know how to use her powers, if she has them.

"Weird," I murmur.

Her eyes bulge. "Weird? Kinda like someone arguing you don't deserve respect or bodily autonomy? Like, damn. If I wanted to deal with that kind of attitude, I'd visit my grandmother. I'm sure Kalamata is nice this time of year."

"I didn't—no, I'm not used to ghosts of your caliber. Most ghosts I meet are like…glimpses of their former selves. They have a routine they stick to, they can't have drawn-out conversations, they get confused and angry easily."

"Maybe that's because you suck to be around."

"Okay." I close my eyes and hold up my hands defensively. "I'm sorry. What I'm trying to tell you is that you're a ghost that plays music, so you fit the criteria for what everyone is looking for."

"But I'm not killing people. I haven't even, like, hit a person since the second grade, and that was because Ricky stole my chifles during snacktime."

"Yeah, my parents aren't the type of people to stop and think and have a conversation with a ghost. They find you, you get sucked up in the cap-can."

"Well…" She scoffs and shakes her head, frustrated. "What the hell am I supposed to do?"

I shrug. "My advice would be to skip town."

"But I can't. I…" She trails off, eyes wide and unblinking. Quiet panic seeps into her voice. "My parents…they must be so worried about me."

Pieces of my heart shatter when she says this, so sad, so defeated. In this moment, she's not only a ghost, but she's also a teenage girl like me. Clearly she's had some type of severe memory loss, perhaps brought on by some traumatic brain injury she experienced before her death. She's not like other ghosts I've caught. Her memory may be lost in parts, but her soul and personality aren't abstracted. This was a person.

Is a person.

"I need to get home," she says, standing upright.

I frown. "You can't go home. Did you not hear me? My parents are looking for ghosts."

"But I can't stay here," she cries out. "My mom, she probably thinks I'm—she probably thinks I'm gone-gone."

"You are gone-gone," I whisper.

She can't meet my eyes.

"I'm sorry. I don't know how I can help you, and I don't think I can. You'll have to figure out how to manage on your own. You've been doing…okay this whole time, right?"

"That was because I didn't realize how *long* it's been. You have to help me. I have to get out of here. I have to—"

"Cyrus, you can't leave here. *Literally.* If you can't fly or turn invisible or phase through walls, you're going to get caught. Besides, do you remember where you lived? Where your parents are?"

She points to her temple, face twisting in confused expression. "I remember what—what my house looks like. Pictures. It's all fuzzy pictures."

"Okay. Well, I can show you the way out, but I strongly advise you *not* to leave until you have a solid plan."

"You gotta help me, then. If you're a ghost hunter, you know how to evade other ghost hunters, right?"

I hesitate. "I could probably come up with something. But…I'm also in the middle of this other thing—hunting for a killer ghost."

"Right. I don't think you could pencil me into your schedule. I mean, between your bizarre cosplay and school, how will you ever find the time to help me?"

I sigh and pinch the bridge of my nose. This conversation exhausts me.

She shakes her head. "You can't wander in here and upend my entire life and not help me. L-look, what if—what if I help you? With your ghost thing?"

"How will you be able to help me without powers?"

"I don't know. We'll figure it out as we go. Oh—oh, what if you came here straight after school? We could meet up here and then go looking for it."

"I'd have to come here every day after school if we're ever going to get ahead of my parents…" I trail off, crossing my arms. "I'll need to think of some excuse."

"High school musical."

"What?"

She takes a deep breath. "Every fall, the high school puts on a musical. Figure out which one it is and say you're going to be in it. Problem solved."

"Damn." I'm a bit taken aback by the suddenness of her response. "Am I jogging your memory or something?"

"I don't—I don't remember a few things. Like how I got in here. Or how I died. But it's not like I'm working with a total blank slate here."

I'm sure a talented psychiatrist could help her work through her memory loss, but I have no idea where to begin with this. Besides, my phone won't stop buzzing in my pocket. I check it, expecting it to be Tomai with an update on my shoes.

But it's not.

It's Simon.

SIMON: Hey where are you? Isn't school out by now???

I check the time: 4:15. Spirits above, school has been out for forty-five minutes. How did I waste so much time?! And wait— I'm supposed to be grounded!

ME: I had to stay late because I was working on a project with some classmates

I hold my breath as I await his reply.

SIMON: Oh cool. Well, not cool. You should've told me. But I won't tell if you do me a favor.

SIMON: Could you go and pick up some things for the house? I have a web conference with some of the other Apostles so I can't go.

ME: Yes I can. Text me a list please!

Whew. Narrowly avoided my own doom there, but I had better get my ass out of here and go to the grocery store pronto.

I look up at Cyrus. "I have to go."

"And you're going to *leave* me here?"

"I have no choice. I can't protect you if you don't have powers."

"But…" She trails off again, eyes wide with worry. "If it's been a year since someone last came in here… What if you don't come back? What if more of my memories disappear?"

In her desperation, she reaches out as if to grab my hand. A yelp of surprise catches in the back of my throat and I shrink away in fear. Those mournful eyes swallow me whole and my body is racked with guilt. I can't imagine what it's like to live without human contact for a year like she did, but I can't let her touch me.

"I-I'm sorry," I whisper. "I'm sorry. It's—it's not your fault." It's not a great explanation for my reaction, but I don't have time to explain this to her right now. "I-I'm not used to touching ghosts. But look, if you're offering, I'll take all the help I can get."

"So you'll come back?"

"Yes."

"And you'll help me find my parents? You promise?"

I place one hand over my heart, the other high in the air. "Scout's honor."

She crosses her arms, her eyes surveying my body as though trying to calculate whether I'm lying to her. Then she nods, accepting my decision.

"Can you help me break the padlocks on the doors?"

She winces and hisses between clenched teeth. "I don't think there's anything I can use in here to, y'know, cut a padlock. This place has been ransacked of tools."

"Seriously?" I whisper, my stomach somersaulting in horror. No. But that means... "But that means I'm going to have to climb back down that horrible ladder."

"There's a *ladder*? Like, a working, functional ladder?"

I sigh. "I wouldn't say it's functional, but yeah. You want me to show you?"

"Please."

I'm a little nervous to turn my back to her, but I swallow my courage and lead her from the theater, back up the stairs.

"So..." she says, and the sound of her voice almost spooks me. "Where you from?"

"West Province. Mountain Ridge."

"Damn. Long way from home—whoa, *careful!*"

I narrowly avoid a hole in the stairs. "Shit!"

"You good?"

"Y-yeah. Thanks."

"So your family moved out here to catch these ghosts?"

"They're relocating the business altogether. Things were a little tougher back home."

She reaches the landing alongside me. "Oh yeah? Lot of competition?"

"You could say that." I navigate to the staircase, my phone lighting the way. "See this? This leads up to the roof."

"You gotta be shitting me. That door was open this whole time?"

"Afraid so. Come on."

I lead her up the cursed staircase, out onto the roof. Her eyes widen with surprise, and although her lungs don't work anymore, she gulps down a big breath of fresh air. She smiles and closes her eyes, tilting her head back to face the sun, perfectly blissful.

She's...kinda...

No. Nope. I'm not going to say it.

"You know, when you told me it had been a year, I didn't believe you. But now that I'm up here"—she wraps her arms around herself in a bear hug—"I dunno, it's like I'm realizing it's been awhile since I've seen the sun. Feels good. Nice."

"You can hang out up here a little longer, but don't get too close to the edge of the roof. I don't want someone seeing you from the street."

In theory, because she's a ghost, she should be able to conceal herself from non ghost hunters. But because she has no control over her powers, I'm not willing to run that risk. We're going to have to be extraordinarily careful.

"Can you hold the ladder for me as I go down?"

I remove the dreaded heels once more and climb onto the first few rungs. She holds the top firmly in place, and when she looks at me, her gaze is so tender, I have to look away.

"Hey, uh, I'm sorry I insulted your outfit earlier."

"Are you being nice to me to make sure I come back?"

"Figured it wouldn't hurt." She grins. "But nah. You seem like the type of person who can keep your word. I'm not worried anymore."

Nervously, I mutter goodbye to her and proceed down, struggling not to think too hard about what she said. I may be the type of person that keeps her word, but I'm not sure I'm the same type of person that can protect her.

Although I really hope I can.

In the 1960s, mediums, powerful individuals capable of helping spirits cross over, suggested to the Council something blasphemous: instead of forcing spirits from their haunted dwellings, allowing them to take control of their own afterlives. The Head Apostle during this era, Nataya Brown, was enraged by this radicalism, largely invoked by Leorna Giles, a famous medium at the time.

—Peggy Harthorne, *My Year of Ghosts: An Anthropological Account of Life with the Spirit Whisperers in the West Province* (1978)

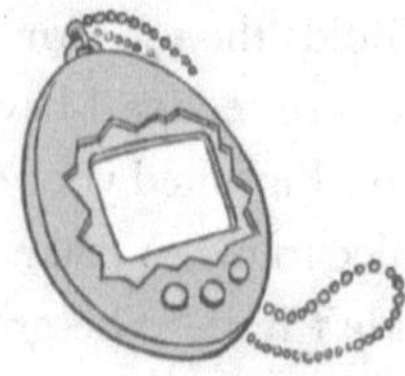

Chapter Eleven

The only saving grace from today's shittiness is that I've managed to change clothes and wipe the makeup off my face in the grocery store bathroom. I was not about to walk around this place looking like a succubus past her prime.

I can already tell I'm going to be the one carrying most of this investigation, and if that's the case we're doomed. I found the ghost I was looking for, but I didn't find the right one, and I have no other leads.

I fester in my thoughts as I debate what kind of stupid vegan butter (Mom and I both eat this) to choose and try to find a packet of chicken thighs that aren't as expensive. Fifteen dollars for six thighs? What, are these chickens free-range? Did they grow up on Ol' MacDonald's farm? Is this how much people pay for food here? Shit, no wonder we're poor. I add that to my cart and snag a package of Band-Aids from the pharmacy as well. When I finish buying the groceries, I slap a couple Band-Aids on the backs of my ankles and wobble home, but everything still hurts.

My heart hits my stomach when I see my parents' car is already in the driveway. *Damn it, Tomai. did you find my shoes?* I have no idea how I'm going to explain my way out of this, but if I do, I'll be the most accomplished bullshitter ever.

Luckily, when I stumble through the door, no one is right there waiting for me. I scramble into the kitchen, dump the groceries on the counter, and sprint for my room while my blistered heels can still carry me. I rip off the cursed shoes and chuck them under my bed skirt, out of sight, and out of mind. Good thing, too, because no less than five seconds later, Mom calls for me.

"Melody? Melody!"

I shake out my arms and legs, trying to calm my jittering nerves. Suddenly the weight of everything I've done today hits me like a ton of bricks. I skipped school for the first time ever. I dressed up in the tackiest, most atrocious outfit I've ever worn. I inadvertently formed a partnership with a ghost, directly going against the written code of the *Thistlefeayr Tomes* and the word of the Council. My inner badass has been unleashed, but my suppressed Goody Two-shoes persona is writhing in guilt-induced agony.

Then again, I've got nothing left to lose.

"Melody Yuluna Myere! Why are these groceries sitting out on the counter?"

Before I exit, I notice the Band-Aids on my ankles have wilted away. *Socks.* I need socks.

"A minute!" I tell her, stumbling back into my room.

I throw open my dresser drawer, grab the thickest pair of socks I can find, and frantically tug them onto my feet. I can hear her coming down the hallway, her foot stomps growing ever louder, till finally, she appears in my doorway. She appears tired, a bit disheveled, her eyes puffy. Hunts where children have died are always the hardest for my mother.

"Sweetheart," she says, lowering her voice, "you can't leave groceries out on the counter. Eggs and chicken need to go in the fridge, pronto." Her eyes trail downward and land on my socks. "Aren't those your winter socks?"

"Y-yeah. I'm feeling super cold today."

"Cold? In those jeans and that button-up?"

"Y-yeah. I don't think I'm used to the coastal climate."

She gives me a weird look but shrugs her shoulders and steps away from the door. "Go help Simon with groceries and prepping for dinner. Your dad and I have to talk about strategy in the lab."

The lab. Wait. Shit. The EMF reader. The Phantom Prod Lite. The bag of blessed salt that I've buried in the bottom of my backpack. All things I stole from the lab but haven't had the chance to return yet. I'll be lucky if they don't do inventory while they're down there—Mom and Dad like to set aside some time to test out all their equipment each week and make sure that nothing needs replacing. I try my best to keep a neutral expression on my face as I follow Mom down the hallway and enter the kitchen, but as soon as I do, Simon arches a brow. Damn Simon. He always knows when something's up.

"Hey," he says stiffly, looking me up and down. "How was your day?"

"Fine," I say, unloading the bags and putting things away in the cupboards.

"Did prepping for that project go okay?"

"What project?"

He gives me a look. "You told me you were meeting with other kids after school to discuss a project?"

"Oh," I say. Shit. I forgot I texted him that. With a nervous laugh, I nod. "Uh, yeah. We mostly hung out, honestly. We were too distracted to discuss school."

He gives a small smile. At least, I think he does. The corners of his lips barely move. "Well, good to hear you're already making friends. I was worried the transition would be rough for you."

"*You* were worried about me?" The incredulous statement flies out of my mouth before I have a chance to stop it.

Simon's eyebrows arch, and he blinks a few times. He nods slowly and moves to wash his hands in the kitchen sink.

As he begins to lather with soap, he says quietly, "I know things have been rough for you since the Hunt."

"Because my parents told you?"

He nods. "They keep me in the loop where they can."

"Oh, great," I reply sarcastically. "So you know I got dumped."

"Amongst other things, yes." He shuts off the water and shakes some of the droplets from his hands before moving to grab a dish towel. "Mountain Ridge people are very…"

"Rude? Snobby? Passive-aggressive?"

"All of the above." He smiles. "The culture there is different from here. I can tell already. Stronger sense of community. When you've been through what these people have been through, there's no other choice but to unify."

A pang hits my chest when I think about the three boys who died—how Cyrus teared up over Tyreese, a boy she had known her whole life. I've never lost anyone, unless you count my paternal grandparents, but that was years ago, and they didn't have a good relationship with Dad or me. I couldn't imagine what it would be like to lose someone you've known for your whole life, who you were used to seeing every single day.

"Mom… Mom doesn't look too well."

"Yes. It's been a rough day," he admits with a heavy sigh. "From what she tells me, they spent today looking at crime scene photos and reviewing the statements from families of the victims, as well as visiting where the killings took place. They're going to go investigate some of the sewers tomorrow."

Tomorrow… The clock is ticking faster than I would like. Cyrus and I are going to have to work fast.

"Did… Did they mention anything about the case to you at all?"

"Not in great detail, no. Not my department," he says dismissively, collecting the things he needs for tonight's dinner from cupboards and the fridge. "Why?"

"I can't help but think about what my friend told me—about hearing a song the night of one of the murders. But that doesn't make sense, right? Wraiths don't do that?"

Simon stops to consider this, deep in thought. "Like I said the other night, only young wraiths can do that, and they're extremely rare. Besides, from the state the bodies were found in, we aren't dealing with young wraiths. We're dealing with an experienced ghost."

"And it's for *sure* a wraith? Could a phantom eat people?"

"I would have to look into that," he replies, and then he stops. He points an accusatory finger at me. "No, Melody. Your parents told you to stay out of it. I can't be putting ideas in your head. Dean will have my hide."

"I was just asking! If I'm not allowed on this mission, how am I expected to grow as a hunter?"

"You're not—you need to focus on school and your whole transition here right now."

"You're not my dad."

"No, but I am your godfather." A decision my parents made which baffles me to this day.

"You only bring that up when it's convenient."

"Please. When else would be a good time to bring it up? It's the only trump card I have." He tears the plastic wrap from the package of chicken breasts and lays each one neatly on the cutting board, then moves to wash his hands again. "Can you grab the chili and adobo seasoning from the spice rack?"

I go over to the oven and retrieve the spices. With freshly washed hands, he unsnaps the lid to each of the containers and begins to season the chicken.

"What are we having?"

"Tacos. I don't know. We have shells, a head of lettuce, cheese, and tomatoes. Speaking of the tomatoes, can you chop those up for me?"

"Uhh…" The equipment—the EMF reader, the Phantom Prod Lite. I'm going to have to put those back, but I can't do it if my parents are down there already.

"Let me rephrase," he says. "That was an order, *not* a request. Please chop up the tomatoes."

With a heavy sigh, I roll up my sleeves, yank open the fridge, and retrieve the beefsteak tomatoes I got from the store. I had hoped when I got home, I'd be able to get off my feet, but I guess I'll have to suffer for a little while longer.

We welcome couples and families from all walks of life. Here at Little Sandy Acres, we believe that everyone deserves to have fun in the sun.

—"Fun in the Sun for Everyone," Oceanview Travel Industry, brochure (2000)

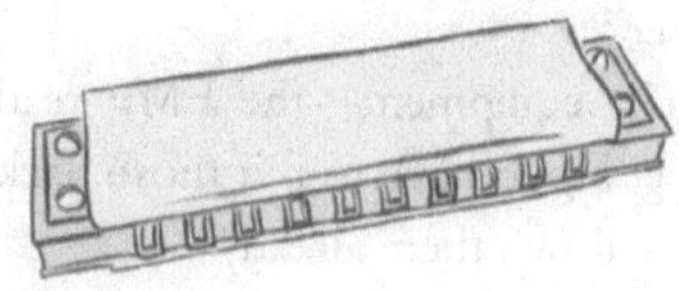

Chapter Twelve

Even after sitting down and eating dinner, my feet are still screaming in pain, so I do my best to limp off to my bedroom and start my homework—well, the homework for the classes I was present for, at least. Mom and Dad went to watch TV, so if they haven't done inventory by now, they probably aren't doing it tonight. I might try to sneak down there to put the stuff back, after everyone's gone to sleep. Hopefully Simon's a heavy sleeper. In between Precalc problems, I text Tomai about my shoes. Thankfully, they respond within a couple of minutes.

TOMAI: YES I got them. I had to sneak off to the bathroom to grab them and thankfully no one stopped me and lectured me about using the gender-neutral bathroom instead lol

ME: THANK THE SPIRITS!!! Can you bring them to me tomorrow?

TOMAI: For sure. How did today go btw?

My fingers fly across my phone's keyboard as I eagerly type a response, but then I pause. I don't know how Tomai would react to me teaming up with the ghost they thought was responsible for all the murders. Also, what if Tomai knows who Cyrus is? If I can't guarantee her safety, what would be the point in telling them about her? With all these questions floating around, I think it's best I keep this to myself for now.

ME: **Dead end**

TOMAI: **WHAT? Really? Shiiiiiit well I thought for sure you would've found somethin. Oh well. Any ideas on where to go next?**

ME: **My parents are going to start investigating some of the sewers so I guess I have to figure out how to get in**

TOMAI: **Oh ew :-P can't help you there. I guess open up a manhole and go down?**

Right, but how do I open a manhole cover by myself? That feels like something you need special tools for. I search the web for answers, and I see a video of a waste worker opening one with a crowbar, but I have never seen a crowbar in real life. I thought they were only items you found in horror games. Another video says you could use a screwdriver, but I'm not too keen on stealing *more* stuff from my parents, even something as small as that. If Cyrus could figure out how to use her powers, we might be able to get it open, but I'm not so sure.

As I do my homework and muse about the next stages of my investigation, something clatters from down the hall. Takes me a minute to register that it's the sound of dishes in the sink. It's followed by the sound of men's voices and laughter. Dad and Simon? I stop my scribbling and set my pencil down on my notebook, trying to listen more. Their voices are as soft as the autumn breeze outside my window.

"I've missed those tacos. Totally took me back." Dad's voice.

"Oh please. They were not, and have never been, good." But Simon laughs, and his laugh sounds…different. Musical, almost. "But I'm happy I'm around to cook you and Rachel some semi-decent food."

Tacos… Simon used to cook for my dad? In what lifetime? Come to think of it, didn't Dad say he had eaten Simon's steak fries before, too? And Simon mentioned they knew each other when they were younger, that they went to Oceanview…that he knew my dad before he met my mother. But if my parents met at the academy, then that means Simon must've known my dad since high school, right? Why is there so much history between them but I don't know anything about it?

I creep over to the door and press my ear against it to listen closer. Their voices are still faint, but slightly louder than before.

"Sorry if Melody is being a little…"

"She's fine. She's a teenage girl. If she didn't have an attitude, I'd think something was seriously wrong." Simon sighs. "Although—"

"No—"

"Don't interrupt me." Simon huffs. "You're being too harsh on her. I'm not saying let her help, but I am saying you shouldn't shut her down like you did last night."

"I didn't mean to shut her down."

"That's what it felt like to her. She said it felt like you were insulting her."

"She…did?"

Another huff. "Yes, Dean. Yes. You might want to watch the things you say."

"You and Rachel both say that."

"For good reason."

Dad chuckles sheepishly. Then he sighs. "I… I don't want her getting hurt again, Simon. Maybe if we had some will-o'-wisp to deal with, I would let her handle it. But…no. I can't. I can't make that mistake again."

"It wasn't yours, it was mine. And I'm going to have to live with that for the rest of my life."

"Well…we followed the word of the Council. I think they're more responsible than anything."

Suddenly I feel as though I'm suspended in a dark pool of water. My ears are clogged with the sound of blood rushing through my body, my vision is fuzzy, and my heart trembles within my chest as though it's about to give out. I'm trying so hard to grasp what was said, but I can't believe it.

Simon… Simon and Dad knew there was a wraith in that house, the night of my First Hunt? They knew, and they didn't bother to send me in with a Phantom Prod? But why? Why would they do that knowing how dangerous wraiths are?

I shrink away from the door. I don't want to hear any more of this. My body trembles with rage even after I return to the safety of my bed. If Dad and Simon knew, I have no idea how Mom didn't know, which means that possibly all the adults in my life—including the ones that I was supposed to trust the most—made the decision that almost resulted in my death.

How could they have done this to me?

It is against the Will of the Ancestors for spirit whisperers to consort with souls that belong to the Beyond. Any sort of fraternization is considered oppositional to our faith's mission, which is to ensure that they cross over. I know that there are those who believe we can all coexist, but coexistence is only going to ensure chaos.

—Nataya Brown, Head Apostle, 1969 interview in *Radical Spirits: Ghost Hunter Politics in the 1960s and '70s*, dir. Genevieve Plottergirth (2005)

Chapter Thirteen

The next morning, I wake up before everyone else. I creep into the basement lab to return my EMF and Prod. Once the items are back in their safe places on the shelf, I rub my bleary eyes, crack open Mom's laptop, and type in her password—my name followed by my birthday. Whenever my parents work on a more complicated mission, Mom will take whatever files or information she's been sent and compile it into a folder on her desktop.

I find what I'm looking for: MURKMORE WRAITH INF. I'm guessing INF is an abbreviation for infestation?

Scrolling through briefly, I find several folders—way more than usual. I skim past every image (crime scene photos, dead bodies, no thanks) and highlight two files: victims.pdf and sightings_locations.pdf. I log into my email account, and I send myself the files. After deleting the browser history, I shut the laptop and scurry back to bed and sleep for three more hours until my alarm goes off.

Simon makes coffee and breakfast again—this time, a bell-pepper-and-egg hash brown bowl. He smiles at me and he's friendly, but I can't look him in the eye for fear of being found out. I mumble something about needing to go to school early for the project again and bound out the door before he can force me to sit down and chat.

Tomai is waiting for me outside the main gates, my beloved shoes in hand. I grin, my excitement bubbling over, and I rush to them.

"My precious babies!" I sigh as I clutch them to my chest. "I'll never leave you again!"

"Damn, girl. They're just shoes."

"Want to take a guess as to how much these cost?"

"Nope," Tomai says with a grin, stepping back. They cross their arms and run a hand over their pink hair, an excited expression on their face. "What's your plan for today? Any other big escapes I gotta stress about?"

"Thankfully no, not today." I sigh, unzip my backpack, and shove my white sneakers inside. "I'm going to try to get into the sewers after school. See if I can find anything."

"Oh, right, the sewers. You're seriously going down there?"

"Unfortunately."

"Eww." Tomai scrunches up their nose, their eyes big and disgusted behind their glasses. "Well, as much as I'd love to join you on your little adventure today, I can't. Stage crew has a meeting."

"Stage crew?"

"Y'know, for the musical?"

"Oh. Oh, that's right." An embarrassed heat fills my cheeks, but then I remember what advice Cyrus gave me yesterday. "What's the musical going to be?"

"It's *Gargs and Dwarves*. Terribly sexist, but still a classic. Sets are going to be killer this year." They rub their hands together. "Why, did you want to help out?"

"No, um, I was thinking I could use the musical as a cover for the investigation. So like, if I'm out late after school or at night, I could tell my parents I'm in the musical."

The excitement vanishes from Tomai's face. "Oh." They replace it with a more neutral expression, nodding slowly. "That makes sense. I can cover for you if needed."

"I appreciate it."

"So…the Lennox Theater. You said you didn't find anything there. Were you saying that because your parents were hovering over your shoulder, or was it true?"

For the briefest of moments, I pray my expression doesn't betray the words coming out of my mouth. "Oh, no. They weren't in my room. I, uh, didn't find anything. It was spooky though."

"Really?" Their eyes glitter with excitement. "How so? Like, was there any evidence a ghost had been there before?"

Maybe a tidbit of truth wouldn't hurt? "Uh…some. Ectoplasm and stuff. But that doesn't necessarily mean a ghost is still living there."

"What does ectoplasm look like?"

"It's…blue and gooey. Kind of like slime, or Silly Putty in terms of texture. Maybe a bit stickier? At least when it's fresh. Ghosts will often secrete the substance and it will trail on the ground behind them or be left behind on surfaces they touch."

"Gross. But if a ghost was there at one point, is there any chance it will return?"

A hard feeling emerges in my stomach, stubborn and solid, like I've swallowed a rock. I can't tell if Tomai is asking questions to be curious, or if they don't believe me. I have a hard time telling the difference after having dated Brynne, who had this sort of…dualism to the way she spoke. Mom said she was passive-aggressive, but I didn't see that until after we broke up.

"Uh, no," I reply awkwardly.

It's rude, but I try to look at my phone so I can seem like I'm growing bored with the conversation, and maybe we'll switch to something else.

Thankfully Tomai takes the hint. "Oh, wait. You're probably going to need the homework from yesterday." The bell rings, and Tomai winces at the irritating noise. They reach into their backpack and withdraw their agenda. "Can you give this back to me at lunch?"

"You're a lifesaver. Seriously."

"No," Tomai says, grinning from ear to ear, "*you're* a lifesaver—once you get this ghost, that is."

They give a two-fingered salute before heading into the school. From what I've gathered, their first-hour class is on the opposite end of the building, so they have to book it if they want to make it before the bell rings. Thankfully, I only have to stroll down the hall for my Northern Province History class. I enter the school and am walking past a row of lockers when I feel something…intense. Like I'm being watched. Call it a hunter's instinct, but my head starts swiveling in all directions, trying to figure out what's giving me this bad vibe.

When I look over my shoulder, Ms. Ruder is standing there. Arms crossed, shoulders squared, staring me down like some sort of anime villain challenging me to a duel. It's honestly as comical as it is threatening, but I don't dare laugh near this woman.

"Melody," she says, her tone of voice calm as her eyes glare at me with a burning hatred; the sort of expression you'd reserve for someone who ran over your dog.

What did I do to this lady other than exist?

"Glad to see you're back in school today. Tomai said you weren't feeling too well."

"Th-that's correct," I say with a nervous laugh. I squeeze the straps of my backpack a little too hard and can feel my knuckles growing white. "I always get sick around the start of school."

"How unfortunate." She walks over, her gaze confident, her eyes not diminishing in intensity.

Uh-oh. *Uh-oh.* Each step she takes, my heart sinks farther and farther into my gut.

"You know though, the next time your mom comes to the school to pick you up, she needs to sign you out at the front desk, okay?"

"Huh?"

"Your mom? Tomai said your mom came to pick you up"— she strokes her chin—"but when I talked to the front office, you weren't on the sign-out sheet. They said they would call your parents to assure you had been picked up, but I told them no, they're probably very busy."

The upper half of my body is completely rigid, the bottom half is trembling like a Jenga tower about to collapse. Holy shit. She knows. She *knows* I skipped school yesterday. Spirits above, of course I would be caught by someone like her. Why did I choose her class to skip? What was I thinking?

She yawns and covers her mouth as she does. "Next time you get 'sick,' please try your best to suffer through my class first. There's a lot of material you'll need to catch up on today."

I hold up the agenda Tomai gave me. "I'm already on it."

"Splendid."

She doesn't smile. Delivers one final chilling gaze and brushes past me. I listen to the sound of her freshly polished loafers squishing against the floor and wait till she turns the corner before releasing the biggest sigh of relief. Even though she's not near me anymore, my ribs squeeze my lungs like a boa constrictor crushing a mouse. I try to take a few deep breaths, hoping I can stave off the impending panic attack. All this secret-keeping and mystery solving is not good for my long-term health.

"Oh my God, Melody, are you okay?"

I look up to see Jackie approaching me with her gaggle of friends, flanking her on either side in perfect formation. She's wearing an airy tennis dress with a pleated skirt, the school logo emblazoned across the front. Her braids are pulled back in a severe ponytail, baby hairs swooped into sweet little curls around her widow's peak. Her big, big eyes blink at me rapidly, azure and glimmering, and for the briefest of moments, she reminds me of Brynne. She had the biggest blue eyes out of anyone I know, till I met Jackie.

She places a comforting hand on my arm and gives it a squeeze. "Girl, you looked like you were getting chewed out by Ms. Ruder."

"Why does she have it out for you?" one of the girls—I think her name is Phoebe, she's in my second-hour Precalc class—asks with a snicker.

"Oh my God, Phoebe," another girl chastises her, swatting her playfully. "It's not funny. Stop laughing."

"Don't let it get to you," Jackie says, her smile kind and disarming. "Come on. You should walk with us to History."

I don't know why Jackie is inviting me, but I know I shouldn't turn her down. It's better for me to make friends with the sharks on the high school food chain than to make enemies. Then again, maybe she's not a shark—or at least not a megalodon like Brinkley. Maybe I'm thinking the worst of people again and she's a genuinely nice person.

The same girl who scolded Phoebe speaks again, looking at me pointedly. "I love how you do your makeup. Covers up your birthmarks well."

"Oh, those aren't—those aren't birthmarks. They're scars. But thanks."

"Scars?" Phoebe whispers, and Jackie rolls her eyes. I can tell Phoebe is the one in the group with no filter. "What gave you scars like that?"

"Oh my God, Phoebe, you can't just ask someone why they have scars."

"Maybe she wouldn't mind telling me, *Tam-ar-ah*," she responds snarkily, sticking out her tongue. "Besides, I wasn't acting like they were a bad thing! They're badass. Not that I would want them of course, but—"

"Phoebe, the time to remove your foot from your mouth is now," Jackie says coolly, brushing her braids over her shoulder. She purses her lips and glances at me, and I can't tell if she's trying to sympathize with my situation or show she's annoyed with her. "Totally not a question you need to answer."

For some reason this helps the tightness in my chest loosen. "Thanks."

"How're you adjusting? I see you've been hanging around—what's their name—Tomai."

"It's been…good," I say, but I'm deeply suspicious of why she's showing an interest in me.

Intrinsically I know somehow, someway, I have done something wrong to attract her attention. Or maybe she's fishing for hot goss on the murders or something, I don't know. No amount of nice, pearly-white smiles can make me think this girl has good intentions.

"Cool, cool. Well, as the student body president, I would be remiss if I didn't check in with you and make sure you're doing okay." She smiles. "But like, totally let me know if Ms. Ruder keeps bothering you. I can always talk to my mom about it."

"Th-thanks, Jackie."

"No worries. So hey, are you coming to the pep rally?"

"Pep rally?" I ask, confused.

"On Friday after school in the gym."

Phoebe shakes her head. "It's on the beach. The gym flooded during the stormy season, remember? They're still cleaning up."

"Oh, that's right. Beach. Even better! Anyways, we get out early, do a few cheers; it's a good time. The townsfolk show up too," she says. "And at my place after, we're having a little get-together. You're welcome to come. Tomai included."

"Oh," I say. "Uh, thank you. That's…super nice of you."

"Of course! Do you want my number? I can send you the details."

We exchange numbers quickly. Suspicion still lurks at the back of my mind, but when the bell rings, I bury it down deep. Our History teacher turns the morning announcements on as I take my seat. In my pocket, my phone vibrates, and I check it, my panicked heart assuming it's Mom or Dad or Simon somehow discovering that the lab equipment had been touched.

But no.

It's a Photobooth notification.

Brynne Matthews posted for the first time in a while.

Despite her vanity, Brynne wasn't an avid user of social media. She found my desire to post pics from our dates "frustrating" and "time-consuming," so for the most part, when we were together, I was careful to limit the number of pictures I took with her…even on our anniversary.

But there she is, at the entrance of our—*my*—old school. She's wearing the sunflower dress I got her for her birthday last year; the one I spent most of my allowance on because I knew how much she loved looking at it in the store window. Those little flower-petal-shaped lips of hers, stained a shade of glittering pink, turn upward in a playful smirk. Her arms are wrapped around the neck of Tamblyn, one of the girls she became a *little* too close to in Mathletes. When we were together, I repeatedly told her how uncomfortable I was with their friendship, but she struck me down every time.

The caption: **We look so cute together haha**

And the first comment is Tamblyn's reply: Love you <3

Which I guess makes it official, because there are swarms of our former mutual friends commenting "Congratulations" and partaking in their cuteness as well. It's a hub of disgustingly gross happy feelings that makes my stomach churn like a cauldron full of acid.

I know it's been six months since we broke up—but somehow when I see this, all the awful feelings I had resurface like a picked-open scab. This is *more* than just a relationship announcement post. Tamblyn casually told her that she loves her in that comments section, which means this has been going on for far longer than I've known. Is it possible they kept it on the downlow until they knew I was gone? What's even worse is seeing all of our friends—people who *knew* how much I disliked Tamblyn—congratulating them and acting all cool with it. Like losing Brynne to her was an inevitability that everyone knew about, and I was just the last to know.

If I had bothered to eat anything this morning, I would barf right now.

It's funny how you disrespect my opinion, Madame Apostle, when you know our Foremost Matriarch herself was a medium. We are spoken of in sacred terms in the text of the Tomes, *and yet, you will do everything in your power to silence me. And I think that is because you're afraid. You're afraid your theories of the Beyond are wrong, and that these technologies—ones that you advocated for so diligently and mercilessly—bring more harm than good.*

—Leorna Giles, medium/ghost advocate, to Head Apostle Evelyn Graow, 1976 televised debate in *Radical Spirits: Ghost Hunter Politics in the 1960s and '70s*, dir. Genevieve Plottergirth (2005)

Chapter Fourteen

After school, I'm able to return to the Lennox without issue—and this time, in an outfit appropriate for climbing: heavy-duty sweatshirt, plain T-shirt, and my thickest pair of jeans. I'm ready to get down and dirty, which is probably best since I'm heading into a sewer.

I skirt around the back side of the theater and look at the ladder. To my surprise, Cyrus is already climbing down. In the faint sunlight, she looks a lot less blue than she does in darkness. This is normal for ghosts—they tend to desaturate when exposed to light. The brighter the day, the blander they look.

"How did you know I was here? I thought you had no concept of how time passes."

"Found a clock in the back office last night. Also, I remember what time school gets out. Stand back."

She jumps down from the last few rungs of the ladder and lands safely on the ground. She stares at her feet for a little bit too long, then looks back up at me with wide, wondrous eyes. I have to avert my gaze a little because they're so…pretty—a deep mahogany brown, timeless and soulful like the trees in the forests outside Mountain Ridge.

"Hey, you know how ghosts can phase through things? Have you ever heard of a ghost phasing through the ground and falling to the center of the earth?" She shivers and rubs her arms. "That would be so freaky."

"No I haven't, and…" I look her up and down.

She grins and folds her arms across her chest. "What, are you checking me out?"

"Don't—don't be ridiculous. I was checking out your outfit."

"Because it looks cool?"

"No. Because we're about to go into a sewer and you're dressed like a businessperson who got lost on their way to the dive bar."

In death, Cyrus wears an immaculately pressed suit with oxfords. She's regal, refined, and dripping with confidence. The suit must have been tailored, because it conforms to her stocky shape quite well—breathable, but not too bulky. A pair of Ray-Bans are permanently tucked into the neckline of her shirt, which is unbuttoned at the top. Her hair is shaved along the sides, leaving only a little tuft square along the center of her head which she pulls back into a small, spiky ponytail. Her shaved hairstyle shows off her ears, which have small tattoos curling around them: on the left side, a treble clef, and on the right side, a pair of feathers—what bird, I don't know. The one thing I do know is she oozes cool, which isn't a surprise to me, because musicians always ooze cool.

For some reason, it pisses me off. Ghosts aren't supposed to be cool, or talented, or ridiculously attractive. They're supposed to be soulless husks of their living selves, like grown-ass adults who waste away at their corporate jobs in sunless cubicles.

"Ohh, I see. You're intimidated by my strong sense of style."

"I didn't say that. I think it's—funny. It's funny," I repeat, as if trying to convince her I wasn't eating all the eye candy she has to offer. *Spirits, what's wrong with me?* "Did you dress like this every day when you were alive?"

"No. This was for homecoming. In case you didn't pick up on it, I'm a plaid shirt and jeans kinda gal. Or I was." That same anguished expression from yesterday resurfaces. "Um…do you know what happened to my parents at all? Did you look them up?"

"I—no, I'm sorry." After I overhead Dad's conversation with Simon, I curled up in a tight little ball on my bed and lay there the rest of the night like the useless lump I am. But I don't know how to tell her that. "I-I can do that, though. Maybe after this is over."

I shuffle in place, uncomfortable. She squeezes her eyes shut, and in the silent moments that follow, I want nothing more than to take away her pain. I give her the time she needs to recollect herself. When her eyes snap open again, there's a renewed sense of determination on her face.

"What's the plan?"

"We're going to find a manhole, climb inside, and see what we can find."

"That's…that's it?" She trails off, uncertain. "How do you know we're not going to run into your parents?"

"Because they're probably heading home by now. According to their case files, they're going to be entering closer to City Hall, where another one of the bodies was found. That's the east side of the island. They get the nice steps, and we get the creepy ladder to hell."

"Okay. So…manhole." Cyrus points to one that sits in the center of the alleyway, adjacent to the abandoned dumpsters. "There we go. How do you plan to get it open?"

"I'm not going to open it. You are."

"What? How?"

"It can't be that hard. Besides, you have to figure out how to use your powers."

"My powers? You want me to lift it, like, with my mind? Like telepathy?"

"It's telekinesis, not telepathy. Telepathy is when you can read the thoughts of other people, and you aren't a shade, so you wouldn't have that power." I gesture to the manhole again. "Come on, we don't have much time."

She wrings her hands. "How do I know that your parents aren't waiting down there for me?"

"Seriously? My family and I don't need to lead you into a sewer like this. We could've gotten some pliers and snipped the lock off the front door. It's not hard to capture a ghost that can't phase through walls."

"Rude."

"My parents also don't want me involved in this investigation. Like, at all."

"What? Why?"

"Unimportant."

She snorts. "Uh, okay, weirdo."

"We have to figure out what kind of powers you have anyways. Even if I help you return to your parents, which I *will*, you need to learn how to get around and avoid human detection."

"What kind of ghost do you think I am, anyway?"

"I'm… I'm honestly not sure."

That's another thing that bothers me yet again. What kind of ghost *is* Cyrus? More importantly, how did she die? If she's wearing her homecoming outfit, that means she died on the day of homecoming. So many mysteries to uncover in one person, and as tasteless as it is to admit it, I'm kind of excited to learn more about her. What if she is some sort of rare ghost that I've discovered? A new type that somehow emerged on this isolated little island?

"Circling back to our manhole problem, how do you expect me to get it open? How do I use my powers?" She wiggles her fingers. "Is it like a magician thing?"

"Maybe?"

She wiggles her fingers in the direction of the manhole. Nothing happens, but it sure looks silly. I can't help but giggle. She shoots me a rude look.

"Are you going to help, or are you going to mock me?"

I cup my hand over my mouth to stifle my giggles. "I— sorry."

"Don't you *dare* laugh, dude." Her eyes are wide with anger, but her mouth trembles, on the verge of breaking into laughter. "At least I'm trying. What have you contributed to our expedition so far?"

"Uh, I figured out where we're supposed to go?"

"Shit." She gives one more dramatic finger wiggle before her arms drop to her sides. "I got nothing."

"You're not trying."

"Hard to concentrate with all that giggling."

"Okay, okay, I'm sorry."

I smile and shake my head. Cautiously, I shuffle closer to her. Talking to her feels cozy and familiar, but that doesn't mean I entirely trust getting this close to a ghost. Yesterday's romp through the moldy theater didn't do anything to alleviate my fears of being attacked.

"Can you show me how to move my hands the way you want me to?"

Uh-oh. Touch her? Like…hold her hand? The last time a ghost touched me, they removed 42 percent of the skin from my face. Nervously, I glance up at her, but her expression seems neutral, not sinister in the least. Okay. So maybe she's not going to tear me limb from limb. But that doesn't change the fact I'll be holding a girl's hand for the first time since Brynne dumped me. A superhot butch's hand. Maybe my fears are more complicated than I thought.

But she's patient with me, waits for me to take her by the hand. My heart lurches in my chest like it's been thrown through the windshield of a car, but I ground myself. *I am safe. I am safe. I am safe.* She won't hurt me. Her hand is cold and clammy, but almost refreshing, like a drink of ice water on a hot day. Huh. I lead her over to the manhole and lift her arm, then adjust her palm so it's perpendicular to the ground—fingertips pointed toward the sky. When I saw witches lifting things back in Mountain Ridge, they always kept their hands pointed up, so maybe it works like that? But nothing happens. I place my hand on the small of her back and tilt her body down and forward, so she's directly facing the manhole cover. Still nothing.

"Are you going to give any instruction, or are you just gonna be touchy-feely?"

I scramble away from her like she's lit me on fire. "Y-you're the one that asked me to touch you!"

She arches a brow, but the smirk on her face doesn't dissipate. "I asked you to *show* me how you wanted me to do it. But don't worry, I appreciate the hands-on instruction."

Oh no. She thinks I'm flirting with her. This ghost totally thinks I'm flirting with her. Worse, she's liking it. Is she into me? I can't have that happen. The number of rules from the *Tomes* I'm breaking just by associating with her is enough to fill me with guilt. No matter how nice she is, or how cute that grin of hers is, I will not be tempted.

Or at least, I'll try my hardest not to be.

My voice quiets to a passive-aggressive mutter. "I… I mean, you should be feeling something. Some sort of energy in the air."

"You say this as fact?"

"No. I—ugh. When I see young ghosts do this, they generally point or gesture at things to get them to move. Um, let's try having you point at the manhole cover."

Cyrus stands rigidly, arm stretched, finger now pointing toward the ground. "Like this?"

"Yes."

A pause.

"I feel nothing."

"You're not concentrating." I can't help it. I stand shoulder to shoulder with her, extend my arm parallel to hers, and grab her wrist. I close my eyes. The texture of the ectoplasm soaks into my palm, thin like a layer of mucus, but soft and not slimy. Cool, yet comforting. So, so strange. "You have to *feel* the world around you."

"Should I close my eyes like you?"

"If it helps."

I open my eyes a smidge to see her squeezing her eyes shut in full determination mode. She scrunches up her face into this tight knot, and I have to stop myself from thinking it's cute. I close my eyes again.

"Think about every particle, every molecule, every atom around us right now. Feel it from the top of your head, down to the tips of your toes."

"Like meditation?"

"Shh. You're not concentrating."

She takes a deep breath—although she doesn't need to. At first, there's nothing but the faint sound of wind scattering the fallen leaves and a car driving by in the distance. Then, slowly, I hear it: the rattling of metal. I open my eyes a pinch, and the cover is trembling in place. I lift Cyrus's arm and she lifts the cover till it's hovering about an inch or two above the hole. The muscles in her arm are trembling, like it's becoming too much for her. She grits her teeth like she's in pain.

I sweep her arm to the side and the manhole cover falls to the left of its original place. Her arm gives out, and the hefty metal falls to the ground with a mighty thud. She exhales again and, as she does, falls to her knees. Her body shudders and convulses, and for a moment the panic swells within the back of my throat again. Did I push her too far? Could I have hurt her? Is it possible to hurt a ghost like that?

"Hey, are you okay?" I touch her shoulder.

Somehow her body seems warmer than before. That's…interesting. I didn't know using their powers could result in a ghost's body temperature fluctuating.

"I'm fine…but that took a lot out of me." She pounds her fist against her chest rhythmically, nodding her head, like she's trying to come down from a panic attack. "Man. That sucked."

I rub her shoulder reassuringly. Spirits, I can scarcely feel it through the thick fabric of her blazer, but her broad shoulders seem so toned. For the briefest of moments, I wonder what it would be like to hug her—how tight and warm I'd feel within those thick arms of hers.

I bet it'd feel different than holding Brynne.

"You did good."

"I *did* do good, didn't I?" She offers me a grin. "And I have powers."

"You do! I told you you did!"

"Well, I didn't believe you until now. Huh." She flexes her hands, astounded by her newfound abilities. "Bet it won't be long until I can like, move buildings and shit."

"Uh yeah, I wouldn't go that far." I grab her hand and pull her to her feet. "Ready for our descent into darkness?"

She nods. "Let's catch this ghost."

"Climate change this, climate change that," Stu Foster says. "The climate's always been changing. It's nothing new and nothing we have to prepare for. A bunch of yuppie scare tactics from folks who think they're smarter than the rest of us."

—Howard Bonevue, "Citizens Express Discontentment Over Proposed Greenery Changes," *The Sunshine Standard* (30 Mar. 2017)

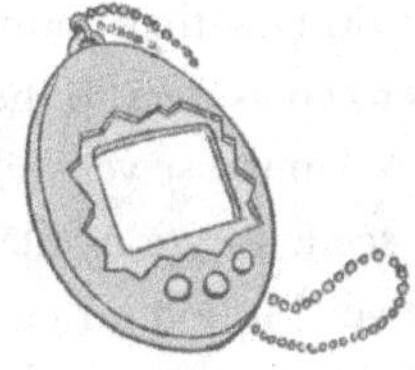

Chapter Fifteen

I imagined a sewer to smell worse, but oddly enough, it doesn't. It's…damp—kinda like how the rain smells when it first begins to pour. Faint notes of salt. Almost like the sea-breeze-scented detergent Dad uses to do laundry. Maybe there's something about being surrounded by the ocean that makes this all smell better? Or is it just that for some reason, there's not as much trash down here?

Super concerning that the streets of Murkmore are filthier than the sewers.

The concrete interior of the sewer appears to be covered with either a thin layer of lichen, or shit. It's slimy to the touch and makes me want to hurl, but I manage to grit my teeth and swallow down the bile at the back of my throat.

"Did you bring hand sanitizer?" Cyrus asks, wrinkling her nose with disgust.

"No." I didn't, because I come unprepared every single time, like an idiot. I'm surprised I remembered to charge my phone at school so that when I used my flashlight down here, my battery wouldn't die.

I flick on the flashlight and see what lies ahead of us: a canal leading to an intersection that branches off in four directions, the waters low but fast moving. The sounds of its trickling and babbling fill my ears. Along the sides of the tunnel are narrow pathways and a few bridges that connect some of the canals together, allowing us to cross over to the other side.

"Do you know *where* in the sewer we're supposed to go?"

I open the crime scene locations file on my phone and look for the map of the sewer I found earlier today.

"Okay, so one of the victims was found on…the north side of the island."

"The north side?" She considers this for a moment. "You got your maps app pulled up?"

I show her the map of the island. I'm surprised this thing works when we're twelve feet under. She squints, touching the screen a few times as if to reorient the app's focus.

"Got it."

"Got it? How? Do you remember?"

She taps her forehead. "Coming back to me a little bit. But I think—emphasis on *think*—I know where to go, and it's a bit of a trek. We better get moving."

She forges on ahead with a confident swagger, completely unbothered. Cyrus and I walk alongside each other in total silence, the light of my phone bouncing over the water waves. When we round a corner, I catch a glimpse of my shadow on the wall, but hers is missing. So weird to be walking next to someone and yet they don't cast a shadow. She doesn't seem to notice though. If anything, she's more focused on the water coursing through the canal, milk-white froth bubbling at the surface. Her eyes are as wide as moons. Don't tell me she's afraid of water? She's afraid of water and she agreed to follow me all the way down here? Spirits above, now I feel awful. Part of me wants to take hold of her hand again, but I know I can't be that bold.

I can't.

I can't get that close to someone again.

"What's your big plan once you come across these wraiths?" she asks. "You gonna season them into the next afterlife?"

"Ha ha, you're *so* funny. And no, this is only a scouting mission. I need a cap-can and a full Phantom Prod if I ever want to bring a wraith down, and I can't take those from my parents without them noticing."

She scratches her head. "Yeah, why're you doing this behind their backs, anyways?"

"I prefer to think of it as helping from the shadows."

"That sounds more ominous than 'doing it behind their back.' But you do you."

The scars on my cheeks burn furiously. I don't know how to tell a non-ghost hunter about my First Sacred Hunt, how I failed, and how my failure ruined my family's life. It feels so ultra specific to my own culture that I'm not sure she would understand. Besides, even if we've decided to be allies, Cyrus is still a stranger to me. I don't know if I want to tell her about all my embarrassing failures within the past year. Once this is over, I'm supposed to help her find her family, figure out how she died, and after that, we'll go our separate ways.

"I need to prove to them I know what I'm doing. That's all."

"Ohh, so it's a situation where you want to join the family business and they won't let you?" She nods. "I get it."

"You can relate?"

"Oh, absolutely not. My dad runs a restaurant in town and wanted me to take it over when I got older. But I can't cook for shit and I'm also way more into music than I could ever be into cooking."

"You sounded good on the violin yesterday. How long have you been playing?"

"About as long as I've been playing piano. So…ten years?" She squeezes her eyes shut to think, counts on her fingers, then nods vigorously. "Yeah. About ten years."

"Piano *and* violin? How many instruments do you play?"

She grins, her expression almost bashful. "I can play about six. Piano, violin, guitar, trumpet, rondador, and my personal favorite, harmonica. When we visit my abuelo in the winters, I get to play around on a marimba, which is basically a big xylophone. Oh, and when I had a working computer, made some tunes in DAW."

"Wow. A real modern-day Mozart."

Suddenly a cold expression crosses her face. "Well, if I wasn't dead, I would be. Now I suck at being a ghost."

I almost say, "You'll get the hang of it!" but it would feel too weird to tell her that. Like, "Now you have all the time in the world to figure out how to move manhole covers," as if that's some riveting, exciting life compared to the dreams she pursued before. I take a few moments to gather my thoughts before replying.

"I guess it doesn't come as naturally as I thought it would," I say. "Don't beat yourself up for that."

"Not what I was…never mind." She shakes her head.

I don't know what I said that was so wrong, but I bite my lip and decide perhaps it's better I don't speak anymore. We continue down the dark corridor for several more minutes. I'm glancing at the map of the sewer on my phone when suddenly an odd feeling hits me… While this is a perfect environment for a wraith to thrive in, dark and cool as it is, it begs the question: why would a body be found down here? Wraiths, like most ghosts, are sedentary creatures. Unless they're being forced out, they don't migrate to claim other territories. So that would mean the person found down here *came* down here.

Why?

I open the victims file in my email.

"What are you doing?"

"Checking something."

I scroll through the document. Each entry has a photo, name, age, occupation, and brief description of injuries and where the body was found. I grimace as I scroll past the boys my age, and carefully look for the one found in the sewers. I find him: Parker Kim, twenty-nine years old. Marine biologist. He was found in this section of the sewer system, but his lab partner, Thad Stevens, was found in a separate area—that's where my parents are investigating today. Strange. Nothing in the file indicates there's a research facility or lab on this island, so I guess they must have been from the mainland, surveying the area? That could also explain why they decided to split up, to cover more ground.

But that doesn't explain why either of them would be down in the sewers. What made these guys want to come down here?

"Melody, what's up?" Cyrus stops dead in her tracks, eyeing me warily. "You're too close to the edge."

Spirits. I didn't realize it, but I'm only an inch or two away from the edge of the walkway beside the canal. Cyrus places a hand on my arm and pulls me closer to her. She loops around to my other side, providing a barrier between me and the water. She's…protective of me. She'd stand between me and this canal although she's clearly afraid of it. Maybe she doesn't think anything bad would happen to her if she fell in, but still, this makes my heart flutter within my chest like a wild bird desperate to break free from its cage.

"You good?" she asks.

"I was thinking about how weird it was for a body to be found down here. Because wraiths—if wraiths were living down here, they wouldn't move. They aren't like wolves. They don't go hunt then return to their den."

"So what would motivate them to leave?"

I sigh. "I don't know. If it wasn't obvious, I'm a pretty amateur detective, and my brain is more than a little fried with everything that's been going on."

"Like what?"

"Well, for one, I moved to a new town. Two, I found a ghost. Three, my family's Apostle moved in with us, and—"

"Your what?"

"It's a ghost hunter thing. Families are assigned these people called Apostles whose job is to educate us on the *Thistlefeayr Tomes*—basically, the equivalency of the Bible or the Quran or the fae's *Spring Chronicles*—and to teach us about different spirits and the ways of our people."

"Like your own personal priest?"

"Kinda. It's hard for me to compare being a ghost hunter to any other religion," I say. "Apostles are not only religious leaders—they're historians, cultural experts. Simon isn't only a guy who can wax poetic about passages in the *Tomes*, he's also a professional at identifying different types of spirits and tracing family lineages. But they usually don't live with their families; that's an old-school thing. And they typically aren't limited to one family anymore, since y'know, the religious needs of families differ. But we got 'lucky,' and now he lives with us."

"And you don't like him?"

I sigh. "I don't know what to think about him. He's—he's difficult to read. He always has been. And he's snarkier than most."

"Did he choose to move out here with you guys, or he didn't have a choice?"

I shrug my shoulders. "He could've asked the Council for a reassignment. But I guess he didn't want to. There's too much history for him to start over elsewhere."

Too much history I don't know about, apparently. I recall last night, when I overheard Simon and Dad's conversation: how much they had laughed, how they shared memories from the past. Feels weird to think of my parents as people, and not just as my parents.

"Yeah, that's gotta be weird. Ghost hunters in general seem kinda weird. No offense."

"None taken," I reply, although I definitely, on some level, take some.

"Especially since, like, you apparently think I don't deserve rights and should be sent to bottle-jail or whatever it is ghost hunters do with spirits."

"You're not sent to bottle-jail. You're only put into the EctoChamber until you can be sent through the Ingress."

"What is the Ingress?"

"It's—it's a device that connects our metaphysical world to the spiritual realm. You power it up, it accelerates superfast—kinda acts like a little wormhole."

"Wait, really? Could you go between the human world and the spiritual realm?"

"No, not like that. Humans can't go into the spiritual realm. The Ingress is a small device, not capable of transporting a human. From what we know of the spiritual realm, it's completely unsustainable. It's like being out in space—no air, water, anything."

Cyrus stops in her tracks. A pained expression crosses her face.

"So you send them there? Even though there's nothing?"

"It's better for them there. Peaceful. They get to be with other spirits and interact with them as well. And they don't have to worry about the human realm."

Cyrus shakes her head. Her shoulders stiffen and she stares at the ground. I anticipated the conversation going this way, but I'm not about to shut down all questions she may have. Non ghost hunters have their own theories of how the afterlife is supposed to work—especially ones like Cyrus, who wears a cross—and when you try to tell them that idea is wrong, they can be reactive. I've gotten used to it by now, and while the hostility can be frustrating, that doesn't mean I shouldn't try to explain it to those who truly want to try to understand it.

"I know it's uncomfortable," I say, "but it's better for them to be safe and protected than to suffer endlessly in the human plane of existence. Before we had technologies such as the Ingress, ghost hunters would keep the spirits for years, endlessly searching for ways to help them cross over. And there is great suffering in keeping souls captive. Putting spirits through that sort of trauma can—"

"Trauma, you mean like kidnapping them by sucking them into a glorified trash can?"

"No. And again, you cannot kidnap a ghost. You don't live like people. You're literally haunting an abandoned theater. That is very on brand for a ghost."

"But you think of me as less than you?"

Less than? I hadn't even given that a thought. I don't think of her as less than me. It's just that…

"Ghosts are different from human beings for a reason," I tell her. "They're compelled to relive their memories or to pursue their goals from when they were alive. They lose themselves eventually."

"What if I told you that that won't happen to me?"

"That's"—I shake my head—"that's not possible. I'm sorry."

"Well, it's going to have to be, because if I disappear on my mom again, she might chase me into the afterlife." She chuckles a little, but her eyes are sad. "God, a whole year. She's going to be so mad when I show up again."

I try to speak as gently as I can. "Cyrus, I don't think you get it. Ghosts…lose themselves. I mean, you lost quite a bit of your memory, as well as your sense of time."

"That's because I was alone."

"No, not because you were alone. It happens to every ghost at one point or another."

"Maybe I'm a special type of ghost. I mean, there's gotta be hundreds of kinds, right?"

"No. Um, so…" I trail off, trying to think of a way to explain this. "You know how for biology, we've got taxonomy: kingdom, phylum, class? Same thing for ghosts, but simplified. Four classes—wraiths, phantoms, shades, will-o'-wisps—and then subtypes. For example, banshees are a subtype of wraith specific to Ireland. You can only be a banshee *if* you died in Ireland, and *if* you died while mourning a family member. It's a specific, rare type of ghost. This is why it's so important we figure out how you died."

"So you can determine exactly when I turn into a monster?"

"So I can understand how much time you have left."

When I say it out loud, my voice sounds so hollow. Cyrus flinches. She hangs her head low.

"Christ," she mutters. "You don't have much of a filter, do you?"

"I'm sorry—"

"You're not, so don't tell me that."

"If you don't want to figure out how you died, you could've said so."

"Maybe I don't want to remember, Melody. Did you think about that?" She squeezes her eyes shut and runs a hand through her hair. "You're kind of a jackass."

"I'm just trying to help."

She rolls her eyes. "I didn't realize ghost hunters had such a God complex."

"What?"

"You think the more you know about me, the more capable you are of helping me. Fixing me. You never stop to question *why* you should. Or if you should."

"Because…"

"Because you think I'm a monster?"

"I don't think you're a monster. You're just a ghost, and as the Apostles have said and as I've seen, certain kinds of ghosts *can* be dangerous—"

"And you blindly follow everything they tell you?"

"Faith isn't blind."

"It is when you don't question it." She glares at me like I'm scum on the bottom of her shoe. "I'm only going to say this one more time. You need to stop acting like I'm not a person. Because I am, and you know that, and I get it makes you extremely uncomfortable, but it's the truth. So maybe your book, your Apostles, your beliefs—maybe they're a little bit wrong. I've had to work through the same shit, you know."

I recoil, embarrassed but also deeply ashamed. But honestly? Asking me to unpack my beliefs while standing in a stinky sewer is way too much. I shake my head and keep going.

When we arrive, it's a little bit darker. Through the storm drains, it looks like the sun is slowly setting—the consequences of summer shifting into fall. And there's nothing here. A few bloodstains on the walls, but they're more like splatters and sprinkles; there's barely any evidence a body was here.

"Grody," Cyrus comments, and to my astonishment, she presses her finger against the stain and tries to rub it off, but it doesn't budge. She shudders and furiously wipes her hand against the leg of her pants. "Sick."

"I mean, it's dried on. But yeah, I wouldn't recommend touching remnants of a crime scene."

I approach some of the stains, scrunching up my face. Kinda weird that when they cleaned up the body they didn't also clean up the blood down here, right? I peer down at the base of the wall, and the light from my phone catches something twinkling in the faint light. I crouch so I can get a closer look.

An…earring? A little gold bow-shaped earring, glittering yet tarnished by muck, with a large diamond serving as the center of the bow. Wait a minute. That's not muck.

Blood. There's blood on it.

"Who would lose an earring down here?" Cyrus asks, confused.

"It's a sewer, with a storm drain right above it. That's not too unusual, right? Things fall off, get lost, flushed away…"

Cyrus smirks. "Sounds like you're trying to convince yourself that's not important."

"I don't…" I squirm, looking at the glob of unmentionably bad scum on the surface of the earring. "I don't want to touch it."

"I guess I will," Cyrus says, but she winces as she reaches for it.

Something about this…doesn't seem right. I shine my flashlight onto the wall, then up through the storm drain overhead. The underside of the grate looks oddly discolored, and that's when I realize there're bloodstains on it, too. But the body was found down here.

Why would there be blood splatters on the storm drain?

My flashlight traces the walls, highlighting small patches and spots of blood smeared into the cement. The pathway crosses over our heads, to the wall beside us. How did blood get all the way up there?

"Hey, so you said a wraith doesn't drag food back to their den, right?"

"Right…"

"Are we both wondering why the hell there's blood on that drain?"

Gruesome as it is, I try to picture it: the sloppy remains of a slain person sitting atop the sewer grate, the steaming entrails and blood dripping and falling into the sewer below. But that doesn't explain the blood on the walls down here, nor on the ceiling above us. Wraiths may be messy when they kill, but not like this. There's more blood on the other side of this sewer than on the side where the body was found.

"Yeah. I mean…his body was found down here, but if there's blood on that sewer drain—"

"Then he had to have been dragged down here."

Or he could've struggled and wound up down here, but given the blood on the ceiling, that's unlikely. It's almost like he was played with in midair. But wraiths don't do that, and I don't even think ghosts, in general, are capable of doing that. From my experience, they're only able to lift small objects, maybe ones that are at best twenty or twenty-five pounds.

Then again, no better way to find out than using a ghost, right?

"Can you lift me and hold me over the canal, close to where those blood spots are?"

Cyrus's eyes widen. "What?"

"Okay, you don't have to hold me over the water, but try to get me as close to the ceiling as you can."

She frowns. "No."

"I'm trying to figure out if a ghost is powerful enough to lift a body over this area."

"What if I drop you and you roll over into the canal?"

"Don't worry. I'm a good swimmer."

"Melody—"

"Please?"

"If you fall in and drown, you better not hold it against me in your afterlife," she huffs.

I set my phone on the ground, flashlight pointed up. With shaking hands, Cyrus attempts to lift me, but she can only move me a few inches off the ground before her body gives out. My body tilts headfirst. The sound of my palms slapping against the tiled ground is deafening, and I wince as red-hot pain radiates through my body.

"Melody!"

"I'm fine," I whisper, shakily climbing to my feet.

Ouch. My knee throbs. Probably going to have a massive bruise later. I pick up my cell phone and examine the patterns on the walls and ceiling. More blood is splattered above us than anywhere else, in an arc pattern, almost like someone sliced open an artery. This ghost killed him in midair, but that's not possible. Even if it *did* manage to hold the victim above the canal long enough to slice open his neck, it would've dropped him in the canal. And given that wraiths want to eat, it wouldn't have carelessly wasted food like that. I explain all of this to Cyrus, who listens, bewildered.

"This…doesn't make sense."

"It's like… It's like someone who wasn't super knowledgeable about ghosts was trying to plant…"

Evidence.

Someone is trying to plant evidence.

I rub my hands all over the walls vigorously. Nothing. I squeeze my eyes shut in disgust and run my hand over the ground. Nothing.

There is no ectoplasm here.

"There's no evidence that a ghost has ever been here, is there?" Cyrus whispers.

My body trembles furiously, and my eyes widen with horror. There's grime on my hands, but it's dirt and soot and probably something unmentionable. It reeks, but it's not ectoplasm. It's not blue. It's not sticky.

"If this murder happened only a few months ago, and a wraith is allegedly still on the loose, there is absolutely no way there wouldn't be ectoplasm covering this place," I tell her. "So that means—"

"Someone killed this guy down here, and they were somehow able to kill him in midair."

I nod. "And, they covered his body with ectoplasm so it would look like a wraith did it. All of the bodies had ectoplasm on them."

Cyrus throws up her hands in frustration. She laughs breathlessly as she paces back and forth, but her eyes are full of terror.

"You're telling me there's an *actual* killer on the loose? An actual serial killer? Here? In Murkmore?"

"It sure seems like it. But why would someone pretend to be a wraith? Why go to that kind of trouble?"

"I don't know!" she cries out. "M-maybe we shouldn't rush to conclusions. I mean, wouldn't the police have figured that out already? W-wouldn't a coroner's report figure that…"

She's hyperventilating. She's already dead, she has no need to breathe, and yet she's hyperventilating. She tears into her hair, trying to catch her breath, but it's not working. Her chest heaves and heaves and heaves. I touch her shoulder to comfort her. She squeezes her cross necklace and slowly tries to take deeper breaths. In my head, I try to recall everything that has transpired so far. Reports of mysterious singing. *Singing*. But Cyrus doesn't sing, or at least, I've never heard her sing.

Oh no.

"Cyrus…you died a year ago, right? Which was…probably before the murders started?"

"I…yeah, I think so." She scratches her head so ferociously, if she was alive, her scalp would be bleeding. "Y-yeah. About then. Beginning of junior year. H-h-homecoming."

"Okay. And there are a lot of people in town that knew you were a musician, right?"

"Yes! Jesus! I hate to brag and all, but I was like, a once-in-a-lifetime talent." She pauses, then corrects herself. "Still am, honestly."

"Okay, so what we have here…is a serial killer going around…singing songs at night…and trying to blame this on a ghost."

It takes her a moment to consider everything I'm saying. Then her eyes widen with horror at the realization.

"No," she says. "*No.* You're joking."

"I'm not. Someone is framing you for this."

"But—but didn't you say the bodies were covered in ectoplasm?"

"You can get ectoplasm from anywhere. You can order it online. I knew people back in Mountain Ridge who used to put some of it in the mulch of their gardens to help keep the soil damp in the summers."

She clenches a fist and presses it against her mouth. Her entire body is trembling so hard, the outline of her form blurs at the edges. Watching her, something inside me stirs—this terrible, righteous urge to protect her. I squeeze her hands and pull her closer to me. Carelessly, I run my hand through her hair, and while she seems stunned by this, her expression softens. She reaches up to touch my hand, and only after she briefly squeezes it do I allow it to fall.

"We need to figure out what happened on the night you died."

There are certain radicals who insist ghosts can be kept as pets. To that, I would like to ask them if they're prepared to be hit by a variety of random flying objects when they disrupt a poltergeist's routine. There's no safe way for all of us to coexist. But in the Beyond, they are free to be themselves, as they were in life. That is the way it should be.

—Adalia Verony, Spirit Whisperer Supreme Winner, 1980 interview in *Radical Spirits: Ghost Hunter Politics in the 1960s and '70s,* dir. Genevieve Plottergirth (2005)

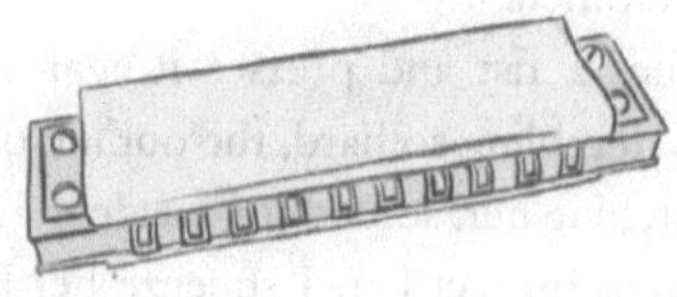

Chapter Sixteen

"No, really. I remember getting to the dance, and then after that, everything's a blur."

We're walking through the sewers, heading back to our original destination and trying to piece together what happened. Some of her memory is being jogged, although not all of it, because of course, we could never be so lucky. It's so much darker now than before, but thankfully, my phone doesn't show any texts from the parental units, so I'm still in the clear. I texted Simon earlier this afternoon to let him know I was attending an informational session for the musical. Hopefully he won't harp on me for being grounded, but he hasn't called it out yet. Through the grates of the storm drains above us, the muddy-orange shades of the sunset blend with the early beginnings of the navy night sky. It's started to feel cold down here.

"I know it's hard, but it's important you try to recall as many details as you can."

"Because you think I was murdered? Okay, first of all, why would someone want to murder me? Other than for being too cute and too talented?"

I point at her. "That? That right there."

"Arrogance isn't grounds for murder."

"It *is* grounds for someone to hate you."

"Remember what I said earlier about you having no filter? Dial it back a notch."

"Sorry." I take a deep breath. "We have to think hard—like if you had to make a list of die-hard enemies, who do you think you'd pick? Did you have a falling out with a friend? Dump someone at the dance?"

"No…I definitely didn't do that. And I…hmm. I think I went to the dance with my friends? I can't remember getting there."

"Do you remember being around your friends at all?"

She pauses, then, "Yeah."

"Okay. And you were with them all night, or…?"

"I… I think I got…separated from them?" Cyrus rubs her temples. "I don't remember why. I don't think it was a fight, but I'm not sure."

Well, *that* doesn't sound promising. "Okay, so you don't remember if you were fighting with your friends or not. What about enemies in general? Frenemies? Foes? People you shoulder-checked in the hallway while walking to class? That kid who stole your snack in the second grade or whatever?"

Cyrus blinks. "Ricky?"

"Yeah, him."

"How the hell did you remember that?"

Because I'm high-key obsessed with you. "Uh, because it was funny."

She smirks. "Well, nothing like that. But now that you mention it, a lot of the girls disliked me."

"What? Why?"

"Because I'm… I'm butch," she says slowly. "You know that, right?"

"Are you saying people here are homophobic?"

I'm not getting that vibe. They have gender-neutral bathrooms at the school. Homophobia is pervasive everywhere, but I don't think the culture here is hostile.

"Not homophobic. *Butchphobic.* There're a lot of queer people here, believe it or not. All I'm saying is a lot of girls—queer or straight—don't like butches. When I was in middle school, people would tell me to my face how ugly and mannish they thought I was, and if a girl found out I liked her? She'd be *so* embarrassed. To a point where it felt like I committed a crime against her if I so much as looked in her direction. Don't get me started on all the looks I'd get in the girls' restroom. There were times I was asked to leave."

"But you're a girl."

"Yep. I know. Between that and the hypersexualization? I could not catch a break."

"Hypersexualization…?"

"Maybe that's not the right word. But…there's this assumption that because I'm so masculine presenting, I want to be a dude, or act like one. That I see all women as sexual objects, and I'm—well, that I'm down to fuck, no feelings involved. But I'm not like that, and I've made that clear to every person I've ever dated, only to find out they were trying to use me as a quick way to lose their V card. Sometimes I'd… I'd give in. I'd hope they'd stick around, but they never did."

I know what it's like—to do things for someone before you're ready, out of the hopes they'll stick around longer. That was pretty much the entirety of my relationship with Brynne.

"That's *vile.*"

"It is, but what can you do? Tried to dress more femininely; hated it. It's not me. Honestly, Melody, it's hard as hell, but I like who I am. I wouldn't want to be anyone else." She examines her cuticles and squishes them down. "Dating may be impossible, but it's their loss. At least I can spend more time on music. I'll have plenty of time for groupies later."

She plays it off like a joke, but I can tell she's hurt. I don't know what to say. I didn't have an understanding of this. I'm pretty femme, and truth be told, I didn't know too many butch or masc girls in Mountain Ridge. I didn't realize until now there might've been a reason for that. No one has ever vocalized that they felt my presence was dangerous. Her gender presentation has never felt threatening to me. I love her style; I love the way she carries herself. It's who she is.

"I'm sorry. That sounds…rough."

"Yeah. If you're looking for a killer, parsing through half the girls in senior year sounds a bit much."

"Although, if the earring we found has anything to do with it, then it's worth looking into."

I trail off, realizing we've arrived back where we started from. Cyrus nods and gestures for me to go up first, which I do. I look around the alleyway, and thankfully, there's no one waiting for us. I have no idea why I thought there would be, but after all the weirdness we've come across these past few days, it'd be the least surprising thing to have happened. I watch Cyrus climb up the ladder and extend a hand to help her out.

"Thanks," she says with a small smile. Her hands move to brush the dirt off her clothes even though they're still perfectly clean. Perks of being a ghost. "So…"

"Let's go inside, then we can figure out what to do next."

Somehow, someway, that ladder holds us once more as we climb and head into the building. We retreat to the main theater where we first met. I take a sip from the water bottle in my backpack and anxiously check my phone, but still no texts. I'm beginning to worry that something happened to my parents, but I bury those nervous feelings as much as I can. Spirits know I don't need another thing to freak out over right now. *Practice what you learned in therapy.* Count to five on each breath in, five on each breath out. It's not as good as a meditation session, but it helps.

Cyrus sits on the floor of the stage and sighs, although a wistful smirk plays at the corner of her mouth. "All right, so you're back to square one for the second day in a row. And my life—or should I say afterlife?—has been getting progressively worse since I met you yesterday."

To my surprise, I can't help but laugh. Her smirk finally breaks into a wide grin, the dimples on the surface of her apple-shaped cheeks shiny like a cherub from a Renaissance-era painting. Something about her smile and the mischievous twinkle in her eyes stirs a strange feeling in the pit of my stomach—but again: ghost. Absolutely out of the question, no matter how attractive Cyrus is. Besides, I'm not sure these feelings are genuine, or if it's a by-product of me missing Brynne.

And, y'know, figuring out that she finally started dating the girl she told me not to worry about.

"How can you laugh when you've caused me so much sorrow?" Cyrus says in faux outrage, placing a hand against her chest.

"Comes with the job."

"So what do we do? What's our next step?"

"Let's...take a look at that earring. Can we... Can we wash it first?"

She sighs. "Hand me your water bottle."

Reluctantly, I pass it over to her. She brings the open edge of the bottle a little too close to the earring.

"I do not want E. coli touching that water bottle."

"Jeez!" she says, but she holds it a little higher before pouring the water over it.

Grimacing, she scrapes away some of the dirt and grime with her fingernail until it looks somewhat presentable. She holds it close to her nose, sniffs it, and makes a face.

"Spirits," I say, gagging. "Why did you do that?"

"Because I'm letting the impulsive thoughts win today." She sets it down on the floor between the two of us. "Now what do we do?"

"Uh… I mean…now that it's a little cleaner"—I lean in closer—"it looks…kinda new."

"So?"

"Uh… I guess if the jewelry was old, then it would be an old lady doing all these things."

Her eyebrows rise. "Y'know, I do have a theory or two on which old lady might be a vampire in this town."

"How do you remember that but not where you live or how you died?"

"Ghost brain works in mysterious ways, I guess."

I think that's a crock of bullshit, but I won't push it. "I don't think it's a vampire who did this. Their kills are cleaner. And vampires can order blood from a donor bank, so why bother?"

"Because the hunt makes them feel more alive?"

"I *really* don't think it's a vampire."

"Okay, but to be clear, I am not taking that off the table."

"Fair enough. I mean…it's kinda cutesy. Preppy. Who do you know in Murkmore that fits that aesthetic?"

"Hmm… I could probably draft up a list, but I'd need something to jog my memory—like access to social media or something. But isn't it getting late?"

Paranoid, I check my phone again, but no texts. Still, she's right. It's almost five. I don't think my parents would believe me if a musical information session went much longer than this.

But Cyrus is still vulnerable.

"I don't think it's safe for you here," I tell her quietly. "If I'm right, and someone is framing you for the murders, then my parents are going to be looking for every obvious place a musical ghost would hide."

She considers this with a wry smile. "Therefore I should hide in the least obvious place."

"No—what's that smile you got?"

"A ghost hunter wouldn't expect a ghost to freely roam their own house, correct?"

My jaw drops, but I can't help smiling at the wackiness of her statement and how she delivers it with so much confidence. "You want to stay with me? You're insane."

"Not insane. A creative problem solver."

"I don't know how I'd sneak you into my house. You don't know how to phase through walls."

"You're gonna have to figure it out because I'm not staying here. At least…not anymore."

She sighs and wistfully looks around the room. If this place has been her home for a year, I can't imagine how much it hurts to leave it behind. It stung when we left our old house, but for Cyrus, this theater has been a refuge to her. For as much as she's lost her memories while living here, she's also protected herself from the chaos of the outside. It both hindered her and protected her.

"This place means a lot to you, doesn't it?"

Her eyes are misty. "I played my first recital here. Piano. I was seven. The most nervous I had ever been in my life. I lost my sheet music somewhere in the car and I burst into tears backstage."

"No!"

"Yeah. My dad looked and looked but he couldn't find the pages until after. He told me to do my best, and when I got out on this stage, I was so nervous. Shaking from the waist down.

Took a seat on the bench. And it all came to me." She smiles. "It was the first time I discovered how great it was to lose yourself. Music helps me do that. Then it helps me find myself again."

As I look out upon the rows of seats, I try to picture the smiling faces of parents and family members, coming here for a nice afternoon to celebrate their children's musical talents. I imagine the warmth of the lights and the childish whispers you'd hear backstage and the feeling of excitement settling like an all-consuming fog over the space. The countless number of films screened here. The way this place must have been, at its peak, so critical and beloved by this community.

And, like her, I feel sad we're leaving too.

"I know we're burning what little daylight we have left, but...do you mind if I play one last song here?" Her voice is hoarse. "To say goodbye?"

"Sure. Sorry I'm not much of an audience, though."

"Hey. You'll do," she says, grinning as she stands.

She retreats backstage and retrieves a stool, along with her violin and bow. She glances at me pointedly, indicating that the stage is hers now, and I descend. I find a seat in the front row, and when I plop down, a cloud of dust escapes into the air. Yet despite its age and poor care, the texture is soft and velvety.

Cyrus tunes her instrument, playing a few experimental notes, and then her body relaxes. She closes her eyes and adjusts her posture so she's standing as tall and proud as she possibly can. Then the bow slides across the strings, and her fingers begin to move, and the theater is completely immersed in the power of her song.

It begins quiet and sweet, before building in volume. When Cyrus slides the bow across the strings, she moves her whole body in time with the music, swaying from side to side to the rhythm, a dance she's completely lost in. Even with her eyes closed, her expression communicates everything she's feeling—at first, anguish, her facial features scrunched up, but somewhere in the middle of the song, they begin to relax. Her eyebrows lift, and the corners of her mouth turn up in gentle delight.

I'm lost in her performance, but not enough to ignore the sounds of something in the theater…a metal tinkering—a quiet pattering. What is that? At the back of the stage the curtains are fluttering, as if a breeze was moving through the space. It ripples outward, shaking the tops of the seats. Cyrus's music grows in intensity, each staccato note succinct; the discarded pages of sheet music lift from the floor and whirl around her in a tornado, spinning as fast as the pace of her song. The stage lights overhead rattle and flicker erratically. But the most unusual, fascinating thing is this hazy blue miasma that manifests in the air above her, squiggly lines of energy reminiscent of the aurora borealis. It shimmers and twinkles in the light, a detached constellation of stars and Milky Ways. It's wonderful and ethereal, and I become as enraptured with the visuals as I do her song.

That's when it hits me: this is telekinesis. She struggles to use her powers without my help, but when she's playing this piece, it's like she's removed some sort of blockage. Is it possible her powers can only be accessed through music? She had played a little bit when we first met, but her powers weren't drawn out of her like this. Does it have something to do with the length of the piece, or the emotions she experiences as she plays?

Her song builds to a crescendo, and as she plays the sweet, lingering final note, her eyes slowly open. The papers swirling around her gently fall like snow, and the theater goes dark. All that's left is her, me, and my endless fascination. I can't deny it any longer. I'm burning up for her faster than a meteor hurling through Earth's atmosphere.

I leap to my feet and cheer till my throat is hoarse and my hands sting from clapping so hard. She smiles bashfully as she lowers her instrument and takes in the chaotic mess she's left on the stage. Then her humble expression falters, and her eyebrows shoot up in pure surprise.

"What the heck happened?" she asks.

"You," I tell her. "You did it. Your telekinesis is influenced by your music. That makes so much more sense."

"Does that finally help you narrow down what ghost type I am?"

"Not really, no." It's giving poltergeist, but she's still too coherent to be one.

"Oh." Her expression deflates, and she glances at the floor. "Did you…like the song?"

"Y'know, I'm not a big classical music fan, but…yes." I smile. "I liked it. And I liked how much you enjoyed playing."

Her cheeks bloom blue, and for a moment I'm worried I've been caught. Then she glances down at the instrument in her hands and nods in the direction of backstage. I follow her into the dimly lit space, full of junk and dusty wooden pallets and flimsy decorations lost to time. The case for her violin sits atop a crate. Scattered on the floor are various reels of film. She rehomes her instrument in its case with delicate care.

"So," she says, "how are you planning on sneaking me into your house?"

"You got any extra clothes?"

If I put heavy, dark clothes on her, that might hide her glow— and also make her look more like a human person. I could tell Simon I was inviting a friend over for a project, then pretend the friend went home and he didn't notice it.

Cyrus tugs at the collar of her shirt. "Nope. This is all I got."

"Damn." Then again, even if I covered her in the thickest clothes, Simon would still notice a drop in the temperature. "You know, if you were more skilled with your powers, I would suggest that you maybe possess an object. I could put the object into my backpack and sneak you inside."

"Possess? How would I do that?"

"I don't know, Cyrus," I reply, blinking. "I'm not a ghost."

"You are *so* helpful. Truly."

"We've figured out your powers are connected to your music… I don't know, are there any songs about possession you can play?"

"Songs about possession? Stalking, maybe. But not possession." She considers this for a moment, then snaps her fingers. "Got it. But you gotta find an object for me to possess, first."

"Uhh…"

Ghosts can throw objects, but they can typically only possess technological items—i.e., a computer, television, or cell phone. But who knows what kind of trouble she could get up to inside my phone, especially when she's so inexperienced. I could end up with a totally fried device. Still, her livelihood—or deadlihood—is far more important than the displeasure of going a few days without Photobooth. In fact, given what I know about Brynne, I would welcome it at this point.

With a reluctant sigh, I reach into my pocket and withdraw my phone, then extend it toward her. She looks at it in disbelief.

"Your phone?"

"You need something compatible with your electronegativity. That means any sort of electronics."

"Wait, really?" Her jaw drops open, her eyes sparkling with childlike wonder. "Does that mean I could like—possess a car?"

"In theory, but your powers are nowhere near that strong. Sorry to rush you, but we're burning what little free time I've got until my parents demand to know where I'm at. Whatever you're going to try, let's try it now."

Cyrus takes a deep breath and reaches into the pocket of her pants. She withdraws this small, shiny metallic thing: a harmonica.

"You carry that around with you?"

She doesn't answer me. Instead, she closes her eyes and presses the instrument to her lips. The first notes are bright but aggressively present, piercing the air without any of the delicacy her violin had. The notes do not ebb in their flow; they are punctual and demand to take up space. But her song is rich and soulful, and she moves with it nonetheless. This time, the blue light does not hover over her, but instead emanates from her body—I guess whatever this electromagnetic spectacle is, with a smaller instrument, it doesn't have the ability to get away from her. But that appears to be exactly what she needs, because when she reaches out and grabs my phone, her body evaporates, dissolving inside of it.

The harmonica clatters to the ground, discarded. Carefully, I squat and pick it up. My phone buzzes and vibrates for a few minutes, the screen flickering, brightness adjusting, before finally falling silent and still.

Oh no. Where is she?

I try a couple of different apps on my phone and they're still completely functional, but there's no sign of Cyrus. Can a ghost get stuck inside an object they've possessed? If she's stuck, is there a way I can get her out? Is there a way I could try to communicate with her? I stew in silence for several minutes, brainstorming different possibilities.

Then, biting my lip, I open up the Notes app on my phone and type into it.

CYRUS? YOU THERE?

The screen flickers. A new sentence appears next to mine.

YEAH BUT THIS IS PRETTY WEIRD.
YOU GONNA BE OKAY?
I THINK SO BUT PLEASE HURRY.
OK I'LL HEAD HOME AS FAST AS I CAN

I turn on my heel, but the sight of Cyrus's beloved violin, so delicately tucked away in its case, stops me. She *loves* this violin, with her entire heart and soul. I carefully close the lid and snap the latches on, sealing it from whatever threats may come across it. I take the harmonica and tuck it away inside my backpack, pocket my phone, and then, case in hand, I head for the roof for the last time.

Our people care so much about saving souls when they are in fact soulless. That is a sickness that I cannot hope to correct during my lifetime, but I pray the Tomes *will guide us to a healthier future.*

    —Leorna Giles, 1968 interview in *Radical Spirits: Ghost Hunter Politics in the 1960s and '70s,* dir. Genevieve Plottergirth (2005)

Chapter Seventeen

Out of all my years removing ghosts from homes, never did I think I would be sneaking one into my *own* home. My parents' car is not there, but Simon's is. I open the door ever so gently and step in quietly, hoping I can make it to my room before he can spot me. But he's already there, sitting in the living room, a book on his lap despite the TV being tuned to the evening news. Glasses hang from a golden chain around his neck that glitters in the light of the living room lamp.

"Hey," he says, a smile on his face. "I was getting worried."

His eyes immediately move to the violin case I'm carrying. Droplets of sweat break out along my hairline, threatening to roll down my face and blow my cover completely. When I gulp down my nervousness, his expression shifts. Spirits, I've already failed.

"My friend forgot this at school and asked me to bring it to them tomorrow."

"What is that, a violin? Is this musical going to have a live orchestra?"

"Y-yeah," I say. "They go all out."

I shrug my backpack off my shoulders. My phone radiates heat inside my pocket, and I wonder if this is Cyrus's way of communicating how frustrated she is. But I have to play it cool, right? If I run off to my bedroom now, a suspicious instrument in hand, isn't Simon going to know that I'm up to something?

I head over and sit on the couch beside his armchair, pretending to be interested in what's on TV. Then do a double take. My *parents* are on TV. Talking to an anchor who appears to be in her midforties, but whose hair is perfectly coiffed and coiled like she's straight from the 1980s. I guess these local stations can't afford a modern-day stylist.

Actually, that's generous thinking; she probably does her hair herself.

Mom is in the middle of answering the anchor's question. She appears as sweaty as I am at this moment, is trying to hide behind a timid smile.

"We're doing everything we can to end this town's nightmare. Tomorrow we're investigating rumors of a ghost at the Lennox Theater, and we hope to have some more information in the coming days."

"How would you recommend citizens of the town stay safe?" the anchor asks, her eyes troubled.

Dad chimes in. "We recommend everyone stay indoors at night as much as possible, preferably from 7 p.m. onward. Never go anywhere alone. And if you hear any music or singing while walking outside, you should call the police immediately."

"Music?" the anchor repeats. "Curious. What have you heard?"

I stare at the fuzzy image of my parents on the screen. They exchange sheepish looks. No. They can't possibly be using the information *I* gave them, right?

Mom confirms my suspicions. "We've discovered that on the nights before the bodies were found, people heard music playing. So, if you hear music, that's a sign you need to find shelter—and call the police."

I'm sorry, I thought they didn't *want* my help. But when they hit a dead end, they're willing to take it? Nice. Real nice, Mom and Dad.

"Oh, I'm sorry. I forgot to tell you they were going to be home late tonight. It's only you and me for dinner." He looks at me with a small smile. "What do you feel like having? I promise I won't make you sit through tacos again."

"I don't mind tacos," I tell him.

"You don't?" His brow furrows in confusion. "You seemed so upset last night."

"I did?"

"You were pushing food around your plate and you barely said a word."

I shrug. "I was tired, I guess."

"Well, we can order something in, if you'd like."

"I'd rather not, sorry." I stand up and move closer to the hallway. "I have a ton of homework to do. And because of the meeting, I'm a little behind."

"How did it go, by the way?"

"It was fine."

I hope my curt response will get him to leave me alone, but he appears blissfully unaware of my frustration. "What musical is it?"

"*Gargs and Dwarves.* I'm interested in the part of Adalia." I know enough about the musical to know there are two major female leads, at least.

"Ahh, that's such a good role for you—especially since you're an alto."

I'm completely bewildered he knows this, and I guess that shows on my face because he says, "I came to your sophomore year musical performance. When you were doing *Into the Witch-Wood*."

"Oh. I forgot about that. Anyways"—I shuffle in place awkwardly—"homework."

"Do you want me to fix you a plate of food?"

I can't help but wince. *Too many damn questions from this man.* He can try to be as nice as he wants, but I haven't forgotten the words he exchanged last night with Dad. And, the thought of eating leftover tacos—those they so keenly reminisced over—makes my stomach churn.

"No thanks, I'm good."

I make a beeline for my bedroom. By the time I shut and lock the door, my phone feels like it's burning a hole in my pocket. I fish it out and throw it onto the bed. A blue vapor wisps from the power port. Anxiously, I double-check my door—for sure, locked. Then I rush over to my window and draw the blinds. By the time I turn around, the blue vapor is forming a cloud, one that resembles a person. Slowly, piece by piece, Cyrus rematerializes, a disturbed expression on her face.

"Whoa," I whisper, tiptoeing over to her. "Are you okay?"

"It's like being trapped inside a sauna," she says hoarsely. "In the most humid place on Earth."

"That explains why you were freaking scalding me."

"Why are you talking so quietly?"

"Because Simon is home. He's out in the living room. And I told him I had to do homework." I nervously reach for my phone—still hot to the touch, but thankfully, still functional. "My parents are out, so we're all good for now. But if you have to hide, can you possess something again?"

She stammers wordlessly and spreads her hands in exasperation. After taking a deep breath she ruffles her hair, which surprisingly looks wet. I didn't think ghosts could...be wet. Didn't think they could be dry or damp either. Another interesting facet of her ghostiness I didn't anticipate.

"Okay, okay," I say, waving a dismissive hand. "You're going to have to hide in the closet if my parents come back."

"I don't know if I can hide in the closet. I did it until I was ten, and going back in again doesn't seem appealing to me."

I roll my eyes. "Har, har. Very funny."

"It *was* funny, and I would appreciate a little more laughter."

I reach for my backpack and unzip it, unloading all my things, including her harmonica. I offer it to her and she murmurs her thanks before pocketing it once more. I rearrange my textbooks and various notebooks on my bed, preparing to buckle down for a few nights' worth of homework—I didn't do much last night because there wasn't much to do, since I missed class. And Ms. Ruder was right: she *did* have a lot of materials to go over. Serves me right for skipping. Then again, how lucky am I to get a buttload of homework the one time I've ever skipped in my life?

Cyrus wanders around my room, examining the various posters and pictures I've affixed to my walls. She admires a series of drawings I've tacked to the bulletin board beside my closet. For a long time I was interested in styling clothes and costume designing. Back when I did theater (before Brynne, of course) I helped with the costume department on occasion and would research different fashion styles for various eras or how to best illustrate a theme through clothing choices. It's why my outfits can sometimes be a little weird and over the top. Weird things can be embarrassing and make you stand out too much, sure, but for me it feels like a safe way to push myself out of my comfort zone. Clothes are clothes. You can take them off, replace them, and rearrange them any way you like. When the breakup depression hit, I pretty much spent all my time in sweats and oversized crewnecks. Funny enough, yesterday was the first day I decided to experiment with fashion again. And as stupid as some of my choices were yesterday, it was also…kinda fun.

"Clothing designs?" she asks.

"Stylist stuff," I reply. "I can't sew anything, but I love to put together collages and mood boards."

"Oh, cool. Nice designs. We could've used someone like you on the musicals."

"You worked on the musicals at school, too?" I wonder if that means she knows Tomai, since they're a part of the stage crew.

Cyrus nods. "Any time I could play something, I'd do it. Orchestra during the year, marching band in the summer, fall musical, spring play."

"Of course you did."

She grins. "Did you honestly expect anything less?"

"Guess not." I prop my chin up on my hand. "But yeah. I used to be in musicals too, at my old school. I stopped doing them because I got too busy. I'd play mostly bit parts, but I liked to help out the costume department too."

"Nice. So you can sing?"

I wave my hand a little. "Kinda sorta? I guess I can carry a tune."

"Ahh, so you're less interested in the onstage stuff, and more interested in the behind-the-scenes things."

"I wouldn't say either-or. I liked doing both. It was fun. Styling and designing clothes can be fun. But I'm more into makeup than anything else."

"Like regular everyday makeup or special effects makeup?"

"I've wanted to get into special effects makeup, but the materials are expensive." I look down at my homework. "I'm sorry, do you mind?"

"Are you really doing homework at a time like this?"

I sigh and lay down my pencil. "I need to maintain *some* semblance of normalcy. My grades don't have to suffer because we've decided to hunt down a cannibal serial killer. Besides, if they do, people are going to catch on."

"You want me to kinda…hang out, while you do your homework in silence?"

I sigh again. "I don't know what you want from me, Cyrus. But you can't leave this room, and I still have stuff to get done."

She comes and sits on the bed beside me, twiddling her thumbs, clearly bored out of her mind. But I'm bothered by her proximity. When I'm looking at her from the side, I can trace the individual lines of her strong profile—the long downward slope of her nose, the roundness of her cheerful cheeks. Cyrus has a striking quality to her beauty, but from how she acts and what she's told me about her life, she doesn't seem to understand that.

Or maybe I'm the only one who thinks that way?

Nervously, I tear out a sheet of notebook paper and pass it to her along with a pen, then slide my phone over to her.

"Try to see if you can comb through social media and start writing down the names of girls you want me to look into."

"Roger that."

She takes the supplies, along with one of the textbooks I'm not using, and scribbles down some names. I flip idly through the pages of my History textbook and begin to highlight the key dates and names. A few minutes pass, the two of us jotting things down in blissful silence, before Cyrus speaks again.

"Who is, uh, Brynne?"

"What?" My pencil falls from my hand and clatters against my notebook.

"When I was in the phone, it was weird, but I could like, see your files and stuff. And for however long it took you to walk back home—I mean, I was bored and had nothing to do."

"You looked through my files?"

I pick up my pencil once more and return to furiously copying down notes. The lines are so harsh and heavy that they almost break through the paper. *I have to get this done; I have to get this done. I don't have time for this.* Why is she so eager to know more about Brynne anyways? I think back to the way she smiled at me earlier today. Oh no. Is she gauging whether I'm single? Are we going to have this conversation right now?

"Sorry. And no, I didn't…look through your files, but I did go through your Photobooth. I was trying to see if somehow I could use the search bar, but all that came up was your feed. And I saw her picture and everything. That was your ex?"

"Yeah. We broke up last year."

"Makes sense. She wears a *lot* of purple."

"What's your deal with the color purple? You said that about my eye shadow when we first met, too."

"Ecuadorean mom. Purple is associated with death."

Well, breaking up with Brynne kinda did make me want to die, so maybe that superstition checks out. I'm about to open my mouth to crack a joke when I notice Cyrus looks a little…off.

"Why didn't you tell me you were queer?" she asks.

"I've only known you for like, two days. I figured it would come up eventually. I don't usually tell people I'm queer right out of the gate. Why does it matter?"

She laughs. "I kinda feel dumb because I gave you this big lecture on how people treated me for being butch."

"I don't think it was dumb. You're only telling me your experience, right?"

Her eyes seem so serious. Wow, she feels bad? Why?

"I can tell you I've never had a moment where I felt unwelcome in a women's restroom like you have. And up until last year, I never felt like someone would die of embarrassment if they knew I was in love with them."

"But…Brynne made you feel that way?"

"Brynne—I don't know." That's a lie. I do know.

Her exact words were that I was *too much* for her. Turns out being a traumatized, sad sack of shit is a real deal-breaker.

"We were together for almost two years. Then she moved on to the girl I was always worried about her hooking up with: Tamblyn." I scrunch up my face in disgust as I say her name.

"They made it Photobooth official today, but they've been together way longer than that."

"But you haven't taken down your photos of her?"

"You looked at my profile too?"

"Again, lots of time to kill."

"Why would I take down pictures? They're just pictures."

Memories of when I was a happier, healthier, prettier person. Who didn't have scars on her face. Who didn't feel like a turd personified. Who didn't live in fear of what had happened to her, and what was going to happen next. Those photos mean something to me even if they're painful to look at now. No matter how angry I am at Brynne and how horrible her behavior was post breakup, I'm not going to get rid of them. It's my right to have them. Besides, it's normal to want to keep photos of your ex, right? Maybe one day, when my heart doesn't feel like a shattered vase that's been glued back together, they'll only remind me of the good times. They'll make me laugh, not fill me with regret.

I'm looking forward to that day—hoping it comes sooner rather than later.

"Nothing, it's just"—she laughs—"you're a bigger person than me. When I broke up with my cheating ex? Oh, her shit got deleted. It was like we had never met. I even got my friends to delete group pics."

"You had a cheating ex?"

Cyrus nods. "Yeah. It was mostly virtual though—like, on SnapIt. She lived on the mainland, and I could only go and see her once a month, when my dad would give me my allowance and I could get on the ferry. I don't know how I was expecting that to work out. But then again, I was thirteen. Everything seemed so serious when I was thirteen." She averts her eyes, her expression melancholic. "Anyways, sorry to distract you. I was curious. It sucks to get dumped."

"I loved her."

Suddenly the silence between us is so thick and heavy, and I've no idea why those words left my mouth. I guess I feel like I have to say it out loud because if I don't, it's like it wasn't true. Like it never happened. Like it wasn't a feeling she shared with me. Like it was some one-sided situation I invested way too much time in. Because if it wasn't one-sided—if she loved me as much as I loved her—how could she leave me so easily when things got hard? Aren't you supposed to support your partner through hard times?

I mean, I don't think Dad had ever loved Mom harder than when she had heart surgery. That happened when I was thirteen. Even after being attacked by that wraith, I don't think anything has ever rocked me as hard as seeing that line of scar tissue, red and raw, running right down the center of her chest. I spent that summer waiting beside her bed trying not to cry, watching as so many tubes and machines tried to keep her alive.

When she was awake, she couldn't open her eyes because her entire body was so bruised from being torn apart and put back together, but even while sleeping, she found the strength to hold my hand. At thirteen, I didn't know I liked girls yet, but I knew I still needed my mom, and I had been so scared of losing her. At thirteen, I had struggled with body image issues for some time and had gotten used to seeing my body as a self-targeting emotional weapon, but when compounded with the fact that my mom's issues were genetic, I also came to see it as a physical one.

While I struggled during this time, Dad took it in stride. He held her hand every day, chauffeured her to every follow-up appointment with the biggest smile on his face, and learned new heart-healthy recipes to cook. He attended every single doctor's appointment she had, took notes, challenged them, questioned them. Did whatever he needed to improve her quality of care. Not to compare traumas or anything, but I think what Mom went through was way worse than me dealing with this bout of trauma-induced depression. Theoretically, it's easier to deal with, but

Brynne didn't want to *try* to invest the effort. Visited me only once during my two-week hospital stay, scarcely responded to my texts, and quickly came up with excuses to avoid coming over to my house.

Almost two damn years. Too much for her.

And maybe too much for Cyrus, because the shock hasn't faded. She sucks air through her teeth with a hiss and strokes her chin. "Damn. Was the breakup recent?"

"Well it's been six months, but she announced that she was dating the girl she told me not to worry about. And apparently, they're in love."

"Wow! *Wow*," Cyrus responds, completely offended. "You're handling this better than I would."

"I mean, she doesn't owe me anything. We've broken up."

"She's dating the girl you accused her of having a thing for. Bro, I would drag her."

"If our old friends cared, then I would. But when we broke up, they took her side."

"*Gross.*" She shudders violently in disgust, as if a mouse just ran across her toes. "Good thing you got away from them. And I thought Murkmore was full of scum."

She scribbles down something on her sheet of notebook paper. I keep taking notes for a few more minutes, but the tension between us remains.

"Do you remember if you had someone?" I ask.

"Huh?"

"That you were dating. Before you kicked the bucket."

For some reason, asking her this question hurts more than admitting I loved Brynne. Selfishly, I don't want the answer to be yes, because I don't want to worry about her hurrying off to someone else and forgetting about me when this is all over. My voice comes out hoarser than I intended it to. But Cyrus doesn't seem to notice this. She only chuckles and scratches the back of her head.

"Oh, no. I was way too focused on music. I was trying to practice for one of these open auditions for a music school in Empire City: Strengstorm. Had my audition and everything, man. Was supposed to be before Christmas."

"Strengstorm?"

That's one of the premiere art schools in the country. The best-of-the-best dancers, artists, filmmakers, musicians, and actors are recruited from all over the world. I was interested in it when I was still doing theater. (Before Brynne, obvi.) From what I've seen of Cyrus's work so far, I mean, I'm not surprised, but I *am* profoundly impressed she was able to secure an audition in her junior year.

She was a shoo-in.

Until someone decided to take that away from her.

This solemnness, heavy with the weight of knowing too much too young, overtakes my body in a swift wave. For a few moments, it renders me speechless, until finally, I nod, regain feeling in my jaw, and say, "They would've been lucky to have you."

I don't understand. How have they not found the ghosts yet? Why do we have to implement an island-wide curfew? Good tax dollars were spent hiring these people, and they haven't made any kind of progress.

—Name redacted for privacy purposes, *Murkmore Evening News* (5 Sept. 2024)

Chapter Eighteen

My alarm doesn't wake me up the next morning, but rather the knocking of someone's hand against my door. I'm halfway through a snore, completely disoriented. My face is planted on top of one of my textbooks, and my body is lying sideways across the bed. I can't believe it. I fell asleep while doing homework. That's a first. I push back the blanket covering my body—I don't remember wrapping myself in it before dozing off. Did Cyrus do this?

"Melody?" Mom knocks again.

I rub my bleary eyes, yawning and trying to get accustomed to the world around me, but then I remember Cyrus is supposed to be here. And yet, she's nowhere to be seen. *Oh shit.* My eyes scan the room. I check if the window's open, thinking maybe she climbed out and escaped in the night, but the blinds remain shut. Slowly, my gut sinking lower, I approach my bedroom door, unlock it, and come face-to-face with my mother.

She looks more tired than she did yesterday, gray circles underlining her eyes. Yet despite her obvious exhaustion, it seems she's been up for some time, because she's wearing the gray coveralls she often wears on missions. She smiles at me gently, then grimaces at my disheveled mess of a bed.

"Sweetie," she says in a tone of voice that's both surprised and concerned. "Did you fall asleep doing homework?"

"Y-yeah."

She frowns and places the back of her hand against my forehead to check for a fever. "You feeling okay? Simon told me you didn't come out for dinner last night, and I was going to get you to eat something, but your bedroom light was off."

"I'm fine. I didn't feel hungry."

I yawn again and check the time on my phone. It's not glitching, so Cyrus probably isn't inside. About fifteen minutes till my normal wake-up time. Huh. At least I didn't oversleep.

"Your father and I are going on another stakeout tonight. We've asked Simon to join us, so you'll be on your own. Call Simon if something happens, all right? He's staying in the car and keeping an eye on things while we work."

"I'm not going to call Simon," I snap, and my nastiness surprises me.

Mom's expression softens. "I know this change has been frustrating."

"To say the least."

"But he cares about you, and he's trying. He was worried when you didn't come out of your room last night. Said you were on the phone talking to someone."

"On the phone—" *Cyrus, idiot.* My tone eases. "O-oh, yeah. I was talking with Tomai."

"I'm glad you're making friends."

"Yeah."

"I'm not asking you to be Simon's best friend or anything, but please don't shut him down if he asks you to eat something."

"Why are you guys so obsessed with me building some kind of friendship with Simon? What, you're finally taking the word of the *Tomes* seriously?"

"Nothing of the sort. We're—well, we're a family. We always have been."

"Families aren't supposed to have strangers in them."

"Simon is less of a stranger to you than your own grandparents. And welcoming strangers into the fold—honey, that's how families work. Strangers find each other, and they bond, and they become one." She meshes her fingers together in a cat's cradle pose as if to demonstrate, but I'm only getting the ick. "Family is as much blood as it is what you make of it."

"You guys can be buddy-buddy with Simon if you want, but I don't have any memories I'd care to reminisce over."

Mom frowns. "Memories of…what?"

"I overheard Simon and Dad talking about the tacos. Dad was saying how they were exactly like he remembered them, or something."

"You heard that?"

"You *know* about that? That Dad had some secret life with Simon?"

"What?" I hear Dad from the kitchen, clearly caught mid eavesdrop.

My blood boils. First, they woke me up, then they lectured me about being nicer to Simon, and now they're eavesdropping? What the hell is going on with all the adults in my life? Why are they being so weird?

"Dad, if you want to join in on the conversation, you should come over here instead of hiding behind a corner."

Dad shuffles down the hallway with a steaming thermos in hand. He looks as tired as Mom does, brown eyes a little bloodshot, the five-o'clock shadow on his face obvious. He takes a tentative sip and looks between me and Mom, then into my room. He makes a stink face.

"Did you stay up all night doing homework?"

"I fell asleep, but never mind that. Why are you and Mom so weirdly obsessed with Simon?"

Some unknown expression crosses Dad's face. He seems almost…hurt? "What do you mean?"

"I mean first thing after I wake up I'm getting a lecture on being nicer to Simon. Not so much as a *hi, how are you, good morning,* any of that."

"Maybe because you're being standoffish, and also, refusing to eat meals?" Dad arches a brow and takes another sip from his thermos. "I don't like that you locked yourself in your room all night."

"If it was a problem, he should've knocked," I huff, crossing my arms. "I was busy, and then I fell asleep. It's not my fault I didn't eat. I was busy after school with the musical and everything."

"Musical?" Dad repeats, incredulous. "You're trying out for that?"

"Yes," I say. "I want to get back into theater."

Mom smiles politely, but her posture is rigid, like she's bracing for impact. "That's wonderful, honey."

"What about school?" Dad asks, confused, his tone slightly more hostile. His brow furrows. "Melody, you've got to work on applications for academies. I don't want you to get distracted by a musical. I remember how much time those took away from you."

Mom elbows Dad and casts a threatening, wide-eyed stare, but he's oblivious to it, of course.

"I know this move is an opportunity for you to reinvent yourself," he says, "but I don't want you to lose focus because your mom and I are busy."

"*We,*" Mom says through gritted teeth, "think it's great that you are *putting yourself out there again.*"

Mom's eager to throw me a pity party, Dad is eager to shut me down, and I'm eager to go back to bed and catch up on those last ten minutes of precious, blissful sleep. But my phone alarm goes off, breaking the tension. I switch it off quickly. *Still no glitching.* My heartbeat rumbles and sputters like a motorcycle engine. *Where is she?*

"Well, there goes that discussion," Mom says, directing a disappointed look at Dad. She places a hand on his shoulder. "Come on. She has to get ready for school."

"Okay," Dad says, then points at me sternly. "But we gotta have a talk about this later on."

I shrug my shoulders in response. Nothing pisses Dad off more than nonchalance. He rolls his eyes and follows my mother's hissing behest, back down the hallway, but not before shouting one final order over his shoulder.

"And *eat* something!"

I know I should, but I feel as grossly full as I did yesterday. If I tried to eat something I'm pretty sure I'd wind up painting the bathroom with my own vomit. With a huff, I shut my door and lock it, then gather and organize my homework to put in my backpack. Maybe if I'm lucky, I'll get some of this done in between classes, and I can finally catch up. But first, I have to find my ghost friend, who seems to have mysteriously vanished without a trace. I shove a notebook into the back pocket. *Maybe she took off in the dead of night to try to find her family.* Drop pens into my pencil pouch and zip it shut. *Maybe I'm on my own now.* Close up the books and cram them in as best I can. *Maybe I was wrong to help her in the way I did.* Crumpled between the wall and my bedspread is a sheet of paper, and I grab it, thinking it's a misplaced math page. But no. It's the sheet of paper I gave Cyrus last night to write down the names of the girls.

Girls Who Would Want Me Dead
Tif-

But then it's scratched out and erased, like she couldn't finish the name, or changed her mind. She had access to my phone for most of last night, and she was supposed to be using it to write down the names of potential suspects. Even with access to social media, she couldn't come up with anyone? Was she unable to jog her own memory, or did she get distracted by something else?

Or maybe she didn't do it because she was never planning on helping me to begin with. Maybe she's gone and I was right not to trust her.

As I'm making my bed, a soft hissing sound, like compressed air leaving an inflatable, fills my ears. I spin around in the direction of the sound, and from the corner of my open closet, I see the ghostly blue fumes trail up from behind a stack of boxes. In mere seconds—a profound improvement—Cyrus reappears.

"Where the hell were you?" I hiss.

"While you were catching up on beauty rest, I figured we shouldn't rely on your phone as a means of transporting me around." She crouches down and picks up her harmonica, which I'm only now realizing she dropped at the entrance of the closet. "Since, y'know, you need it. And I happened to find something useful…"

She reaches back into one of the boxes and withdraws an egg-shaped device. No way.

"A Tamawotchi?"

"The one and only," she says with a grin, tossing it up in the air and catching it. Show-off. "And it's got a key chain, so you can put it on your backpack. Super incognito."

"What if you become one of the little monsters? Do you know how hard it is to keep one of those things alive?"

She arches her brow suspiciously. "I never had any problems with mine."

"Oh, of course you didn't, Child Prodigy. Put it on my backpack," I tell her as I walk over to my dresser. "I gotta get ready for the day."

Thankfully, while I'm in the shower, my parents and Simon leave for the day. I wrap up my wet hair in a towel before walking back into the bedroom. Cyrus is sitting on my bed. She spots the towel, blushes, and averts her gaze.

"Sorry," I mutter under my breath. "I gotta get changed."

"No worries."

"Thanks. Oh, uh, can you check if my parents left me any coffee?"

"Will do." She smiles softly as she leaves.

I close the door behind her, but even with us separated by a door, my heart still shudders with the intensity of a woodpecker carving out a home in an elm tree. *Note to self: take your clothes to the bathroom with you next time.* I put on my outfit for the day— shortalls with a striped pink shirt and black-cat tights. It's so profoundly cute I'm euphoric when I look at myself in the mirror. I check the weather for the day and figure out there'll be showers later in the evening, possibly late afternoon, so I pack a yellow windbreaker in my backpack.

After blow-drying my hair, I head into the kitchen, where a steaming mug of coffee awaits. I grab some milk from the fridge and add a bit to it. She's currently rummaging through the cabinets. She turns back to look at me and appraises me, her eyes glancing up and down. It's such a subtle gesture, but for some reason, this makes me feel all tingly.

"What?" I ask her.

"Nothing. You look cute today."

I'm about to melt into a puddle of goo. I'm so embarrassed of myself. Am I truly that desperate for these itty-bitty phrases of affirmation? Why does her saying that make my knees tremble?

"Th-thank you. Um, what're you looking for?" I ask as I take a sip of coffee.

"I don't know. You got any cereal, or anything?"

"Why? You don't eat."

"It's not for me, it's for you," Cyrus says, rolling her eyes. "Duh."

"I don't—"

"Your parents are right. You should eat, while your mortal body still needs it. If you ever end up dead, trust me, you're going to miss wanting to eat. It does nothing for me like it did before."

"You can't taste?"

"Not really. Back at the theater I remember finding some popcorn and trying to heat that up, but it felt like…like wet paper in my mouth. It's horrible. I *loved* food. I grew up in a Greek-Ecuadorean family. We *always* had good food, no matter which one of my parents was cooking. Spanakopita, llapingachos, all kinds of stuff."

I'm still hesitant. My stomach grumbles but I place my hand over it to stifle the sound. "I mean, I'm kinda running late."

"You're going to run even later if you pass out because you don't eat something. Look, what about an apple? A banana?" She gestures to the fruit basket that Simon carefully stocked a few days ago. "You got options. Might as well take them."

Begrudgingly, I reach for a speckled-brown banana and peel back its layers. When I bite into it, it's soft and sweet. But not as sweet as that triumphant little grin on her face.

"Let Fantasticals move to the island? Honey, they've been on this island," Etheria Green says. *"This island used to be a fishing giant, an immigration hub, and a major cargo shipper. Bigoted rules couldn't stop people from making big money back in the day. Glad they're gone, though. It's about time."*

—Howard Bonevue, "Ghost Hunters Moving In Late Fall; Will Address Island's Ghost Problem," *The Sunshine Standard* (10 Aug. 2024)

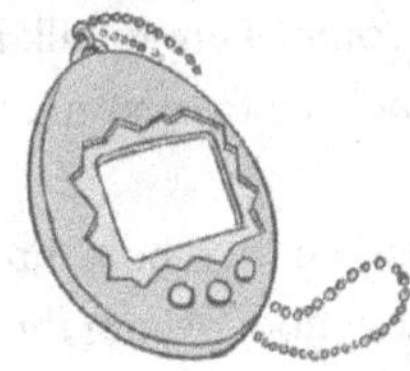

Chapter Nineteen

After breakfast, Cyrus plays another tune on her harmonica and shrinks inside the Tamawotchi. I'm about to step out the door when I remember that—in all likelihood—someone dangerous could potentially attack us. I think given the circumstances, even my parents would want me to have some form of protection, so I head back to the basement and grab my Phantom Prod Lite before we depart, shoving it into my backpack. While I don't feel great, I certainly feel safer. I bump into Tomai outside of the entrance of the school.

"Hey," they say. "You look like shit."

I rub my tired eyes. I didn't bother to put on makeup this morning. "It's been a time."

"And not a good one, apparently—not that I'd expect crawling around inside a sewer to have any kind of benefit."

A pang ruptures my chest and I mumble uncomfortably, "Didn't find anything."

Tomai narrows their eyes, and for several moments, they stare at me in tense silence. I flinch, and their eyes widen with realization. I want to shrink inside myself and disappear completely.

"You're lying," Tomai whispers, and I place a finger against my lips, but their voice grows louder. "Oh my God, I *knew* you were lying!"

"*Shhh!* Can we go somewhere to talk in private?"

Tomai's teeth clench in frustration. "To the storage room, madam."

They grab my wrist, and we bolt through the hallway to get to the other end of the school. Along the way we pass Jackie and her friends. We blow by them so fast I can't say hello, and she stares after us in confusion, big blue eyes unblinking. *Damn it, Tomai, you're going to blow my cover.* Once we're in the familiar storage room, Tomai closes the doors behind us. They fold their arms across their chest as they turn to face me, eyes wide with excitement.

"So," I say, taking a deep breath, "it's not a ghost."

"It's *not* a ghost?"

"No. I think it's…an actual person."

"Like a human person or a Fantastical person?"

Inhale, exhale. "Fantastical."

I launch into my explanation of the previous day's events—finding the blood splatters, the mysterious lone earring, the complete lack of ectoplasm. Predictably, Tomai's excitement dissipates, shifting from wonder to fear.

"I don't know if you have a dark sense of humor or something, but this isn't funny," Tomai responds. "And I can be pretty naive, but even I have to call bullshit on this one."

"I'm not joking."

Tomai squints their eyes, staring me down as if performing some sort of high-tech body scan. After a few moments of not finding any tells, their shoulders slump forward, their jaw slack.

"You're really not."

"Nope."

"There's a cannibal here?" Tomai drags their hands over their face, their eyes darting from side to side. "You're telling me the day I was walking home alone, I could've been *eaten* by someone?"

"Afraid so."

"W-wait! What about the singing I heard from the theater?"

I bite my lip. "They were probably near the theater. But there was nothing in there."

Tomai snaps their fingers and points at me. "Liar."

"W-what? I'm not lying."

"You bit your lip."

"That doesn't mean I'm lying."

Now they're furious, their cheeks darkening, nostrils flaring. "Melody, what the hell? Do you know how serious this is? If there's someone going around eating people, do you know how many of us could be targeted? Especially me!"

"Why you?"

Tomai grinds their jaw and lifts their fingers. From small, near-invisible pores, gentle strings emerge, white and gossamer like silk—*spider silk*. Ohh. Tomai is an arachne: a spider person. The strings, wet and soft, dangle limply from their fingers. With their other hand, Tomai wipes them off, grimacing at the sticky texture.

"And it's not just me."

I'm flabbergasted. The Fantastical-free zone rules on Murkmore weren't lifted until recently, so this means some families have been living here in secret all this time. "Wh-who else is there?"

"Some werewolves and vampires—all Fantastical races with histories of 'cannibalism.' If the cops know a ghost didn't do this, who do you think they're going to blame next? Do you think the cops in this town will be kind? They hate Fantasticals. What do you think is going to happen to us if we're discovered? It's going to be a witch hunt like no other—no, not a witch hunt, a bloodbath." Tomai narrows their eyes, their voice dropping to a grave tone. "So you had best tell me everything."

My heart skitters in my chest as I glance down at the Tamawotchi dangling from my backpack. *Cyrus.* I don't want to give away her cover, but I don't want to forsake Tomai any more than I already have. They've helped me out a lot, and I don't want them to feel like this is a one-sided friendship, especially when their own safety is on the line.

I unclip the Tamawotchi from my backpack. As my finger cleans away the smudges on the screen, the sprite of a young girl appears, living within the monochromatic, pixelated world. The device burns my palm, and I can't tell if Cyrus is giving me permission to tell Tomai or not.

"I'm sorry," I whisper. "But we can trust them."

Tomai glares at me like I'm insane, and honestly, I don't blame them for it. With a deep breath, I hug the toy against my chest, pressing it as close to my heart as possible.

"When I went to the theater, there *was* a ghost. But she's not a wraith. And she's not like any ghost I've ever met. You probably know her. Her name is Cyrus."

Tomai's eyes widen for a moment, then they shake their head, their pupils frozen. I can't tell whether they're surprised or angry—or maybe it's disgust, because they recoil as if I slapped them across the face. Tomai scoffs, stutters, closes their mouth again, and holds up a finger. They take a few steps back from me, and their voice lowers to a venomous hiss.

"I don't know who the hell told you about Cyrus, but that *also* isn't funny."

I can't help but smile. Someone *knew* her. Someone saw her when she was flesh and bone and blood and had her whole life ahead of her. "You know Cyrus?"

"Who the—do I know Cyrus? Yeah, I know Cyrus. *Knew* her. She was my best friend," Tomai says, shaking. "And I know damn well she's not a ghost, because if she was, there's no way she wouldn't have come home by now."

My heart plummets to my stomach. I didn't think about that—about how Cyrus, in her amnesiac state, left behind more than her parents. She left behind an entire community of people who loved her their entire lives.

"So…" I struggle to recall what Cyrus told me. "You were with her at the homecoming dance that night?"

"Yes."

"Then what happened? How did you get separated?"

"Because I was *molting*! You know, skin-shedding?" Tomai's breath catches in their chest, and their eyes well with tears. "I-I had to go to the bathroom to hide it, and she saw me and left the bathroom before I finished cleaning up. When I came out, the other people in orchestra said she wasn't feeling well and had gone home."

Why would Cyrus have left the bathroom? "Did she know you were an arachne before?"

"I don't—look, th-this isn't funny, Melody. This is fucked up. How could you possibly know about her? What, was she in your parents' files or something?"

"No, she wasn't." And now I'm beginning to wonder *why* she wasn't. "Give me a second. I can explain."

I unclip the Tamawotchi from my backpack and set it on the ground. But nothing happens. Tomai stares at me, their expression transforming from anguish to fury, their eyes growing redder and smaller and wetter as the moments pass by. My heart pounds in my chest. *Cyrus, get out of there.* But the device remains still. I have no idea why she isn't coming out. Is she too nervous to reveal herself to Tomai? Or are her powers acting up again?

Tomai tosses their head in aggravation. "Are you done with whatever the hell this weird performance is?'

"No—wait a minute." *The harmonica.* I unzip my backpack and retrieve it from beside my pencil pouch. I have no idea if my playing this thing is going to coax her spirit from the toy she's inhabiting, but it's my last chance. If Tomai walks out of this room thinking I've made all this shit up, there's no telling what they'll do next.

"Who…"

Their face lightens to a pale almond hue, their eyes stunned. They recognize this instrument. Their mouth falls open softly, a fish flopping on dry land, and they say nothing as I fumble with the instrument and try to position it against my lips. Thin traces of blue ectoplasm fill the holes, and with a grimace I wipe them away before placing it against my mouth once more. This is more awkward than I thought it would be. Like, how hard do I have to press this against my mouth to make a sound? I blow into one of the holes, and a single discordant note blurts out. Tomai winces, their grief-stricken trance breaking for a moment so they can put their hands over their ears. My stomach somersaults as I try to blow another note, and then another, each more awkward than the last. A tingling sensation fills my mouth and I have to smack my lips together to get it to go away. Damn it. Cyrus makes this look so effortless. Who would have thought it took actual talent to be a musician?

The Tamawotchi emits a succession of high-pitched, distorted beeps. Blue ethereal vapor seeps from the toy's crevices. Tomai's mouth drops open, and I keep playing, my lips feebly huffing and puffing into the ten holes as fast as I can manage. When Cyrus rematerializes, she appraises me with a smug expression and a heavy sigh.

"I came out of hiding to rescue you from your own embarrassment. Fork it over, girl."

With trembling hands, I pass it to her, and she pockets it once more. Tomai lets out an incomprehensible squawk, like their words and breath have collectively failed them, and Cyrus turns to face them. Tomai's hands fling toward their face but their eyes remain wide open—trembling, wet, taking in all of her. Cyrus's form seems to vibrate in place, the edges of her body rippling like a VHS tape in reverse. Several moments pass between all of us, suspended in silence and grief, before Cyrus speaks again, a soft grin on her face.

"So how much does the orchestra suck without me?"

At only fourteen years old, freshman Cyrus Paredes-Pantazis was selected for the East Province Band, an honor bestowed only on the most talented, hardworking of music students. Paredes-Pantazis is the first person on Murkmore to ever be selected for a seat, and only the third fourteen-year-old in the Province Band's fifty-four-year history. But for Paredes-Pantazis, this is only the beginning. "Tell Strengstorm to hit me up," she says with a laugh.

—Howard Bonevue, "Freshman Selected for East Province Band: The First Ever to Represent Murkmore," *The Sunshine Standard* (8 Oct. 2020)

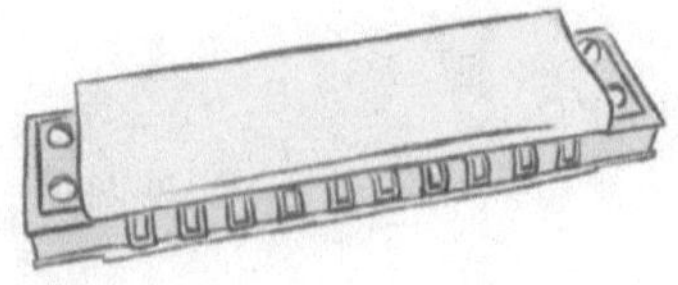

Chapter Twenty

There are no words. How could there be, when your dead best friend is standing right before you in all her glory? A strangled sound halfway between a sob and a shriek of surprise escapes Tomai's lips. Wobbly knees struggle to remain upright. Cyrus nods slowly, reaching out her hand. Trembling, Tomai reaches to touch it—flinches—and then gently rubs the surface, as if to acknowledge yes, yes, she's real. This is not a dream. But still they don't embrace. The tension is thicker than a brick wall, and I want nothing more than to sledgehammer it down, but it's not my place. They need to have their moment.

Eventually, Tomai finds the courage to speak. "Y-you… How long have you…"

"About a year. I was in the theater."

Tomai laughs breathlessly. "Oh my God. And I walked right past it."

"It's okay—"

"Don't tell me it's okay!" Sobs escape their body in rolling waves. "I went to the dance with you on Friday and buried you on Monday. I carried your casket to the cemetery from the church. I held your mom's hand when she cried at the kitchen table—I...!"

Their breath gives out in convulsive shudders and they stagger backward, hands on their hips. They pace across the floor, inconsolable, tears continuing to drip down their face. All their grief resurfaces in this moment, and I want to take the pain away, but I don't want their words to hurt Cyrus, either.

"Tomai, please don't be angry," I beg. "Cyrus lost all track of time when she was hiding out in the theater. She thought only several hours had passed. And she didn't know she was a ghost, either. She's had a lot of memory loss issues in general."

"Didn't know she was a ghost," Tomai sputters. "If that isn't the most on-brand fucking thing for you. You're glowing, dude! And blue! How did you not notice?!"

Cyrus cracks a smile. "I know."

"D-don't *smile* at me, you jackass!" Snot bubbles out of their nostrils, and the tears are falling so hard and fast that they can't keep their eyes open. "You think this is funny? This isn't funny, this—"

Cyrus's arms close around Tomai in a tight embrace, and shaking, the two of them collapse to their knees. Tomai sobs and buries their face against her shoulder, and Cyrus rocks them back and forth in her arms.

"I'm sorry," Tomai whispers between tears. "I'm sorry I didn't tell you I was an arachne. I'm sorry I didn't look harder for you that night—"

"Whoa, whoa, what?" Cyrus holds Tomai at arm's length, her brow furrowed.

Tomai glances at me. "You weren't kidding when you said she was dealing with memory loss."

Cyrus laughs. "I think…" Her face twists in a frustrated expression. One eye squeezes shut. "I think I remember what happened."

My heart leaps with joy. "You do?"

"Don't get too excited." Cyrus rubs her temples. "You and I… We went to the dance together, right Tomai?"

"Yes, yes."

"And you… You rushed off into the bathroom, right? And I followed to make sure you were okay."

"Right." Tomai wipes their eyes. "Y-you came in, and you saw the skin on my neck…peeling off—that I was molting. Then you left."

Cyrus tilts her head. "I don't remember being angry."

"I don't know if you were or not. You disappeared. And all this time I"—Tomai warbles—"I thought it was because I lied to you about who I was."

"I… I'm so sorry I left you. I'm sure I didn't—I mean, I don't think I was upset about that, but I don't remember." She squeezes her necklace in one fist. "You should know I don't want you to hide yourself from me. Gender rebels for life and all of that."

"Gender fucking rebels for life!" Tomai laughs, hugging her again. They look at me. "We're aware it's cringe. It's a self-aware joke, just to be clear."

"I figured."

As Cyrus rocks Tomai back and forth in her arms, her head turns, and her brown eyes meet mine.

Thank you, she mouths.

At that moment, the morning bell rings, leaving us with less than five minutes to get to our first class. We exchange sheepish looks with one another. It feels ridiculous to go to class and pretend like everything is fine when these two just reunited after a year apart.

Tomai doesn't want Cyrus to go. Their entire body is stiff, like they're in rigor mortis. An anguish I'm lucky enough to have never experienced surfaces in their soft-brown eyes. Must feel like a knife to the gut, to meet your dead friend again and be separated from her once more.

Cyrus recognizes this, because she offers a simple, reassuring smile. She reaches out and pats Tomai's shoulder. "I'm not going to disappear on you again—not like I did that night."

Tears well up in Tomai's eyes. They throw their arms around Cyrus, sobbing and laughing. Cyrus wraps their arms around them once more.

Maybe it'll be okay if we're late to class this once.

After Tomai calms down, Cyrus returns to the Tamawotchi and we shuffle down the hallway in the direction of our class. The halls, for now, are completely silent save for the muffled sounds of kids talking over the top of the morning announcements in their classrooms. Tomai smiles and sniffles as they wipe the tears from their face. I want to make a joke or say something to help them feel better, but guilt keeps my lips sealed shut. I'm ashamed of lying to Tomai, even if I did it for good reason. Had I known how they felt about Cyrus, maybe I would've been able to tell them sooner.

I guess an apology is worth a try, however pathetic it may be. "I'm sorry I couldn't be honest with you. I needed to keep her a secret as best I could."

"I get it," Tomai says, and I'm not sure they do, but I appreciate that they're trying to make peace with it. "If anyone knew you'd found a ghost…"

"Right."

"And she's…not…responsible? Right?"

"No," I say, surprised by the certainty in my voice. "Like I said, she didn't leave the theater the entire time. It was locked, and she doesn't know how to phase through walls."

"Phase through walls?"

"Usually, ghosts can pass through solid objects. But not her, for some reason. At least, I'm not sure. She still can't remember how she ended up in the theater."

Tomai considers this. "Maybe she did and forgot how."

"What would make you think that?"

"Her violin disappeared from her room after the funeral. Her mother wondered where it had gone, but we never found it. And she didn't bring it with us to homecoming, because, duh, why would she have done that?"

I always wondered why Cyrus had her violin and harmonica with her. I've imagined Cyrus, waking up in her ghostlike state, dazed and confused—panicked. Maybe traumatic memory loss made her forget everything that happened. After my attack, my memory was fuzzy as well. Took a lot of therapy sessions to try to retrain my brain and fill some of those gaps.

Tomai shakes their head. "To think of her…all alone in that theater. She was probably afraid."

"I don't think she was. She seemed super chill when I first met her. In fact, I think she was more afraid of me."

Tomai shrugs. "You don't know her like I do."

Wow, that stings. But I'm going to let it slide. They're right. I don't. But I want to. And if I want any hope of getting to know her better, we need to figure this out, and fast.

"Tomai," I ask, "do you know what happened to Cyrus? What her official cause of death was?"

"I do." Tomai breathes a shaky sigh, and in their eyes, grief resurfaces. Reliving the worst moment of their life. "They said the official cause of death was—"

Fear tickles the back of my neck when I hear the curt, high-pitched shriek of a whistle. I find Ms. Ruder standing before me, whistle perched on the edge of her lips, a yardstick in her grasp. She smacks it firmly against the palm of her hand before allowing the whistle to drop from her mouth.

"Gentlepeople." Her words are courteous although her tone is anything but. "Pray tell, why are you not in class this morning?"

"Sorry, Ms. Ruder," Tomai says, wiping their eyes. "I've been having kind of a rough morning, and—and we were talking."

To my surprise, Ruder's expression softens. "Is that so?"

"Yes, ma'am."

"Well…" She scratches the back of her head with the yardstick, her face scrunched up in mild annoyance. "Don't let it happen again, I suppose. Get to class, Tomai."

Tomai resumes walking down the hallway, and I trail after them, but Ruder shakes her head. Points at me with her yardstick.

"Just Tomai. Not you. Don't look at them—*you*, Ms. Myere. You're coming with me."

"I have to get to class," I insist.

"*Ehhh*." She mimics an obnoxious buzzer sound and shakes her head.

Without another word, she motions for me to follow her. I cast an apologetic glance in Tomai's direction before shuffling off to what I can only presume is my doom. I can't seem to catch a break with this lady. Anger bubbles inside my body like a festering wound, but I manage to keep it together until we pass the office. Wait. We *passed* the office. It takes me a second to register we're heading in the direction of her classroom. Why? I thought she was taking me to detention or to Redd's office or something.

Ruder flicks on the classroom light, which buzzes overhead. I guess she doesn't have a homeroom class. She gestures for me to pull up a chair, and I sit down across from her desk. For a few moments, she ignores me, messing around with her email and double-checking a few things on her computer before finally turning her attention back.

"You've certainly made quite a mess of things, young lady." She spreads her hands, as if waiting for me to say something.

But I'm as confused as I usually am. "We were only talking."

"I know that's not what you were doing."

Ruder sighs. She seems more tired than angry. She takes a sip of stale coffee (I mean, it has to be, there's no steam coming off it) from a mug labeled *WORLD'S BEST ENGLISH TEACHER*—an obvious ploy to get a better grade in her class.

"And all I'm trying to tell you, as I've tried to tell you from the beginning, is that you shouldn't discuss these sorts of things on school grounds."

"We weren't talking about the ghosts," I say carefully, the gears in my head turning faster. How much does Ruder know about me and what I've been doing? *What* does she know? "We…were talking about Cyrus."

"Cyrus?" she says, and for a moment her expression brightens, before disintegrating into grief. "Oh. That's right. They were best friends, weren't they?"

"Yeah."

"Cyrus…" she repeats, trailing off. She shakes her head as if to snap herself out of it. "If that's all that this was about…then I'm sorry to have misunderstood."

"Why can't I talk about the ghosts?" I cross my legs and clasp my hands around my knees, trying to remain poised even as my body wants to quake with fear.

She *knows* something.

Ruder arches a brow but says nothing. I shrug my shoulders and blather on.

"If Tomai is my friend, why can't we talk about it together? It's not like I'm broadcasting details of the investigation on the morning announcements. It's a private conversation."

"Surely you know how fast gossip can spread?" Ruder says with a smarmy smirk, but her eyes hold a grave seriousness, piercing through me and affixing me to my seat like a stake through a heart. "Especially in high school in a small town."

I shrug my shoulders, trying to play it cool. "Gossip is gossip."

"Words can be wielded as weapons, and if certain people heard certain pieces of information, they might be able to use them as such. It would be wise of you to learn that sooner, not later."

At those words, every synapse in my brain ignites, driven by a single emotion: panic. Deep, deadly panic. She doesn't only know that I've skipped school. She knows beyond a shadow of a doubt that I'm continuing my investigation.

She's trying to let me know that people are watching me. Does that mean they already know about Cyrus?

"Rumor has it," Ruder says quietly, "they found sheet music lying on the stage in the Lennox Theater."

She...

She knows.

"Y-you," I whisper, unable to keep my strength any longer. The air leaves my body so quickly I immediately feel as though I'm drowning. "You know?"

She nods. "I know nothing."

I twist around in my seat and look toward the door. Wide open, but no one standing there. Are there cameras in here? Are we being spied on? What is she so afraid of?

"Anyway," she says, her voice suddenly louder, "that project you were working on with Tomai, you know the one?" She stares at me knowingly, and I nod, trying to keep up. "I'll need to see your work by Friday, before the pep rally." She puts extra emphasis on the last two words.

The project...the pep rally. The project she's referring to is the investigation into the boys' deaths. And the pep rally...

Whoever is making Ms. Ruder act all scared and suspicious must be planning something for the pep rally.

That's our last chance to get this right.

Her mouth sets in a hard, firm line. "Understand?"

"Yes, ma'am."

"Good," she says, leaning back in her chair with a heavy sigh.

"So…could Tomai and I leave early today to work on the project?"

Ruder rolls her eyes. She moves over to a file cabinet beside her desk and withdraws a pink slip, which she fills out swiftly. She hands me the hall pass.

"I'm not going to dismiss you outright," she says. "But you can certainly go to the library—and I won't ask questions about where you go after that."

Even though he's lived in places like Jewel West and Empire City, Redd can't imagine his future in any other place. "I can't think of anywhere else I'd want to spend the rest of my life. Sure it's small, but Murkmore is a lovely community. Always has been," he says.

—Howard Bonevue, "'Good to Be Back.' An Exclusive Interview with Jamal Redd, TV Star and Murkmore Native," *The Sunshine Standard* (30 Jun. 2005)

Chapter Twenty-One

When the bell rings, Tomai and I head to the library with the pass, and after fifteen minutes, we skedaddle. We leave through the same exit I did on the day I snuck out to the Lennox the first time, and book it across campus until we're free. Even then, we don't stop running. We're huffing and puffing the whole way down the sidewalk on the way to my place, and thankfully, the driveway is empty. Who would've thought Ms. Ruder would cut us a break?

Maybe that mug has some truth to it, although I'm not willing to accept that as fact yet.

After we kick off our shoes, I lead Tomai into my bedroom. I draw the blinds shut, then triple-check the locks on every door and window in the house, closing some of the curtains. The house feels bleak and depressing without natural light, but it's a small price to pay for privacy from, um, bloodthirsty stalkers. Besides, with those storm clouds rolling in from the distance, it's not going to be nice outside for much longer.

"Melody!" Cyrus calls out.

I sprint back into the room to find Tomai and Cyrus sitting on the bed. Tomai is scrolling through something on their phone. I wave my hands at them.

"I was trying to make sure no one could look in and see us."

"You really think someone could be spying on us right now?" Tomai asks.

"Ms. Ruder more or less implied someone's been spying on us this whole time." I sit pretzel-style on the floor. "I'm taking all the precautions."

"Okay, so…where do we start?"

That's a good question. Where *do* we start? I think of everything that we know. Cyrus died around homecoming last year. Five people were killed, two of which were adults, and for some reason those two bodies were found in the sewers. Suspicious reports of music on the nights of some of the deaths.

"Tomai…the music you heard from the theater the night—Wendell, right?"

"Yes," Tomai says, somber. "The night Wendell died."

"Right. Well, Cyrus has been hiding out at the theater since she died, but she wasn't the one singing. Do you sing?"

Cyrus shakes her head. "I can carry a tune, but my voice is gross."

"I can attest to the truth of this statement," Tomai says. "She hits all the right notes but sounds like a gargoyle while doing it—all gravelly and smoky in the worst ways possible. It's kinda sad. Cursed to be the greatest musician with every instrument except her own voice."

I bite my lip, glancing between Cyrus and Tomai. "Tomai…you said earlier, before we were stopped by Ms. Ruder, that you knew her official cause of death."

"I did." Tomai wets their lips. "Drowning."

At this, I hold my breath, half expecting Cyrus's memory to explode with recognition, to remember all the details of what happened.

But instead, she scrunches up her nose in disbelief and spreads her hands. "*Drowning?* Like I went for a swim, and drowned?"

"That's what they said," Tomai says. "The police and the coroner's report—"

"But I don't know how to swim. I spent my entire life refusing to learn, because *sharks*, and now you're telling me that night was the one time I decided to try?"

"I don't *know*," Tomai says. "That's what I've been trying to figure out. I don't know what would've possessed you to go anywhere *near* water."

Drowning. Cyrus died by drowning. But she didn't know how to swim, so she wouldn't have had any reason to go near water.

I take another deep breath and pinch the bridge of my nose. "I think Cyrus's death and the cannibal are interconnected."

"Interconnected?" Tomai repeats.

"Do you think this is a coincidence? Cyrus the musical prodigy dies, people start hearing music, people get murdered, and somehow, the entire town becomes convinced they're infested with wraiths, despite having never seen one, and no other ghostly activity to report. Ghosts may not reveal themselves to humans often, but this is a stretch."

"Well, duh, Melody. But that means someone tried to *make* Cyrus a ghost. Or they were willing to risk killing Cyrus to try to see if she became a ghost. Which is—I mean, holy shit. Holy shit. Can someone make a ghost?"

I bite my lip. I don't know the answer to that. Most ghosts happen randomly. Like, not everyone in the world is going to become a ghost when they pass. I've never heard of someone making a ghost, but I think it's dependent on the circumstances of the individual's death. There's only one person who would know the answer to that question, and it's Simon—Simon, who I've been treating like trash, and who is also out helping my parents on their mission tonight.

"Never mind that," Cyrus interjects breathlessly. She taps her finger against her breastbone as she speaks. "We have to focus on the earring. I think that's a good starting point. Melody, did you…?"

"Right here."

I dig into my backpack and withdraw the little earring from the plastic bag I found last night. I pass it to Tomai, who holds it close to their face. They wrinkle their nose in frustration and peer back at Cyrus and me, profoundly disappointed.

"I don't think this is much of a lead, guys."

"It's not," Cyrus admits. "But it's what we've got. Who do you think would wear something this tacky?"

"Could be anyone," Tomai says. "That's the problem. And tacky? I kinda like this. It's cute."

"Sparkly," I add.

Cyrus rolls her eyes. "Okay, okay. *Ooh, shiny*. I get it."

"Wow, lot of heat behind that statement. Not a big fan of jewelry?" I ask, grinning.

Tomai rolls their eyes. "I keep telling Cyrus she's not a real lesbian because she doesn't wear a thumb ring."

"We've been over this. Rings get in the way of playing instruments."

"Not for everyone."

"But for *me,* they would, and I'd have to take them off every time. Forgive me for not giving into a stereotype and letting the entire community down."

"Wait a minute," Tomai says. "Melody said *shiny. Shiny.* Do we think this is a real diamond in the center or cubic zirconia?"

"This is clearly party jewelry," Cyrus says.

"No." Tomai shakes their head. "We can't tell from looking at it if it's cubic zirconia or not. If this is a real diamond—and it's a honking big one—then it probably belongs to a rich girl, which is going to narrow down our search exponentially, because everyone here is poor as dirt."

"Bet," Cyrus says. "We take it to a jeweler, and if it's a diamond, that'll help us figure out who our suspects are."

"No," I cut in. "We can't do that."

"Why not?"

"Because what if someone—the killer, or my parents—sees us at a jeweler trying to get a suspicious earring evaluated? We have to figure this out on our own."

"Then the internet is the next best resource we have," Tomai says as they withdraw their phone from their pocket.

Cyrus's eyes widen. "Wait, Tom. What if we did a reverse image search on that?"

"A reverse—because a picture we take ourselves is not going to show up with results on a reverse image search?"

"That's not true. Remember that time we went to AniEast, on the mainland? And you saw someone wearing that *Titanic Tiger Force* shirt and you were trying to figure out where we could get it from?"

"Oh!" Tomai cries out, the memory coming back to them. "Yeah, we *did* use a reverse image search for that. But that was with an app…" Tomai trails off, their fingers flying across their phone screen, presumably trying to download the app again. "That was a wicked cool shirt."

"It was." Cyrus smiles at me. "You know *Titanic Tiger Force?*"

"No? Is that a cartoon?"

"A cartoon—listen to her. A cartoon."

"It's an anime," Tomai interjects. "So yes, technically a cartoon."

"It's a masterpiece," Cyrus says.

"Cartoons can be masterpieces."

"We can watch all you want of it later, once we finally come up with a suspect list. Tomai, are you ready to take a photo of this thing?" I hold up the earring.

Tomai nods, raises their phone, and carefully snaps a pic. After more button-pressing and a few moments of silence, Tomai finally urges us to look over their shoulder. A series of photos pop up on-screen, including some that are bizarrely inaccurate—namely, a feather earring, a sequined sweater, and most interestingly, a vintage teddy bear from 1978. Of the closer matches, a few look like knockoffs based on their size and the placement of the diamond, but after a several minutes of careful analysis, we finally find it.

A carbon copy of our earring, crisper and cleaner, seated in the bed of a pink-velvet-covered jewelry box: a half carat, worth more than all the shoes in my closet combined.

Tomai clutches their chest when they see the price listed at the bottom of the screen. "Sweet Lord. *Big* money."

"For something as tacky as this, yes," Cyrus says. "At least we've figured it out. It's probably one of the rich girls. So, that means…"

"Who are the wealthy people in town?" I ask.

Tomai and Cyrus take a minute to consider this.

"Jackie's family," Tomai says. "For sure."

"Jackie?" My eyes nearly pop out of my head. "But her mom is the principal."

"Principals make hella bank," Tomai replies. "And on top of that, her dad is a TV judge."

"He *played* a TV judge," Cyrus says, rolling her eyes. "You know the show *Law Inc?*"

I nod. It was one of my mom's favorites back in the day, although I don't remember too much about it. It was something she'd leave on in the background when she was working on shipping souls through the Ingress.

"Brinkley would be on the list, too," Tomai says.

Cyrus sighs. "You know, Brinkley would probably be my top choice."

"Huh? Why Brinkley?"

Tomai grins. "Because Cyrus hit on her at a cast party one time—"

"For the thousandth time, I didn't know she had a boyfriend—"

"Chairs were thrown, fists went flying; it was absolute chaos," Tomai says. "Brinkley has hated her ever since."

"I swear everyone at that party was grounded by their parents for two months."

"Sophomore year," Tomai adds cheerily. "One helluva time."

"How do we know their parents weren't involved or something?"

Cyrus snorts. "Melody, what grown-ass woman would wear this?"

"I don't know… She might have a point," Tomai says.

Cyrus shakes her head. "But the guys that were killed were mostly students. Three people, right? Marcus, Wendell, and Tyreese. And then two marine biologists that ended up in the sewers somehow. Did we figure out why the marine biologists were here? They were from the mainland, right?"

I nod. "Yep. They were from the mainland. And they came after Marcus and Wendell had been picked off."

"For some reason, those two felt motivated to come here…" Cyrus trails off, pinching the bridge of her nose. "It doesn't make any sense."

"Let's focus on the students," I suggest. "Wendell, Tyreese, and Marcus. Who would want them dead between Brinkley and Jackie? *Assuming* it's Brinkley and Jackie, and not other members of their family. Did either of them date any of those boys? Is this like a revenge story?"

Tomai shakes their head. "I don't…" Their eyes widen. "Wait. Jackie dated Marcus."

"She *did?*" Cyrus cries.

"It was last year, remember?" Tomai stops. "Oh. Oh no. You don't remember. Because it was after…"

"After I died?"

"Yeah…" Tomai mumbles. "They were together at the start of last year, and then in the winter, they broke up because he hooked up with Sylvia Chadwick at a party. She was so devastated she didn't come to school for an entire week."

"But did she date Wendell? Or Tyreese?"

"No. I don't know what her deal would be with those two." They scratch their chin again. "Wendell was the captain of the coed tennis team. Tyreese was the student body president before…" They trail off. "Oh. Oh shit, guys."

"Oh shit, what?" I ask.

"Jackie. It's gotta be Jackie. She killed Marcus to get revenge for humiliating her, then she killed Wendell to become tennis team captain, and then she killed Tyreese to get his position as the student body president." Their eyes are fearful, but they laugh. "Oh my God, did we solve a fucking murder mystery?"

"We don't know if Brinkley had motivation to kill the others, do we?" I ask.

"No. Because she didn't," Tomai says.

I shake my head. "I think we should explore all of the possibilities first."

I don't want to wreck their joy, but there's something about this that seems a little too easy. Sweet, nice Jackie was the one who killed those boys and two grown men? The past couple of days have taught me that stranger things have happened, but at the same time, it's weird to think a girl our age would be living a double life as a serial killer.

"Unconvinced?" Cyrus asks, and when I nod, she says, "Maybe our next step is to figure out who the earring belongs to?"

"Already on it." Tomai holds up their phone to me, revealing an Photobooth timeline. "I'll sleuth on Brinkley if you do Jackie."

"What are you doing?" Cyrus asks.

"To figure out who owns that earring, we have to figure out if either of them were wearing it the day of the murder."

"Oh my God, that's genius," Cyrus says, clapping her hands together. "Melody, when did the one guy in the sewer die again? The one you and I went to investigate?"

"Parker Kim? Um…" I try to pull up his record on my phone and find the date. "March 12."

"March 12, March 12, March 12…" Tomai trails off, laser-focusing on scrolling through the timeline.

I sit down beside them and open the app on my phone, only to be assaulted by another photo of Brynne and Tamblyn. *Ugh.* Not cheek kisses. Not cliché cheek kisses. The kind of photo I would have begged her to take when we were first going out, and she would've told me it was too corny to post.

Well, Brynne, guess what? You look corny as hell.

Cyrus squints at my phone. "You should block her."

"Block who?" Tomai asks.

"No one," I reply, hastily typing Jackie's name into the search bar. Somehow when Cyrus squeezes my shoulder, I feel a little better. "Let's get to work."

And we do. We scroll through Photobooth for hours, zooming in on photos, deleting any accidental likes, and swallowing any resentment we have for their lavish lifestyles. Brinkley, the daughter of a prominent lawyer, got a pink Lexus for her sixteenth birthday. It was used, sure, but it was still a nice, *very* expensive car. Jackie's family throws parties every season, which the whole town is invited to. Pictures and pictures of kids in swimsuits, jumping over a rock wall into the turquoise pool below. People perusing a catered BBQ lunch, complete with all the fixings. Dancing and running around in the massive multiacre front yard with glowsticks while a trained professional shoots off fireworks. The kind of event that has its own hashtag.

"Someone loves showing off," I mutter.

Tomai asks, "Who? Jackie? I mean, yeah, but her parties are the bomb."

"Can confirm," Cyrus says. "Would be sad if she was the one who killed me though."

That's another part of this mystery we're nowhere close to solving. Cyrus died by drowning, but she wouldn't have gone anywhere near water. Did she actually drown, or did someone murder her and then tamper with the coroner's report? And if Jackie killed her, was it so she could set all of this up?

Tomai nods. "Yeah. A real bummer."

"I kinda want it to be Brinkley."

Tomai sputters into hysterical laughter, but I stare at Cyrus reproachfully. "That is *not* funny."

"It's a little funny." Cyrus winks and elbows me, and I resist the urge to smile at her.

All jokes aside, after a few hours of searching, we have nothing. There are other diamond earrings, but none in the shape of a bow. We go back further, thinking maybe they might have worn them to the winter formal, but nothing pops up there either. Tomai's the first to give up. They drop their phone on their lap and bury their face in their hands, muttering quietly to themselves.

"You've got to be kidding me. *Something* has to be here." I furiously scroll back through Jackie's pictures, trying to find something, *anything* that could connect her to this hellish nightmare. But no. Nothing but that stupid, shimmery smile and perfect glowing skin and all the things I will never have. With a frustrated growl, I throw my phone on my bed.

Cyrus pats my knee reassuringly. "We didn't think it was going to be that easy, did we?"

"Kinda, yeah. If the killer is someone our age, I mean, they can't be a criminal mastermind. I barely made it through Algebra II last year, and you're telling me one of them is smart enough to be a serial killer? As if."

"What if they have people working with them?" Tomai suggests. "What if we're wrong in assuming there's one killer? Or in assuming they wore the earring? What if they lent the earring to a friend? To create a red herring or something."

"A red herring?" Cyrus crinkles her nose.

"In mystery novels, red herrings are like—like distracting bits of clues that make it *seem* like something happened one way, when it could've been another way. Just because Colonel Mustard was the last one seen holding a candlestick doesn't mean he used that candlestick to kill Mr. Boddy."

"What?" Cyrus asks, still confused.

"This is why you should've come to Grandma's board game nights. *Clue*, Cyrus. The game *Clue*."

I refrain from mentioning I have no idea what the game is. Instead, I stew over the possibilities Tomai has introduced. Tomai is saying even *if* the earring belonged to Jackie, it doesn't mean she was the one who was wearing it in the sewer when the victims were murdered. It could've been someone else.

Maybe this is all pointless. Maybe we're nowhere closer to solving this mystery than we were a few days ago.

Before I can open my mouth to say anything else, I hear the locks tumbling in the front door.

Some parts of our culture will have you believe that ghost hunting was a practice with pure intentions, but history has demonstrated that is not the case. For as long as there have been ghost hunters, there have been people who have tried to control the spirits to their own benefit. Some ancient civilizations, as well as rogue factions, specialized in the creation of wraiths. Oftentimes, this was a brutal process, which commonly began with stealing children from rival groups.
—Penelope Snowde, *Wicked Work: The Dark History Behind Ghost Hunting & Its Ancient Practices* (2013)

Chapter Twenty-Two

Shit. It could be Simon or my parents, but they're not supposed to be home yet. That means it could also be someone else—someone I don't care to meet. I lunge for my backpack and dig through it to find the Phantom Prod Lite, then flick it on, purple lights sparkling. Tomai and Cyrus both shrink away from me as I move past them to the door. The front door squeaks open. *Shit.* I creep down the hallway, the device crackling in my hands like a bolt of lightning ready to strike. When I turn the corner, Simon is the only person in the hall, looking disheveled and somewhat sweaty.

"What are you *doing?*" he cries out, seeing the device in my hand.

I flick it off. "Nothing."

"Is that from your parents' lab?" He shrugs his coat off his shoulders, all the while staring at me in disbelief.

"No," I say unconvincingly. "What are you doing here?"

"What am I doing here—I live here."

"Weren't you supposed to be with Mom and Dad?"

"We agreed I should stop at home to make sure you had something to eat and got home safely. We're out of leftovers, and you've been coming home late almost every night." He stares at the Phantom Prod Lite in my grasp. "And now I'm wondering why."

"I'm not a baby," I say, hoping to redirect the conversation. "You don't have to come home and cook for me."

He stares at me, long and hard, for several moments. Something surfaces in his eyes—is it guilt? Is it shame? He sighs, his posture stiff, but his head hanging low. He runs a hand through his raven hair.

"Well, I'm here now." He glances at his phone, as if to check the time. "How are you home so early?"

"My teacher let us out early. I have a friend over and we're working on a project." I hope he doesn't bring up that I'm technically grounded.

"Oh." His face brightens. "You have a friend over. That's great. Would they like to stay for dinner?"

"Probably not. Besides, don't we have a mandated curfew or something?"

"Well…" He rolls up his sleeves and heads into the kitchen. I trail after him. "That's too bad. If you want, I can slice up some apples and throw some peanut butter on them?"

My stomach grumbles longingly in response. *Traitor.* Simon can't help but laugh, making my embarrassed cheeks burn hotter. He gathers the apples from the fridge and washes them in the sink. Their ruby-red skin, damp with water droplets, glitters like a lost trinket discovered in a cavern, and I can't wait to sink my teeth into a slice. Simon looks over his shoulder with a concerned expression and pats the apples dry with paper towels.

He nods in the direction of the door. "You should get back to your friend. I can bring these to you."

"No!" I cry out, and then say more quietly, "No. This is… This is perfect. I actually have a question to ask you."

"For your project?"

"For my project." I drum my fingertips against the scuffed countertops. "Can someone…make a ghost?"

He looks over his shoulder, completely bewildered. "*Make* a ghost?"

"Yeah."

"Sure, I guess. It's not that hard to *make* a ghost," he replies, considering this seriously. "It's not that hard to make a wraith. All you have to do is torture a soul to death. Why?"

Torture a soul to death? My heart stumbles in my chest like a runner tripping on their shoelaces. Someone could've tortured Cyrus and made her the way she is? They tortured her, and *then* they drowned her?

"Can you give me a little more information?"

Simon looks at me knowingly, and there's this glint shimmering in his eyes that implies he knows what I'm trying to do. But thankfully he doesn't push it. He sighs and keeps talking, his voice barely audible over the sound of him chopping apple slices.

"Making a wraith requires some dark, *dark* ritualism—ancient practices I only learned a little about in early stages of my training as an Apostle. The more pain inflicted on a person before they die, the more traumatic the death, the higher the chance that person will become a wraith. If you're practicing the rituals and kill someone only by slitting their throat—a relatively quick way to die—you're not going to get a wraith. You'd be lucky to get a will-o'-wisp. But if you…" His breathing sounds shallow, as if he's uncomfortable. I wonder what he's seen. What he's studied.

Clearly, it doesn't sit well with him. "If you prolong their suffering, then your chances improve."

"What kind of person, other than an Apostle, would know how to make a ghost?"

"A ghost hunter. An older one. Someone who was around before knowledge about these practices was banned. Melody, how does this fit into your project again?"

"Uhh—Lit and Comp. Comparing and contrasting different art forms. Since ghost hunting is an art form in and of itself."

"Right, but what would you be comparing it to? Witchcraft?"

"It's for my project."

"Melody." He sets down the knife. "You have to stop this. You have to."

"I don't have to answer to you."

"No, you do, because I am still an adult in your life who cares about you and your safety. You have to stop poking and prying and prodding into this case, and asking random questions about ghost hunter rituals, and—"

"You are our family's Apostle. I am asking questions that I would ask *any* Apostle."

"Would you ask me these same questions if your parents were home?"

"I thought you were sad because I shut you out. Now I let you in and it pisses you off?"

That gets him to flinch. "This is not letting me in, Melody. I'm a person, not an encyclopedia."

"Answering my questions is your freaking job. That's the whole reason you're here, in case you've forgotten. You're not a personal chef or a maid or whatever the hell it is you're doing."

"What?"

"Why are you *so* obsessed with me? Why are you making me food? Why are you asking me so many questions, every single day? Why are you trying to be my parent?"

"I'm not trying to be your parent, I'm—"

"You know, if you *really* wanted to be a good parental figure, you shouldn't have let me walk into that house. You knew," I hiss, my voice so low and grave I'm scaring myself. Or maybe I'm scared to finally speak up. That must be the reason my hands are trembling. "You knew there was a wraith in there, didn't you?"

Simon leans back against the counter as if he can't stand without the support. Dark circles ring the undersides of his tired eyes, and while I'm waiting for some sort of malicious glint to surface in them, I only find sadness—deep, deep sadness, as uncomfortable as it is unfamiliar. He takes a deep breath and rubs his hands over his face, trying to compose himself. Rain begins to patter against the window, steady and soft like cat footprints.

His fingers don't leave his face when he asks the question. Distant thunder almost drowns out the sound of his voice as he speaks. "How did you find out?"

"I overheard you and Dad talking. I guess one good thing has come from the two of you being buddy-buddy lately."

"I..." Simon clasps his hands together and casts a pleading stare in my direction. "Look, Dean made a mistake because I misjudged something. It's my fault and not your parents'. If you gave us a chance to explain, maybe you would understand..."

He continues talking in that diplomatic way of his, but at this point, the sound of his voice becomes a low humming in my ears. I can't understand a word he says. My heart plummets through my chest, sinking into the pit of my stomach. *All* of them knew? Not only Dad and Simon, but Mom too? And Mom let them do it? Instinctively my hand touches my face, tracing the web of scarred skin that once was perfect and smooth and not symbolic of everything wrong in my life. But my scars aren't the problem. It's my parents. They're the reason everything went wrong.

I stomp out of the kitchen and back into my room, ignoring Simon's pleas to stay, to talk this out. Tomai and Cyrus appear alarmed, and I know they've probably heard most of the argument. My eyes burn with embarrassed tears, and I rub the heels of my palms against them a little too aggressively, sniffling.

Tomai stands up, pulling on their backpack. "I should go."

"No. We have to keep working."

"I have to head home," Tomai says, their cheeks flushed. "I'm sorry. We can absolutely keep working on this tomorrow." They lower their voice. "Cyrus is safe for now, and that's what matters anyways."

"No, it doesn't," I retort. "Ruder told me we only have until the pep rally to figure this out. Something is going to happen at the pep rally, and that means someone else is probably going to die!"

"We can't figure it out when you're clearly in the middle of a family crisis," Tomai says in a hushed whisper. "And if I don't leave now, that will raise more suspicion for whoever is watching us. Besides, I want to hit the road before the storm hits."

Tomai places a hand on my shoulder, and the weight of it is surprising. I know what they're trying to say without the words leaving their mouth. *Give it a rest.* But they don't know what this case means to me; they don't know that it's my one pathway to redemption. They pick up the rest of their things and shuffle out the door, leaving Cyrus and me to sit in silence.

"Great," I snap. "That's frickin' great. We're back to square one."

"Tomai is right," Cyrus says. "We have to give it a rest. We've hit a dead end. And you're tired."

"I'm not tired," I say, like a petulant kindergartner who missed naptime.

"Yes, you are. You didn't get a lot of sleep last night." She pats the bed, encouraging me to sit beside her. "Take a breather."

But I can't. I pace the floor, my nerves alight and tingly, like I've been flash frozen in a block of ice and defrosted in a microwave. I wring my hands and nibble on my knuckles. Cyrus shakes her head.

"Melody. Sit. What can I do to help you relax?"

"Find the killer."

"Okay." She takes a deep breath. "We are not going to find the killer by stressing and fretting about it. I still think we're close, right?"

I stop pacing. "Close? We're nowhere near close. This earring might not be a useful clue anymore, and—"

There's a sudden knock on my door.

"Go away, Simon!"

"It's not Simon," Dad's gruff voice echoes from the other side of the door. "It's us."

"No, dude, that's what I'm saying. It was bullshit," Dani (laughs). "Families nowadays don't even keep Apostles in their homes all that often anymore. You're essentially homeless or bouncing between your families and the housing the Council assigns for you. And for what? For a lifetime of loneliness. We used to be rewarded for our service, man. The Council needs to get with the times before they lose all their recruits."

—Theo Luchez and Dani Montero, "Apostle Apostasy: Former Religious Leaders Angry," *Confessions of a Half-Baked Heretic,* www.halfbakedhereticpodcast.com (1 Jan. 2019)

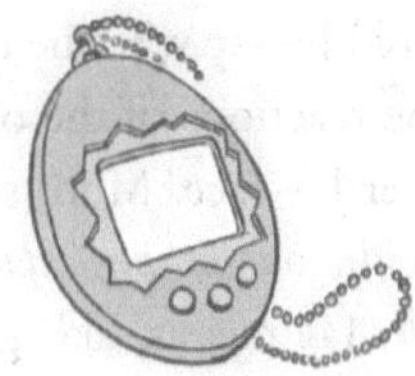

Chapter Twenty-Three

Immediately Cyrus scrambles to hide in the closet. *Shit.* Her harmonica is still in my backpack. There's no way she's going to be able to get into the Tamawotchi. I rush over and try to close the doors as fast as I can. My parents burst in, Simon standing sheepishly behind them.

"What the hell?" I shout. "I was changing!"

"Tough," Dad says. "You want to talk, we got answers."

"What are you doing here?" I kick aside some piles of discarded clothes on the floor, rearranging them into an even bigger pile. "Don't you have work or something?"

"We *did.* We finished early. There're traces of ectoplasm in the theater, but definitely no ghosts there. Nothing popped up on the EMF reader." Mom crosses her arms. "Honey, I think it's time we had a family discussion."

"Yes. Let's. As a *family*," I sneer.

Simon hovers in the background, his face red and blotchy. He's been crying? Spirits above, he's making me look like an asshole.

"Simon is a part of that family," Mom insists.

I snort. "Since when?"

"Since we got back together." Dad rolls back his shoulders, completely unbothered by the truth bomb he just detonated in the room.

Literally, it feels like a bomb exploded; has my hearing gone completely fuzzy or did he say what he did? My eyes widen with horror when I see the reactions of the other adults. Simon sighs and drags a hand over his face. Mom slowly turns her head to look at Dad with an *Are you fucking kidding me?* expression. Back together. *Back together?* He means, like, got their friendship back together, right? Or is he telling me he and Mom are getting a divorce and he's dating Simon?

"No tact," Simon chides him. "No tact whatsoever."

"How long were we going to keep dancing around this?" Dad asks them, raising his hands defensively. "I mean, she's clearly upset and isn't going to—"

"We didn't think you'd *drop* the information like that," Mom says. "We were supposed to have a conversation about this once we had all settled in and closed this case."

"Dad"—little black dots dance in front of my eyes, and as the words leave my lips, I fear I'll pass out—"you're...gay?"

"What? No! No, I'm not gay. I love your mother."

Simon snorts. "*Hello?*"

Dad's cheeks redden. Mom and Simon exchange shit-eating smirks. "Well, I love you *both*, but—Si, Rach, help me out here."

"Wait a second, Dad, you're...*bi?*"

Dad nods.

"I didn't know that."

"When would that have come up, kiddo?" Dad scratches the back of his head.

"Uh, maybe when I came out?"

Dad shrugs. "Didn't feel important."

"Are you kidding me? That would've been the *best* time to tell me."

"Hey," Dad says, "coming out of the closet is never convenient—you know that. Like right now? This is not convenient."

He places his hands on his hips and stares hard at the floor. Oh. Oh Spirits. This is *really* hard for him. My anger subsides a little at his vulnerability, but it still makes me mad. I mean, Dad knows I'm bi too—and he didn't feel safe enough to come out to me? To be honest with me? I don't know what that means for our relationship. I stand stupefied, until Simon finally decides to speak.

"Um…" He looks at Mom for approval, and she nods encouragingly. "Your father and I have known each other a long time, Melody—since before I took my vows to become an Apostle, before he met your mom. We dated for a time when we were young. Broke up shortly after starting our freshman year at the academy."

Mom… Mom and Dad started dating when they were at the academy. "So…did…Dad leave you for Mom?"

Simon and Dad exchange confused looks, as if trying to recall exactly what happened back then. Mom blushes with embarrassment and combs her fingers through her hair.

"No?" she suggests.

"No," Simon agrees. "I mean, it sure didn't help you and Dean were getting close to each other, but there were other things that led to the deterioration of our relationship back then."

Mom smirks. "He had all those weird work hours, remember?"

"*Spirits*, that's right!"

"So you were jealous my parents started dating, and became our family's Apostle?"

"No," Mom says. "He finished his training, and because someone in the Council knew him as your father's best friend, he was assigned to our family."

Simon nods. "Right. Last year, when we were prepping for your First Sacred Hunt, we happened to reconnect. At first it was casual, we didn't want to tell you, but then…everything fell apart all at once. You had to move here, and well… We had spent so much time working on ourselves and reconnecting, and I didn't want all that to go to waste, so I came along. I understand if this isn't great. Trust us, we planned for things to go so much differently than this."

"'We?' Mom, are you okay with this?"

"Yes." Mom smiles. "I am. The three of us had a discussion before we agreed to pursue this—several, actually."

"So…you're polyamorous?" I ask, and Mom nods. "What, are you dating Simon too?"

"No. I'm your dad's wife. Simon is your dad's boyfriend." Mom considers this. "Well, I suppose I'm monogamous, and your dad is polyamorous. But I'm not as familiar with the lingo. I only see love for what it is."

"This is… Wow, this is…" I'm stunned. Flabbergasted. Bamboozled.

This was *not* what I expected. But it certainly explains a lot— why Simon and Dad have been so close, why Mom is insistent I get along with Simon, and why Simon randomly rushed to move in here. If Simon hadn't moved with us to Murkmore, they would've had to break up. I know Dad well enough to know he does not have the patience nor the attention span for long-distance relationships. He's the kind of man whose night is ruined if he isn't served water within two minutes of sitting down at a restaurant—I would know, I've seen it happen. But…

"Wait a minute," I say. "Apostles aren't supposed to be in relationships. That's against the rules of the *Tomes*."

"And as I've told you, I don't believe every single word of the *Tomes*. Some of those rules were wrought from ancient cultural practices that prioritized the cultivation of a nuclear family above all else." Of course he would give the most Apostle-y response possible. Typical Simon. "Many don't agree with that rhetoric anymore either."

"I know this must be so confusing for you, dear," Mom murmurs. "Can we please sit down and talk about this?"

In the fallout of this truth bomb, I almost forgot what we were originally supposed to discuss: the night of my First Sacred Hunt. I gnaw on the inside of my cheek.

"Yeah. We need to have a talk about how you all conspired to send me into that hell house."

They flinch, but I don't care. These adults, who I trusted and loved (except for Simon), were the ones who made the decision to let me go in there with a wraith, *knowingly*. I need an explanation for this betrayal. Otherwise, I don't know how I'm going to continue living under the same roof with them. Spirits, I'd swim across the strait if I couldn't hop a ferry.

We enter the kitchen and take a seat at the table, where the peanut butter apples wait for us, ornately arranged on a plate in the shape of a chrysanthemum. We've been in my room talking for so long, the edges of the apples have started to oxidize and wilt, turning a soft, sugary brown. I pop one into my mouth regardless.

Simon folds his hands on the tabletop. "Again, I cannot express how sorry I am for what happened to you, and how we misjudged things."

"We need you to know," Dad adds softly, "everything that's happened since is not your fault."

"I know that," I say, although I don't. "I want to know *why* you did it."

Simon shivers in his seat. He looks at my mother, his eyes suddenly wet. "Rachel, I don't…"

"Well…" Mom rubs his shoulder and looks at me. "I don't…know how to tell you this. This is so, so hard. But um…we sent you into the house because we thought you would be able to handle it. Because…we thought you were a medium."

"A…" I trail off. "A medium?"

"This isn't something that's mentioned much in the *Tomes*, but there are people within our culture called mediums," Simon explains quietly. "Iliony, our first matriarch, was technically a medium."

"Right, but…" I trail off, considering this.

Mediums are people who can converse with spirits and heal them so they can cross into the Beyond. No Ingress, no cap-can, no special rituals—no nothing. To my knowledge, they simply do this by talking with them, and possibly helping them resolve any unfinished business. But I couldn't be—*could I?* At once I feel like I'm rolling beneath the waves of a tumultuous, stormy sea. My head throbs as the air leaves my lungs. I think about Cyrus. How I was able to touch her, and how her coldness didn't bother me. How I was able to converse with her, despite never having been able to converse with ghosts in the past. Maybe Cyrus isn't the only special one. Maybe I am too. And maybe by my finding her, I was able to help her reconnect to her past self.

"But why do you think I'm a medium? I thought they were only born in specific circumstances."

Simon juts in. "Because you were. The most common way they come about is when…when a pregnant woman is possessed by a ghost."

Mom can't raise her head to look at me. "I shouldn't have been working. Your father had begged me not to do it, but…I didn't like feeling useless. I still don't."

She rubs her eyes, trying to clear some of the tears that drip from them. I've seen my mom laid up in a hospital bed, barely conscious, but I have never seen her look as wounded as she does now.

"I was tired, and distraught, and didn't notice the phantom when it crept up on me."

Whoa…she was possessed? While pregnant? That's…horrifying. Possessions can be extremely distressing to the human psyche. When you're possessed, the ghost suppresses your consciousness, which means they are effectively "switching off" parts of your nervous system. People can stop breathing—or worse, their hearts will stop altogether. If you're pregnant and fall victim to a possession, that could be a death sentence. I'm wondering how much worse this made my mother's heart condition.

"It was an accident," Dad tells her.

He squeezes her hand firmly, and the way he looks at her… He hurts for her in ways that I can't imagine. In ways I hope I will never experience myself.

"I was right on the cusp of my second trimester, and when we got to the hospital, the doctors said there was an extremely high chance I would miscarry. I had to be on bed rest for the remainder of the pregnancy." Mom's voice shakes.

Simon reaches across the table and grabs a napkin, which she graciously accepts.

"But you came along and you were a healthy little baby girl, and we were all over the moon." She dabs at her eyes and takes a deep breath, as if trying to suppress the sniffles and gulping sobs that threaten to escape her body. "But when you were little, you seemed…off."

"Off?" I whisper.

"From the time you could walk and talk, you used to come into the lab and chat with the spirits in the EctoChamber." Dad smiles fondly at the memory. "You were such a chatterbox. You'd talk and talk and talk with them. And one day, Simon was over, and he connected the dots. That's why we let you go on so many missions with us when you were a kid."

"She was so intuitive, wasn't she?" Mom asks him, her eyes shining with tears. "Spirits, she picked up on things fast."

"You did," Dad says softly. "We really believed you had a gift."

Believed. I know he doesn't mean anything malicious when he says this, but it hurts all the same. My parents believed I was special—and maybe I am, but because of my failure, they no longer feel that way.

I swallow back a lump in my throat, but my voice still quakes. "If you knew all of this, why wouldn't you tell me?"

"Historically, in order for mediums to truly activate their talents, they have to…be put into a high-stakes situation. If you'd known there was a wraith in there, it could've ruined the opportunity for you to activate your powers, so you had to face it alone," Simon says quietly. "Based on your performance in your parents' missions, we were so sure you would be able to handle it. But…"

"We made a horrible mistake, and we never should have put you through that." Mom blows her nose as the tears continue to stream down her face. "And for that, we are so sorry."

My heartbeat catches in my throat and my legs jitter underneath the table. *A medium, a medium. I could be a medium.* "Are you sure you were wrong? Maybe what happened that night was a fluke."

I helped Cyrus get her memory back. I helped her use her powers. Am I supposed to believe that's all coincidence?

"Well, if a wraith couldn't help you bring out your powers, it's unlikely you are a medium," Simon says politely. "Like I said, mediums have to be put in high-stakes situations for their powers to be triggered. What could have been more high stakes than that?"

Oh, Simon. I can think of a few things.

The lower half of my body feels heavy, and if I wasn't sitting in a chair right now, I could sink right through the center of the earth. I can't believe my parents have been living with the weight of this secret for seventeen years. They believed I was special—that I was someone who had, for lack of a better term, ghost hunting superpowers. Now they believe they were wrong, and their mistake left me with hideous scars all over my face. But what makes this all worse?

They knew they made me feel worthless, and yet, I still feel like I'm competing for their approval. That's all I've been doing since we got here.

"We're sorry, Mel," Dad whispers. He squeezes Mom's hand. "We can't tell you how sorry we are."

"That's…it? That's all you're going to say? Sorry?"

"We thought we were doing what was best for you," Simon says.

"Did you?" I ask. "Are you the one with the fucked-up face, Simon?"

"Melody," Mom says. "We know we can't ever make this up to you, but—"

"That's right. You can't make this up to me. *Ever.*" My hands grip the edges of the table, and I swear if I had the strength, I would flip the damn thing over. "My entire life was ruined because of your mistake. And you guys are still punishing me for *my* failure. You won't even let me go on this mission."

"We don't want you to get hurt," Dad cries out.

"If you cared about making me feel better, you'd let me help."

"Melody," Mom protests, "we can't. I know when you're obsessed, and I know you won't rest until you go after those ghosts. And I'm sorry, but we can't take that risk again."

"But it's my life."

"And you are our daughter. Our *only* daughter. When the mission isn't as high risk, we're happy to have you join us again. But…honey"—Mom shakes her head, folding her hands together—"I think *not* working on missions, especially high-profile ones like this, is a good thing for you. You used to have your entire life mapped out for you, and then you went through all those big, traumatic changes. You have a lot about yourself that you need to figure out. You need to understand this is good for you in many ways. It's not only meant to keep you safe. It's essential to your own growth."

"Oh. I'm so glad you get to decide what's best for me, after sending me to my absolute rock bottom. I'm *so* glad you expect me to trust your judgment now."

"We are your parents—"

"Well, you suck at being parents." I shrug my shoulders.

They are stunned. Wide-eyed. Mom touches a hand to her chest, and the look of hurt on her face is worse than anything I've ever seen before, but it doesn't make me empathize with her; it only makes me angrier.

"I'm sorry, are you surprised? You kept the fact I'm a medium from me, you didn't tell me about why everything happened when you were the ones who set it up to begin with, and now, Dad has a boyfriend who's *living with us*. All things no one told me about; you just expected me to deal with it. Well, you know what? You can't say sorry and think I'm not going to resent you for this. You always told me I have to live with the consequences of my actions. And you're going to have to live with this."

I push my chair back from the table and head for my bedroom, then slam the door shut. To my surprise, no one comes after me. I can hear them murmuring amongst themselves in the kitchen. The sound of Mom weeping softly, and Simon trying to comfort her. But their sadness only angers me further. How can they sit there and cry and expect me to forgive them? They think they ruined my life, but what they don't seem to understand is that *I don't have one anymore*! My girlfriend dumped me, my friends ditched me, and any sense of purpose I had left with them!

Could've been a medium, but *no*! I can't even have that! And I can't continue to have the family dynamic I grew up with, either.

I sink down to the floor. My chest feels like it's been seized by eight hundred hands, all squeezing my heart and rib cage so hard they could crack. Maybe that wouldn't be so bad. Maybe they'll crack and splinter parts of my body, and little foul festering wounds will grow and abscess and I can finally be out of my misery. The rage, the rage, the *rage* is so painful I want to scream. I ball up my hands into fists and smack them into the sides of my head, gritting my teeth as I rock back and forth on the floor. The energy has to go somewhere, and what's a few extra bruises on my skull? Maybe I can knock myself the hell out. Maybe I can—

"Melody?" Rattling echoes through the closet, along with the scraping sounds of wire hangers. "Is it safe to come out now?"

I don't say anything. She comes out anyway. Her hands are deep in her pockets, and her shoulders are bunched up. She's nervous, but she's trying to hide it.

"How much did you hear?"

"A lot of it," she says quietly. "You're some kind of superpowered ghost hunter, I guess. Congratulations?"

"Funny," I say, my voice biting back harshly.

She flinches.

"Because I'm *not* a medium, and my parents risked my life to see if I was one. And also, my dad is dating Simon." I shudder in disgust. Of all the men he could choose to be with, did it have to be the one I hate most? "They've lost their minds."

"Parents are nuts," Cyrus agrees, smirking. "The stories I could tell you about my mom. She had a mental breakdown when I cut my hair short for the first time in middle school. And don't even get me started on the time I got my tattoos."

"Cool."

"Not into talking much right now. That's okay." She takes a deep breath and sits on the bed. "At least they were trying to be honest with you."

I turn to face her, my face contorted in disgust. "What?"

"Now you know the truth about everything," she says. "At least they finally owned up to it."

"I'm sorry—you think this is a good thing? That they lied to me for this long and they're only now choosing to admit it?"

"I don't think them keeping secrets is a good thing at all," she replies. "But I think it's good they were honest. It had to have been hard for them."

I snort. "Hard for them? Are you serious?"

"I mean, yeah. They were responsible for putting their one and only daughter through a traumatizing event."

"Are you on *their* side right now?" The words blister my tongue, and I struggle to keep my voice down. All I want to do is explode, but with my family right outside my door, I can't do that. I have to keep it together.

"I'm taking no one's side, Melody. Calm down."

"Don't tell me to be calm. There's a serial killer on the loose, and people's lives are on the line! And you know, you've spent a lot of time dismissing me and telling me how my people are full of shit—"

"Your people *literally* believe that I don't deserve to continue existing! You expect me to *not* call that out?"

"*I* am not like my people! I don't blindly believe everything they've taught me!"

"You sure about that? Because you seem to have a hard time letting go."

"This is the culture I was raised in. I can't unlearn everything overnight. But I know you shouldn't be sent through the Ingress; I know that's wrong!"

"Why? Because I'm special?" She watches my face, and I cannot hide my shame. "See, that's the problem. I don't care if you think I'm 'special.' I don't care if I'm the only ghost of my type to have ever walked the planet. Any conscious creature deserves a fate better than that. How are you investigating a murder and you don't know right from wrong?" She laughs in disbelief, running a hand through her hair. "You're upset right now that your parents haven't treated you like a person with actual thoughts and feelings and they don't respect your wishes, but you're continuing to defend your people's practices?"

"I'm *not* defending them. I didn't suck you into a cap-can and put you into an EctoChamber, so I think it's wrong of you to act like I'm on the same level as every other ghost hunter."

"Not kidnapping me and shoving me through some space wormhole is the *bare minimum* for respecting someone as a person. And lower your voice. Your parents are still in this friggin' house!"

I bury my face in my hands and try to take a deep breath. One, two, three, four, five. Hold. One, two, three, four, five. Exhale. Like my therapist taught me. Cyrus reaches out to touch my shoulder, but I shrug away, and I don't know why. I could use a freaking hug right now. It would feel nice, especially from her. But I don't think I deserve it.

The hurt from my rejection is palpable in her voice. "I know you're tired. I know you're frustrated. Believe me, if I could wave a magic wand and somehow figure this all out—my death, everything—I would."

"You haven't exactly been trying." My hands drop from my face as a hurt, disturbed scowl crosses her lips.

"The hell do you mean, I haven't been trying?"

"You keep making jokes about your death and being so flippant about it."

"That's unfair of you to say. I've been trying. Do you know what it's like to have amnesia? It sucks. I feel like I'm walking around in a fog all the time."

"If you spent half the effort trying to remember what happened to you that you did making jokes, we'd *actually* be somewhere in this investigation."

"W-wow." Laughter, taut with disbelief, escapes her lips, and she shakes her head. "If you think I'm that useless, maybe I should leave."

"You know what? Maybe you should."

Shock floods her face. The outline of her body quivers in the dusky light of my room. She opens her mouth as if to say something else, but then—

She vanishes.

I wipe away some of the tears from my face in disbelief. When did she learn how to turn invisible? I spin around and around in my room, looking for her, but I don't feel anything. There's no chill in the air. Nothing that would indicate the presence of a ghost. She's truly left me alone. And when she left the room, she took all the anger with her.

I take a deep breath. My chest still hurts. But I can't relax when there's work to do and a murder to solve.

I try to think about the things I know. I know that Parker Kim was murdered—and not by a ghost, based off where the body was initially found and where I discovered the bloodstains. I know I found this earring at the scene of the crime. I know it's expensive. I don't know who owns it, and I don't know who could've been wearing it when they murdered Parker Kim. Heck, I don't even know if Jackie or Brinkley are the true owners of this earring, but they're about my only leads, and Jackie for sure has a motive for three of the victims.

Jackie was nice to me from the start. The one who greeted me on the first day of school, who curiously continues to be kind to me. Hard to think someone so sweet could be so sinister. Then again it was hard for me to believe that Brynne was such a vindictive bitch, but I came around. I came around *hard*.

I send a quick text to Jackie and ask her if she's around, saying I need help with my History homework. It's five o'clock, but the town curfew only kicks in at seven, so I hold my breath, awaiting her reply. Within minutes, she invites me to come over. I locate my Phantom Prod Lite and put it into my purse.

I'm going to get to the bottom of this mystery, even if it kills me.

It's gonna be a wet one, folks.

—Sal Rodriguez, Weather Report, *Murkmore Evening News* (6 Sept. 2024)

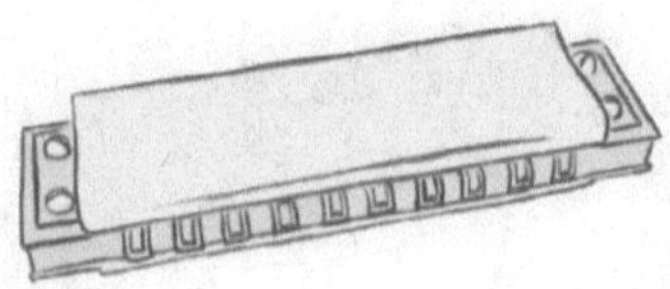

Chapter Twenty-Four

"Melody! Come on in."

Jackie steps aside to let me in, and I shuffle into the house, my arms pinned against my sides. I can't let her see the pools of sweat that have accumulated underneath them. I hauled ass over here, and the walkway up to her front door is a mile long, all lined with cobblestones and perfectly maintained white rose bushes. Like, we get it: your family owns the biggest chunk of land on the shittiest island in existence. Big whoop.

The entrance is grand and massive, as to be expected from one of the richest girls in town. Everything—from the dark mahogany floors to the collection of gold-framed family photos—reeks of old money. Through the shadowy corridor to the left, a smartly dressed butler emerges, his palms turned upward and outstretched. I balk in confusion and glance over at Jackie.

"Oh, he wants to take your jacket. Thanks, Sebastian."

Of course Jackie's family has a butler named Sebastian. I wriggle my jacket off my shoulders and pass it to him. He doesn't acknowledge me with so much as a polite nod before whisking it away. *Creepy.* What, are the help not allowed to talk?

Jackie smiles and squeezes my arm. "I'm glad you messaged me."

"Sorry it was so last minute."

"No worries! I was struggling with the assignment too. And like, since Pheebs and Tam started working at Cups and Scoops after school, I have no one else to study with. This is great!"

She guides me up the winding staircase. The railing has been polished so well I can see my face in it. The air reeks of lemon-scented furniture polish, and it wafts through my nostrils into the back of my mouth, causing my eyes to water. I swallow back the urge to cough as we navigate our way to her bedroom.

The ceiling in her room is cavernous and tall enough to hold a shimmering chandelier, which hovers precariously close to the top of her four-poster canopy bed. And the thing looks *heavy*— my anxiety could never. Posters of Black models, music artists, and athletes are plastered all over her walls alongside family photos. It's wild seeing pictures of her dad, knowing he used to be on TV. In one photo, she sits on his shoulders, arms spread as wide as her gap-toothed grin. Such a cute smile.

Shame she won't be smiling once I reveal her secrets.

We sit on the bed, which is so soft I sink into it like quicksand. I reach out to grab ahold of the tufted headboard to steady myself, and the texture is luxurious like velvet. This bed must be worth more than my parents' car. I copy her posture, swinging my legs around to the center of the bed and propping myself up. I'm still sinking, but I'm sitting up a little better now. Jackie retrieves her homework from her vanity while I fish around in my backpack for mine. I open my textbook to the first page of the homework and hope I don't seem too nervous. Is it smart to be in such close proximity to a murderer? Will she have the upper hand if she tries something?

"What is the point of learning all the specifics about the Intrahuman Fantastical Treaty of '46?" she grumbles aloud. "I'd rather take some class on how to do my taxes than this. At least then I'd be using it."

"I took a personal finance course last summer. It was a good experience."

"Aww, that sounds nice. Mountain Ridge must have everything cool."

"It's pretty cool." The people are shit, though. "But it's good to have a change."

It has been, honestly. While I've been concerned with redeeming my rep, there's not a part of me that misses Mountain Ridge. I'm not doing any of this to win *those* people back. I'm only doing this for myself. I have to prove I'm worth something. I have to fulfill the promise I made to myself.

Jackie looks at me incredulously, vivid-blue eyes blinking. "Even though you moved to a town where a bunch of people have died really brutal deaths?"

"Uh…" She's got me there.

I pretend to fixate on the answer to one of my History problems and show it to her, but she doesn't seem interested. She stares at me with an uncomfortable intensity and sets down her mechanical pencil on the bed, only for it to get lost in the wrinkles and folds of her stupidly fluffy duvet.

"Do you think your parents are going to find the wraiths anytime soon?"

"I think so," I murmur with uncertainty. I avert my eyes for a second and move on to the next problem in the textbook. "It's interesting. When they were investigating the sewers…they found something."

"What?" her eyes widen. "Like, another body?"

"No. They found an earring."

I pull out my phone and show her a picture of the earring, my heart pounding in my chest, thinking I've pulled a gotcha. I expect her to recoil, to hiss, to glower, but her expression is blank, her brow furrowed, profoundly confused. Her eyelashes bat against her cheeks and she tilts her head to the side. My heart stutters within my chest. This wasn't what I expected. What's her game here?

"That's so weird," she says. "That looks like a nice earring—way too nice to be down in the sewer."

I frown, confused. She's either a good actor, or she's never seen this earring before.

"Why do you have that photo anyways?" she asks, reaching for a water bottle on her nightstand. "I thought your parents weren't letting you help in the investigation."

"They…aren't. They don't know I took that photo." As soon as the words leave my mouth, regret bubbles in the pit of my stomach. Why did I mention that? It's like I admitted no one else knows I'm here. "I've been trying to piece together things on my own."

"Oh?" She pauses to take a sip of her water. "Really?"

"Y-yeah."

"So where do you think the wraiths are hiding?"

If I'm going to continue to work as a detective, then I'm going to need to work on my poker face, because Jackie realizes right away that something is off.

"What? What is it?"

"I shouldn't say."

Jackie makes a zipping motion across her lips, her gaze serious, but not threatening. "I won't tell a single soul. Honest."

This is a gamble, but maybe if I feed her a little more information, I can get her to slip up. I can figure out if she has any tells. "Well…I don't think it's wraiths at all."

"You think so too?" Her hands fly upward and cover her mouth for a moment, then she flaps them excitedly and shakes her head. "Ohh, Melody, you're giving me *chills*, girl!"

"O-oh," I say in faux surprise, laughing to hide my nervousness. "I'm glad I'm not the only one with this theory."

"I keep thinking about it, and it's—I mean, it's *so* weird, right? We've never had a problem with ghosts before. People here don't die in tragic ways. In fact, they don't usually die on the island at all. Like, they get airlifted to different hospitals, or ferried away to hospice care. We don't even have a graveyard here." The matter-of-fact way she's talking, combined with the breezy pitch of her voice, chills me. "Not to mention what happened to Cyrus. It all feels weirdly connected."

"Cyrus…"

Jackie winces. "Tomai's best friend Cyrus. She died last year, before the wraith attacks. I'm sorry, I thought you knew about her."

"I know *of* her, I just don't know much about her," I admit.

Guilt wells inside of me as I think back to our argument. The things I said to her. The way I've been prioritizing my feelings and desires, with little regard for how she feels.

"Tomai hasn't opened up to me about that. I heard from some other people that she drowned, though, right?"

Jackie shudders. A dark look crosses her face and she exhales slowly. To my surprise, a tear wells in her eye, and she wipes it away. For a moment my ambition subsides, and a nagging feeling of guilt resurfaces in my stomach. The closer I get to the truth, the more old wounds I reopen.

"Sorry. It's hard to think about. It was so sad." She rubs her arms like she's cold, her gaze far away. "Cyrus was… God, you never met a person more talented. Or kind. We were in orchestra, but we didn't spend a lot of time together, and truth be told, I regret that. People treated her like shit, and she took it all with a smile on her face."

"She said that."

"What?"

"Uh, I mean, Tomai said Cyrus had said people were awful to her," I stammer. "But look, it's okay. You don't have to tell me if you don't want to."

Suddenly, even after yearning to know the answer for so long, I'm too afraid to know it. Especially if Jackie is tearing up over it. I don't want to picture what happened to Cyrus. It'll be engraved on the tombstone of my brain for the rest of my life. I've been so selfish. *I* don't even want to remember my run-in with the wraith, and this entire time, I've been pressuring her to remember her death.

That's really fucked up of me.

"I can. So that night… Cyrus wasn't feeling too well. Rumor was someone spiked her drink, which is weird, because, I mean, I don't know who would've done that. Or why. Like, no one else was spiked that night that I know of." Jackie scratches her head. "I'm still hung up on that, honestly. Because that means another girl must have spiked her drink, right? I mean, none of the boys were going to go for Cyrus. We've got some real sleazeballs at our school, but I don't think they'd—I mean, shit."

"How do you know her drink was spiked?"

"She was like, *really* out of it. I remember she stumbled out of the bathroom, and I asked her if she was okay, and she insisted she was… I didn't… I didn't think anything of it at the time," Jackie admits, her voice hoarse. "I figured someone was passing around a flask and she drank too much. But her eyelids were fluttering, and she seemed sleepy. Then she got freaked out about something and insisted she had to leave and that her mom was going to pick her up. And I saw some of the other orchestra kids begging her to stay but she left anyway."

"The teachers didn't notice?"

Jackie shrugs. "They noticed too late."

"So… So she tried to walk home, and…"

"Right. Um…" Jackie drags a hand over her face as she takes in a shuddery breath. "She disappeared. There was an all-out search party for her, and like a week later, her body washed up on the shore. Tamarah was there, and she said the body was covered in abrasions. Deep puncture holes. They said she had fallen from a cliff on the north shore and drowned and that her body was cut up by the rocks in the water, but…"

"But what?"

"Cyrus was afraid of that cliffside. Like, deathly afraid of it. When we were in the third grade, we went there for a picnic, and there were a bunch of kids that liked jumping off the side and into the water—there're no rocks on either side of the cliff, just that peak. But someone tried to push her over it. She had a huge meltdown and didn't come to school for like, a week."

A nauseous belch crawls up my throat, and I have to fight to keep it down. I think about the day we went into the sewers. How she protected me from falling into the canal, but was so nervous—so freaked out. She was afraid of water but wanted to ensure my safety.

Luckily, Jackie doesn't notice my discomfort. "A lot of kids hold parties there because like, it's *so* far away from the center of town. Takes a while for the cops to break up a party. But she never went to them, because she was worried some asshole would pressure her to go cliff diving again. She wouldn't go near those cliffs unless someone forced her to." Jackie rolls her eyes. "I tried to tell the investigators when they came to our school, but they didn't listen. Ruled it an accident days later. Tell you the truth, I think all of this is like, *so* far above their pay grade."

My chest tightens. I picture Cyrus in the grasp of some malicious force, the pure terror welling in her eyes as they tossed her over the edge. Her face, clouded by murky waters, those gorgeous brown eyes forever closed. She didn't drown.

She was pushed off a cliff.

Which means…

… No. *No. No, no, no.*

"Jackie, I'm sorry, I have to go."

I abruptly try to climb off the bed, but the motion causes her water bottle to spill all over her shorts and bare legs. She gasps in surprise, and immediately tries to dry herself off with the duvet. As I stammer my apologies, I notice something about her skin. It's…shiny. Shimmery. Where have I seen that before?

"It's okay," she says through a clenched jaw.

"You're a…"

"A selkie," she responds, and her voice is oddly quiet. "Well, half selkie. If water touches my skin, it gets like this."

Selkies are half-seal half-human creatures, similar to mermaids except they're capable of living on land, too, since they can shape-shift depending on how wet or dry their environment is. I knew that there were other Fantasticals living on the island, but never did I think the principal's daughter would be one of them. Which one of her parents is the selkie? Huh. I've also never noticed this until now, but Jackie has slightly webbed fingers. There's this thin membrane stretching between the bottoms of each of them, with tiny little blue and red veins running through. They're kinda pretty to look at. With a frustrated grunt, she peels away the duvet from her skin, and I notice something on the underside of it: blue goo.

Goo, like ectoplasm.

Spirits above.

Jackie's body secretes goo like ectoplasm, which means she's the killer—but this doesn't make sense. Selkies—selkies don't *eat* people. Why would a selkie want to eat humans? That's not in their nature. The gears in my head continue to turn, and I resist the urge to gasp when I realize what the answer is.

What's the common thread, aside from music? Males. Every single person that was eaten was male. And…wait a second. This whole time we've been looking for someone who's been playing music, but what did Tomai tell me the day we met? They had heard *singing*. What did Cyrus say over and over again? She can't sing well. She wouldn't have been singing.

Sirens sing, and sirens eat men.

Jackie isn't a selkie. She's a siren.

But sirens are reclusive and haven't integrated into society like other Fantasticals. Now it makes sense why Parker Kim and his partner Thad Stevens, two marine biologists, were here. Somehow, someway, they caught wind of what was going on in Murkmore and came to investigate, only to meet their deaths.

Shock electrocutes my spine and rattles all the nerve endings in my body. My voice hardens. "You're absolutely sure you don't know whose earring that is?"

"What? No. Why?" She stares at me. There's a look of disgust on her face I'm all too familiar with—the kind that shows up when you commit a severe social faux pas. "Are you feeling okay?"

"Not really."

"I can't help this, y'know," Jackie says with a nervous laugh, averting her eyes. Her cheeks burn. "I know it's gross, but—"

"I'm not bothered by that."

"Seems like you are."

Briefly, a wave of shame washes over me. "I'm sorry. I don't handle death well. I shouldn't have asked you to tell me about what happened to Cyrus. Um, I—I need to find a bathroom. I'm going to be sick."

I sprint from that room like my heels are on fire. My heartbeat echoes in my ears as I stumble down the hallway, toward the stairs. I see what I think is a person's shadow—Sebastian. *Shit.* I can't leave the way I came in.

I'm fucked.

Panicked, I start throwing open doors, revealing little studies and tidied guest bedrooms, until finally, I find a bathroom. I lock the door and lean against it, my entire body trembling in fear. Spirits above. I left my backpack in Jackie's room, which means I left my phone in there. Stupid, stupid! I slap the sides of my head, ready to disperse into a rage episode, but then I catch my breath. *Stop it, Melody. You got yourself into this mess, and only you can get yourself out.* Inhale, exhale. Count back from twenty.

Think.

When I first approached Jackie's house, it looked like there was a window beside a trellis. If I can figure out what window that trellis rested on, I might have a chance of shimmying down it. It might not hold my weight, but I'd rather take my chances outside than in here.

I shake out my hands, trying to quiet my nerves. Jackie hasn't followed me—or hasn't found me yet. I survey the porcelain and marble-laden bathroom. The opulence is insane. How deep is that soaker tub? Is this supposed to be a guest bathroom or something? My eyes are taking in all the little details and tastefully assembled I when I notice—

There's another door.

I walk over and open it, expecting it to be a linen closet, but instead, I'm greeted with yet another cavernous bedroom. Wooden beams crisscross their way across the vaulted ceiling. A king-size bed rests in the center of the room, atop a colorful artisan rug. Half-folded clothes lay on the comforter. A lived-in space, but no one is in here right now.

Is this her parents' room? Ew. Out of all the places I could pick, it had to be my principal's bedroom?

Although part of me wants to keep looking for an exit, there's another part of me—call it intuition—that's compelled to venture further. Maybe it's because I spy the vanity in the back corner, along with a jewelry box encrusted with jade jewels. My heart lurches within my chest. *The earring.* It's a long shot, but I've come this far, so I'm not giving up now. If it's in that box, I'm damn well going to find it.

I tiptoe over and crack open the lid like a greedy pirate. Pushing aside bangles and necklaces, I search for the one thing that could unravel this whole mystery. But I don't see it. I've emptied everything from the box, and I don't see the other earring. *Shit.* I grab it and tilt it upside down, shaking it. Something rattles. *Bingo.* I set it back on the vanity and press on the sides, then on the bottom, and that's when I hear something click.

The jewelry box has a false bottom.

I push down harder, popping up the edges until I can sneak a fingernail underneath and pry it up. It comes away with a loud *POP!* Like an exploding soda can. That's when I see it.

The other earring. But wait, that means…

"Melody?" Jackie calls.

It's not Jackie. It's Redd. She's the killer.

"Melody?" I have no time to lose.

I pocket the other earring and sprint back into the bathroom, then shut the door behind me. I drop to my knees in front of the toilet and make a gagging noise right as Jackie cracks open the bathroom door.

"You poor thing!" she cries out, rushing over to me. "Oh my God, you weren't kidding!"

I wipe at my perfectly clean mouth, although honestly, if I stay in this house much longer, I might actually hurl. I tell her I have to go home—never have I been more thankful for the fact there's a curfew. She offers to walk me out, and we retrieve my backpack before she leads me back to the foyer. But as we descend the steps, there's someone waiting for us below—two people, in fact.

Principal Redd stands shoulder to shoulder with Sebastian. Her skin glimmers in the faint auburn glow of the crystal pendants mounted to the walls. Her smile is as warm and polite as it's ever been, but her eyes are deeply unkind and cold.

"Hello, Melody," Principal Redd murmurs. "Good to see you again."

"H-hi," I stammer, hoping my face doesn't look too flushed, but it's no use.

I clearly look nervous; I can feel the sweat beads along my hairline and the heat radiating from my face. And as Ms. Ruder told me—or implied—the killer was watching us.

"My dear," she purrs like a cat who's caught its prey, "you don't look so good."

"She's heading home," Jackie interjects. "She's not feeling well. And um, Sebastian, you might want to send Shirley up to clean Mom's bathroom."

Oh fuck, Jackie, *why* would you say that? Something in Redd's eyes shifts, and the malice deepens. Shit, shit, shit.

She knows.

"In this rain?" Principal Redd frowns. "Oh no, my dear. It's far too dangerous. There isn't a sidewalk around here, and the roads fill with water easily. You'll be drenched, and that can lead to hypothermia. With all that sweat on your forehead, you already look like you're running a fever." She turns over her shoulder and speaks to Sebastian. "Could you get her jacket and take her home?"

She's playing nice. Why? If she's the killer, and she knows what *I* know—or what I *think* I know—why would she offer to take me home?

"I'm fine," I insist, smiling as broadly as I can. "I'm from Mountain Ridge, after all. I love the rain."

"Aww," she comments affectionately, like someone holding a puppy for the first time. "Sweet girl, you have no idea how bad things can get on this island when it rains. Sebastian will take you."

Sebastian nods and brusquely makes his way to the hall closet. I stand there, trying not to shiver in fear. Jackie remains cordial, chatting to me about sending some of the homework answers over text later, oblivious to the fact her mother may be a stone-cold serial killer. Principal Redd's piercing gaze holds me the entire time, as if she's imagining every way she could spit roast me, deep-fry me in a vat of oil, maybe slice me up and make me into a cheesesteak. Sebastian returns with my jacket, and I take a little too much time to put it on. The smile on Principal Redd's face grows wider and wider. Jackie bids me goodbye, cheerful as ever. Principal Redd leads her back upstairs, insisting she needs her help with something, leaving me to my fate.

I watch helplessly as Jackie leaves. Two fingers press against the small of my back, and Sebastian pushes me along without looking at me. I slowly march out of the foyer, down a hallway, and out the side door into the garage. Sebastian grabs my shoulder, pulling me to a stop. He uses the keys to unlock the car door, and then holds it open. I stand there motionlessly.

"Get in," he says gruffly.

"Y-you don't have to drive me home," I somehow find the courage to stammer. "I can call my parents."

"You won't be calling anyone." He motions for me to pass the phone over to him. "Get in the car."

Take note, folks: when a ghost is in an electric object, it can lead to some serious problems!

—Hal Loffskarr, "YOWCH – All About Possessions of Electrical Objects," *Ghost Hunting for the Non Ghost Hunter* (2010)

Chapter Twenty-Five

I bite my lip so hard I taste copper. Sebastian's gaze is so cold. A dead fish has more emotion. I shuffle over. Tears well in my eyes, and with shaking hands, I give him my phone. His grip tightens around it, and I swear I hear it crack under the pressure. He orders me to sit, then buckles me in. I take a deep breath, inhaling and exhaling through my nose. He climbs into the driver's seat beside me, turns on the car, and we're off, slowly driving through the slick roads. The windshield wipers can barely clear enough space for us to see the path ahead.

I turn to look at him. "You don't have to do this."

Silence.

"You can't keep doing this. You're gonna get caught. I don't know what she's paying you, but it's not worth a life in prison."

He doesn't respond. Keeps his eyes focused on the road. I eye the lock on the door. If I eject my seat belt, maybe I can get the door open in time to tuck and roll? But as soon as I reach for the seat belt, he revs the engine and speeds up. I press down on my heels to prevent myself from being thrown against the dashboard. My forehead stops a mere inch away.

"Don't try it," he says.

My breath catches in my throat. Regret floods my body as the tears spill out from my eyes. No one is coming for me; no one other than Jackie knows I was there. I should've listened to my parents. I should've listened to Tomai. I should've listened to Cyrus. So many warnings and caution signs I could've paid attention to, but I was prideful, and arrogant, and honestly, really fucking sad. I was so desperate to stop feeling like a loser, I was willing to lose my life over it. I'm no detective, and I'm no hero, and I'm not smart enough to figure out how to save myself. Worse, I played the victim the whole time. Cyrus didn't deserve to be treated like that. She didn't deserve to hear the things I said. She didn't deserve to be used like some kind of pawn in a game. She's so much more than that. She's a person—a wonderful, beautiful, fantastic person who deserves an apology and to know what she means to me.

Tears bite at my eyes and blur my vision. I have to find a way out of this. I can't be yet another thing that traumatizes Cyrus, or Tomai. And also, even if my parents are on my shit list right now, I can't traumatize them either.

But how do I fight him? It's not like I have a weapon on— oh wait. I *do*.

I faux sniffle, turning my head away to look out the window. I've never seen this part of Murkmore before—never knew it existed. It's dark and full of dense trees. The moon is the only thing illuminating the road, casting silver light that shimmers against the asphalt. Is this what Cyrus saw the night she died? As I gaze into the nothingness, my fingers reach down to gently pull on the zipper of my backpack. My Phantom Prod Lite is right inside, nestled in the front pocket. I have it halfway opened when fingers grab fistfuls of my hair. I scream as he presses my face against the dashboard. I struggle feebly, one of my arms pinned, the other helplessly reaching upward to swat at the hand that grips the steering wheel, but I can't reach. He slams me into it— *one, two, three*—and I screech as pain explodes in my head.

"You're not going to try anything," he snaps as I sob in agony. "Do you understand me?" He shoves me back into my seat with a scoff. "I could bury you in these woods, but I'm being generous out of consideration for your family." He reaches inside his sport coat and withdraws a bowie knife, waving it at me briefly before tucking it away once more. "Try anything again, and this thing is going in your rib cage. The last girl I did this to squealed like a stuck pig." A cruel smile twists across his lips. "She was about as round as one, too."

This *fucker*. Principal Redd must've been the one to drug Cyrus at the dance, and Sebastian was the one who kidnapped her when she tried to find her mom. I shiver in my seat, eyes wide, the blood pounding in my ears, my head throbbing from the pain. With trembling hands, I touch a small gash on my forehead; the blood is sticky to the touch.

He chuckles at my fear and reaches for the audio controls, flipping on music. The sound of an '80s pop-rock song, complete with a raging synthesizer, crackles to life. He drums his fingertips against the steering wheel and sings along under his breath, chillingly cavalier while driving me to my death. All I can think of is Cyrus. How alone did she feel when this man drove her up this winding road?

The radio crackles as the song continues to play. Weirdly, I think I hear the voice of a girl speaking over the male vocals, but then Sebastian reaches across to fiddle with the controls, and the music returns to normal. My heart thrums in my chest. Could it be? The crackling resumes, and the voice sounds louder over the din. With an aggravated grunt, he switches it off. A few moments of tense silence pass before the crackling starts again, now devoid of music.

"What the hell is with this damn thing?" he mutters, flicking the power button on and off.

A spark bursts from behind the power button, stinging his fingers. He yelps and withdraws his hand. The sparks continue, blue and bright, effervescent like bubbles in soda. *Pop, pop, pop!* The engine whirs shrilly, and Sebastian begins to cuss out loud, pressing down on the brake. The car speeds up instead of decelerating. Sweat breaks out on his forehead. He tries to correct, but the steering wheel doesn't budge.

"What the *fuck*?!" Sebastian roars, rattling the steering wheel with both hands and slamming on the brakes again.

The radio grows louder and louder, and I swear I hear someone giggling. Sebastian tries to remove the keys from the ignition, but the sparks shock him, and he howls in pain. He screams and starts tugging on his seat belt, but it won't budge. He casts a horrific look in my direction, lips peeled back in a snarl, the whites of his eyes nearly swallowing his irises whole— a rabid wolf ready to bite.

"What did you do, you little freak!?"

The music cuts out, but the radio is still on.

A soft whisper slices through the air like a knife: "Boo."

After Leorna discovered she was a medium, her high school sweetheart, Jeremiah Young, passed away in a car accident. He became a poltergeist, but after seeing his ability to continue a coherent conversation, Leorna begged their parents to not capture him. Sadly, they went against her wishes, and he was sent to the Beyond. Leorna has often cited this tragic event as the inciting incident for her activist career.

—Maroony Snow, *Speak Loud, Don't Whisper: A Biography of Medium Leorna Giles* (2015)

Chapter Twenty-Six

We come to a screeching halt, and I brace myself as I'm thrown against the dash. Sebastian isn't so lucky. His head collides with the steering wheel, knocking him out cold. Smoke, chalky and gray, rises from underneath the hood. I tug on my seat belt, and thankfully, it comes loose. I scramble to grab my phone. The door locks click open, and I stumble outside, falling to my knees. My fingers sink into the wet, muddy earth as I rise to my feet. The rain has stopped. The forest is quiet.

But the radio still crackles.

"Shut the door," Cyrus says.

"The—"

"*Shut. The. Door.*"

Confused, I close the passenger door. Sebastian raises his head slowly, his eyes delirious. He watches me and screams in protest. The car locks automatically, and through the window, I can see the hand brake shift down. Smoke continues to rise from the hood, growing darker by the second, till it blends in with the night. The engine is on fire. Sebastian screams and fights, but he's firmly held in place by his seat belt.

Then smoke fills the cabin.

The man inside screams as he wrestles with his seat belt. A blue mist trails out of the exhaust pipe, and piece by piece, Cyrus materializes in front of me. She lifts her fingers to her forehead, her brows knitting in concentration as she focuses on the car. The hand brake snaps out of place and the engine growls, then roars as the car rockets over the side of the hill. A thunderous crash erupts through the peaceful night, and I cling to Cyrus, completely spooked. Drat. My backpack was in that stupid car.

"How?" I whisper, tears dripping from my eyes. "I didn't—I didn't know you were with me."

"In your phone, dum-dum."

"But I didn't see you enter it."

"Well, if you did, you probably would've yelled at me to get out." She smirks.

Spirits, how I thought I wouldn't see that sweet smile again. But the moment is short-lived. Raucous shouting, filled with expletives, cuts through the night once more.

Oh shit. He's not dead.

She squeezes my hand. "We gotta go."

I turn to leave, but my knees give out. She squats and helps me to my feet, has me wrap my arm around her shoulders. More raindrops hit my head—the storm is starting again. I don't think I'm injured, but the shock has drained my energy. My breathing is shallow and I have tunnel vision. It's like the night with the wraith all over again. I weep like a child. Cyrus only squeezes me tighter.

"You can't walk, can you?"

"N-no."

"Okay. Shit." She grunts, shifting under my weight. "We gotta get you out of this rain."

I hadn't noticed I was shivering until now. Cyrus stops and turns our bodies to the side, and we limp into the darkness of the woods. The entangled branches form a canopy above us, making it so I only catch glimpses of the moon. She helps me over every root we come across, moving forward determinedly, as if she has a destination in mind. It's clear she knows this place well. After a little while, we emerge into a clearing, where a small wooden shack rests. A *Keep Out* sign is affixed to the outside, scrawled in childlike writing.

Cyrus nods in the direction of downhill. "Tomai lives down the road from here. This is where a lot of the kids in their neighborhood used to play."

For a moment I want to ask her to take us to Tomai, but the exhaustion hits when she opens the door. The shack smells of old leaves and mildew, but at least it's somewhat dry. Old milk crates lie around, crayon drawings are pinned to the wall. Discarded toy army soldiers and Polly Pockets litter the floor. Cyrus picks up a blanket and shakes off some dirt, then wraps it around my shoulders and ushers me to sit down on a torn-up beanbag. I watch as she lays another blanket on the floor, and I notice something.

"What's that on your hands?"

"Nothing."

"Cyrus," I snap, my voice taut and thinned by the tears I am trying so hard to hold back. "Show me."

She sighs and approaches slowly. She crouches at my level, and when I see them, I can't help but sob, consumed by grief. Now I finally understand. I understand everything, and the weight of that knowledge hurts me more than my parents' betrayal ever could. The human skin recedes from her wounded fingertips; little glimpses of white bone emerge from the gummy edges where the ectoplasm has begun to build up. Little by little, the skin continues to recede at the pace of sand falling through an hourglass.

Everything makes so much more sense now: Why the blessed salt didn't work on her when we first met. Why she's so coherent and capable. Why her powers are so ridiculously strong when she knows how to use them. Cyrus isn't some new, special type of ghost. She's a wraith. A wraith in the earliest stages of its transformation—a rarity I don't think even the wisest and oldest of Apostles has come across.

The thing I feared the most has come true.

"Wh-why didn't you tell me?" I whisper, the tears rolling down my cheeks. I hiccup, trying to stifle the sound of my sobs, but I can't. "D-did you know this whole time?"

"I didn't know what I was turning into, but I knew it wasn't good. After you found me in the theater, I noticed parts of my body weren't…working quite right. And it was like the more I tried to remember how I died, the worse it was getting."

"B-but…but why?"

"At first it was because I didn't want you to be afraid of me. And then I didn't want you to worry."

"I'm so sorry. I'm so sorry. I'm so—"

"Shh. It's all right now." She speaks softly as she takes my hands in hers.

Her beautiful, scarred hands. The ones that have held me and protected me these past few days. Spirits above, I cannot imagine what this curse will do to her eyes. Her face. Her soul.

It will eat away at everything.

"Melody, listen to me. Whatever happens is going to happen."

"No," I sob and bury my face against her chest, stomping my feet like a child. "No, I can fix this, I can still save you—"

"No. You gotta worry about what you have to finish."

"I can multitask. I promise. I can't let you go." I swallow a hard lump of tears. "I won't."

A pained smile crosses her face. "I appreciate that. But I don't think it's in your control."

"It would be, if I was a medium." I grab my head, gritting my teeth in frustration.

She gently removes my hands, squeezing them again. Her touch is ice cold, but somehow, so comforting. It's funny, the texture of a ghost's skin is almost the same as a human's—maybe a bit damper, slicker, given the layer of ectoplasm they have, but for some reason I like it. I like feeling the grooves in her palms, the small notches and string scars on her fingertips she's accumulated over the years from playing various instruments. It's new yet familiar all at once, and instinctively, I want nothing more than to memorize the patterns traced onto her skin. We'll never get that chance.

I rub my thumb over her hand, and she winces.

"Sorry," she says, and as if suddenly self-conscious, she tries to withdraw her hands. "I know you probably find them gross."

"Why would I?"

"Well…the nubby, bony bits. And then the ectoplasm."

"They're not gross. No part of you is gross." I trace my fingertip over one of her scars, as if trying to memorize it. "I'll figure out a way to fix them before the curse takes you."

She chuckles. "You seem pretty confident for someone who almost got murdered."

"I don't think it's confidence as much as it's stupidity and stubbornness." I wince. "I'm sorry. For earlier, I mean. I was being selfish, and I was angry, and I was taking that out on you."

"It's okay—"

"No, it's not. You deserve better. I let my insecurities get the best of me tonight. Actually, that's been the case ever since you met me."

Tears well in my eyes as I try to figure out how to say what I've needed to tell her all along. I point to the scars on my cheek, which burn as anxiety builds.

"A wraith did this to me. I failed my First Sacred Hunt because of it, and my family and I had to move to this shithole island so that we can redeem ourselves in the eyes of the Council. And well now—now more people may die at this rally, and Brynne is dating someone else, and I still can't get my shit together to save my fucking life."

She hugs me tightly, pulling me off the milk crate. Spirits, I wish I wasn't so pathetic. I wish I wouldn't burden her with all these heavy emotions. I wish I could be the strong person I always thought I was. But I'm not. She lets me cry until my lungs give out, and when I'm quiet, speaks again.

"Are you supposed to have your shit together?" she asks as she rubs small circles on my back. It feels nice. Safe. "I don't think that's a fair expectation to have, y'know? Like, what do you mean by having your shit together?"

"I mean…" I trail off. "I mean…like being a good hunter and knowing what I want to do with my future, and not gaining thirty pounds."

She wrinkles her nose, her expression confused but also annoyed. "*Only* thirty? You're not fat. I mean, you're not remotely what I'd consider plus sized. You're midsized at best."

I twist the ends of my shirt, wringing out some of the excess water. "I know that. But I've always been a bigger girl and I let that get worse. I hate how I look. I lost all the muscles I worked to get, I filled out every area of my face, my body is covered in stretch marks… I feel ugly."

"Wait, you don't think you're pretty?"

In this body? With these scars? "N-no. Not really. Maybe when I put on makeup."

"I'm bigger than you. You think I'm ugly? You think it's bad for me to be fat?"

"No. But it's different for you."

She arches her brow. "Because I'm butch?"

"Because you're already pretty," I say, "so it doesn't matter."

My response catches her off guard. Her eyes bug out and she snickers like a child.

"Girl, be so fucking for real," she says, continuing to laugh. "I don't think anyone has ever called me pretty."

"But you *are*. You're confident, you're talented, you're kind. You—you've got a great smile, dimples, a strong sense of style. Being fat doesn't change any of that."

"But being midsized changes that for you?"

"It changes everything for me. I can't be… I can't…"

I don't know how to describe it, but every time I see the jagged scar that trails down the center of Mom's chest, I feel compelled to cut parts of my body off with scissors. Chop through all the blubbery layers of adipose and spiderwebs of stretch marks until I bleed out on the floor and finally meet the vague beauty standards inscribed in the columns of countless fashion magazines. Not only do I feel ugly, I feel unsafe. I feel like I'm setting myself up to go through the same things she did. I can't take a break. I can't like the body I'm in, because liking it means I'm okay with the consequences.

And I'm not okay with the consequences.

I can look at Cyrus all day long and admire her curves, the squareness of her shoulders, the way her ghostly body feels cool yet soft against my chest when she hugs me—how my heart flutters in my chest like a butterfly caught in a net. Her body is a home, the stuff of strength and goodness and comfort. Mine is a prison that aims to kill me slowly, and I'll never know how much time I'll have.

My lower lip wobbles. She tucks a strand of hair behind my ear and removes a leaf stuck to the top of my head. She chuckles a little bit.

"You know what makes me a good musician? Why I like music?"

I shake my head.

"Because I never pushed myself to be perfect at it. I loved it because it made me feel good. As long as I felt good doing it, it was worth doing. But if you live your life striving for perfection, instead of feeling good, you're going to burn yourself out. You're going to feel like shit. You know what also makes you feel like shit? Blaming and berating yourself for feeling like that. Also, not eating." She squeezes my hands. "We have *good* bodies, Melody. These are the only bodies we'll ever have. And we can both be beautiful—not despite or regardless of how big we are, but *because* of it. You're beautiful."

"Th-thank you."

"I mean it. You're a fox. Straight up."

I laugh. "Thank you."

She wipes a stray tear from my eyes. "You're welcome."

Maybe it's something in the way she's looking at me right now, or maybe it's that she rescued me, but there's this feeling of desire rumbling low in my stomach like thunder. I think it's been there ever since I met her, but up until this moment, I've been able to hold back—to resist that tidal wave of strange emotion. For one reason or another, I can't keep treading water. My feelings for her are too strong.

So maybe it's best to roll with the motions. Maybe it would be okay—just this once—to drown.

I lean forward and kiss her cheek. Cyrus's cheeks turn sapphire blue—the color rushing to fill the tips of her ears. She touches her lipstick-stained cheek, stunned, chuckling a little. A brief wave of shame overcomes me. I kissed her. I *kissed* her. If being her friend was a betrayal to my people, then kissing her is surely heresy.

But would the Spirits hold it against me for doing it when she looks at me like that?

"Wow." She chuckles as she rubs her face, and her eyes are so, so expectant.

I shouldn't do this. I know this. I know this, and yet my heart can't stop somersaulting in joyful acrobatic circles within my chest. And I can't stop staring at those intelligent brown eyes and sensitive little smirk and thinking about how it would feel to run my fingers over the buzzed edges of her hair and trace the intricate lines of her tattoos. Judging from how she's looking at me, she's thinking the same. She places her hands on my cheeks, and I feel this flash of cold, but when her lips press against mine, the heat overwhelms me. Her kiss is forceful, deep, and passionate. A wordless murmur escapes my lips, and she pulls away, rubbing the edges of her mouth with her thumb.

Suddenly I feel like the lights are off inside my brain and there's no one home. She kissed me back. And I loved every single second of it, even knowing she's a ghost—a wraith! Last time I had a wraith this close to my face it didn't end well. I kiss her again—and again, and again—and by the time I make it past three kisses, I'm wrapping my arms around her neck, trying to close every gap that's left between us. She murmurs something underneath her breath, and I break away, breathless.

"You okay?" I ask her, taking her face in my hands. "You okay with this?"

She smiles softly. "That's what I was trying to ask *you*."

"I'm fine! And you're good? You sure? If this is too fast for you, we can—"

"I'm good," she whispers. "As long as you keep kissing me."

I oblige and am ravenous as I do so. I can't hear over the sound of my heart pounding loud in my ears. More kisses lead to fingers sliding under shirts, and when she pulls me onto her lap, her hands holding me steady on the small of my waist, my body shudders at her touch. She smirks as I feverishly lean in for another kiss, leaning back so she's out of reach. Teasing me.

Her thumb rubs my bottom lip. "You would be, like, so easy to possess right now."

I smile. "Too late."

It should be noted that sirens are extremely dangerous individuals, as they have the power to control the flow of water, much like a water mage or witch is able to do. Sirens are a proud people, who have historically held great hostility for bipedal creatures, and have waged countless wars against land-dwelling Fantasticals. Over the years, their numbers have drastically plummeted thanks to their brutal clashes with land dwellers as well as environmental issues such as overfishing and water pollution.

Today, only an estimated twenty clans exist, and although their population counts are low, they show no interest in integrating with the rest of Fantastical society. Sociologists estimate that if the ocean temperatures continue to rise, we could see the end of the entire race as early as 2085, making them a prime candidate for the UN's Endangered Societies List.

—Wendy Wright, "Sirens," The Complete Fantastical Encyclopedia (2020)

Chapter Twenty-Seven

I wake up the next morning to find sunlight streaming through the cracks in between the damp wooden planks overhead. Cyrus lies next to me, her eyes closed, the collar of her shirt loose and crinkled. She looks so soft—so lovingly at peace despite everything that's happened. She doesn't need sleep anymore, so this is a bit of a rarity in itself. I take a mental snapshot of the adorable scene before nudging her awake.

"Hey," she says, her voice groggy. She stretches and yawns. "How'd you sleep?"

"Like ass," I reply, smirking. "My body is sore in places I didn't think it could be."

"You *did* get into a car accident last night. Not to mention what happened afterwards."

A blush rises to my cheeks, and I look at my discarded damp clothes on the other side of the shack. *Heresy, Melody. Heresy of the highest order.* Oh well. I can ask for forgiveness from the Spirits later…if the mood strikes me. Besides, we have to get to work.

"Wait, where are you going?" Cyrus is sitting upright.

"I don't know what time it is, but we have to get out of here."

I pull on my jeans and my shirt, wincing at the uncomfortably wet texture on my dry skin. I guess there's only so much that my clothes could've dried, given the quality of the roof above us.

"The Tamawotchi was in my backpack, which has now been burnt to a crisp, and my phone is dead, so we're kind of out of luck when it comes to hiding you."

"Melody, wait. We may have avoided her little henchman last night, but we're going to have to be extremely careful today. Redd and that guy will be looking for you. Plus, cops are going to be crawling all over the place, and Redd could be buying them off. We need a plan."

I cross my arms and consider this. "I'm all ears."

"We need irrefutable proof that Principal Redd is a siren before you go and make any accusations." Last night I explained everything I knew to Cyrus before we drifted off to sleep.

I sigh. "We need help. We can't do this alone anymore."

If we ever should have done it alone to begin with. And given everything that's happened? We shouldn't have.

"Are you saying we should tell your parents or something?" Cyrus asks, her eyes wide. "Your *ghost hunter* parents?"

"I mean…yes," I say quietly. "Not only to take her down, but because we need to find a way to help you."

Fear washes over me like rain in a thunderstorm. *That's right.* Last night, I learned that Cyrus is a wraith—and her curse is eating away at her hands, removing the bits and pieces of her that make her human. I'm not sure how much longer her body can last, and I don't know how to help her. Cyrus notices my discomfort and tries to tease me.

"You're still going on about that?" Her eyes are sad, but her grin is wide, easygoing. She tucks her arms behind her head and closes her eyes, satisfied. "Girl, you gotta learn how to prioritize. I'm doing awesome. I've unlocked a lot of ghosty powers, and I bagged a pretty hot girl last night."

I blush. "*Stop.*" I crouch down beside her and take her hand. "I promise I'll protect you. But at this point, they're the only ones with the weapons and the brainpower to help."

"Okay. We gotta figure out a way to get back to your house; let's hope they'll be there."

"Right. You know how yesterday, you disappeared? Do you know how you did that? You weren't playing music or anything."

"Aha, you didn't notice. I was tapping my foot against the ground. Seems like as long as I've got a basic beat and some rhythm, I can make it work. Although…only for a little while. I popped into your phone without you noticing, but I don't think I could've held it for much longer than that."

"So the *more* music, and the *louder* the music—"

"And the more *emotional* the song choice, given what happened at the theater the day we left—"

"The better your powers work. Do you think you could turn us both invisible?"

"No better way to find out than to try."

A pang hits my chest. "I'm sorry. I think your harmonica might've been in my backpack."

"Which is burnt to a crisp. Okay, okay…"

She takes my hand and tries to drum a beat against her thigh, but at best, it makes the outline of her body tremble in place, giving it a fuzzier appearance, almost like I'm viewing her through an old-school TV.

"I think you need more musical power. What if you tried singing?"

"I don't sing, Melody."

I put my hands on my hips. "Oh, come on. How bad could you be?"

"You'd be surprised."

I squeeze her hands. "What if I sang with you? Could you try to match my pitch and follow along?"

"I guess it's worth a shot."

I try to figure out the song I remember best and settle on one I sang when I was in the chorus of *West Side Sorcerers*. It's not much, and my voice is definitely rusty, but it seems to do the trick. When I sing the first few notes, she picks up on the tune and joins me. Her voice is rough—I don't think she has the vocal power to hold a note for that long—but she's managing to harmonize well, for someone who doesn't sing. A smile breaks out across my lips and I notice the twinkle in her eyes as we move through the song. Cyrus's grip on me tightens as the edges of her outline fade into nothingness, and I watch as the same vanishing trick races up my arms, until slowly, like a fading photograph, I disappear.

Being invisible is this weird, tingly sensation. My bones feel heavier, but my skin feels prickly—like I'm on the brink of zapping my body with a million static shocks. Despite this exhaustion, my hand squeezes hers tight.

"You can stop now," Cyrus says.

I close my mouth, and we both hold our breath, waiting to see if she can maintain her form. She grunts in frustration.

"You okay?"

"I'm okay, but…" She hisses through tightly clenched teeth. She's in pain. "This is going to be hard."

"What if we keep humming or taking turns?"

"We can try. It's better than nothing."

"What do you think is the fastest way back to my place?"

"Let me try to lead."

Slowly, with our hands tightly interlocked, we maneuver out of the door. I continue to hum as we move along, and when I pause to take a breath, Cyrus joins in. My palm feels slick with sweat and my heartbeat echoes through my chest, pinging off my rib cage like a submarine sonar. She leads us away from the forest, down the hill, toward some of the houses. We slink between the privacy fences of two different yards to get to the street. A cop car rolls by, its windows down, and a little peep of fear escapes my mouth. Cyrus squeezes my hand.

"Keep quiet," she whispers.

I clamp my mouth shut and for a moment, our song seizes. When the cop car turns the corner, we make a break for it. Our shoes scuffle against the sidewalk and gravel crunches underneath our feet as we sprint along. Cyrus guides us through more backyards, across roads, around the corners of buildings. My hand begins to cramp, throbbing in pain from the pressure of being held for so long, but I don't dare let go until we arrive on my street. As long as I'm holding her hand, I'll be okay.

I stand in the center of the sidewalk, panting, gripping my knees for support. Not even my damp clothes can cool the sizzling heat on my body. Ugh. I *desperately* need a shower. Cyrus urges me to keep going. In one giant gulp, I suck air into my lungs and sprint for the house, finally releasing her from my grip. She continues to hum behind me as I grab the fake rock from the landscaping beside the front step and fumble with the keypad to unlock it. My heart climbs up the back of my throat as I scroll through the number lock and enter in my date of birth. When I finish the combination, I tug on it, but it's not opening. It's not— it's not *opening*? They changed the combination to the fake rock?! As I continue to struggle, my skin melts into view, starting at my fingers and inching up my body at the pace of raindrops falling on a windowpane. *Shit, shit, shit.* I'm becoming visible again.

Behind me, tires crunch against gravel, eerily slow, as though they're inching closer to me. *Cop car.* Has to be. I don't dare turn around to face it. Gritting my teeth, I rattle the door handle, completely out of ideas, and desperate to get out of the street before someone spots me.

But then the door opens.

"Melody?"

I look up and see Simon, his eyes wide, face as white as snow. I must look like a mess, with my hair sweaty and tangled, and my clothes damp and smelling of soot. Despite everything that happened between us yesterday, I've never been happier to see him. Gulping back tears, I fling my arms around him, and he ushers me inside then locks the door. I stammer nonsensically, struggling to explain everything I've been hiding these past few days, but I'm also panicking because I don't know if Cyrus made it inside. Simon squeezes my shoulders and demonstrates a deep-breathing technique, and I inhale, inhale, inhale, before exhaling in a gust of wind. I do this about five times until I can finally calm down enough to speak in coherent sentences.

"Where have you been?" he whispers.

He touches the scar along my forehead, the one Sebastian tore into my face. His eyes tremble with fear, like by seeing that wound and my general disheveled appearance, he knows something is horribly wrong.

My face crumples. He shushes me and pulls me close to him, rocking me back and forth in his arms. As he holds me, I tell him everything about Jackie and Principal Redd, about the earring, about the man who almost drove me to my demise. His body stiffens, but he doesn't let go.

"How did you get away?"

I gulp down air. "You need to promise…"

"Promise what?"

"Promise me you won't freak out."

"You went missing and came home all bloody, and you don't think I'm going to freak out?"

"Simon. *Please.* I know I've been awful to you. I know I've turned away your help constantly these past few days. But I need you to be on my side this time and promise me you'll be able to handle *exactly* what I'm telling you."

He nods, his expression gravely serious. "I promise."

A cold hand brushes against mine. Oh good, Cyrus *did* follow us inside, but she's still invisible. I wrap my hand around hers, and I'm well aware that to Simon, it looks like I'm holding air. She trembles in my grasp, and I squeeze her hand, urging her to relax. Slowly, vapor by vapor, she begins to reappear, until she's standing right beside me.

She gives a little nod to Simon. "Sup?"

Simon's eyes are wide; he opens his mouth as if to say something, but then clenches his jaw shut. After a few moments, he releases an exasperated sigh and places his hands on his hips.

"You," he says, "are in big trouble, young lady."

"You just promised me that you wouldn't freak out."

"I am totally calm," he says at a volume that would suggest otherwise. "But this—I *knew* something was going on." His expression shifts from frustration to wonder as he gazes upon Cyrus. His hand hovers over his heart. "What *are* you? Sorry, *who* are you?"

Cyrus bites her lip and nervously shows him her hands. Little wisps and vapors drip from her fingers. The outline of her body quakes.

"I'm Cyrus. And uh, I... I think I'm a wraith."

To my surprise, Simon takes her hands and examines them. He's not afraid to touch the bony bits jutting from the flesh.

"My... I think you're right." An excited laugh escapes his lips, which he doesn't try to restrain. "Spirits, do you know how rare this is? Do you know how special you are?"

"Melody might've mentioned it once or twice," Cyrus says with a wink.

She's gonna be the death of me.

"Well, this is delightful."

"Except for the whole turning into a flesh-eating monster thing."

"Oh, right, right. But you don't experience any kind of craving or bloodlust?"

"Uh, at this time, no, thankfully. No hunger pangs of any sort, really."

"Well then, that's good."

I look at Simon. "Do you think you could help her? Y'know, *stop* her from turning into a wraith? Is there any way to reverse this process?"

"Reverse the…" he repeats slowly, and his face is crestfallen. He looks between the two of us. "I'm sorry, girls, I don't think I know of anything off the top of my head."

"Cyrus has been helping me. And she's going to help me take down Redd. But we need a plan, and I need…"

I'm surprised by the lump of tears rising in my throat. Even though Simon is clearly sympathetic, I don't want him to know how much she means to me. I know that I've crossed a line by getting this close to her—have crossed several lines as of last night, in fact—but Cyrus is right. She's one in a million. Once in a lifetime.

"She doesn't want to go yet, Simon. She doesn't want to go."

Simon nods, understanding. He offers Cyrus his most reassuring smile. "I'm sure I can figure something out. Might take a little bit of research, but then again, research is my specialty."

"That would be—that would be awesome," Cyrus stammers, completely taken aback by his kindness. "Thank you."

I am *also* somewhat surprised by the confidence in his answer, but then again, he kinda owes me one after all the drama he's caused in my family life—or rather, the drama Dad has caused.

You know what, if they want to refer to themselves as one parental unit, then they can collectively owe me one.

"Thank you," I chime in. "Simon, where are my parents?"

"Where do you think they are? They're out looking for you. I could call them, but—"

"Don't," Cyrus says. "If the cops are in on this, they could be bugging the phone lines."

"I have to do *something*. Her parents will hop a ferry and start searching the mainland if they have to." Simon sighs. "I can try to find them. But you two—you have to stay here. No more running off on your own. Okay, Melody?" He pulls on his coat. "I kept my promise, so you can at least give me that."

"Aye, aye, Captain."

"Funny. If you're hungry, there are mini corn dogs in the freezer and some homemade aioli in the fridge. Also, put on a turtleneck or something."

"I'm sorry?"

He points to his neck. "Don't worry; you don't even have to ask. I'll keep that one a secret too."

Bewildered, I reach my hand up to touch my neck, and I can't feel anything except a tender spot. But from the expression on Cyrus's face, and the way her cheeks are turning a deeper shade of blue, I'm able to put two and two together.

It's a hickey.

Simon has seen a hickey on my neck, and for the briefest of seconds, I kinda wish I had burned alive in that car last night.

"Lose the look," Simon says, rolling his eyes. "You are *so* seventeen that I'm getting secondhand embarrassment."

He exits out the front door, locking it behind him. Jaw slack, I turn toward Cyrus, who only offers a sheepish smile in return.

"Sorry. You're good with makeup though, right?"

When asked if she approved of ghost-human relationships during a provincial conference in 1968, Giles declined to take a formal stance on the issue, instead insisting that individuals (including spirits) be allowed to make the decision for themselves. This in itself was a radical statement for the time period, one that convinced Nataya Brown to formally eject her from the next provincial conference.

—Maroony Snow, *Speak Loud, Don't Whisper: A Biography of Leorna Giles* (2015)

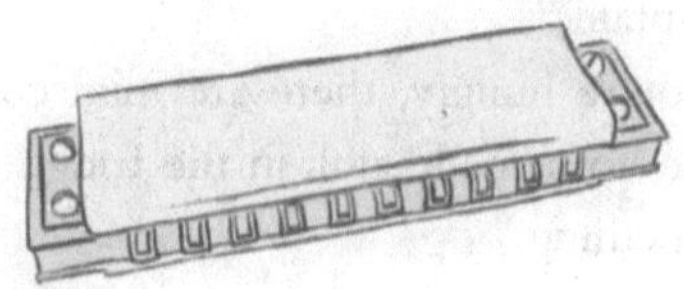

Chapter Twenty-Eight

When Simon returns home with my parents, they are simultaneously overjoyed and pissed. Mom throws her arms around my neck and sobs for what feels like eons, and even Dad is tearful: he can't help but stammer through his apologies. By the time Cyrus reveals herself, though, all those feel-good emotions are gone. Dad looks at her the way he looks at me when I ask for something at Target that's not on sale.

"What the hell is that?" Dad asks.

Simon rolls his eyes. "*Dean.*"

"You're working…with a ghost?" Mom whispers, her eyes wide.

A mischievous smile crosses her lips, like she's somehow thrilled by this secret. I wonder if she's thinking that the fact we're here together proves I'm actually a medium.

Dad remains alarmed. "What the hell kind of ghost is that?"

"She has a name, Dean."

I launch into my account of the past few days: meeting Cyrus, going behind their backs to do the investigation, my face-off with Sebastian. I'm sure to emphasize the fact that Cyrus, baby-wraith extraordinaire, saved my life, and distinctly leave out the part where I had sex with a ghost. Thankfully Simon keeps his word and remains silent, so now I owe him a favor.

Frick.

My parents take this in slowly, their eyes wide with disbelief, but after a few moments of silence, they seem to accept it. Dad rubs his hands together vigorously and stares at the wall, deep in thought.

"Military," he decides.

"Military?" Mom snorts. "And say what? A lady with a bad platinum-blond dye job is a serial killer? They're not going to call in the military for that."

"Where one siren is, many follow. That's how they work," Dad says.

"I don't think Jackie is aware," I say. "She told me she was a selkie, and I think she believes that."

"See, Dean?" Mom says. "We can't call the military. Why is your first thought always to call the military?"

"Because they have bigger, scarier weapons than we do. We're a family of four and our daughter's ghost friend."

"Let's not panic," Simon says, motioning for everyone to calm down. "We can do this. We have weapons of our own here. Besides, with the storm that rolled through last night, I wouldn't be surprised if radio communications were disabled, too—if we could even *find* a radio."

"Do we have proof? Do we have any evidence she was responsible for any of this to begin with?" Dad asks. "I mean, what do we have that connects her to the scene?"

"The earring, the ectoplasm—well, slime—on the bodies. We could have that sent in for testing," Simon replies, folding his hands together. "You're also forgetting we have eyewitness testimonies. I think we have a lot of incriminating evidence."

"That's true. But what motivation? I mean, why would an educator want to kill all those kids? Just so she could eat them? She couldn't eat anyone else?"

Simon snorts. "I'm sorry, you're asking why an educator wouldn't want to kill some unruly teens and eat them?" We all stare at him till he turns red in the face. Flabbergasted, he throws up his hands. "Come on! I am simply stating the obvious."

"No…" Mom murmurs. "It's not obvious. We know sirens like to eat humans and humanoid Fantasticals, but we don't know why she picked the targets she picked. It's so bizarrely hateful I'm having a hard time wrapping my head around it."

Dad strokes the stubble along his chin. "I don't want Melody involved in this anymore. It's too risky."

"Dean," Simon says, and there's this tenderness in his voice that surprises me. I had no idea Simon could sound like anything other than a machine, honestly. "Your daughter is right here, in the room with us, asking you to please help her finish what she started. I know you're afraid—I am too—but the time for us to be divisive and not listen to each other is over. The time for action is now. That's what families do."

Dad looks at me, and there's a graveness in his brown eyes that hurts me. For a moment I think I see tears, but then he ducks his head and sniffs loudly, so I can't tell. My mind flashes back to that fateful moment when he pressed the cloth to my cheeks—how he had desperately tried to get the bleeding to stop. His worst nightmare almost came true for the second time last night.

"You're not going to lose me, Dad."

He flinches and chews on the inside of his cheek. He paces the living room in a circle for a few moments, then finally his sluggish steps cease, and he turns to face me.

"Okay. But I can't promise I'm not going to kick this lady's ass."

Simon rolls his eyes. "He's always one for violence, isn't he?"

Mom laughs.

Once our heartwarming family moment is over, we jump into planning. Dad and Mom suggest we all go to the school before the rally starts tomorrow, so we won't be noticed. I point out that this year, the pep rally isn't being held at the school, but outside at the beach.

"That would be Southwind Beach. It's closest to the school," Cyrus explains.

Dad's eyes widen. "If it's on the beach, that means she's—"

"Bringing other sirens to it," Simon says. "Why else would her teacher… What was her name again?"

"Ms. Ruder," I say.

"Right," Simon says. "Why would she have said something was going to happen at the pep rally?"

"Honestly, I'm not quite sure. She must've been conducting her own investigation, but I think we can figure that out later, yeah?"

Mom scrolls through her phone, presumably reading through some sort of wiki on sirens. "Sirens are strongest when they're close to large bodies of salt water. If the pep rally is on the beach, she's going to be at her most powerful. We may not know what she's planning, but based on that information alone, it can't be good."

"I mean, think about it," Simon says. "She's going to be down at the beach, close to the ocean, where she's strongest, with a *ton* of children surrounding her. And Dean said it himself. Where one siren is, many more follow. So…"

It takes a minute for it to register with us, but when it does, Mom lets out a startled yelp, and her hands move to cover her mouth. Brown eyes tremble. "You—she's going to—"

Eat the kids.

She and her clan are going to eat all the kids at the pep rally.

Simon nods. "She can use her song to lure them into the ocean, and they'll go under in minutes."

Dad shakes his head. "I still think we should call the military. The coast guard—"

"Dean." Simon rolls his eyes.

"Let's focus," I interject. "How can we stop her singing?"

We sit in silence. Dad crosses his arms and stares hard at the floor. Mom sighs, her fingertips tracing the wooden grooves in our table. Simon removes his glasses and pinches the bridge of his nose, squeezing his eyes shut so hard, it's like he's trying to conjure up an answer to appear in front of him.

"Noise?" Cyrus asks.

My family turn to look at her. She gives us a confused look, one eyebrow arched. She gestures to her ears.

"Noise? Like, volume? I thought aquatic creatures hated loud noises. Like whenever my dad took me to the aquarium on the mainland, he always told me not to bang on the glass because it would upset the dolphins."

Simon scrolls through his phone. "That could work. Says here that 'Sirens, like other aquatic creatures, use sonar to communicate with one another as well as navigate.' So making noises would not only interrupt her song, but it would mess with their sonar."

"Do we have a way of making a sound *loud* enough to mess with her hearing?" Dad asks.

"Well, we're going to have to make do with what we have." Mom rubs her hands together excitedly, the spark lighting anew within her eyes. "All we need is sound. It's a pep rally. There's going to be sound—microphones, amps, speakers."

Cyrus nods. "Yep. There will be all of that there for sure."

"You could play music," I say. "If you keep making constant noise, that should be enough for us to take them down."

"Uhh…sure, if I had my harmonica. But that went up in flames last night."

"What about your violin?" The case is still sitting in my closet, probably collecting dust.

"I don't have an acoustic pickup." When we all stare blankly back, she sighs and elaborates. "In order to connect an acoustic violin to an electric amplifier, you need an acoustic pickup. I had a pickup, but I didn't have it with me in my case."

"Well, where did you have it?"

"At my home. My parents' home." She says slowly, as if she's stumbling on the emotional weight of the words, then shakes her head. "It'd be better if I used another instrument—an electric guitar or something."

"We definitely don't have an electric guitar lying around. I haven't owned one since my twenties," Dad says, scratching the back of his head.

"What a rough time that was," Simon grumbles.

"Do you know if your parents still live on the island?" Mom asks.

A distant look glazes over Cyrus's eyes. If her hands weren't above the table, I'd reach across and squeeze one of them to give her some encouragement. It hurts me to see her like this, feeling so small and vulnerable.

"I don't know. I…don't remember where I used to live. I have a lot of memory loss issues in general."

"I was supposed to help her figure that out," I chime in. "But we got distracted with everything else."

Mom's lips turn upward in a soft, gentle smile—the same smile Mom would give me when I'd spill milk on the kitchen counter as a kid learning to pour my own cereal. "Do you remember what your last name is? Or any kind of details about your home?"

"Paredes-Pantazis. The house had…ivy on it, I think?" she chuckles nervously, squeezing her eyes shut. "I know they ran a Greek restaurant in town."

Simon types into his phone. "Paredes-Pantazis… Thank you, Yellow Pages." He looks at us. "Yeah, your parents are still here. I have the address."

"Really?" Her eyes widen. "Sick!"

"Should one of us go over there?" Dad asks. "I don't want you girls driving around by yourselves. Not when there's people looking for you, Mel. Absolutely out of the question."

A nervous expression crosses Cyrus's face and she glances over at me. She doesn't want to go alone with my dad. I can't blame her, either. My dad is a stranger who, up until twenty minutes ago, would've wanted to suck her into a cap-can. Not to mention the last time she was in a car alone with a man, he freaking murdered her.

"I think Cyrus would feel better if I came with," I tell Dad gently, and Cyrus nods. "Besides, I can help explain to her parents what happened."

"I don't—"

Simon casts a sharp glare in Dad's direction. "Do you *really* think strangers are going to invite you, a middle-aged man, into their home? You think you're more nonthreatening than a teenage girl?"

"I don't look threatening. Rach, do I look threatening?"

Mom sighs.

I dunno (sic) *if Mom and Dad will see me the same way again. But I dunno if I want them to.*

—Cyrus Paredes-Pantazis on coming out as a lesbian, diary entry (2016)

Chapter Twenty-Nine

I dress in inconspicuous black clothes: yoga pants, hoodie, baseball cap. Comfortable, but not superfashionable—I look like an emo girl going to watch a softball game while on her period. But my parents insist that I dress like this to avoid drawing attention to myself. I climb into the back seat while Dad drives, and Cyrus possesses my freshly charged phone. The landscape of Murkmore blurs by us, the number of buildings slowly diminishing until we're in a more isolated section of town. Here the terrain is rockier, grittier, and the beach grass is sparse and scraggly. I thought Cyrus said her parents ran a restaurant in town, so what are they doing all the way out here?

It's a small Cape Cod-style home. Shingles are peeling off the roof in places, and the eggshell-blue siding is speckled—probably battered by year after year of torrential rain. A long portico sits adjacent to the home, with a minivan and a pickup truck resting underneath it. On the exterior wall nearest to the driveway, a trellis blooming with wisteria leans; the lilac flowers have faded to a quieter shade of blue gray.

It's peaceful here—so peaceful they probably don't get much company. When we pull into the driveway, a woman exits the house, her shoulders stiff, chin tilted up in a prideful, powerful pose. In one hand she grips a broom. She is stout, with square, firm shoulders; it's obvious she's Cyrus's mother, but unlike her daughter, her raven hair is long and tied upright in a messy bun. Wispy pieces, thin like the shawl wrapped around her body, frame the edges of her soft, oval-shaped face. She pulls her shawl tighter and folds her arms against her chest.

"No soliciting," she says.

I wave my hands. "We're not here to solicit. We're here to—"

"We're not interested."

"It's about your daughter."

Her tone is as sharp as a knife's tip. "If you're a reporter come to ask me questions about my baby girl *again*, you need to—"

"I'm not," I say, gesturing to my clothes with a look of confusion. "I'm—I'm not a reporter. I'm a ghost hunter."

"You…"

Her eyes widen. She looks at the car, then back at me, then sighs. Much like her daughter, when she is frustrated, her shoulders slump forward. Wordlessly, she motions me in the direction of the front door. Dad tells me he's going to keep watch in the car. I follow Mrs. Paredes-Pantazis.

Inside is a mess of boxes full of restaurant pamphlets, old menus, and other related trinkets. Some of these boxes are emblazoned with the logos of food corporations or farmer's markets. Religious iconography—budded crosses and photos of saints I don't recognize—also decorates the walls alongside colorful woven textiles and tapestries. As we make our way to the kitchen, I'm overwhelmed by the smell of basil and other herbs, and when I see the assortment of colorful pots on the counter, I realize why.

"A ghost hunter," she repeats. "Pah. What do you want with me?"

"I…" I reach into my pocket and pull out the phone. "You might want to sit down for this."

With wide, doe-like eyes, Cyrus's mother takes a seat at the table. She's trembling, almost. I set the phone on the table and it vibrates erratically in place. When the blue mist leaks out, she is slack-jawed, her chest shuddering as if she's unable to breathe.

Cyrus looks at her mother. "Hi, Mamá."

Her mother whispers her name, tears dripping from her eyes. She reaches out and hugs her tightly, for what feels like years, then kisses both of her cheeks. Cyrus returns the gesture but says nothing. She doesn't utter a single word, but when her mom holds her, she cries silent tears. Her mother cups her face in her hands and presses their foreheads together, murmuring something in Spanish I can't understand.

"Mi corazón, mi corazón," she sobs, chanting the words like a prayer. "You've returned to me."

I'm so quiet during their conversation you would've thought *I* was the ghost. Cyrus's mom Alondra makes coffee for each of us and sets the *briki*, or coffeepot, in the center of the table, but the drinks remain untouched. For nearly an hour, Cyrus and her mom sit, talking about the past year's events and explaining the circumstances of her death. It's hard for Alondra to make it through the conversation without sobbing or cursing, but she musters up all her strength to do it. Her hands clench fistfuls of damp tissue, and every once in a while, she'll aggressively wipe the tears that fall. By the time we finish explaining what happened and why we're here, she's still confused.

"Why didn't you come home, my love?" she whispers. "Why would you not return to us? ¿Qué pasó?"

Cyrus wipes the tears from her eyes and stares hard at the table. "Because I couldn't remember anything. I thought I was"—there's a tremor in Cyrus's voice that makes her sound like a little kid—"waiting for someone to realize I was stuck in the theater. But no one ever showed up. And now, learning the truth about what happened, I mean…I feel ashamed."

"Ashamed?" I echo, surprised. "What? Why?"

"Because…I left my drink unattended and picked it back up. I made one little mistake and now I've ruined everything. All my chances for getting into Strengstorm, gone."

"Leaving your drink unattended doesn't give *anyone* the right to drug you," I whisper. "That's not your fault, Cyrus. What happened to you was not your fault."

"And by the principal of your school, no less," her mother chimes in, clenching her fists together. "As your oddly dressed friend says, it was not your fault. I would've expected your school to be the one place you were safe."

"And I'm positive Strengstorm would still love to have you," I tell her, "because ghost or not, you are still a once-in-a-lifetime talent."

Cyrus smirks. "Maybe now an eternal talent."

"We can hope." I squeeze her hand, my fingers rubbing the grooves in the knuckles still covered by flesh.

Cyrus's mother raises her eyebrows, noting our intimacy, but doesn't comment on it. Spirits, I am so thankful Dad isn't in here right now. I blush and retract my hand, sliding it underneath the table, and try to refocus my attention on Alondra, but from the corner of my eye, Cyrus's mischievous little grin teases me. She slips her hand below the table to continue holding mine.

"So what's the plan?" Alondra asks.

"I need my acoustic pickup," Cyrus says. "For my violin. We have a plan to take down Redd."

"I have no idea what that is or where it could be."

"That's—that's okay," she says, her voice thin with nervousness. "Did you put my stuff into boxes? Can we look at it?"

Alondra's mouth sets in a thin, firm line. She pushes back from the table and walks off down the hallway. Confused, Cyrus and I exchange glances before we leave our seats and follow her. She ascends the stairs like a woman possessed, perfectly poised, her hand gripping the railing every step of the way. When she reaches the landing, she turns left and opens a door there.

Alondra scoldingly looks at Cyrus. "And you thought I would've gotten rid of your stuff."

Her room is perfectly preserved—at least, that's what I'm assuming, given the look of shock on Cyrus's face as she steps into it. On her desk there're stray papers from some sort of homework assignment she never finished. Tacked to the walls are a ridiculous number of posters of musicians obscuring the eggshell-blue paint that lies underneath, along with flags from Greece and Ecuador. But the biggest surprise is the small collection of stuffed animals sitting on her bookshelf, alongside awards from numerous competitions. Cyrus immediately snatches a little Dalmatian toy off the shelf and hugs it to her chest. She buries her nose against its head.

"I can still smell it," she whispers.

For the next hour, Cyrus, Alondra, and I tear apart the absolute jungle that is Cyrus's walk-in closet. It's like she didn't know hangers existed. Musical sheets, adorned with countless little notes, lay across every flat surface. Clothes litter the floor, and there isn't a hamper in sight. I wonder if this means her mother let these dirty clothes fester here all this time.

That's not something I want to think about.

With a grunt, Alondra pulls a twenty-five-gallon plastic storage bin from its spot below a shelf and out into the center of the space. She cracks open the lid and for a moment I swear little clouds of dust flutter out like moths. Maybe those *were* moths. Uh-oh.

"If it's anywhere, it should be in here." She clicks her tongue against her teeth as she fumbles around in the bin. "You need to stay better organized."

"Wow, only been back in your life for three hours and you're already lecturing me about the mess I've made. You sure don't miss a beat, Mamá."

To which Alondra delivers a resounding smack on the back of her daughter's shoulder, and Cyrus cackles with laughter in response.

A smile tugs at the corner of Alondra's lips as she continues to dig around in the container. "Now's not the time for your jokes. Where is this thing?"

Cyrus leans over and peers into the box. "Sick! Found it."

And she withdraws what I can only describe as… Wow, that really *is* a doohickey—a thread, thin like those on headphones, with an aux cord at one end and some sort of clippy-hooky thing on the other. It's hard to imagine something as small and simple as this is what's going to save our asses tomorrow when we have to face off against Principal Redd, but anything's worth a shot when there's so much at stake.

Cyrus examines it for a moment, then nods. "Yep, this should work."

"Great." I check the time. It's almost when school will be out. I don't want to be out of my house when I know Redd isn't working at the school. Plus, in all likelihood, there'll be more cops on the road in the evening. "We should go."

"Oh." A soft expression crosses her face. She looks toward Alondra. "I'm sorry. I… I need to make sure I see this through to the end."

"Well…I guess the worst thing I can fear as a parent of a ghost is a ghost hunter." She arches a brow and smirks at me. I think I know where Cyrus gets her wily nature from. "You do what you need to do, *mija*. And then you come home to us, okay?"

For a moment, Cyrus glances down at her injured fingers. She's wondering if she can make that promise to her mom. But if she can't, I will.

"I'll bring her home safe," I tell Alondra. "And then maybe I can try some of that great Greek-Ecuadorean food Cyrus mentioned?"

There's a twinkle in her eye. "Looking forward to it."

Oddly enough, while siren society is deeply patriarchal, women are often the ones leading the clans. An estimated one in five hundred children born every year in these populations are male, a figure that has been consistent for the past several centuries. To the sirens, in the realm of warfare, there is no greater insult than killing the enemy's sons, as they are highly valuable...

—Thalia Lee, *Sirens Screaming: An Anthropological Account of a Community Ravaged by Environmental Disaster* (2015)

Chapter Thirty

When the bell rings at school the next day, I have never been more excited, and by excited, I mean eager to throw up. Sitting in the back of my parents' SUV, I watch as students exit out the side and front doors of the building, whooping cheerfully. Some make their way to the main road, while the majority proceed to the beach, blissfully unaware of the chaos about to befall them this afternoon. Mom and Dad nod affirmatively before I jump out of the car, violin case in hand. Today, I'm dressed as I normally would be, but my sunglasses are on, and a pair of earplugs are jammed into my pants pocket. When Redd belts out her lil' siren song, I won't be bewitched.

Tomai finds me in the crowd but doesn't look at me directly. I used Mom's phone to find them on Facebook and message them last night so they could help us. As the person elected by the office to help with audio setup on the beach, they're going to help me connect Cyrus's violin to the system.

My grip tightens on the handle of the case. "We'll be good, right?"

Tomai nods, focused on walking the path ahead of them. "As long as Redd doesn't check the equipment—which, I don't know why she would."

I place my sizzling phone in their outstretched palm, and a little pang of fear reverberates through my chest. Cyrus is holed up inside of it now, but when Redd takes the stage, we'll be ready. We continue to walk past the school grounds, down the road, to the little hill that leads us to the shore before I pass the violin case to Tomai and we part ways.

Dozens of metal bleachers sit on the beach, six to a row, with the stage and podium resting in front of them. From the stage, amp and microphone cables wind and twist their paths through the sand, connecting to a couple of electric generators sitting a safe distance away. Band students dressed in uniform, cheerleaders holding pom-poms, and ROTC kids clasping provincial flags scramble to their seats, close to the front. Some of the townsfolk also filter in, carrying beach chairs and blankets.

I hope Cyrus can get her powers under control today without going overboard. Last night after we got home and she stopped possessing my phone, I noticed her hands looked worse for wear—like the skin had receded to the top knuckle on her fingers. It seems like her powers could be making things worse, which means not only do *we* not have a lot of time, but she doesn't have long until her humanity is gone for good.

I stay at the back of the crowd, watching above the sand dunes and looking out toward the blue waters of the ocean. The waves are unusually foamy today, rolling in erratic motions. The water seems oddly stormy compared to the sunny sky overhead. I could swear I see glimpses of shimmering scales sparkle in the light before diving beneath the surface. If there're other sirens out there, they are far away right now. Here's hoping they'll stay away. I keep my eyes on Tomai, still down in the front, diligently connecting strings and cords. No one is bothering to supervise them. Good. That'll make this so much easier.

"I knew this would be chaos," a familiar voice mutters underneath her breath, and I resist the urge to look in her direction.

My stomach lurches in fear. *Redd.* I watch as she descends the wooden steps, past the bleachers, toward the podium. I reach into the pocket of my pants and fumble for my earplugs, then subtly cram them in. Tomai anxiously glances in my direction, then returns to prepping the cables. Thankfully there are so many boxes in front of them I don't think anyone can see the violin case. Tomai finishes what they're doing and wipes their silk-sticky palms on their shorts. Even from this distance, I can make out the nervous sweat glistening on their skin in the sparkling afternoon sun. They shuffle off to their seat, joining one of the front rows of bleachers. Out of the corner of my eye, I notice my parents' car pull up alongside the curb. More kids settle in around me, and I shift and wiggle in my seat to keep Redd in my sight.

"Young lady, you need to take those glasses off right now."

Confused, I turn in the direction of the voice. It's Mr. Ernest, the teacher who tried to stop me from leaving the school the other day.

"But the sun hurts my eyes," I whine.

He opens his mouth as if to say something, but to my surprise, someone comes to my rescue. Ms. Ruder. She places a hand on his shoulder and smiles firmly up at him. He flinches at her touch, as if fearful.

"She's wearing sunglasses outside. That's fully appropriate."

She places her hand against his back and ushers him to where the teachers are sitting. I'm so grateful she's on my side today. Shrill feedback from the speaker pierces the air, and some of the kids murmur their discontentment. Redd stands at the podium, microphone in hand. A plastic water bottle sits within reach. My stomach churns as I fold my trembling hands on my lap. This is not going to be good.

"Good afternoon, Murkmore Marauders! Who is ready to show off their school pride?"

Polite cheering echoes from the crowd. Smatterings of applause. The usual. Redd nods, as if unbothered by all of this. She clears her throat before speaking again, a polite smile on her lips.

"I know you were expecting a fully rousing day of festivities. But I'm afraid this year, there's been a change of plan."

The students exchange confused looks. Ms. Ruder stiffens in her seat, her eyes wide. Redd's smile doesn't falter.

"Yes. It's unfortunate our school has been plagued by so much tragedy. Then again, none of us are strangers to it, are we?"

Her smile seems to widen, almost unnaturally so. She surveys the crowd, which is murmuring nervously.

"When the fishing industry sank, this town may as well have sank with it. Sunk right into the sea. That would've been preferable."

She paces the stage, microphone still in hand.

"But even when you knew there were no more fish left to harvest sustainably, you kept going. 'To persevere.' Isn't that the Murkmore way?"

She stops and faces the crowd. The smile has evaporated from her face.

"Except none of you ever considered how the Murkmore way might be hurting others. That your greed, and reckless desire to never give up could lead to devastating consequences for others."

A girl breaks away from her seat and scrambles onto the stage. It's Jackie. Her bright-blue eyes are wide with alarm as she urgently whispers to her mother, parts of her muffled speech amplified by the microphone. I wonder if she's begun to put two and two together since my disappearance. Redd gazes lovingly at her daughter and strokes her cheek, but Jackie stiffens at her touch, as if frozen in place. Her brow furrows, lips pressed together in a thin line, and even from this distance, her knees visibly begin to tremble, her body teetering like a wispy willow tree in a ferocious wind.

"Jackie. Many of you know Jackie, my daughter. Captain of the tennis team, thanks to Wendell's death. Took over as class president when Tyreese died. And last year, she made first chair in the orchestra, after our school's golden girl, Cyrus, passed away."

She looks back at the crowd.

"My daughter has far surpassed my expectations—has lived out more dreams than I could've ever hoped to have, at such a young age. Isn't that worth applauding?"

Jackie shakes her head and whispers "No" under her breath, but some of the kids clap their hands, thinking this is a joke. More concerned expressions emerge on the faces of students and teachers, a few of whom have anxiously stood up. Ruder is one of them. Her eyes have laser-focused onto the stage, mouth in a firm line. Gripped tight in her hand is her handy tape measure, like she's about to use it as a weapon. Redd laughs haughtily at it all, clearly deeply amused.

"Yes, yes. You see, I didn't grow up in Murkmore. At least not right in it."

Her arm swings wide, gesturing to the vast open expanse of blue behind her.

"There. That is where I lived. With my people. What was left of them."

Jackie whimpers, begging her to stop. Her voice grows in volume, but Redd ignores her. Gritting her teeth, Jackie firmly demands that she stop. In a flash, Redd releases Jackie, then backhands her. The feedback from the microphone clashes with Jackie's scream as she collapses. The crowd cries out. Murmurs and hisses of "Siren" ripple through the crowd. More teachers, parents, and townsfolk scramble to their feet. A woman wails, so hysterical I have to wonder if she's the mother of one of the victims. Ruder shouts something I can't understand. Redd ignores it. She clicks her tongue against her teeth.

"You see, Murkmorians, your overfishing meant my people had less to eat. You caused a mass famine that took so many of us to our graves. So many young children. Many of them didn't have the privilege to grow as old as you, my love."

Redd casts a disgusted look at her daughter.

"My child may sympathize with you, but she doesn't know better. I suppose this is what I get for raising her amongst you, rather than returning to our people."

Jackie sobs. Her piercing eyes glare at her mother with complex hatred. She stumbles to her feet, her hand pressed against her wounded cheek, which is beginning to swell.

"Mom!" Her sobs are splintered by her screams. "Please!"

Redd sighs, tired by her daughter's opposition. The waves behind swell. The shimmering I saw earlier wasn't an illusion or some trick of the light. There's *something* out there, bobbing in the background: sirens, hungry and lying in wait, but the crowd hasn't noticed them yet. Redd migrates back to the podium and, with her free hand, unscrews the lid to her water bottle to take a sip. Her lipstick smudges but she gulps it down like it's the elixir of youth. With a satisfied sigh, she smacks her lips together before continuing.

"The famine forced my family onto your land so that we wouldn't starve to death. I grew up amongst you—living in the shadows, weak. Over the years I watched as you grew greedier and greedier. Your own businesses have struggled, and yet you abandon your lifeblood to shop at the big-box stores on the mainland. Your children are falling behind, and yet you refuse to invest in their education. Any cultural institutions you've had have been lost to time. And no matter how hard I tried to fit in with you, I simply couldn't help myself. Your pathetic, desperate struggle to stay here by any means necessary makes no sense to me. That my society would collapse, while your people thrive, is not right. Your children are your future: your only hope. It seems only right that I take them away from you!"

A cruel smile teases across her lips. A few adults break free from the stands and charge the stage, but Redd tips the water bottle over, spilling the contents from its mouth. She whistles and wiggles her fingers, coaxing the water close to her before freezing it in midair, completely solidifying it. Her song escapes her lips, muffled by my earplugs, and as she sings, and around me, a few people stiffen and their eyes darken. When I look at the girl standing next to me, her pupils are now solar eclipses, wide and all-consuming. For a moment, my head feels light and fuzzy like a caterpillar, but with the earplugs in, I'm able to concentrate and push through.

Other people aren't so lucky though. Her voice rolls over them in waves, flooding the bleachers row by row. The teachers closest to the podium collapse to their knees, jaws slack. I recognize this tune. It's the same one Tomai told me they heard the night Wendell died: *aah-aah-ah, ohh-ohh-oh.* Redd's vocal runs are both haunting and bewitching, climbing up and down scales effortlessly. She doesn't pause to take a breath.

She taps the rigid, icy glob, and it shatters, erupting in a series of spiky ice shards. They fly at the incapacitated adults, striking a few in the head, knocking them over. Kids in the back rows of bleachers are far enough away that they're not impacted by her song, so when they see this, they scream and leap to their feet. They scramble up the hill, colliding with one another in chaos. The people closest to the stage are still transfixed. Redd whistles sharply midsong, and with a flick of her wrist, they all stand, then begin a sluggish march toward the ocean.

At this moment, my parents and Simon, armed with their Phantom Prods, purple lights crackling, exit the car and rush forward. They wrestle with the bewitched, pulling them back from the ocean and jamming earplugs in to prevent them from going farther. I watch it all unfold as a blue mist rises from the boxes near the sound equipment. She seems like she's moving slower than usual. *Come on, Cyrus. Now's the time.*

About a dozen siren heads rise up in the distance, bobbing weightlessly above the raucous waves. They swim a little closer to the shoreline, enough to be able to stand in the shallow waters. Then their mouths open, and they join Redd's song. They are so loud, the air around us vibrates with their energy. Beaming with pride, Redd spills a little more water from her bottle, suspending it once more. Then she yanks Jackie to her feet and pins her arms behind her back. Jackie sobs as her mother drags her down the steps of the stage, heading in the direction of the ocean. Oh shit. She's gonna drag Jackie in with her. Once they get into those waves, there's no getting her back.

I whip out my Phantom Prod and press a button to extend it, then press another button to activate its electrical powers. After double-checking the placement of my earplugs, I push through the crowd, dodging people as I make my way toward them. Redd's attention snaps to my parents, who are wrestling with another student desperate to enter his watery grave.

"Dad!" I shout. "Watch out!"

He doesn't hear me, but Mom sees my mouth moving. She elbows Dad and points toward Redd, who has stretched out her water to the length of a whip. She sings a shrill note and flicks her wrist, whipping it at him. He narrowly avoids being hit, and it cracks against the sand with a thunderous boom, leaving a jagged dent. My parents take the kid and scramble away as fast as possible.

Enraged, Jackie screams wordlessly at her mother, but from the deranged look on Redd's face—she's gone. Her eyes are hollow as she gazes upon the girl that was once her daughter. As her lips pull back in a snarl, I realize now that Jackie is only an obstacle standing between her and her sick game of revenge.

"Jackie!" I cry out. "Come on! You have to fight her! Fight *hard!*"

With a sick twist of her head, Redd faces me. I expect her lips to curl back in a disgusted snarl, but instead her smile spreads wider, wider, wider, until it twists halfway up to her cheekbones, her cracking lips almost threatening to peel off her face. Her teeth have transformed into rows and rows of tiny spears. The pupils of her eyes, fishlike and bobbing in the endless sea of white, split and scatter in multiple directions.

With a singular song note, she twists her arm back and her water whip with it, and as she whirls it around in a circle above her head, it grows larger and larger—an absolute laser disc of death that will shred me into neat little ribbons. I know that if it connects, it will slice clean through me. Redd's voice grows in volume and power, undulating rapidly, inhumanly. The faster she performs her vocal runs, the faster the lasso spins. But I can't run away—Cyrus needs my help. Her blue outline is getting more and more corporeal. Tomai army-crawls across the sand over to the sound controls, their head tucked almost completely between their arms, trying to avoid Redd's wrath. If she turns around, she'll see them.

I cup a hand around my mouth and call out to her: "Sorry about your car! How's your henchman holding up by the way?"

That does it. Her lip twitches, and with a furious string of notes, she cracks the water whip forward. It soars over my head and I dive from the bleachers onto a nearby dune, narrowly avoiding its touch. Grits of sand fly into my eyes, nearly blinding me, and I rub them away. When I look back, the water has sliced cleanly through the metal. *Water magic is no joke, huh?*

"This time," Redd shouts, "I won't miss!"

With surprising agility, she twists the lasso and snaps it forward once more. It comes sailing over my head, like a flying saucer hovering to land. I can't get away fast enough. I squeeze my eyes shut. But I feel no water—nothing wrapping around my body, severing me in two.

Instead, I hear the agonizing scream of a woman.

Why should we show mercy to those who do not grant the same to the land upon which they live?

—Nicole Redd in an email to [name redacted], subject line "Family Reunion" (13 May 2021)

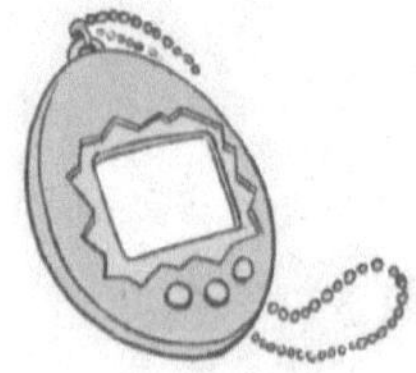

Chapter Thirty-One

When I open my eyes, standing before me is Ms. Ruder, the water whip wrapped tightly around her bicep, embedded above her elbow. Blood pulses from the wound, gushing downward, staining the sand maroon. Ruder grinds her teeth so hard I fear she might whittle them down to a pulp. I scramble to my feet. Instinctively, I reach for the whip to pull it off her, but then I remember, razor-sharp. It'll cut me if I touch her. Helplessly, I stare at my teacher, who's now perspiring and whimpering in pain.

Redd pulls the water whip back to her slowly, and in painstaking increments, it slices through Ruder's skin. Blubbery flesh shreds from bone, blood erupting from the gash. Ruder convulses, collapsing to her knees. She hugs her arm as tight as she can without hurting herself, howling in pain.

Redd presses her lips together in a mocking pout. "Aww, Ruder, you weren't trying to be a hero, were you?"

Jackie screams for her mother to stop. My hands shake. Ruder's chest heaves as if her heart is about to give out. We're seconds away from her arm being severed from her body—seconds away, and after that, Jackie and I are next.

But then the sweet sound of a violin slices through the air.

I look up to find Cyrus, her chin pressed firmly against her beloved instrument, her bow delicately sliding across the strings, the notes electrified and demanding. Her pupils laser-focus on Redd with a hatred that sharply contradicts the soothing melody she plays. Behind her, Tomai hovers by the audio controls, and they crank the dial, the volume increasing. A flurry of notes, as quick as they are cutthroat, echo through the air, Cyrus's hands moving with expert precision.

The look on Redd's face tells all. Her scowl stretches from cheek to cheek, and she presses a hand against her head firmly, gritting her teeth. She attempts to trill out a few notes, but the overwhelming volume of the violin drowns out her voice. Bewildered, she tosses her head from side to side, as if doing so would prevent the notes from rattling her brain—from scrambling all the signals in her nervous system. Unfortunately for her, it's no use. The water whip loosens its grip, its outline fluttering and dripping, but somehow still stable. Ruder pulls her mangled arm from its clutches.

In the water, the other sirens are also flustered, their songs weakening, mouths slowly closing in frustration as they struggle to fight back against the waves of sound crashing over them. Enraged, a couple sirens throw back their heads and screech, the salt water filling their mouths. Waves slip over their heads and some of them disappear below the surface, while the others remain. With the sirens' song interrupted, some of the kids snap out of their trance, and Mom motions them toward the street, away from the chaos. Dad and Simon pull screaming kids from the water and push them back to shore.

I unzip my sweatshirt and wrap Ruder's arm in it, pressing it against her chest to try to stop the bleeding.

"Go," I tell her. "We've got this."

She falters, her shoulders squared as if she's about to stand her ground. I shake my head again. *No.* After a reluctant pause, she nods, her mouth set in a firm line, before bounding up the steps, out of sight. In the distance, the sound of emergency sirens echoes. I guess if you cause mass chaos, not even paying off the police can save you from the consequences of your actions.

When she realizes some of her people have fled, Redd shrinks away from us, blue eyes wide. Her water whip follows her, hovering above her head. She shoves her daughter away, wincing at the pain caused by Cyrus's music. A growl rips from her throat, drowned out by the sweetest of the high notes.

Jackie pleads for her mother one last time. "Mom, *stop*. Stop this. This is *our* town. These are *our* people."

Redd closes her eyes. Her fingers curl into a clenching fist, and I know she's made her decision. She will not be coming back from this. Even if she stepped down now, there's no way she's going to avoid spending the rest of her life in prison.

Something in her posture shifts, and luckily, Cyrus notices this when I do. This time she plays a sharp, angry note. Redd snarls wordlessly, and this time, both hands fly upward to dig into her scalp. Loose strands of frizzy blond hair break away from her formerly perfect bun. Her song comes out in garbled growls, unable to connect or maintain a melody. Cyrus's music is too powerful—too disorienting for her to handle. The melodies overpower Redd's discordant song with ease. The water whip wobbles in midair before splattering against the ground in defeat.

Then Cyrus winces, and I notice something. Her skin is receding again. The bones of her fingers are now completely exposed, slick and damp with blue ectoplasm. It causes her to slip and lose her grip on her bow a few times, creating jarring notes. My heart catches in my throat, and my mouth opens to call her name, but no sound comes out.

"Looks like this is our swan song, Principal Redd," Cyrus calls out.

Redd turns to face her in staggering steps, her body quaking like a time bomb on the verge of exploding. In the ocean, Simon is pummeled by a wave and slips underneath. Dad cries out and rushes in to save him. Mom notices Cyrus's hands but looks at me anxiously. I nod and motion for her to go help Dad and Simon, and she sprints toward them. Somehow, in all of this chaos, Cyrus's eyes meet mine.

She winks at me. "Make sure you cheer real loud. If I'm gonna go out, I'm gonna go out rocking her world." She turns to Tomai. "You got this?"

In response, Tomai cranks the stereo to max, and electric sparks leap from the speakers. Popping and sizzling noises erupt like fireworks, and the sound system catches fire, thin threads of smoke drifting up from the equipment. Cyrus pulls the bow across her strings, releasing a flourish of sound. In the water, the remaining sirens shriek in fury. Some try to sing, but the notes are pathetic and disjointed, like stray cats begging for scraps in an alleyway.

Tomai presses their hands against their ears, and I can't help but wince as well, but this song—this song, *this song*. Maybe it's because of how loud it is, but I don't think I've ever heard anything quite as powerful. The harmonic notes strike with the urgency of a knight slashing his sword at a fiery dragon: relentless as the wraith's curse consumes more and more of Cyrus's skin. Redd's head bows low, her agonized groans becoming less and less human. She attempts to take another step toward the stage and shrieks in pain, collapsing to her knees.

"I can't fucking *hear* you! What was that?" The bombastic timbre of Cyrus's laughter clashes with the legato strumming of the strings; as the notes form chords, as the chords form her final song.

Her blue light ignites, engulfing her body, fully demonstrating the extent of her power. Above, her blue aurora glows bright and proud, spreading out to create a haze overhead that's so large it rivals the cumulus clouds. Each note creates a shockwave that rattles the ground with such vibrato, we struggle to stand. The curse continues to consume her fingers, exposing part of her hands, which tremble violently. Somehow, she stays in tune. Redd, although sweating profusely, regains enough energy that she can laugh. Even the sirens in the water seem to be moving a little bit faster. Redd cackles hideously, her chest heaving as she tries to get back up. After a few moments of struggle, she staggers to her feet.

I don't know what I can do, but I have to do something.

And I have a hunch I *can* do something.

I race for the stage, trying to hop above the ground whenever the shockwave threatens to topple me over. Tomai's eyes widen when I approach, their mouth forming the words, "What are you *doing*?" The closer and closer I get to the speakers, the more my ears feel like they're bleeding, but I grit my teeth and push through. I climb up, and the force of Cyrus's power hits me, nearly threatening to throw me backward. I gulp for air and crawl onto the stage, slowly staggering to my feet.

Perspiration drips from Cyrus's brow and her body continues to quake. I grip onto the back of her blazer, hovering behind her, and slowly, I begin to hum the melody. Redd's vengeful smile curls downward in an aghast scowl. My hand moves to Cyrus's shoulder, my voice growing louder, beginning to sing the notes. It's not perfect, but it's enough to keep Redd at bay. Simon and my parents escape the water and head in Redd's direction, their weapons held high like soldiers charging into battle.

As it turns out, my hunch was right. Although the bones of Cyrus's hands are completely exposed now, the curse has stopped consuming them. For some reason, if I keep my hands on her, she won't lose herself. She looks over her shoulder at me, her smile growing bolder, her hands now making more determined movements, building to a crescendo unlike any other.

It's the performance of a lifetime.

Dad swipes at Redd with the Phantom Prod, and she's unable to defend herself. It connects with her stomach and she spurts up a chunk of hot blood before collapsing to her knees. Simon reaches into the pocket of his cargo pants and pulls out a net, which he tosses to Mom, throwing it over Redd's head. Mom snatches it, securing her side, then tosses to Dad. Redd screeches, her hands trying to claw through the mesh, but she's unable to break through. Mascara streams down her cheeks in asymmetrical rivers, and she howls in agony. The few remaining sirens make no effort to help her, and instead retreat below the waves. The cold cruelty of this act stuns me somewhat, but then I remember she promised them a feast, and they got their asses handed to them instead.

Yeah, I wouldn't be so keen on saving her either.

Cars and people gather on the hills above us. Sobbing parents hug their traumatized children, and friend groups reunite in joyful cheers. Blue and red lights sparkle on the street overlooking the beach; the cops have finally arrived and will maybe, just maybe, earn the tax dollars they've been paid today. Some kids begin to cheer and clap in time to the music, encouraging Cyrus along. Over my shoulder, the last defeated siren returns to the ocean and disappears, lost to the depths.

Dad gives Cyrus a thumbs-up—the best approval one can hope to receive from a suburbanite dad. Cyrus nods. The bow waves back and forth across the strings, and she finishes with a flurry. Panting, she collapses to her knees, and I fall with her, my hand not leaving her shoulder. She carefully lays down her bow and presses her forehead against the stage as though praying to the heavens, laughing breathlessly.

"Holy shit," she breathes. "We did it. We did it, Melody."

I laugh as tears form in my eyes, press my head against her shoulder, and take in the moment.

The seas may still be stormy, but the sky has never looked brighter.

Tomai turns off the still-smoking speaker system, and those of us who've been fighting Redd collectively breathe a sigh of relief. Cops scramble down the hill toward my exasperated parents. Redd wrestles and snarls like a rabid raccoon stuck in a trash can, and the cops quickly wrap tape around her mouth to prevent her from singing. Jackie looks on, devastated. Mom rubs her back soothingly, and Jackie collapses into her arms with a sob. My heart hurts for her so badly. She didn't deserve any of this.

Cyrus's hand reaches up to touch mine, and I give it a squeeze.

"Don't tell me you were worried," she says, chuckling.

"Never doubted you for a second. Only wanted to give you a little boost."

"Sure, sure."

She sits upright now, and slowly, I remove my hand from her shoulder. The curse doesn't continue to eat away at her, and I breathe a shaky sigh of relief. She looks at her hands, then back at me.

"Melody…I think this is it. This is your power."

"What? No," I protest. "If I had powers, I'd be able to help you cross over. That's what a medium is supposed to do."

She shakes her head. "I don't think that's the case. What if you're an amplifier? You make my powers stronger."

I think back to the events of the past few days. How when she moved the manhole cover for the first time, she hadn't even played music; I held onto her and directed her, as I did just now. When we needed to turn invisible, I sang while holding her hand. And if I played her harmonica, I could get her out of the phone.

It all seems so much more obvious now that I'm thinking about it. Maybe I really *am* a medium.

But helping spirits use their powers is probably *not* what my ancestors had in mind.

"That was fucking *baller*," Tomai cheers, climbing up onto the stage beside us. They wrap an arm around each of our shoulders, squeezing us tight. "Cyrus, you played like a madwoman."

"I know! That should've been my audition tape for Strengstorm." She looks up at the hills, where the crowd has gathered. "Huh. You think someone got it on video?"

We burst into hysterics, knowing she's completely serious. I'm wheezing by the time the tears are streaming down my face. For the first time in months, both the town of Murkmore and I are at peace.

"He was always such a stickler for routine," Shelly laughs. Ralph—or rather, what remains of his spirit—is a poltergeist, a particular type of ghost which is conditioned to repeat the same routines they lived in life. But Ralph is special in that his schedule is almost identical to that of a day when he was retired and alive. The only trouble? He doesn't talk. But Shelly says that Ralph doesn't need words. "The fact that some subconscious part of his soul is here, living with me, like it's an unshakable part of himself—well that's true love. I've loved this man for fifty years. It won't be any trouble to love him the rest of my life."

—Tyreena Nkosi, *Eternal Love: Dating and Living with Specters* (2009)

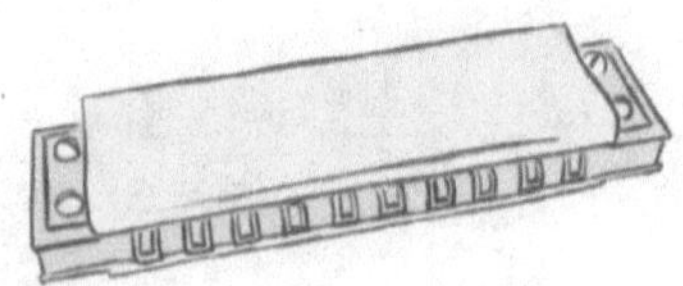

Chapter Thirty-Two

"Mom, Dad, Simon. I think I've found them."

It's a familiar scene. A decrepit house with rotten floorboards, paper peeling from the walls. Daylight streams in through the windows, and the moss and mildew on them casts a green glow inside. A stench of sulfur permeates the air—or is that raw sewage? Ugh. The houses out in the East Province need some work. Such a shame, too. This one has a wraparound porch. I can picture *so* many barbecues out there.

Mom's voice crackles over my radio. "Okay!"

She's not bothered. For safety's sake—and for the purpose of my First (Second?) Sacred Hunt retest—I'm wearing a helmet with a camera strapped to it, so they're all following along with me. I walk into the living room and step over a gaping hole that drops about two feet down into the house's crumbling foundation. Earthworms glisten in the fresh mud below, damp from the rain last night.

Giggles fill the air. My EMF reader pings and I dial down the sound. Inhale, count to five. Exhale, count to five. This isn't my first rodeo and it's far from my last. Circling around the couch, I see them. Two twin boys—phantoms—not much older than five, play with decaying wooden cars on top of the rug. One kicks his heels as he *vrooms* and crashes his car into the other's. They look at me in unison.

"Who're you?" one demands, scrunching up his nose. I recognize him as Timothy. "No girls allowed. Didn't you see the sign on the door?"

I smile at them both. "Must've missed it."

Their mother told us they would be like this. She's in her eighties now, living in a retirement community close to the shoreline. Her little boys died from influenza, and she could never bear to hire a ghost hunter to get rid of them—besides that, these two are tricky, and almost never revealed themselves to nonhunters. When she got news about what we had done in Murkmore, she reached out and asked us to help.

"Well," the other boy, Todd, huffs, "You're a blockhead. Because we put it up there and everything."

Predictably, as phantoms, they're irritable because their routine has been interrupted. Fairly normal behavior, and no cause for concern.

"It's not nice to call someone a blockhead." I sit cross-legged on the floor and reach into my satchel. My EMF reader continues to tick nervously, but I ignore it. "So, what're you playing?"

"Cops and robbers."

"Oh, wow. Looks like a fun game. Have you guys been playing for very long?"

They exchange a look, lower lips protruding, before shrugging their shoulders.

"We dunno," Todd says. "We're waiting on Mama to come home."

"Mama?" I ask.

"Uh-huh! She said she was gonna make fish 'n' chips tonight. When Mama makes fish 'n' chips, she brings home a *big* one"— Timothy stretches his hands wide as if to demonstrate—"and she slices it up into the yummiest pieces you've ever seen. They're the size of my wrist!"

Poor babies. All this time they've been waiting for their mother to come back with their favorite food. She had suspected as much. My fingers graze the greasy paper bag I've stowed away inside my satchel, and I draw it out. She made fresh cod and chips for them this morning, way before the sun came up.

"Your mama asked me to bring you this."

Their eyes widen with excitement, and with joyful cheers, they dig into the bag, tear into the fish, and shove fistfuls of chips into their mouths. Ghosts don't need to eat, but they're ravenous all the same, and soon enough, their last meal is nearly gone. Their blue forms grow hazier and hazier, evaporating with each mouthful they chew, but they are not afraid. Those little smiles stay plastered across their lips as they swallow bite after bite.

It won't be much longer now.

"Where is Mama?" Todd asks, his voice heavy with sleep. "How come she isn't here with us?"

"She wanted to be." She did, but unfortunately, she's on hospice, and the machines keeping her alive aren't portable. "She wanted me to tell you she's sorry, and she loves you very much."

Tears well in my eyes when I look at their rapidly disappearing little faces. They curl up on the floor like they're going to take a long nap.

"She says she'll be coming to see you again soon."

Timothy yawns. "Tell her we love her too."

Their bodies fade into white mists, and they evaporate. The house, which had previously felt cold, is now as warm as a hug. I settle into it, taking a deep breath, and wipe away some of my tears.

Simon's voice crackles over my speaker. "Good job, Melody. I've got the footage and stopped the recording."

I take a deep breath. "And?"

"Well, we still have to send it off to the Council to see what they say…but I think you've passed with flying colors. Congratulations!"

The sound of my parents and Simon cheering erupts over the walkie-talkie, and I cheer as well, pumping a fist into the air.

Then I gasp. "Wait."

"What? You okay?"

"When's the next ferry back to Murkmore? It's Cleanup Day."

After Redd was captured a couple months ago, the city council hosted a town hall session, and everyone came together to advocate for an environmental revitalization of the town and protection of the wildlife inhabiting its shores. Tomai spoke at the event and discussed the amount of work left to be done, and in response, the mayor gifted the Beautification Committee a shiny new budget. Like, they had enough money to buy the trash pickers with the nice little grippy thingies at the end, and on top of that, the committee will be working with other council members to spruce up the town and add more green spaces. Today is the third Cleanup Day, and we're finally on the beach, so I am beyond excited.

I check my look in the mirror and try not to be too disappointed. Sure, a windbreaker and threadbare jeans isn't my cutest assembled outfit, but when you're going to pick up trash in late fall, it'll have to do. After tying my hair in a ponytail, I'm finally ready to go. Outside my window, Tomai's car pulls up. Mercury is clearly not in retrograde today, because I am ready and on time for once—even after suffering through a ferry ride this morning!

I grab my rattiest pair of sneakers and pull them on as I make my way toward the front door. On the couch in the living room, my parents and Simon nestle together in a cuddle pile. Simon leans against my dad's shoulder while my mom's legs are stretched out across them both. They're laughing at something on TV but stop when they see me pass.

"Oh, Melody," Simon says, wriggling out from underneath Mom, "don't forget to bring Cyrus her new salve."

Simon researched ways for Cyrus's curse to be slowed down, and he ended up finding a method online. Every couple of weeks he breaks out a giant soup pot and throws a bunch of herbs and Vaseline jelly into it, and the whole house stinks like antibiotic ointment, medicinal and sour. She can rub it on different parts of her body and it reverses the wraith curse. After three days of using that stuff, her hands were fully healed.

I follow Simon into the kitchen and he reaches into a cabinet to retrieve a little plastic container, which he passes to me. I tuck it into my messenger bag and get ready to leave again, but Mom stops me, a smile on her face.

"What time are you going to be back tonight?"

"Uhh…probably ten-thirty-ish?"

"Ten-ish would be better," Dad says.

"Okay, then ten-ish."

"Sunscreen?" Mom asks. "I know it's overcast, but you can still get sunburns."

"Tomai's got enough sunscreen for everyone."

Simon pipes up again. "Do you have your Phantom Prod Lite?"

I rummage around in my bag to check. "Yep."

"Are you going out to eat?" Dad asks, and *Spirits above, I have to go*. Before I can answer, he reaches for his wallet on the console table. "Here. Take a twenty. Don't spend it all in one place. Or do."

I laugh as I take it from him. "Thanks, Dad. Mom. Simon. I'll see you all tonight."

I scurry out the front door as fast as I can, and a cool gust of wind nips at my heels. Jackie rolls down the window and leans out, smiling. Since everything went down, she's been hanging out with us more.

"You were so close to being on time today!" she says, laughing. "I was rooting for you!"

"I know! The parental units were parental uniting!"

I squeeze into the back seat, right next to Cyrus. She's dressed in a muscle tank and some cargo shorts today. A backward cap sits on her head, emblazoned with the Strengstorm logo. Her cross necklace is tucked behind the neckline of her shirt. Even though she's a ghost, she's still wearing a seat belt, which I find adorable.

I'm so incredibly happy to see her face. You'd think after everything that happened, we'd be all over each other (believe me, I would like *nothing* more), but she's been busy. During the day, she's trying to make sure she can graduate with all of us on time, and at nights when she's not working on music, she's helping at her family's restaurant. She submitted her application to Strengstorm, and they invited her to audition in the spring. I'm frustrated we haven't spent a lot of time together, and I also worry about what our relationship is going to look like when she goes there. (I say when, and not if, because are you kidding me? She's getting in.)

But this is her future, and I want her to live it to the fullest. It's what she deserves.

"For what it's worth," she says, "I don't mind waiting for you."

I smile at her. "I appreciate that."

"Hey, wait a minute," Tomai says. "Didn't you have your test this morning?"

"I did. And I passed."

Everyone cheers, the force of their voices rattling the car. As Tomai backs out of my driveway, I'm overcome with this urge to hold her hand. Before I can reach for it, her fingers weave through mine, squeezing them tight. I ignore the cheesy grin that Tomai and Jackie share in the front seat, and instead scoot closer to her. When I lean my head against her shoulder, she's as soft and cool as an oasis.

"I'm so proud of you," she whispers.

For once, I'm proud of me, too.

"Tomai, go long!"

With a heavy sigh, Tomai drops their trash picker, and it clatters against the boardwalk. Laughing, Cyrus whips back her arm and slings the Frisbee through the air. Strings of silk fly from Tomai's hands, wrapping around the disc with expert precision.

"If you want me to go long, you're going to have to throw it a lot harder than that, girl."

We've been on the boardwalk for the past two hours: me, Tomai, Cyrus, Jackie, and a couple of her friends, Tamarah and Phoebe. Ms. Ruder, who is supervising us, is camped out on a beach chair on the shoreline, guarding our cooler and eight completely full trash bags. Her arm is covered in compression bandages—still healing from her injury at the battle, but getting better.

After the battle on the beach, Ruder explained that last year when the gym flooded, Redd had tripped and fallen in a puddle. When she went to the bathroom to get cleaned up, Ruder noticed she was secreting goo. Redd gave her the same explanation Jackie had given me: that she was a selkie.

"My partner is a selkie," Ruder said. "And that is *not* what selkie secretions look like."

After a couple of the boys died, she became suspicious and started looking closer at Redd's behavior. Finally, she pieced it together, but had no tangible evidence to connect Redd to any of the crimes. She worried with the anti-Fantastical laws in place, if she told the cops what she'd seen, she and her partner would face retaliation. Plus in her investigation she'd discovered Redd had paid off some of the cops and convinced them to tamper with the forensic evidence from the crime scenes. That's why everyone thought the siren slime was ectoplasm.

Tell the wrong cop, and they would've ended up dead themselves.

Since the investigation died down, I've discovered she's chill outside of school hours. I guess even she knows how to let loose occasionally. Although her version of "let loose" appears to be reading sapphic romance books.

We all laugh when Tomai throws the Frisbee back to Cyrus. She leaps for it, but it flies right over her head, landing on the sand a few feet away.

"I have been *sincerely* humbled," she says with a grin. "Are we calling it? Dinnertime?"

"I thought you didn't eat anymore? Why're you getting all excited?" Tomai says with a teasing smile.

They elbow her and she deflects with a laugh, but it's hard to avoid the blue spreading across her cheeks. On the horizon, the sun glows orange and shades of purple, ready to kiss the day goodbye. Wind ripples across the sand, and I shudder at its coldness. I blow into my hands and rub them together, and Jackie does the same. Hard to believe All Hallows' Eve is only a few days away. When I exhale again, a cloud forms in midair.

Cyrus jogs up to me. "You freezing?"

"A little."

"Food'll warm you up. Are you busy? We could swing by the restaurant. Special tonight is moussaka."

"I'd love to."

Once we get rid of the trash and say goodbye to everyone, we walk over to her family's restaurant downtown and have a quick meal with her parents. I don't know them all well, but they're sweet to me, and plus, they make killer food. I leave that restaurant with my belly full every time, and tonight is no exception.

Hand in hand, Cyrus and I walk through the streets, listening to the intermittent cries of the gulls and chirps of the cicadas in the reeds. Autumn-leaf wreaths hang from the doors of businesses, and electric candelabras sit on the sill of every window in preparation for the holiday. A few stands have been erected along Main Street for vendors preparing to sell their goods. As spooky as it is, it's also peaceful.

"How've things been going with your audition piece? Have you decided what one you want to play yet? And what instrument?"

"Yes! Violin, of course. And the song is *Jota de Pablo, Opus 52*." She stops, and an odd look crosses her face. "Um, do you want to go look at the stars?"

"Look at the stars?" I repeat dryly, arching a brow. "Is that a euphemism for something?"

"No, no—wait, how would that be a euphemism for anything?"

"I don't know, you tell me."

She laughs. "No. I meant stargazing, as in *looking* at stars. On top of the Lennox?"

"The Lennox? Spirits. Sure."

I feel like she's planning something, but I don't push it. We walk toward the old theater. The sidewalks are cleaner now that new trash cans and recycling bins have been installed. And the Lennox itself is looking better and better. They took down the boards on the windows. Rumor has it it's going to become Murkmore's new public library and community center. We make our way to the back of the building and shimmy up the ladder as carefully as we can. Unfortunately, while the windows are getting fixed up, this ladder hasn't been so lucky.

"Every time we come here, we're flirting with death," I tell her when I swing my leg over the threshold of the building. 'Least I'm wearing my worst pair of jeans today. Don't have to care too much about tearing them.

"*You* are. I'm not. Ghost and all."

"I don't know. Remember that time you asked me about falling through the center of the earth? What if you fell from here and hit the ground so hard you kept falling?"

She shudders and laughs, then walks over to the edge and sits down. She gestures for me to take a seat beside her, and I join her as carefully as I can. Her arm wraps around my lower back and she squeezes me close, then leans her head against my shoulder. We sit in silence for several moments, watching the night sky grow taller; the expanse of stars comes into focus, twinkling against the violet blanket they're stitched upon. It's gorgeous, but I still don't understand why we're here.

Finally she speaks. "I'm sorry I haven't been the best at communicating lately. My bad."

"Admitting you're not the best at something? Since I met you, I've never known you to be humble. What's going on?" I laugh when I ask her this, but inside, my heart aches, like it's prematurely preparing for the worst.

"Nothing."

"No, not nothing. What's up?"

She takes a deep breath. "Well, uh, I wanted to say I know this hasn't been easy, and I appreciate you sticking it out."

"Hasn't been easy?"

She smirks. "Don't be coy. You know what I mean. We haven't gone on dates, and we don't spend a lot of one-on-one time together."

"I won't say it's been easy, but you've had to catch up on your entire life. School, family, friends—I'm only one piece of the pie. I don't mind being the smallest sliver."

"But you're not, Melody. You're not the smallest sliver. I want you to be like—like a whole quarter of the pie, at least."

I squirm. "Is the pie big enough?"

"It's a *very* big pie. And it's gotten even bigger since I finished some of my retests. I won't be balls-to-the-wall busy with school stuff anymore. And now that I know Strengstorm is letting me audition, and I know what piece I'm performing…" She averts her eyes, she's so nervous. "I want us to spend *more* time together, and I'm committing to that."

"It wouldn't be too much for you?" My stomach churns. "You brought me here to have this big conversation, and—I mean, if it *is* too much, I would understand."

"No! Melody, I don't think you're too much at all." She squeezes my hand. "You're special to me. I've just never done this before. I had an official girlfriend when I was thirteen, and flings with random girls after that, and—I don't know what I'm doing. I don't want to mess things up."

"Tell you the truth? I don't know what I'm doing either."

I mean that. It's beyond clear to me now that the relationship I had with Brynne was unhealthy. I deserved, and continue to deserve, better. It's two years of my life I'm never going to get back, but it's two years of my life I've learned from. Can grow from. In the short time I've been with Cyrus, despite how few dates we've been on, I've gotten a glimpse at what things *should* be like.

But I want more than the glimpse. I want the whole package.

I want to hold her hand through the hallway as she walks me to class.

I want to lie on her bed and listen to her play all the songs the world has to offer.

I want nights like this.

And she does too.

Finally, Cyrus is brave enough to face me. Navy fills her cheeks. Her brown eyes shimmer with a gentle hopefulness that makes my heart go pitter-patter. Spirits above, she is *so* cute, and I am in *so* much trouble. Her hand slides over my own, and I relish the sensation of her touch. She leans in closer, her lips inches from mine, her eyelids low and sultry. A once-in-a-lifetime talent? More like a once-in-a-lifetime flirt. She's got me wrapped around her little finger and she knows it, but I love every second of it. I think I can see her blue aura swirling around us, fuzzy in the corners of my eyes, but I'm too mesmerized by her to truly pay attention. Blue, blue, blue. This beautiful girl can paint my whole world blue if she wants to. I wouldn't mind.

"So we're in agreement? More date nights?" she murmurs.

I smile. "For sure."

Her hands tenderly cradle my face, and I lean in close. Then she kisses me once, hard, and full of feeling.

My heart sings the sweetest song I've ever heard.

GLOSSARY

Apostles (noun)

A religious organization consisting of the most pious of ghost hunters. An Apostle is assigned to each ghost-hunting family to ensure they are following the Way of the *Tomes* and to guide them in other spiritual practices. In many ways, they are seen as members of the family. Some Apostles will go as far as to live with their assigned families.

arachne (noun)

A half-human, half-spider Fantastical. Although commonly thought of as being human on top, spider on the bottom, arachne people can have a variety of different body types and abilities.

banshee (noun)

A rare type of wraith only found in Ireland. Always feminine presenting.

Beyond, the (noun)

Another world for the spiritual realm. The Beyond is an alternative dimension akin to outer space: there is no air, water, or way to sustain life. Spirits are channeled through the Ingress to be sent here.

cap-can (noun)

A backpack that is connected to a hose which is designed for capturing ghosts. Although these devices are supplied with battery packs, they are also powered and operated through a ghost hunter's manipulation of electromagnetic forces. By manipulating these forces, the ghost hunter can power the internal engine of the cap-can and cancel out the ghosts' abilities to use their own powers.

curse (noun)

The process of a spirit or soul turning into a wraith.

EctoChamber (noun)

An object that resembles an oversized light bulb capable of holding hundreds of captured souls at a single time. For ghost hunters, this is a place to store captured spirits until they're ready to send them through the Ingress.

ectochitis (noun)

A disease similar to bronchitis, caused when too many ectoplasmic mold spores enter the lungs and cause a bacterial infection. Highly treatable with antibiotics, bed rest, and fresh air.

ectoplasm (noun)

Residue left behind by ghosts. Generally blue, sticky like mucus, and always damp. Often creates mold spores when left in an area for too long.

Fantastical (noun)

A person of fantasy heritage—i.e., descended from a mythical, fantasy, or otherwise superpowered creature. Encompasses werewolves, witches, ghost hunters, arachne, selkies, mermaids, sirens, vampires, and others.

Fantastical descent (noun)

An umbrella term referring to a person who is a descendent of a Fantastical.

First Sacred Hunt (noun)

A religious coming-of-age ceremony in which a ghost hunter, typically between fifteen to seventeen years of age, must capture their first ghost. Also referred to as First Hunt.

ghost hunting (verb)

The act of searching for and capturing ghosts to aid them in crossing to the Beyond. Also referred to as *hunting*.

Ingress, the (noun)

A portal (of sorts) that attempts to connect captured souls to the spirit realm, but often leaves them in limbo—particularly if they're spirits with unmet desires.

Passing Certificate (noun)

A certificate awarded to ghost hunters after successfully completing their First Sacred Hunt. Often, this certificate serves as a prerequisite for applying to formal training schools such as academies as well as apprenticeship programs.

poltergeist (noun)

The most humanoid of the ghost types. They are completely unaware that they are ghosts and engage in activities from their everyday routines as members of the living. Any interference in their routine is often met with cataclysmic rage.

salting (verb)

A practice that consists of sprinkling salt in small increments in order to ward off spirits.

siren (noun)

Similar to mermaids, sirens reside in water but—unlike mermaids—are capable of living above land. They are a fierce and proud race whose populations have been reduced due to environmental disasters and physical conflicts. They are known for their "siren song," with which they are able to hypnotize their victims, and are capable of using water magic. Out of all aquatic-based Fantasticals, they are the strongest.

selkie (noun)

A half-human, half-seal Fantastical capable of residing on both water and land. They are typically good natured and are known for their physical beauty.

Shade (noun)

A type of ghost, able to use telepathy to manipulate the minds of those who invade its territory.

shipping (verb)

The process of sending souls through the Ingress/to the Beyond.

Spirits Ancestral (noun)

A religious phrase referring exclusively to the relatives of ghost hunters.

Spirits in Sanctity (noun)

A religious phrase referring to blessed or "good" spirits. This is a contested phrase within the *Tomes*, as many ghost hunters do not believe that any ghost can be good.

Spirits of the Beyond (noun)

A religious phrase referring to spirits who have crossed over to the Beyond.

spirit whisperer (noun)

Another word for ghost hunters. Usually used in religious context.

Thistlefeayr Tomes (noun)

A collection of stories and fables written by the Ancient Ones, or the first ghost hunters. This is a religious text meant to teach morality, ghost hunting, and other sacred ideas.

will-o'-wisp (noun)

The weakest of all the ghost types, will-o'-wisps exist as amorphous blobs and, unlike phantoms, do no exhibit any human characteristics or mannerisms. These spirits are most known for engaging in annoying practices such as messing with electronics.

wraith (noun)

A ghost that died tragically and was left to wander the earth. Usually takes a few decades or centuries for them to reach their full potential as wraiths. They are carnivorous and typically impervious to salting, making them especially dangerous.

ACKNOWLEDGEMENTS

In comparison to previous works I've released, *Haunting Melody* was written after my formal PTSD diagnosis and subsequent treatment. The struggles Melody endures in this book are similar to my own, which arguably makes this my most personal work so far and is special to me because of that.

Thank you so much to my Tiny Ghost fam, including Josh, Reuben, Dana, Jeremy, Thomas, and Lewis, for all your support, guidance, and pride in this project. Thank you to our sensitivity reader, Heather Howland, for your work on this story, and for your much-valued help and insight. Also, thank you to Alex Moore for bringing my girls to life and creating yet another banger cover.

A big, big thank you is owed to Ian, who supported me during some of the darkest times in my life. Thank you for being the shoulder to cry on when I was at my lowest moments. You encouraged me to hold on for one more day when I thought things weren't going to get any better. You were right. They did.

To the therapists I've had now and in the future: thank you for showing me that healing is hard, but worth it. Thank you for teaching me it's okay to rely on others to make it through the day. Thank you for always saying how much you loved my smile and laughing at my jokes in sessions.

Thank you to Angela, for always being so supportive and hyping me up when I'm trying a little too hard to stay humble. You know how to make a girl feel confident. Cody, Aurora, Rachel—love you now and always. Rue, would it be an acknowledgements section written by me if I didn't thank you? I don't think so, haha. To Jenna Miller, thank you for your kindness, your helpful advice, and our many trips for ice cream.

Thank you to everyone who has blogged, read, or reviewed *Haunting Melody*. Your support has meant everything to me, and I sincerely hope that this story resonated with you!

As always, thank you to my family, for everything.

ABOUT THE AUTHOR

Minnesota native Chloe Spencer is an award-winning writer, indie gamedev, and filmmaker. She is the author of Monstersona, Duality, and the upcoming 2024 paranormal mystery-romance Haunting Melody. In her spare time, she enjoys playing video games, trying her best at Pilates, and cuddling with her cats. She holds a BA in Journalism from the University of Oregon and an MFA in Film and Television from SCAD Atlanta. You can find more about her at www.chloespenceronline.com.

A ROMANCE TO HOWL HOME ABOUT

BOOKS ONE AND TWO IN THE BESTSELLING THE ALPHA'S SON SERIES ARE NOW AVAILABLE!

AVAILABLE IN PRINT, EBOOK, & AUDIOBOOK

WWW.TINYGHOSTPRESS.COM
@TINYGHOSTPRESS

MORE BOOKS FROM TINY GHOST PRESS

AVAILABLE NOW WHEREVER BOOKS ARE SOLD

FOR MORE SPOOKY QUEER STORIES SIGN UP FOR OUR NEWSLETTER AND FOLLOW US ON SOCIAL MEDIA

WWW.TINYGHOSTPRESS.COM
@TINYGHOSTPRESS

www.ingramcontent.com/pod-product-compliance
Lightning Source LLC
Chambersburg PA
CBHW011553190726
48287CB00010B/2869